AS CATCH CAN

AS CATCH CAN

VINCENT ZANDRI

DELACORTE PRESS

Published by
Delacorte Press
Random House, Inc.
1540 Broadway
New York, New York 10036

The trademark Delacorte Press® is registered in the U.S. Patent and Trademark Office.

Library of Congress Cataloging in Publication Data
Zandri, Vincent.
As catch can / by Vincent Zandri.
p. cm.
ISBN 0-385-33310-2
I. Title.
PS3576.A52A8   1999
813'.54—dc21   98-35731
CIP

Manufactured in the United States of America
Published simultaneously in Canada

January 1999

10 9 8 7 6 5 4 3 2 1

BVG

FOR JIMMY VINES

ACKNOWLEDGMENTS

Thank you to former Green Haven Warden David Harris for sharing his intimate knowledge of the inner workings of the New York prison system and New York politicos. I would also like to thank the New York State Department of Corrections for researching and preparing certain formerly classified documents that helped me create this novel. Also thank you to my readers Dan Slote, Jim O'Connor, and Doug Butler. A special thanks to my editor, Jacob Hoye, for his encouragement and confidence. Finally, I extend my gratitude and love to my sons, Jack and Harrison, and to my wife, Megan.

AS CATCH CAN

Stone walls do not a prison make,
Nor iron bars a cage;
Minds innocent and quiet take
That for an hermitage.
If I have my freedom in my love,
And in my soul am free,
Angels alone, that soar above,
Enjoy such liberty.

—RICHARD LOVELACE, 1649

BOOK ONE

GREEN HAVEN PRISON

Statement given by Robert Logan, the senior corrections officer in charge of the transportation of convicted cop-killer Eduard Vasquez at the time of his escape:

You wanna know about Vasquez, well I'll tell you about Vasquez. He looked like death twisted inside out. That dentist did a real job on him, or so I thought at the time. What I didn't know was that Vasquez was one hell of a faker, one hell of an actor. You should have seen him sitting in the backseat of that station wagon, all bound up in shackles and cuffs— skin white, lips swelled, gauze stuffed inside his cheeks. Blood and spit were running down his chin. His eyes were glazed and puffed up. That toothache must have been a real headache now that A. J. Royale, the butcher of Newburgh, had gotten to him. No way could Vasquez escape. But then, how could I make any goddamned sense out of the feeling I'd had since we'd started out? The feeling that told me he was going to make the break?

But here's how it really happened:

My partner, Bernie Mastriano, he drove the station wagon while I adjusted the rearview mirror to just the right angle so I could get a better look at Vasquez in the backseat without turning every ten seconds. He was suckin' air like there's no tomorrow. His feet and hands were bound up and he was locked up in that cage and you could see the pain all over his face. He just put his head back on the seat, opened his mouth wide, let his tongue hang out like a sick puppy. He didn't seem so tough then. He seemed kind of stupid and pathetic, not at all like the crazy bastard who pumped three caps into the back of that rookie cop's head back in '88. Vasquez kept suckin' up that air like it somehow relieved the pain from the hole A. J. Royale left in his mouth. Then out of nowhere he doubled over, threw his head between his legs, started heaving blood all over the floor.

Mastriano screamed, "I think he's having a fucking heart attack."

I told him to shut up, stop the car.

"A fucking heart attack," he said.

"Damn it, Bernie," I said, "pull the car over before somebody gets hurt." Sometimes you gotta pound things into Mastriano's head. He pulled the wagon onto the shoulder of Route 84, killed the engine. Then he pulled Vasquez out of the car and laid him out on the field next to the road.

I was right behind him.

When I got down on my knees to see if Vasquez had swallowed his tongue, the black van pulled up behind the station wagon. The back doors of the van swung open. There they were. Three of the hugest dudes you ever saw—in black ski masks, packing shotguns.

Mastriano went for his sidearm. But he took a shot in the head with the butt end of a shotgun, hit the ground cold. I got up and went after the son-of-a-bitch. I guess I didn't see it coming either. I went down, right next to Vasquez. They kicked me in the face, in the forehead. See that purple-and-black shit above my eye?

One of those masked bastards knelt down, reached into my pockets, felt around for the keys to Vasquez's handcuffs and ankle shackles. But here's what really got to me: When Vasquez was free, he jumped up. When those shackles were off, he spun around to his knees, got up, spit out that bloody gauze, let out a laugh. "Hey boss," he said, "you fell for the whole thing, hook, line, and fucking sinker. Just like that, boss."

I rolled over onto my side in the high grass, jammed my knees into my chest. I couldn't work up the air to talk. But my ears were still good. "Lock 'em up," Vasquez said. They cuffed Mastriano and me together with my own handcuffs, shoved us into the front seat of the wagon. Vasquez ordered one of his men to take the wheel. But before we pulled away, he leaned his head inside the open window. "No hard feelings, boss," he said. "Hope this don't fuck up the promotion."

The last thing I remembered before waking up at the gravel pit was Mastriano's piece coming down hard on my right temple.

CHAPTER ONE

Nineteen ninety-seven was the year Green Haven Prison went insane. The winter hadn't produced a single snowstorm that lasted for more than an hour before turning to rain and slush, and what should have been covered with a velvety-smooth blanket of white went on being gray and lifeless and pitiful, as if God Himself saw to it that the twenty-five hundred inmates and corrections officers living and working inside nine concrete cell blocks never once forgot where they were and why they were put there in the first place.

But for a man living and working inside an iron house, you didn't take snow for granted. A fresh dose of snow always broke the endless monotony, pumping good vibrations throughout the facility so that even the hardest inmates showed wide ear-to-ear smiles on their scarred faces. And happy faces meant that, for maybe a day or so, you wouldn't have a prisoner shivved square in the chest or a shit-thrower tossing a handful of shit and piss at an unsuspecting officer or an HIV-positive lifer spitting a mouthful of blood at his cheating honey or a young queer wrapping a sheet around his neck and tying it to the overhead light fixture. What you might get instead was two thousand men joining in song, the gentle hum radiating against the concrete walls like music by moonlight while flakes of white snow drifted slowly down to earth.

What we got that winter, instead of snow, was rain and slush and bone-hard, damp cold. From New Year's to Easter alone, we had six shivvings that resulted in four deaths and two badly rearranged faces. We had seventeen beatings that resulted in one death, and one nineteen-year-old inmate who (mysteriously) fell from the third-floor gallery in F-Block and who would now do life inside an infirmary, taking his meals through IV.

That winter we had two ODs, one death by hanging, an inmate who somehow got his wife pregnant during visiting hours, and another who acquired a good old-fashioned dose of the clap. To make a dismal matter even worse, we also had a group of twelve corrections officers who attracted national attention with their own arrests after a bachelor party turned ugly. The short of it was that my COs thought it would be funny to pelt unsuspecting passersby with raw eggs from the open windows of the school bus they'd rented for the occasion. One elderly citizen, who stood outside his car on a side street in Newburgh and protested, was given a special dose of humiliation. (As of this writing, his suit against Green Haven Prison and the State of New York is pending.)

But these were not the most serious things that happened during that winter.

We also had an increase in the inner-prison drug and contraband trade, in the form of pot, crack, heroin, liquid hormones, and assorted pharmaceuticals. I was personally forced to retire a record number of COs, not because I wanted them gone (I didn't have enough support staff to run the prison as it was), but because the Commissioner of Corrections for the State of New York had sent down his official mandate. And what's more, the winter of 1997 was the first I had spent without my wife, Fran, in more than twenty-five years—although by then nothing more could be done for her.

To add insult to an otherwise uncauterized injury, we had been cheated of our spring. Even the anticipation of spring rains and fresh muddy yards and good sleeping weather (there is no climate control inside a concrete prison cell) had been taken from the men who occupied the walls of Green Haven Prison. The heat of summer took over early with all the force of martial law, and what was supposed to be a "green haven" turned into a broiler oven. What little green vegetation there was within the concrete–and–razor-wire barriers turned brown and died. Even the baseball diamond cracked and heaved, like the blood that thickens and cakes on the upper lip after it oozes from the nostrils of a man's nose when his body writhes and convulses during an execution by lethal injection. (For anyone believing lethal injection is the humanitarian way out, think again. I've witnessed three, and during all three, the men convulsed, choked, snapped their own ribs, and bled from the nose and mouth.)

In May of the year 1997, my prison smelled only of low morale, treason, and pity. And it tasted of sweat, shit, concrete, and human decay. And my God, it was hot. But as for me, Jack Marconi, the keeper . . . the warden . . . the superintendent in charge of all things living and dying inside the iron house?

I did the only thing I could do under circumstances best left in God's hands.

I blamed the fucking weather.

CHAPTER TWO

Green Haven reached the boiling point on a sweltering afternoon in May with the escape of convicted cop-killer Eduard Vasquez. Since I couldn't very well blame the weather on a notorious killer who had practically been handed the keys to the front door, I found myself sitting on the edge of the desk in my office on the second floor of our administration building, holding my head in my hands. I had managed to take control of the situation as best I could (according to SOP) so that it had been only twenty minutes since I'd ordered a general lockdown of the nine blocks. Now, instead of holding my head in my hands, I had to take the steps necessary to get my head together.

I'd just seen Robert Logan, one of the two COs held at gunpoint when Vasquez had escaped from their custody four hours before. Dan Sloat, my First Deputy Superintendent for Security (and my second in command), was on his way downstairs to meet up with a detective from the Stormville PD. Stormville, along with the New York State police, were making preparations to head up the pursuit for Vasquez, at least to the outer fringes of their jurisdiction.

In the meantime, I had more pressing matters to attend to.

I turned to my secretary, Val Antonelli. "What do you mean the file's missing?"

"I mean Vasquez's file is gone, outta here," she said.

"Stormville will want information," I said. "Photos, rap sheets, next of kin. All of it."

"Maybe Vasquez signed it out before he left this morning."

"I don't need jokes, Val," I said. "I need that file."

"Raising your voice does not change the fact that it's hot in here or that the bacon cheeseburger I had for lunch is coming up on me or that Vasquez's file is missing," she said.

Val sat in my swivel-back chair in the middle of the room with her legs crossed tight at the knees, making last-minute corrections to her freehand transcription of Robert Logan's statement. "I'll see if a folder was signed out this morning," she said. "For all I know it's in the filing bin downstairs."

"Try to get it before you leave tonight," I said.

"We've got copies on microfilm anyway, boss," Val said. "So it really doesn't matter if the file's missing or not."

I took a hot, sour breath and stared up at the cracks in the plaster ceiling of my fifty-five-year-old office—a square-shaped room inside a maximum security prison that had housed German POWs during World War II. Now it housed close to twenty-five hundred permanent inmates and transients on their way upstate to Attica or further downstate to Sing Sing.

Most of my prisoners were black and Latino. Kids mostly, with rap sheets so long they'd wear you out just getting past the list of youthful offences. Murderers and gangland killers and torture experts and organized professional killers. Some men with nothing on the outside but poverty and death, but some with beautiful cars and houses and beautiful women in furs who came to visit every day and bank accounts that would make the governor look like a pauper. Evil, mean-spirited killers, but likable killers, too. Tough killers and not-so-tough killers and killers who gave up being men altogether to take hormone injections, as if spending the rest of their God-given days inside five airplane-hangar-size buildings were enough to eradicate the man, give birth to something distorted and freakish.

Inside the sweat-covered concrete walls and razor-wire fences you'd find weight lifters, junkies, drunks, health-food addicts, junk-food junkies, thin men, fat men, small and tall men, Muslims, Catholics, Five-Percenters, Buddhists, Jews, serial killers, man-eaters, motherfuckers, child fuckers, and animal fuckers. You'd find bankers, accountants, lawyers, professors, teachers, architects, welfare cases, preachers, pimps, and you'd find high school graduates and college graduates and illiterate men who'd skipped school altogether and inmates so out of it they couldn't tell you what month it was. Not far down the gallery from them you'd find the queers and steers and crybabies with long French braids, false eyelashes, thick red lips, and tattoos of broken hearts on their freshly shaved ass cheeks. Men with names like Black Jack, Lizard Leonard, and Ricky Too-Sweet. Butchers with baby-blue teardrops tattooed on the soft skin below their left eyeballs (one for each of their victims); men who'd arrived in the 1940s with all the piss and spunk of youth and who now, in their old age, would never consider leaving the comforting walls behind. There were cons and jokesters and pranksters and chronic masturbators and victims of circumstance, and men who did nothing wrong at all except to hire the wrong lawyer, and kids who suffered so much for their mistakes that at night you could hear the echoes of their sobs as they called out for their mamas and you'd gladly wrench your broken heart out of your chest if only it would get them a fair shake in life.

But by 1997 a new breed of inmate had infected Green Haven Prison, a new generation of criminal born of the sewers of New York and raised in the streets. Teenage men who never really had a mother or a father or a home or the chance for an education. Men (not boys) who seemed almost happy to go to prison because, for the first time in their lives, they felt safe and protected by the thirty-foot-high concrete walls. Men who enjoyed the prison life for the free sex, booze, food, drugs, and medical attention. Tough young men who freaked at the sight of a dentist's drill because they'd never seen one before. Young men whose life expectancy shot up dramatically from twenty-one to the ripe old age of forty because they now had iron bars and concrete walls to separate them from the killers they'd dissed along the way.

I was their warden.

I was their keeper, their mother and their father.

Which is why, for me, the matter of Eduard Vasquez's escape was such a serious offense. I had signed the release form allowing him to visit a dentist on the outside. As the keeper of Green Haven, I was directly responsible. It was my decision and my decision only. What I mean is, I could have said no. But then, I couldn't just deny a prisoner his right to proper dental care if that's what he wanted. That was the rule in New York State. As the keeper, my job was not rehabilitation. My job was to see that society was protected from its prisoners. But get this: It was also my job to see that a man who'd shot a New York City cop at point-blank range maintained a pearly-white smile.

I was well aware that Vasquez knew his rights. All the prisoners knew their rights better than did the men who incarcerated them. It was simply a matter of the prisoners knowing more about their civil liberties than did the guards who locked them down every night. At Green Haven Prison in the spring of 1997 ignorance ruled, and ignorance was never bliss.

And when it came to making an executive decision based on an inmate's civil liberties, there was never any right or wrong. There was only wrong and more wrong. But then, Vasquez had been a good prisoner (that is, he didn't go around stabbing or raping anybody) and I'd had no reason to believe he would escape. Anyway, I didn't make the rules in the first place, I only competed with them.

The hot sun poured into my office through the old square-shaped, single-paned windows. Even though Wash Pelton, the commissioner of corrections, had declared it a general cost-saving rule to leave the air conditioners dormant until June, I turned mine on and breathed in the cool, stale air.

I turned back to Val, watched her push up the sleeves of her cream-colored cashmere V-neck sweater.

"Okay," I said. "Give it to me straight. What do you think about Logan's statement?"

Val straightened her legs and spread her arms to catch the cool breeze from the air conditioner. She stood up from the leather chair and stretched her short solid body by reaching for the stars, a habit of hers I never got tired of admiring. "In my opinion," she said, "Logan is one lying son of a bitch . . . if you'll excuse my French."

I slid off the desk, stuffed my hands into my pockets. "My thoughts exactly," I said. I was relying on my gut feeling. I'd never had an escape before. I'd never had any choice but to accept the word of my officers as the gospel truth, no matter what I suspected otherwise. Besides the missing file, I thought, the only thing to go on was Logan's unmarked face.

I asked Val, "You notice any marks on Logan's mug?"

"For a man who got smacked over the head with a gun," she said, stuffing her notepad under her left arm like a purse, "he seemed in pretty good shape."

"Perfect shape," I said, "other than that small bruise on his forehead."

We said nothing for a second or two while the cold air filled the room like the invisible vapors in a gas chamber.

The phone rang.

Val took it at my desk. "Superintendent's office," she said, looking directly at me with the wide eyes that told me someone I didn't want to talk to was on the line. "Pelton," she said cupping her hand over the mouthpiece.

"Christ," I whispered. "He wanted two more men cut from the staff by Friday. Two more men when I don't have enough officers now." I took my charcoal-colored suit jacket off the hanger in the closet and held it by the lapel.

"What do I tell him?"

"Tell him I'm not here," I answered. "Something is definitely not right. I've got a missing prisoner, a missing file, and a possibly phony statement. I might even have a quack for a dentist. What I definitely have is a real problem when Pelton gets word I signed the release for Vasquez to walk."

"What'll I tell Pelton about the escape?" Val said, her hand pressed tightly against the phone. "He's gonna want something, an explanation at least."

I slipped on my jacket, pulling the cuffs to make the shirtsleeves taut. I looked into the small mirror on the back of the closet door, ran my hands through my black hair, pressed my fingers down over my mustache. "Tell him I had a dentist's appointment," I said, looking into my own brown eyes but quickly looking away. "Then try to find Vasquez's file, even if you have to get it off the microfilm."

"I can't tell him you went to the dentist."

"Why not?" I said, turning away from the mirror to face Val. "I have teeth."

"He'll know it's a lie," she said. "You know I hate it when I have to lie for you."

"Okay, then tell him the truth," I said.

"What truth?" she said, pressing her hand even harder against the receiver.

"That I don't want to talk with him right now because I don't feel like firing anyone."

Val pressed her lips together and stared me down. She knew she had to lie for me whether she liked it or not. She took a quick breath, composed herself, and took her hand off the receiver. She brought it to her mouth, spoke slowly, barely moving her thick, red lips. "Mr. Marconi just left for the dentist, Mr. Pelton. Is there a message?"

As I opened the door to the office, she stuck her tongue out at me.

"You mad at me?" I whispered.

She raised her middle finger high, as if the tongue hadn't been enough.

CHAPTER THREE

Like all maximum security penitentiaries in New York State, the bowels of Green Haven are gray, dark, and completely devoid of life. The narrow tunnels and corridors that connect the nine cell blocks are lit only with caged lightbulbs mounted high on the concrete walls. The concrete-paneled ceiling is flat and featureless, like a bunker. Looking around, you have the distinct, claustrophobic sensation of moving toward a dungeon or torture chamber rather than the "Home-Sweet-Home" of a few thousand inmates. Other than the thick, bright-yellow line that runs along the center of the concrete floor, all is gray, cold, and lifeless.

Here's what I used to think, but never spoke up about: Gray is not the color of rehabilitation; gray is the color of incarceration, pure and simple. Incarceration was my job, and Green Haven provided the perfect working environment.

Then there was the odor, the worm smell that coated the interiors like a vapor so thick you tasted it on your lips and tongue as much as you inhaled it, and when you first came to the prison you might have gagged on the foul air. It was an odor that began in the cells, from toilets that could not flush and from shit-throwers who refused to flush the toilets that could. The smells came from the mess-hall galleys where nutritious meals of yellow potato salad, rice pilaf, beans, chicken patties, and Kool-Aid for twenty-five hundred inmates were being prepped for supper and served on styrofoam trays with plastic spoons. The smells came from inmates who showered only twice a week, even after spending entire afternoons at the weight-lifting platforms or in the dark corners of the laundry giving blow jobs or something much worse to the skinny young boys who had no way of defending themselves.

Coming to the end of the first corridor into A-Block, I walked past the square window embedded inside the steel door that accessed A-Yard. The window was thick and reinforced with heavy-gauge chicken wire. There was a crack in the upper right-hand corner of the glass where an inmate had punched it. Outside, the weight-lifting platforms were now empty (a separate platform each for the Muslims, Catholics, Latinos, Five-Percenters, even Buddhists), as were the basketball and handball courts, while the COs took the late afternoon head count. Even with the bright sun shining down on the flat, hard-packed earth, all was colorless, lifeless.

All was burning hot.

Once past A-Block, I crossed through another tunnel that brought me to F- and G-Blocks. The guards at the gate, dressed in their prison grays, perked up when they saw me. The gatekeeper signed me in, asked me what I knew about Vasquez's escape. "It's why I'm here," I told him. The short, bald-headed man turned away expressionless, like he should have known better than to pry at a time like this. And he should have. I wasn't one to hold back information from my men, but he knew that nobody's job in this prison was secure anymore, and I think he sensed the tension in my voice.

I climbed the wrought-iron stairway to F- and G-Blocks, the blocks designated "New York City" by inmates and guards alike, with F-Block being the East Side and G-Block the West Side. All around came the sounds of two hundred fifty locked-down prisoners talking, shouting, laughing. "Yo, Warden, I want my fuckin' lawyer, Warden! Yo, Warden." These were the voices I heard, voices that rose above the sounds of metal gates crashing into more metal gates, guards screaming out

orders, bullhorns blasting over a nonstop rumbling that seemed to ema-
nate from some deformed beast that lived far underneath the thick
floor, like a stillbirth or an abortion suddenly come alive.

Sound shocking?

Listen: Prison is not rehabilitation, prison is incarceration. We admit
that now.

I approached Dan Sloat inside Vasquez's now empty cell. "You
talked to Stormville PD yourself, little brother?"

During my three-year tenure as warden, I'd gotten used to calling
Dan little brother because of our age difference, he being five years
younger. Also, he was thinner, happier, better dressed—all those things
I might have been if I had tried hard enough, or if I were still young
enough to care.

Dan tugged on the loose-fitting waist of his brown slacks and ran a
hand through thick, dirty-blond hair. "Marty Schillinger should be here
anytime," he said.

Martin Schillinger was a cop I'd gotten to know as well as any man
can know an undercover cop. A big, slow-moving, middle-aged man, he
rarely tackled much of anything in the small town of Stormville. An
escape was a big deal for him and his department.

Vasquez's cell was immaculate.

The bedsheet and blanket were army-barracks tight. Posters of Latino
women were Scotch-taped to the walls. One of the posters depicted a
woman dressed only in a skimpy G-string and black cowboy boots. She
sported a ten-gallon Stetson and straddled the back of a live tiger instead of a horse. Her naked breasts were plump and taut and slick-
looking. The index finger of her right hand touched the tip of her
tongue. With the other hand she held a chunk of the tiger's fleshy back
like a rein.

In one corner of the ten-by-twelve-foot cell, opposite the exposed
toilet and sink, Vasquez had set up a small shrine with a wooden crucifix and a little plastic statue of the Virgin Mary. A white plastic rosary
was wrapped around the Virgin's shoulders. The objects had been laid
out on a fragile white doily that looked out of place in the cell. Behind
the Virgin, leaning against the wall, was a reproduction of a painting
that showed the agonized face of Christ, His forehead covered with a
crown of thorns. Blood trickled down onto His closed mouth. His eyes

were raised to the heavens. His suffering seemed to complement the cell. As for me, I hadn't been to my Catholic church since Fran had been killed in a hit-and-run accident almost one year ago to the day.

I hadn't prayed either.

Dan looked at me. "What now?" he said.

"Take the bed apart," I said.

A shoe box had been laid out on one side of the small table holding the religious shrine. I opened it and found a shoe-shine rag, a bottle of shoe-leather cleaner, and some black shoe polish. Contraband technically. But stuff I normally ignored unless the prisoner was difficult to deal with. But even a cop-killer like Vasquez could be a peach of an inmate, so long as he had an agenda. And apparently he had.

I opened the can of polish, brought it to my nose, sniffed the oddly pleasant odor of ink and alcohol that immediately reminded me of my father shining his black Florsheims on Sunday mornings before mass. Nothing funny about it. Just shoe polish. I closed the lid on the little tin can, dropped it back into the box, picked up the plastic statue of the Virgin Mary and shook it.

The Virgin Mary was clean.

I picked up the photograph of Jesus, studied it, back and front. I shook it once and then laid it back down on the table.

Jesus was clean, too.

I turned and watched Dan strip down the bunk.

He found nothing when he pulled the sheet off the mattress. He found nothing when he pulled the pillowcase away from the pillow. But when he pulled the mattress off the metal springboard, a manila envelope slid out. "There's something," I said.

Dan bent over and picked up the envelope. He bent back the clasps, opened it, and slid out four eight-by-ten photographs. "Not bad," he said. He handed the envelope to me and sat down on the edge of the stainless-steel toilet like it was a chair.

I looked at the first photo. Blurry but clear enough. A picture of a naked woman's backside. She knelt on the floor, her face buried between a set of pale legs that belonged to a man sitting on the edge of a bed. Her head was turned to the left just slightly, but enough for me to make out a heart-shaped tattoo on her neck, below the left earlobe. Another photo showed the same tattooed woman riding the man in bed. I still couldn't see any faces, but I could make out a kind of jagged scar on the man's neck between his chest and Adam's apple. It looked almost like a birthmark or a burn. The last picture showed the woman lying on her back, legs spread. This time the man's face was buried in her crotch.

Three very bad shots.

One scar.

One heart-shaped tattoo.

If I had to guess, the pictures were stills from a porn flick. No explanations, no faces, no names. Just a heart-shaped tattoo. Maybe just a meaningless pleasure tool for Vasquez. Maybe not.

I slid the photos back into the envelope, bent back the clasp, and handed the package to Dan. "Hold on to these until I figure out what to do with them," I said.

Dan got up from the toilet, the photos in hand. Just then, Detective Martin Schillinger of the Stormville PD showed up outside the bars of the cell, escorted by one of my COs.

"Big Marty," I said.

"Keeper, Dan," he said, pulling out a small notepad from the right-hand pocket of his Burberry trench coat. "Anything good?"

Schillinger wore a trench coat because he thought it enhanced his image as a crime stopper.

"Some nasty photos," I said, nodding at the envelope in Dan's hand. "Kinky stuff. Other than that, nothing."

Dan handed the manila envelope to Marty. He opened the clasp, took a look inside. "I'll take these with me," he said. He seemed to brighten up all of a sudden. "Mind if I take a second look around, Keeper, case there's something you missed?"

I looked at Dan's narrow, clean-shaven face. He made a rolling motion with his brown eyes. "By all means, Detective," I said. "Dan'll set you up with anything you need—a copy of Vasquez's file once we come up with it, photo IDs, the whole kit and caboodle."

"Any distinctive marks on Vasquez's body I should know about, in case he should turn up dead?"

"If I remember right, he had his serial number tattooed on the knuckles of his right hand," Dan said, making a fist with his own right hand and holding it to Marty's face as if to demonstrate.

"He should also be minus one freshly pulled tooth," I added. "Dan will help you with the rest."

"Serial numbers," Schillinger mumbled under his breath as he wrote in his little notebook. "Pulled tooth."

I took a couple of steps to the front of the cramped cell, held on to the bars, the same way Vasquez must have held them ten thousand times before in his eight years as an inmate. I had to wonder what he thought about, how he felt, how he must have run the scenario for springing these walls over and over again until he was too exhausted to think anymore. I imagined him collapsing onto the bunk and maybe falling into a deep sleep. But then all he'd have to wake up to was this cold gray room and these steel bars.

Vasquez was doing life.

But he also knew that since the death penalty had been reinstated by the governor, it was only a matter of time until he was executed by a three-stage, mechanically operated lethal injection. He had murdered a cop after all. And everybody knows New York cops take care of their own.

I felt Marty's hand on my shoulder.

"Can I ask you something, Keeper?"

"Do I have a choice, Marty?" I shrugged his big hand away.

He pulled down on the belt of his trench coat to better accommodate his gut.

"Why'd you let a yo-yo like Vasquez outside the prison?"

I felt like the concrete had been pulled out from under me. Nerves maybe. A man had escaped from my prison. I was responsible. Schillinger was reminding me of that. I'd signed the field-trip release. I might have had the word *liable* tattooed to my forehead. Just a big letter *L* branded right between the eyes.

I took my hands away from the bars.

"Listen, Marty," I said, not looking at him, but at Dan, "you know as well as I do that an inmate has his rights, which include proper dental care. I can't just take away a prisoner's rights even if he has shot a cop in the back of the head execution style, even if that cop had a young wife who was pregnant with their first child, even if that wife can't afford her own dentist now."

Marty's cheeks turned red. I wasn't sure if the sob story had gotten to him or if his pressure was simply up. "I'm just asking," he said.

"My hands are tied, Marty," I said. "And you know it." Which wasn't exactly the truth. We both knew that if I had thought real hard about it, I could have said no to Vasquez's dental visits. I might have taken a few lumps from some civil-libertarian lawyer, but there were worse things in life. Now, if I was considered negligent by the commission up in Albany, I could easily face criminal charges, possibly jail time. It was too late to reverse the past. Now I had to figure out a way to clear myself as quickly and as cleanly as possible. Once I did that, I would get my head back together, get back to the business of running a tight prison.

I took one last look around before I left the cell. It was then, when I looked at the floor, that I found it. Just a crumpled-up envelope. Garbage really. Something that might go unnoticed to Schillinger, but not to me. You see, Vasquez's cell was immaculate. Too immaculate, too clean to be believable to anyone except an outsider like Schillinger. I took another step inside, picked up the crumpled number-ten-size business envelope. At the same time, Schillinger had his back to me as he studied the Virgin Mary, picking her up and putting her down again. Dan stood beside him, supervising.

I gripped the envelope and walked out.

Outside, on the catwalk, I flattened out the envelope as best I could. It was addressed in a kind of hasty handwriting to Eduard Vasquez care of Green Haven Maximum Security Prison, Stormville, New York. It had come from Cassandra Wolf, a name I recognized as belonging to Vasquez's long-time girlfriend. The return address indicated Olancha, a California town I did not recognize.

I stuffed the envelope into my pants pocket and waved Dan over. A CO was posted at the end of the gallery. He held a baton in his right hand and was slapping it against the palm of his left.

"Watch the house till I get back," I said.

"Pelton," he said, tugging on those thin-waisted pants, looking down on me, but not by much. "What about Wash Pelton?"

"Pelton called once already," I said. "He calls again take it, but stall him. Tell him we're doing everything we can to assist the Stormville PD and the state police to see that Vasquez is stopped in his tracks. Make sure he gets all the paper work he needs. Pictures, prints, statements, next of kin, phone numbers, whatever Val can get off the microfilm."

"And if that doesn't work?"

"Then ask him who we contact at the Bureau. He'll love that."

"What about the guards?"

"What guards?"

"The guards he's been on us to can?"

"You have no knowledge about guards," I said. "That's the keeper's territory, so just play dumb."

"Oh yeah," Dan said, smiling now. "And how am I supposed to do that, boss?"

"Just put yourself in my shoes, little brother, and think real hard."

CHAPTER FOUR

I was driving though Newburgh, past the four- and five-story professional buildings in search of a place with the number 684 posted somewhere outside, along with the name A. J. Royale, dentist. I patted out a
Pall Mall, lit it with the silver-plated Zippo engraved with my initials—
J.H.M., Jack Harrison Marconi. The lighter had been a gift from Fran
for my forty-third birthday, not two weeks before the collision that had
taken her life. A year had gone by and I'd spent the better part of those
twelve months trying to get used to the idea of living alone—before I
could ever get used to the *reality* of living alone—so that every time the
image of Fran's face popped into my head, I wasn't rendered as useless
as a sack of rags and bones.

This is what I thought: I had made a big mistake handing over those
photographs to Marty Schillinger. It was, of course, the right thing to
do. SOP. But it's the way Marty took them from Dan and me. So quick
and so willing to stuff them inside that trench coat of his. Like he knew
what was inside the manila envelope without even looking.

There was something else going on inside my brain, too. I couldn't shake the image of that heart-shaped tattoo. No faces or full bodies. Just an orgy of limbs and white flesh, with a heart-shaped tattoo being the only real mark of distinction.

I was still thinking about the tattoo when I located A. J. Royale's two-story brick-and-glass building at 684 North Main Street in Newburgh. Inside the navy-blue-carpeted waiting room, "The Girl from Ipanema" dribbled from Muzak speakers installed in the square acoustical ceiling grid while a woman behind the Formica-covered reception counter was occupied with a self-applied manicure. When she looked up, I saw that her eyes were encircled with a heavy application of black eyeliner, as if she were hiding a set of equally black shiners.

I gave her the best smile I could summon under the circumstances. "I'd like a word with the dentist," I said.

The receptionist looked back down at the fingers on her left hand. Her fingernails were long and sharp, like stilettos, and painted a glossy black like the finish on a cop cruiser. "The dentist is with a patient," she said, swiping at a fingernail with her emery board.

I reached into my back pocket, pulled out my wallet, and flashed her the badge issued when I took over as warden of Green Haven. She'd probably seen enough TV to know a cop has got to flash a badge—any badge—before someone will believe him. She dropped the emery board onto the open appointment ledger. "Is there some kind of problem, Officer?"

I folded up the wallet, stuffed it back into my pocket.

"It depends," I said, trying to appear deliberately evasive. At the same time, I wasn't sure what made me feel more nauseous, the noise of the dentist's drill or "The Girl from Ipanema."

The receptionist stood up from her seat, pulled down on her mini-skirt, and disappeared into a back room. The noise of the drill stopped and suddenly I could hear her talking with someone. But I couldn't make out their words. Then the dentist came out of the room. Wearing a pea-green coverall and baggy pea-green pants, he peeled off his flesh-colored gloves and extended his right hand toward my own.

The hand felt bony and cold.

I don't know why the man should have annoyed me so much right off the bat. It wasn't like I had a right not to like him, or not to give him the slightest of chances. But there was something about him, his mannerisms, his skinny, almost frail body, that seemed to set me off. I mean, he was taller than my five-foot-eight, but I must have had twenty pounds on him in the arms and chest alone. And that handshake, like a dead fish.

"Angel tells me you're a policeman," said the dentist, getting right to the point, which was fine by me.

"A warden actually," I said. "Green Haven in Stormville. I'm here to verify an appointment one of my inmates had today."

"Is that all you wanted to know?" the dentist said, raising his eyebrows. "You could have checked with my receptionist for that."

Stone-faced, Angel went right on sharpening her nails.

"I thought it would be better to hear it from you in person."

"The Girl from Ipanema" finally died and a Manilow song replaced it. Angel ran the emery board over her fingernails in time with the music. Long live rock 'n' roll.

"We took care of an inmate today."

"What was his name?"

"Angel," the dentist said, "do we have a name for the man who had the molar extraction this morning? We'd been performing a series of root canal procedures for quite a while now on that same tooth. But in the end, I couldn't save it."

"Sounds traumatic," I said.

Angel slapped down the emery board and ran down the page of the register from top to bottom and back up again, using her black fingernail as a pointer. Until she came to a name and an appointment she recognized. "Vasquez," she said, rolling the Z off her tongue. "Eduard Vasquez."

"Not an easy extraction," the dentist said. "Do you know what goes into an extraction, Mr. Marconi?"

"Let me guess," I said. "Lots of Novocaine and a pair of vise grips."

The laugh that followed was more fake than Angel's fingernails, but just as sharp. "It's a little more complicated than that I'm afraid. A dentist certainly could not be expected to handle a job of that magnitude inside a prison like Green Haven, not with those horrible medical facilities."

Almost unconsciously, I pulled a cigarette from the pack in my breast pocket.

"Please," said A. J. Royale. "This is a dentist's office."

"The good dentist doesn't believe in the kind of smoking that makes your lungs fry," the receptionist said, glancing up from her self-manicure.

"That'll be enough from you," said the dentist, now nervously scratching at the red skin on his stick-like fingers. "My niece can be a little abrasive at times," he went on. "Tell me, Mr. Marconi, do you have any family?"

I shook my head because, regrettably, Fran and I had never had the time for children. "Look," I said, "was there anything that seemed out of place when Vasquez was here?"

Royale leaned against the reception counter and stuck out his bottom lip as if imitating a pouting child. "Not that I could see," he said. "I get prisoners in here from Green Haven *and* Sing Sing. After a while, they all start looking the same."

"Brown and browner, right?"

"You may say that."

"What about the guards?" I said, trying to keep things moving while I still had enough daylight left in the afternoon.

"Just a couple of *National Geographic* readers," he said. "The usual."

"No one seemed exceptionally nervous? Exceptionally jumpy?"

He looked to the floor. "No," he said. "Not at all."

"You're sure?"

"The good dentist doesn't bother looking at a man's eyes," Angel broke in. She was on a roll and I wanted out of there. A Muzak version of "Send in the Clowns" replaced Manilow. "You've been a big help," I lied, and started for the door.

"Can I ask just what Mr. Vasquez was imprisoned for?" A. J. Royale said.

I stopped and looked over my shoulder. "He pumped a few bullets into a cop's head," I said. "A rookie, just twenty-five years old, married only twelve months to a girl pregnant with their first kid."

"My God," the dentist said. "What a world we live in."

"My God," Angel said. "What a world you live in."

Send in the clowns, I sang to myself. *Don't bother, they're here.*

CHAPTER FIVE

I crossed the Hudson River via the Newburgh Beacon Bridge along Route 84 on my way back toward Green Haven. I drove the Toyota 4-Runner fast, not worrying about speed, worrying instead about the little bit of natural sunlight I had left. I was trying to figure out why Vasquez would have kept a dentist appointment if he was planning an escape.

I put myself in Vasquez's shoes.

If I had planned on escaping, would I have kept a dentist appointment, allowed him to extract my molar? Why not just run? Why go through all that blood, all that pain, for nothing? Maybe the answer didn't lie with Vasquez so much as it lay with A. J. Royale, dentist to the inmates.

Once over the bridge I drove past Lime Kiln Road, keeping my eye out for a grassy field that might match Logan's description. But looking for a grassy field among acres of grassy fields was an exercise in futility. I looked for burned rubber on the road, for tire tracks dug into the soft shoulder. I looked for spots of blood or vomit or torn clothing or clumps of hair. But I knew it was next to impossible to spot something so small from the driver's seat of the 4-Runner. It's just that, with the setting sun, I didn't have the time to get out and comb the area as thoroughly as I wanted.

What I did manage was to drive over the same section of bad road five, maybe six times. But the more I drove the more I found a whole lot of nothing.

With dusk coming on fast, I knew I had no choice but to head back to Lime Kiln Road and the gravel pit that it led to—where Corrections Officers Logan and Mastriano claimed they had gotten the holy hell beaten out of them.

CHAPTER SIX

With the Toyota moving like a bullet shot out of the twilight, I pictured a faceless woman with a heart-shaped tattoo on her bare neck, and I wondered what kind of woman could do such a thing to her body. I had no idea why I should feel that way. As a corrections official, I saw tattoos of every color and shape every day of my working life. You'd think that after all that time I would have gotten used to them. Inmates with tattoos of naked women on their over-pumped biceps or the name of a long lost girlfriend inscribed in the center of a blood-red heart. Some inmates simply had their prison ID tattooed to their knuckles like Vasquez had. For a couple of packs of smokes, an inmate could have his favorite football team or the name of a child he'd never seen or just about any design he desired tattooed on his body. All it took was a sewing needle and some blue ink from a split-open ballpoint pen and, voilà, instant tattoo. I'll never forget the time an inmate was brought to my attention over a stunt he'd pulled on an unsuspecting prisoner who had hired him to tattoo his mother's name on his back. Instead of the name, the inmate had carved out the words

Fuck Me in dark blue letters. *Fuck Me* was not an invitation you wanted to extend inside the iron house, especially on shower days.

When I came to the end of a two-track, I found a couple of kids riding their bikes up and down the banks of the closest gravel pit. The pit was a small, man-made canyon with high, steep walls and a pool of cloudy rainwater that had collected like a small lake in the center. The kids pushed their bikes up the banks of the pit on foot. Once they got to the top, they mounted the bikes, gunned them down the pit wall—feet off the pedals, hands off the brakes—finishing up with a crash through the brown water.

Here's what I decided to do: I got out of the Toyota and walked around a bit until I found fresh tire tracks in the loose, sandy gravel. Beside the tire tracks, I found some footprints that obviously hadn't come from the two kids. The prints were flat and rectangular-shaped. Maybe size eleven or larger.

I moved closer to the pit.

Just over the edge of the pit wall were some bullets and an empty .38 caliber black-plated service revolver. It was partially buried, but the bullets were scattered about, plainly visible even in the fading light. What I could not understand, though, as I took out my hankie and wrapped it around my right hand before lifting the pistol from the dirt was why Vasquez's men would go to the trouble of disarming Logan and Mastriano and unloading the weapon only to toss it a few feet away where anyone with half a brain could find it. Why not just take the weapon with them, add it to their own private armory?

I tucked the recovered pistol into the back of my pants, wrapped the bullets into the hankie, stuffed it into my pocket. Then I called out to the boys. "You seen anybody here today?" I said. "Maybe a couple of cops in a station wagon?"

The boys looked at each other and then looked back at me like I was crazy. They stared at me, but said nothing. Not a word. Tough little guys. I knew the type. They sloshed out of the water and started pushing their bikes back up the pit wall.

"Simple question," I said. "Anybody come driving in here in the past few hours?"

The two boys went on gazing at me with wide eyes and corner-of-the-mouth smiles, as if I were doing handstands in the dirt. The first kid, who wore a red baseball jacket, mounted his bike. The second, smaller kid, who wore aviator sunglasses with mirrored lenses too large for his head, did the same.

"Hey, mister," baseball jacket said. "I got two words for you."

Aviator sunglasses started to laugh like he knew what was coming and I didn't.

"Fuck *and* you." Then the boys took off, side by side, down the gravel pit wall and into the water.

Maybe one day I'd see them in my prison. Then I'd have two words for them. Too *and* bad.

I headed back toward the Toyota. It was time to take care of the inevitable.

I dialed Channel 13 news on my cellular and asked for Chris Collins, the news director and anchorwoman of the small Stormville station. As the keeper I was expected to play my official public relations role, speaking out on the unfortunate escape of convicted cop-killer Eduard Vasquez. But chances were she knew all about the escape, since news of the event must have gone out over the police scanners. And if she knew about it, she must have already formed an opinion.

Anyway, I told Chris Collins most of what I knew. Just the apparent facts—no opinions, conjectures, or even the simplest of thoughts. From Logan's statement I knew that Vasquez had left his cell at nine in the morning, made it to his eleven o'clock appointment in Newburgh for a tooth extraction. From there he had left the dentist escorted by Officers Logan and Mastriano at about eleven forty-five. Sometime around noon, prisoner Vasquez was overtaken by what appeared to be a heart attack. Not long after, he was rescued by three men in black ski masks driving a black van. As the story goes, Officers Logan and Mastriano took a beating, with Mastriano taking the brunt of the punishment. With the two guards knocked unconscious and, somehow, stuffed into the front seat of the wagon, Vasquez's men drove them out to the gravel pit and dumped them. Sometime around one-thirty, Logan managed to pull Mastriano from the car. He then dragged him out to the road. Around two o'clock, he hailed down a car and brought Mastriano to the hospital in Newburgh. Logan called the prison. He was picked up from the hospital and brought directly to my office at my request. Then I sent him home.

"But all I really know," I told Chris Collins, as the sun went down on the gravel pit, "is that Vasquez flew the coop. End of story."

She wanted an interview ASAP. Chris Collins was a tenacious reporter. Visions of Emmy awards in her big black eyes.

"Not convenient," I said.

"Just take five minutes of your time, Keeper," Collins insisted.

"No can do," I said.

"But this is big news—"

I took the cellular away from my face.

"You're giving out, Chris," I said, pretending to lose the signal.

I hit the end button and dialed my office. Val picked up.

"Hello, doll," I said.

"Pelton called," she said. "He really wants to talk."

"You find Vasquez's file?"

"I checked the log," she said. "No one signed it out."

"Forget it," I said. "If it's lost, it's lost; if somebody took it, it's been shredded."

"I managed to make copies from the microfilm. How updated the information is, though, is anybody's guess."

"You and Dan manage to get copies out to Pelton?"

"Yes."

"He try to pump Dan for more information?"

"He wants to know what went wrong."

"How do I know what went wrong?"

"I'm only telling you what he said, boss."

"What else did he say?"

"You were supposed to drop the ax on two more men last Friday. Here it's Monday, and he still hasn't heard anything from you."

"What'd you tell him?"

"That you wouldn't be coming back after the dentist, . . . said you'd be in too much pain to talk or work."

"Listen," I said, pulling out the crumpled envelope I'd found in Vasquez's cell earlier that afternoon. "I want you to write down a California address for me and then look it up in the atlas on the shelf behind my desk." I read off the address to her. "Then I want you to fax to the sheriff in Olancha, California, the same package Dan faxed to Pelton. Tell them to fax the same material to their contact with the FBI."

I could tell Val was writing down my orders.

"Anything else?"

"Just remember that I still love you, Val Antonelli." I smiled even though I was alone.

"Glad to see you're loosening up, boss," she said.

"Glad to know you care," I said. "And don't call me boss."

I hung up.

I folded up the cellular and put it back into the glove compartment of the 4-Runner. But before I turned over the ignition, I decided to get back out of the truck, take one last look at the gravel pit. The wind had picked up now with the coming of night—a dry, hot wind that swirled the sand around and blew it against my face. I looked at the ground, kicked up some of the loose dirt. It was then that I saw something reflecting in the orange half-light of the setting sun. Some kind of flattened metal about the size of my little finger, with a key ring attached to it. I bent over and slid a small twig carefully through the key ring so that I wouldn't get my prints on it. I could see right away that it was the key to a set of handcuffs. Logan's or Mastriano's cuffs, no doubt. I stored the key in my pants pocket along with the six live rounds and the envelope addressed by Cassandra Wolf, Vasquez's girlfriend. Once I got back to the office, I'd put everything under lock and key, then decide what to do with it.

But first I walked back over to the edge of the pit.

This time the boys sat on their bikes in the center of the giant crater, with the dark, murky water coming up past their ankles. I guess they kind of enjoyed the muddy water. I guess it had a way of holding their interest or cooling them down or both. As I pulled a cigarette from my pocket and fired it up, the kid with the aviator sunglasses flipped me the bird. Just a middle finger raised high from a tough little guy. The second time someone had flipped me off in as many hours.

The kid in the red baseball jacket laughed.

I hoped they'd both catch pneumonia. Double pneumonia.

But then I saw Fran's face. Fran, the elementary school teacher. I saw her scolding me for my despicable attitude toward a couple of harmless adolescents.

Harmless, my ass.

CHAPTER SEVEN

Back in September of 1971, during the third day of the Attica riots, a corrections officer by the name of Mike Norman decided to drop out of the madness. No more shivs made from prison-issue razor blades pressed into toothbrushes, no more poles sharpened into spears, no more trenches dug out of D-Yard, no more COs with their throats slit and their cocks cut off. No more tear gas, handcuffs, blindfolds, and burning buildings. No more bonfires, no more helicopters, no more rain, no more suicide.

I was eighteen years old and engaged to be married.

That night, in the middle of D-Yard, Mike Norman curled up his lanky body like an embryo and went to sleep on the ground where twelve of us had been ordered by the rebel inmates to drop. Half a dozen inmates pointed homemade shivs and spears at the backs of our heads. When a young black man with sunglasses and a black do-rag wrapped around his bald head tried to wake Norman, Norman wouldn't budge. He wasn't sick. But then he didn't even appear alive except for the soft breathing. He was just sleeping peacefully, with a slight smile planted on his face, even with that rebel inmate screaming in his ear, "Wake up, motherfucker. Wake up or I'll cut your fucking throat you don't wake up."

He didn't move when the inmate tried to slap that little smile off his baby face, or when the inmate picked up his feet and dragged his skin and bones along the gravel floor of D-Yard. He slept through the state troopers' failed ambush, when they hit and killed two of their own COs. He slept for two full days during the Attica riots of September 1971— the week the nation's entire penal system nearly caught fire.

Me and Washington Pelton, fellow CO, humped Mike Norman around by his hands and feet, keeping him out of harm's way as best we could. The rebel inmates made jokes about the sleeping beauty, taunting us with sinister kisses in the air. I could understand wanting to drop out. We all wanted to drop out. Still, I could not understand how he had managed to sleep through those final impossible hours.

He was asleep on the last day of our incarceration when a rebel inmate cut Wash Pelton's throat with a razor blade. The jagged scar would stay with Pelton for years, like a tattoo gone bad. And he continued to sleep when the state troopers rushed the thirty-foot stone walls and stormed D-Yard, and when I tackled a rebel inmate from behind and plunged a shiv into his neck.

We lost twelve men, during that riot. No one went unscathed, except for sleeping beauty—my buddy. Inmates and officers died all around him. To this day, I can't be sure if he faked that sleep, or if his nerves had given out and truly left him catatonic. But here's the weird thing: Whatever he did, it worked. By dropping out of life, Mike Norman managed to stay alive.

I couldn't decide if Corrections Officer Bernard Mastriano had a different thing going or not.

What was certain was that he had a room in Newburgh General with a color TV mounted high on the wall. When I walked in he was laid out flat on the bed, a clear tube up his nose, an IV stuck into the underside of his right arm. He was alone, knocked out cold. The hospital bed beside his was empty. The fact that I was in the room had nothing to do with visiting hours, which during mealtime were suspended for anyone not belonging to the immediate family. According to the elderly woman with an Italian accent who worked the reception desk, normal visiting hours didn't resume until seven at night. But I flashed her my badge and that's all it took for me to be admitted to the ICU ward.

Before I tried to wake Mastriano, I took a good look at his face and recalled what Logan had said about him being struck in the head with the butt end of a shotgun. From where I stood, the black-haired, fat-faced man didn't have a scratch on him. He looked in better shape than Logan had.

I grabbed his arm just above the needle that supplied his intravenous. I shook it.

Mastriano mumbled a couple of words, opened his eyes, and closed them again. His face was tan and fleshy, the corners of his mouth turned up like he couldn't hold himself back anymore, like he was about to break out into a fit of laughter.

I shook him again, but there was still no response other than some incoherent mumbling. I bent at the knees, put my mouth up to his ear. "Mastriano," I said. "Can you hear me?"

No visible sign that he could.

But at the chance he might be faking it, I went on with what I had to say. "I want to hear about what happened out there today. I want to hear your story. Understand, Mastriano?"

I glanced over my shoulder at the open door. Nurses walked back and forth from room to room, clipboards and plastic water bottles in hand. It was then that I began running my fingers along Mastriano's right temple, feeling for any evidence of a bump or abrasion. I ran my fingertips all through his thick, black hair, felt the cold, bumpy scalp. I would have run my hand through a second time, too, had the doctor not walked in.

"Excuse me," he said. "But is there some kind of problem?"

He was a short, curly-haired young man. A kid really. He wore a tweed suit jacket, khakis, and running shoes. He had a laminated identification card with his photograph and a name I could not make out pinned to his jacket. He carried a clipboard in his right hand and wore a stethoscope around his neck. What he did not wear, however, was the usual knee-length, hospital-white smock.

I took my hands away from Mastriano's scalp and smiled. "Maybe you can help me," I said. "What's this man's diagnosis?"

The doctor reached for the pen in the breast pocket of his blazer. "You related to the patient, sir?"

I pulled out my wallet. But this time, I did not flash my badge. Instead, I showed the good doctor my valid prison ID. "Keeper Marconi of Green Haven Maximum Security," I said. "This man works for me."

This time the doctor took a breath. "When the patient was brought in," he said, "he was already unconscious. The officer who came in with him said he was knocked out cold with the stock end of a shotgun."

"Be honest, Doc," I said. "Did this man take a blow to the skull with a blunt object?"

The doctor let out a breath. "No," he said. "No sign of it that I could see, anyway. What he does have is a couple of bruises to the head, but nothing that would have been caused by the back end of a rifle, at least I don't think so at this point."

"You're certain of this?"

"Pupils aren't uneven. No other lateralizing signs like paralysis, decreased reflexes, descerbrate posturing. In terms of the Glascow scale, I'd say he's a two, maybe a three."

"Glascow?" I asked.

"The medical standard by which we measure the seriousness of a head injury. The higher the score, the worse off you are. In theory, at least."

"What do you think, in theory?" I said.

"His relaxed state could be due to Descorticate Syndrome, which could mean injury to the cortical level of the brain."

"But so far, he shows no real sign of taking that kind of hit, does he?"

"Could be a blood clot, could be a basilar skull fracture, who knows."

"For now you keep him in ICU?"

"We've pumped him up with some Manitol and steroids in case of brain swelling."

"His breathing seems okay."

"Don't see a ventilator, do you?"

Feisty little guy, I thought. *This doctor is a feisty little guy.*

Together we looked at Mastriano for a second or two, like he was about to bound up, say *Gotcha.* He was as still and as stiff as—you guessed it—a statue. The IV dripped slowly and steadily, in sync with the rising and falling of his chest.

"But he still shows no real sign of a concussion," I said, shaking my head.

"Just the sleeping," the doctor said, "which, in itself, could be serious."

We said nothing for a few more seconds, just continued staring at the motionless body. Then I said, "Doctor, can I see you out in the hall?"

"He can't hear us," he said, nodding toward Mastriano.

"Indulge me," I said, now turning for the open door.

Outside we leaned our shoulders up against the white plaster wall. The nurses and interns marched passed us, not giving us a second look. "Doctor," I said, "is there any chance Mister Mastriano could be faking sleep? I mean, maybe he popped some sleeping pills or something."

The doctor let loose with a high-pitched nasal laugh that I assumed was intended to convey my apparent silliness.

"Listen up," I said. "A cop-killer escaped from my prison today and I want to get to the bottom of it."

"I suppose," he said, getting a grip on himself. "But it's awfully tough to do for hours on end. And he's been in ICU for some time now."

"But it is possible?"

"Given the right conditions," he said, "I guess all things are possible. But then, it's not unusual for a man to go into a catatonic state if properly frightened or startled. And from what I understand, that officer has been through a lot. We've drawn some blood. It's being analyzed as we speak. If there's drugs involved, it'll show up."

"What happens next?" I said.

"Tests, tests, and more tests," he said. "That's what we like to do here."

"Tests for what?"

"CSF leak, concussion, epilepsy, a few other assorted maladies. We have a neurologist coming in to check out his brain, put him into an imaging machine, really get into it. We even have to test his vision."

"Do me another favor, will you?" I said.

He nodded and rolled his eyes in a way that told me he was sick of answering my questions.

"Make sure," I said, loud enough for Mastriano to hear me if he *could* hear me, "that I'm notified right away if the officer wakes up."

"He'll be with us for quite a while," the doctor said.

I took out my wallet, slipped out a business card, and handed it to him. Then I leaned into his ear. "Doctor," I whispered, "let's hope your patient makes one hell of a miraculous recovery."

CHAPTER EIGHT

Maybe it had something to do with having Wash Pelton on the brain. Maybe it had something to do with seeing Bernie Mastriano laid up in bed, knocked out cold without the slightest hint of injury. Maybe it had something to do with Vasquez taking off without a trace. Maybe it was all of the above. But as I walked across the massive block-shaped parking lot outside the electronic sliding-glass doors of Newburgh General, the events of the past came back to haunt me in all their timeless brilliance and horror.

Listen: In the world of the Attica survivor, memory never occurs in the past tense.

One second it's May 1997 and the next it's September 1971 all over again.

In my memory I am able to see Mike Norman rolled over onto all fours on the muddy floor of D-Yard, heaving his guts. My blindfold has finally been pulled away and I can see that there is nothing left in Mike's system to throw up onto the mud and gravel. He slumps over onto his left side, his shackled legs and hands tucked up into his chest.

In the yard, with the fires going and the rebel inmates chanting for blood and revenge, we are the innocent angels of the prison system. Mike's face is soaked with sweat and dirt. The three of us—Norman, Pelton, and I—have got to stick together if only to keep each other sane. But I know Norman is fighting a losing battle. His nerves are giving out. And there are rumors about one CO who got locked in a bathroom on the main floor of the administration building while a rebel tossed in kerosene and a lit match. Another man was castrated with a shiv and crucified to the wall in G-Block. I myself have seen COs kicked to within inches of their lives. Before my blindfold was removed, I could only listen to their screams, their moans, the gurgling, and then the silence.

When an inmate walks by with a wood shank as long as a spear, I try to persuade him to remove my cuffs and shackles. My buddy is hurt, I tell him. I've got a right to help my fucking buddy. Pelton tries to stand. He holds his long arms out as if the inmate will unlock the cuffs right then and there. Instead, the inmate uses the dull end of the shank like a nightstick, plows it into Wash's gut. Wash collapses, curls into himself on the ground. I see the inmate's leg lift behind me and I feel the steel in his toe as his boot comes down against my head.

CHAPTER NINE

On the drive back to Green Haven, with John Coltrane playing softly on the radio, my own eyes caught my attention in the rearview mirror. The skin around my brown eyes was heavy and wrinkled. Dark bags were already beginning to form. My mustache was thick and speckled with gray, my widow's peak receding on my forehead. I needed a shave. The knot of my tie had been pushed to one side of my collar. The tension was shooting through the center of my solar plexus and down the backs of my arms, tightening my triceps. Chest and arms and stomach were tight and sore, yet I hadn't pumped iron in five full days.

It's amazing, really, when you think about it, how stress affects people.

By the time I got back to the office, Val had left. My entire staff had gone home to their wives and their kids and their hot suppers. They sipped cocktails—shoes off, feet up on the coffee table—and got a charge out of the daily news that Dan Rather read for them off the Tele•promp•ter. At least that's the way it had been for me not too long ago. I no longer had any of those things or the woman who had given them to me, but I still had my Jamesons. And as I poured a second shot, I pushed away the paperwork that had piled up after I'd left the office that afternoon.

I felt empty inside, my stomach as vacant as Vasquez's cell.

I sat back, put my feet up on the desk, and gazed into the darkness of my second-floor office—a darkness broken only by the white light from the desk lamp and the scattered spotlights moving across the prison grounds like hungry sharks lurking through deep, blue waters.

I took another drink of whiskey and fingered the notes filled with Val's handwriting. Messages from the commissioner. I had no interest in talking with him right now. As I said, I had to avoid him not only because of the escape, but because of the two additional names he wanted slashed from an already diminished list of officers. I could have given him Robert Logan and Bernard Mastriano, but I still couldn't be sure that they weren't telling the truth about Eduard Vasquez's escape.

The white spotlight swept across my floor.

The wall-mounted clock face showed the big hand on the twelve, little hand on the seven.

I knew Wash Pelton would still be in his office. He would be in his office until midnight, maybe later. Maybe he'd sleep on the couch, send out for a fresh suit of clothing. Pelton had a wife, Rhonda, a small blond-haired bull terrier of a woman who acted as public relations officer for the commission—a position Wash had virtually invented for her. She was notorious for her flirting and her drinking. Pelton was notorious for the way he sometimes slapped her sober. But then, like in any bureaucracy, there were a lot of rumors in the corrections department.

I wasn't entirely against Pelton. We'd been good friends early in our careers. Both of us had started out as COs at Attica only weeks before the riot that had nearly taken our lives. Not long after, both Wash and I, along with Mike Norman, had been reassigned by the commission to set up a training program for rookie cops and security guards, not only to better prepare them in the event of another Attica riot, but also to help prevent another riot. In those days, Wash, Mike, and I were no strangers to the bars that lined Broadway in downtown Albany. Justins, the Lark, Jack's Oyster House. Five solid blocks of bars, glaring neon, and the rich fish smell that used to come off the Hudson River in the days before the state cleaned it up. But those were the days before Wash quit the department to get a bachelor's degree and then a law degree and before Rhonda came into his life. When Wash married Rhonda and Albany politics, whatever friendship we had took a backseat.

Now that Fran was gone, Pelton and I once again had more than a few things in common. Like me, he had no children to go home to. No dog, no dinner, no slippers waiting by the door. He was married, but Rhonda didn't seem the type to greet him with open arms and a peck on the cheek. Like me he had his work and his booze, but that's where the similarities ended.

Whiskey and loneliness didn't make us allies.

I recalled the wassail party the Commission had sponsored at the governor's mansion on Eagle Street just five months before. It was the first time I'd gone out on my own to a social function since Fran's death. Now I was caught in a room full of friends, coworkers, and acquaintances with Nat King Cole singing from the grave and colored lights hanging off the walls and wrapped around a gigantic Christmas tree that took up the entire center of the grand living room. Rhonda, as usual, had drunk herself blind, and somehow the booze had caused her to take a liking to me. Or maybe the recent death of my wife had made me more attractive or pitiable; I'm not sure which.

Anyway, I felt this need to get away from it all so I stepped out onto the patio to have a smoke.

Rhonda followed me.

She asked me for a light. But as soon as I lit her smoke, she grabbed onto my arm, pulling me into her with that deceptive bull-terrier strength. She let the lit cigarette fall to the stone patio, puckered up, and laid one on me, just like that, in the middle of the governor's porch. I didn't want to kiss her. But she'd taken me by surprise. I quickly pushed her away.

But by that time we'd been spotted and the damage done.

Not only had Wash seen us, but so had the governor and his first lady. In fact, the entire party had stopped and stared at us through the open, floor-to-ceiling patio doors.

In the months that followed, Wash never once mentioned the incident to me. We dealt with each other on a professional level. He called me for names to scratch from my roster, and I, with all the fight somehow gone out of me since Fran's death, capitulated. I didn't think much about Rhonda after that or about the incident at the governor's mansion. But I knew, deep down, that it must have been eating away at him. And who could blame him?

I decided to wait until morning to place a call. Anything said between us tonight could only lead to a dead end. I lit another cigarette and watched the smoke boil in the white light from the desk lamp until it disappeared in the darkness. I glanced at the framed picture of Fran that I kept on the right side of my desk—the black-and-white photo taken shortly after her graduation from Albany High, the one with her hair pulled back taut and straight, her costume diamond-stud earrings shining in the bright light of the flash, her eyes wide and brown, her mouth curved up at the corners in a subtle smile.

"Okay, Fran," I said. "Here's the rundown. We've got a missing file and an officer who claims he got the holy hell beaten out of him. But he doesn't show any signs of being beaten. We've got another guard who's checked into a hospital after taking a clip to the head with the butt end of a rifle. But the guy appears to be unharmed. He's alive and well, but then, he's out cold like Sleeping Beauty. I checked in with A. J. Royale down in Newburgh and found out that Vasquez did, in fact, make his dentist appointment. I know he had a series of root canal procedures performed to a bad molar and that, in the end, the good dentist had no choice but to pull it. And last, I've got a weapon, a pile of rounds, and the key to Logan's cuffs. I've got an envelope with Cassandra Wolf's address and a package of stills that Marty Schillinger confiscated. I've even got a woman with a heart-shaped tattoo on her neck. That, my love, is where the facts stop and the speculation begins."

I downed my whiskey and poured another shot. I wrapped my hankie around the .38 service revolver, gripped it, and aimed it at the white spotlight as it floated across my window, left to right. I laid the pistol back down and stood each of the six copper-jacketed bullets upright on the desk. I felt the key to the handcuffs. I touched everything with the hankie as though, in the touching, I'd get answers.

Tomorrow I would contact Mike Norman at the Albany Police Department's downtown division on South Pearl Street. I'd see what he could do about dusting the stuff for prints. In the meantime, I'd consider why Logan would have lied in his statement and why he'd be stupid enough to leave evidence lying around the gravel pit, unless, of course, he wanted it found. I knew someone must have been paid off for something, but who, how much, and why?

I needed connections.

Maybe Cassandra Wolf would provide them.

But from the look of things she was in California. And if I had to guess, Vasquez was with her.

I stamped out my cigarette. In the distance I could hear the electronic buzzers sounding off in F- and G-Blocks. I heard the slam of iron gates. Lockdown. Time for evening head count.

"Are there any good officers left in this prison?" I said out loud, my voice strange and tired.

I looked at Fran's photo one last time and brought my fingers to her lips. I downed the rest of my drink and locked the envelope with Cassandra Wolf's address, the .38, the live rounds, and the rest of the evidence inside my briefcase. I stood up with the now weighted-down case in hand and turned out the desk lamp.

By law I should have gone straight to the Stormville police. I should have gotten on the horn with Marty Schillinger and told him what I'd found. But I had a feeling that I'd already made a mistake giving him the stills from Vasquez's cell. Who knew what would happen to those materials now that I'd handed them over to Marty? Who knew what would happen to the evidence from the gravel pit once it was out of my hands for good? It was my ass that was at stake for Vasquez's escape. I remembered having signed six or seven identical releases in the past few months. I could not deny a prisoner his right to receive proper medical care. It was a case of an inmate's civil rights—rights established in the bloody aftermath of Attica. I had had a responsibility then, and I had a responsibility now.

I knew I had to take control of the situation—bring the material to Mike Norman in Albany, have him dust for prints off the record. It was illegal and I knew it. But I wasn't concerned with breaking the law, so long as it meant I could get to the truth quickly, avoid a lengthy investigation, prosecute those involved, save my job, save my ass.

CHAPTER TEN

I couldn't decide if I wanted to hear Sinatra or Billie Holiday. I chose neither. Instead I reached up to the highest shelf beside the fireplace in my living room, behind my four-piece Rogers drum kit (blue-sparkle finish). I pulled out an old album I hadn't spun in ten years: Zoot Sims and Bucky Pizzarelli. I slipped the record out of its sleeve, held the disc up to my face and breathed in the smell of old vinyl, puckered my lips and blew off the excess dust. Then I slipped the relic of an LP onto the turntable and engaged the stylus.

A while back I had refurbished my stereo system with an eight-disc CD player and replaced most of my collection (and it's a big one) with high-tech, more expensive evolutionary clones. But now it felt some-how soothing to hear the scratchiness that always precedes the music on a vinyl disc.

The sound brought me back, made me think of Fran and her funny, giggly laugh. I could almost see her lying on the couch, stocking feet up on the coffee table, head tilted back just so, eyes closed, a glass of red wine in one hand, a cigarette in the other, smoke rings floating all the

way to the ceiling. But then my memory shifted in directions I did not
want it to go and I recalled the black sedan that had come out of
nowhere, blown the traffic light, plowed into the passenger-side door of
my Ford Bronco. . . .

Almost one year ago to the day.

I sat down at the drums and took the brushes in my hands. I thought
about Vasquez as the first song came on and I placed my brushes to the
snare to mimic the licks of the great Max Roach. I also pictured the
heart-shaped tattoo. I thought about the way Schillinger had taken
those photos from me inside Vasquez's empty cell. Maybe I was putting
too much into it, but I felt that, for some reason, Vasquez had left them
for me to find. Let's face it, he knew it was SOP to shake down a cell
after an escape, and we're talking about a very neat man here, a man
who was not the type to overlook details.

I finished out the piece with a quick triplet and a cymbal crash and
returned the brushes to the snare.

I didn't have the heart for drumming tonight. The keeper of time
was too concerned with the keeper of the maximum security joint.

I took a glance at my watch and thought about asking Val over for
some reheated leftovers. But it was nine already and I knew it was too
late to call. But then, I knew she'd be up. Like me, Val was no longer
married, although she did have a twelve-year-old boy from her only
marriage to keep her company. I even went to the wall phone in the
kitchen and picked up the handset. But at the last second, just as I
turned it over in my palm, just as I was about to punch in the numbers,
I pictured her sitting on the couch beside her son—stocking feet up on
the table, a bowl of popcorn between them—and I hung up.

I found the leftover spaghetti in a Tupperware bowl behind a twelve-
pack of Budweiser long neck bottles in the refrigerator. I pulled down a
frying pan from the rack, set it on the burner, turned the dial to me-
dium, and tossed in a tablespoon of butter. When the butter had melted
and the hissing sound was louder than the smooth licks of Bucky Pizzarelli's jazz guitar, I added the spaghetti and fried it until it was finished. I ate while spinning the Zoot Sims album a second time. When I
was through, I put the dishes into the sink and turned out all the lights.
I let the record spin once more. Now that Fran was gone, music kept
me company in the darkness.

I put my head on the pillow, closed my eyes.

I thought about Pelton and his phone messages.

Sooner or later, I'd have to give him an explanation for Vasquez's escape. Sooner or later I'd have to give him two more names to scratch from the guard roster. I pictured Pelton's puffy red face. I pictured his small, bloodshot eyes—eyes that seemed to have died during all the years that had passed since we'd been friends. I pictured his wife, Rhonda, laying one on me on the patio of the governor's home. My mind raced. I pictured those two kids riding their bikes up and down that steep pit wall, their cherubic faces lighting up when they told me to fuck off. I felt the dentist's gentle grip when we shook hands. I thought about a woman on her knees. A woman with a small, heart-shaped tattoo on her neck giving head to a man with no face. I thought about Logan and his lies, or what appeared to be lies, anyway. I saw Mastriano laid out in a hospital bed faking sleep (maybe), a smile plastered on his face. I couldn't help but make a connection between Logan, Mastriano, and Eduard Vasquez, a connection that went beyond corrections officers and their prisoner.

I rolled over onto my side of the bed, put my face in the pillow, tried to forget about the whole thing. I tried to clear my mind and I tried not to think about a homemade shiv pressed up against Wash Pelton's neck back in September 1971 during the Attica riots. I tried not to think about that Buick running the stop sign a year ago. Eventually, I would fall asleep to the angelic sounds of a jazz guitar and a soprano saxophone singing in my ears, like music by moonlight.

CHAPTER ELEVEN

Tuesday morning I was up before my six-thirty alarm. I tuned in to *Good Morning America* on the small color set as I sat on the edge of the bed and slipped into my running shorts and shoes. While I stretched, the local news came on for their small segment.

The headline came at me like a bullet.

"Notorious cop-killer Eduard Vasquez escaped from Green Haven Maximum Security Penitentiary yesterday afternoon," announced the anchorwoman, "after a vanload of shotgun-toting assailants took him away from the officers in charge of transporting him from the prison to the office of A. J. Royale, a Newburgh dentist who often works on inmates. We spoke with Robert Logan, the senior officer involved in the incident."

Logan had his navy-blue Corrections baseball cap pulled far back on his round head. Someone had added gauze and medical tape to the small bruise above his right eye, making it look a lot worse than it had yesterday afternoon when he had given me his statement. Now he was all frowns as he balanced himself with a cane. The bastard was faking it, making it look like he had withstood one hell of a beating in the name of God, country, and duty.

"Those men came up on us with shotguns," he said, his voice trembling, a glassy, wild look in his eyes. "They pressed the barrels against our heads, made us get down on our knees, threatened to shoot us if we didn't do exactly what they said."

He really poured it on.

"Then they beat us. My partner, Bernie Mastriano, got knocked out cold. We were gagged and locked up together with my own cuffs. They stuffed us into the station wagon and hauled us out to the gravel pit. They assaulted us, tortured us, did unspeakable things." Logan looked shamefully to the floor, as though for effect. It was hard to tell whether his tears were genuine or fake. But to me, the report was like a cup of black coffee and just as bitter. I thought, here's Logan's and Mastriano's chance to gain public sentiment before anyone has the true gen about the escape. Here's their shot to get people on their side, to make themselves look like helpless victims.

The report shifted from Green Haven to Newburgh General. There, lying in his bed, just as still and silent as when I'd seen him yesterday afternoon, was Officer Bernard Mastriano. Now he had a white bandage wrapped around his head and an IV in his arm. A heart monitor was clearly visible in the background. If you listened closely, you could hear the steady beats of his heart over the small speaker of my old portable TV.

Many people surrounded Mastriano.

Family and friends. Standing room only. The crowd of people overflowed out into the hall; people were holding lit candles in their hands. A priest wearing a black habit with a purple cassock draped over his shoulders like a scarf stood just a few feet away from the hospital bed. Anchorwoman Chris Collins stood before the camera. Collins was a good-looking woman with dark, nearly black eyes and black hair cut just to her shoulders. This morning she wore a tight-fitting, fire engine–red minidress and matching blazer.

"We're here in the room of Officer Bernard Mastriano," said Collins directly into the TV camera, "one of the men in charge of Eduard Vasquez when he escaped from Green Haven Prison yesterday afternoon while on a routine trip to a dentist in Newburgh. From what we can make out so far, Mastriano was beaten severely about the head with the back end of a shotgun, until rendered unconscious. Now we're going to speak with Dr. Arnold Fleischer, the physician attending Mastriano, to hear the diagnosis."

For a second or two, confusion overtook the report so that Chris Collins was forced to back off and away from the camera. From out of the crowd emerged the doctor I'd spoken with on Monday. I noticed that the little guy hadn't changed his clothes in all that time. The cameraman gave him a full body shot, then panned in. He wore that same tweed jacket, same white button-down shirt, same running shoes. His thick, curly-black hair was mussed up. He wore a stethoscope around his neck. More for show, I thought, than need.

Chris Collins stuffed a microphone in his face. "Can you tell us, Dr. Fleischer, just what you know up to this point about Mr. Mastriano's condition?"

Fleischer bowed his head toward the mike. He came close to pressing his lips against it. "Mr. Mastriano was brought to us yesterday afternoon," he said pensively. "He bled badly from a wound in the back of the head, near the circle of Willis." Fleischer turned his head and pointed out the area on his own body to demonstrate for the viewers. "It then took me several hours to stem the bleeding and suture the lemon-sized wound. Mister Mastriano has never regained consciousness."

"What, then, is his diagnosis, Doctor?" asked the reporter.

"It's difficult for me to speculate, but if he pulls through, there's a good chance that there will have been significant damage to the nervous system."

"Can you speculate as to the extent, Doctor?"

"We'll just have to wait . . . and pray." Fleischer looked to the floor.

Meanwhile the reporter turned back to the camera as the little doctor faded back into the crowd. "There you have it," she said. "A decorated officer of the law, a dedicated son, struck down while in the line of duty. Just what questions does this unfortunate incident raise about the nature of crime and punishment in our community? How safe are our prisons? Just who is responsible for this lapse of security? Should Eduard Vasquez have been allowed outside prison grounds? Is it a habit that wardens allow cop-killers to just roam the city streets when they should be locked away safely behind bars? And if the warden allows a notorious killer like Vasquez out, shouldn't he be certain that his corrections officers are prepared to handle a disaster such as the one that occurred yesterday afternoon, with weapons and a more concentrated support unit?"

The camera faded away from the reporter and zoomed in to Mastriano's room where a short, rather plump woman with jet-black hair and equally black clothing was seated at the bedside, Mastriano's lifeless hand in hers. Mastriano's mother, no doubt. In a word, she looked destroyed. You could see the tears streaming down her face. Either she was putting on an act as good as her son's or she was as fooled as the rest of the people surrounding him.

"This is Chris Collins reporting live from Newburgh General for Newscenter 13. Now back to our live broadcast of *Good Morning America.*"

I don't think five seconds had elapsed before the phone rang.

I got up off the bed, turned off the TV, and picked up the receiver. I said Val instead of hello.

"How'd you guess?"

"I saw the report," I said. "Logan knows full well he's forbidden to make any comments to the press."

"Haven't had your coffee yet, have you, boss?"

"Now I know Logan has got to be lying."

"There's a real problem here, isn't there?"

"If I don't start getting answers before fingers start pointing in all directions, it could mean any one of our asses in a sling."

"When will you be in?"

"Later," I said. "I've got somebody to see up in Albany first."

"Anyone I know?"

"Norman," I said.

There was a sigh.

"Keeper," Val said, "tell Mike I was asking for him."

Val Antonelli and Mike Norman had been something of an item not too long ago, until Mike's moods and his drinking habits became a bit too much. Even though she found it impossible to be his girl, I couldn't help but think that Val had a real soft spot for him. The strange thing, though, was that whenever she mentioned his name, I got sort of jealous. I knew it was silly, juvenile even. But I really couldn't help the way I felt. "Sure thing, Val," I said, my free hand held out in front of my face, fingers crossed. "I'll remember to give Mike Norman your best."

CHAPTER TWELVE

Lt. Mike Norman sat in his office sipping from a coffee mug with the words I LOVE MY JOB! stenciled around the rim in bold black letters. When he took a drink from the mug, you could see the word NOT! imprinted on the bottom in the same lettering.

I hadn't seen him in a few months, but he looked more haggard than usual.

Norman's face was gaunt, like his skin was too tight for his cheekbones. His eyes were heavy and bloodshot, and what should have been a five o'clock shadow looked more like the emergence of a full-grown beard. A wrinkled and tattered blue blazer hung on a metal coat rack attached to the back of the office door. Mike had his shirt sleeves rolled up, and a brown necktie hung down low on his open-collared shirt. A leather shoulder holster wrapped around his thin shoulders like a harness; his .9 millimeter Glock was stuffed under his left arm, grip forward, easy access.

All the New York State cops were using porcelain Glocks now. Just one way to keep up with the underworld competition. A Glock had no safety other than a trigger you depressed twice just to get off the initial round. From there you kept the finger pressure on until the magazine was empty. But once you chambered a round, you practically had to take the pistol apart in order to dechamber it without firing. I think it's fair to say that a Glock is a weapon for a man or woman who shoots for keeps. I'd fired one a couple of times, but never requisitioned one because, to be perfectly frank, they scared the hell out of me. Imagine a guy who's at best a fair-to-middling shot packing a piece without a safety?

Mike and I shook hands and sat down—Mike at his desk, feet up on top, me on the couch by the door.

"How's Val?" he asked. "She still with you?"

So much for keeping her out of this.

"So far," I said.

"You're having a bad week," Mike said, taking a hit off his I LOVE MY JOB! mug, "and it isn't even Tuesday afternoon yet. That's not like the keeper I remember. How'd you manage it?"

"You're the detective," I said, glad that he dropped the Val issue right away. "You tell me."

"Vasquez flew the coop, huh, just like that?"

"Bolted," I said.

Mike gave me one those squinty-eyed, tight-lipped grins cops seem to perfect by their twenty-fifth year on the job. He opened up his bottom drawer, took out a bottle of ginger brandy, added a shot to his coffee, then gave me a wide-eyed look that said, *Join me.*

I nodded, not out of thirst, but out of consideration. Mike put out another mug, poured a shot.

I sat my briefcase on my lap, opened it, and slipped out a large freezer bag containing Logan's .38 along with the live rounds and the key to the cuffs. I dropped the lot onto Norman's desk. Then I set the briefcase back down on the floor and stood up.

"What's all this?" Mike said, leaning forward, elbows on the desk top.

"I prove the only prints on this stuff are Robert Logan's and Bernie Mastriano's," I said, "I prove the story of three shotgun-packing assailants assisting with Vasquez's escape is a lie. A cover-up for something else."

"You got a hunch?"

"More like a theory," I said, staring up at a calendar that occupied an otherwise bare wall to the right-hand side of Norman's desk. "I smell the proverbial rats and they take the form of Logan and Mastriano."

"I saw the morning news," Norman said. "That scene with Mastriano's mother almost had me bawling."

I nodded and looked at the perfect X's Mike had slashed through each of the square calendar days as they'd passed, one after the other. Only five days X'd out so far in May. By the end of the afternoon, there'd be a sixth.

"You think they made up that story about being attacked?"

"I had Logan in my office only a few hours after the escape," I said. "Not a single mark on the guy. I saw Mastriano in the hospital a few hours later and, again, the same story. Not a mark on his baby face."

"Prints or no prints," Norman said, "you're not gonna prove a god-damned thing."

"But it'll be a start," I said.

"So who's running the show down there, anyway?"

"A guy from Stormville PD by the name of Schillinger."

"Don't know him," Norman said. He drank and frowned, either at me or at the cheap brandy in his old coffee. He broke the seal on the freezer bag. Then he pulled out his handkerchief and shrouded the fingers and palm of his right hand before he gripped the pistol. He closed his left eye and sighted in on the short, four-inch barrel. "Don't see many of these anymore. A Gen-U-Ine relic."

"You can help?" I asked. "Off the record?" I pulled out a Pall Mall, lit it with the Zippo. Then I took a sip of the booze and wished I hadn't. Cheap ginger brandy, sold by the gallon for a drinker like Norman who didn't care how bad his medicine tasted.

Mike straightened up, opened his top drawer, and placed the pistol, bullets, and key ring inside. He closed it, locked it. "I can help," he said. "But I get caught, we both go up shit's creek. Obstructing justice, manipulation of evidence just for starters. Some serious fucking charges going to point you in the face like this fucking Glock hiding inside my armpit." He downed his coffee and brandy so that the word NOT! stared me in the face again. This time Mike filled his mug with brandy only.

"I've considered obstruction already," I said. "It's a chance I've got to take before Logan and Mastriano go too far with the press."

"Logan's not supposed to be opening up his mouth, huh?"

"Department rules," I said. "Unwritten, but rules nonetheless."

Mike smiled. "It'll cost you, Keeper. I mean, I'm closing in on retirement, and you know I've still got to maintain my desirable attributes as a detective."

I blew out some smoke slowly. "Name your price," I said.

Mike leaned back, crossed his hands in his lap, looked up at the ceiling. "Don't rush me," he said. "Delicate operation like this takes some thinking over."

I sat down on the armrest of the couch, half sitting, half standing. "Any ideas, copper?"

"Okay," he said, "I've got it."

"Uh-oh," I said. "Last time I saw that look on your face, I had to buy doughnuts every day for the month of July. Summer of '73, I believe it was. We were at the training academy with Wash Pelton. Cost me fifty bucks in lard and caffeine."

"This evidence could save your ass, Keeper," he said. "Worth more than mere doughnuts, wouldn't you say?" There was a wide smile on his face.

"Definitely more than doughnut-serious," I agreed.

"Okay," Norman said, "I've got it. I agree to pull this favor, lunch is on you once a week for the entire summer."

"Burger King, Wendy's, Jack-in-the-Box, McDonald's, Big Kahuna Burger?"

"None of that shit, Marconi."

I looked at the ceiling. The darkness of Norman's office made the roof nearly invisible, like a black sky on an overcast night.

"No choice?"

"No choice, pal."

"Okay," I said. "Name your venue."

Norman thought hard for a second or two. He took another drink from his mug. "Jack's Oyster House, every Friday, twelve noon. Meet me in the bar for drinks. You buy, of course."

Jack's Oyster House was one of the oldest and most expensive eateries on State Street in downtown Albany. Owned by the same

Jewish family for nearly four generations, Jack's was strictly a New York–style, businessman's restaurant where men, dressed in tuxedos and long white aprons, served you Beefeater martinis and bloody porterhouse steaks.

"I can't talk you down?" I said.

"Them's the terms, pal."

"Anyone finds out about this, could get us both in big trouble."

"Not me, pal," he said, raising his hands. "You came in here, threatened me with my life. I felt intimidated, had nightmares, began drinking heavily. . . ." His voice took on a mock quiver.

"You wouldn't rat on an old buddy, would you, Mike?"

"You ever hear Mike Norman call himself a hero, Keeper? You and Pelton the ones who made it to the big time. Me, I passed out at Attica. Commission's never let me live that one down. Nervous breakdown they called it. Catatonic state. Shit, I was a kid, nineteen years old. Those rebel inmates were going to kill us. Changing departments hasn't helped. Now twenty-five fucking years spent in law enforcement and I still can't make it past lieutenant. They gave me this office—this miserable closet in the corner. But you know what? I don't give a rat's ass."

He took another deep swig from the mug.

"For a cop," I said, "you've got a shaky moral foundation and a bad attitude."

Norman nodded thoughtfully, as if that was the point. And I guess it was.

"Questionable at best," he said. Then he took another pull on his brandy. "Tell you what," he went on, "that shit happens and you get busted, I promise to visit you in the can every Friday, twelve noon, with file sandwiches."

"File sandwiches?"

"Yours comes with a file stuffed between the ham and cheese." He planted another smile on that tired, gaunt face.

"Now I see why we've been pals all these years," I said.

"Hey," Mike said, blowing his nose with the same hankie he'd used on Logan's .38, "what the fuck are good friends for?"

CHAPTER THIRTEEN

It's impossible for me to remember everything that happened during those four hopeless days at Attica. Much of it is distorted, the memories jumbled and mixed together. What I do remember has, over the years, taken on all the sharpness and vividness of the present. What I mean is, there are certain events that repeatedly occur in my mind, as if they have nothing to do with the past at all, as though they are always happening over and over again in the present. Whether or not the events actually happened that way doesn't matter anymore. Because when it comes to memories, what counts is not accuracy, but the feelings they call up.

I can still see Mike Norman sitting with his back against the stone wall, his knees pressed up against his chest. Pelton sits beside me, Indian-style. We say nothing, do nothing. We just stare at Mike, who hasn't been sick to his stomach for an hour now, or what seems an hour, anyway. It's hard to tell. The sun is going down over the yard. Bonfires lighting up the night make the yard seem oddly festive, like a carnival of death.

Some of the inmates have been busy hammering together a large platform out of the loose boards and plywood pulled from the physical plant. From here the platform looks like a staging area of some kind. Maybe a gallows. Some of the inmates come into the yard with Ding-Dongs, Twinkies, little bags of potato chips, and other junk looted from the commissary. They offer us nothing to eat, and I know better than to ask. Occasionally a black-and-white chopper makes a flyby, shining bright white spotlights against the gravel floor of the open yard. When it passes, the inmates throw rocks and shout obscenities, as if words alone will bring the chopper down.

What's the fucking point of choppers, I think.

What can they possibly do for us from the air?

Mike Norman hugs his legs and stares straight ahead, but I'm not sure he's seeing anything at all. Wash asks me what we should do about him. Nothing we can do, I say, but wait. But then I see a CO running like a bat out of hell from a gang of six rebel inmates. He is barefoot, dressed only in his uniform trousers. He tries to evade the rebels by attempting to climb from the first-story gallery up to the second-story gallery along the steel bars that run vertically against the face of D-Block. I can see his bare chest and face pressed up against the bars from where I sit. The gang of six inmates comes after him from behind. They claw at him while he panics and holds to those iron bars for his life. But there are too many inmates. They are enraged, crazy. They climb up after the CO, pull him down off the wall. The last I hear of him, he is kicking and screaming and gagging. "They're cutting my throat," he screams. "They're cutting my fucking throat." I close my eyes and try to think of Fran, but it's no use. The bloody gurgling sound is so loud it echoes throughout the yard, reverberates against the insides of my skull, kills the image of Fran.

Then there is nothing.

I go dizzy, like the entire prison has been pulled out from under me. Wash Pelton buries his face in his hands and cries. But it's Mike Norman who takes it the hardest. He passes out, just like that. A little smile forms at the corners of his mouth, a slight, wry, angelic smile. Peaceful. Like he's dreaming a sweet dream.

CHAPTER FOURTEEN

Giles Garvin occupied a single ten-by-twelve cell within a row of five so-called special cells. The cells are situated on a fourth-floor wing of the administration building and accessed primarily by a freight elevator with a closed-circuit camera unit installed in the ceiling. Anyone transported up or down the elevator to and from the special cells is videotaped. For code reasons, there is a fire escape located at the opposite end of this wing that contains a Plexiglas-walled guard shack, video surveillance monitors, padlocked closets with restraining equipment, and tranquilizers. For security reasons, the fire escape is barred off and bolted closed. There is an additional wall of iron bars outside the usual set of bars that enclose the cells. It's because of this second set of vertical iron bars that inmates and guards alike take a certain pride in calling this special place the cage.

The cage houses inmates who pose a greater-than-average threat to the general population. Inmates who get a special kick out of stabbing a fellow inmate directly in the face, for instance. The mutilation that results is the brand or tattoo handed down by a man of power, a man to be respected. Or the men incarcerated in the cage may enjoy getting together with three or four cronies and holding a fat new fish down on all fours, fucking him from behind. Or the caged men may be in the habit of storing two or three days' worth of shit in an unflushed toilet and tossing it at an unsuspecting prison official or visiting lawyer.

The cage not only protects the general population from its more lethal killers. It also serves the opposite function. It protects marked men who wouldn't last a single day in general population from being offed with a shiv to the liver.

Inside the cage these men could be kept under twenty-four-hour supervision—no outside contact, no chow in the mess hall, no television privileges, no visitors, few phone calls, no windows or fresh air. The only exercise is one hour per day of supervised recreation in a fifty-by-fifty gravel-covered yard normally set aside for condemned prisoners. Other than that, the immediate landscape of the caged prisoner is concrete walls and floors; iron bars; stainless-steel toilets, sinks, and bunks, and Plexiglas shields (to cover the cells of the shit throwers).

This was the price of protection.

Garvin's cell was covered with just such a Plexiglas shield. He was a twenty-nine-year-old Latino-and-black mix from the streets of New York City who, before being shipped to Green Haven, used to wait outside grade schools, lure kids into his van, take them for a ride into the country, and touch them a little before he wrapped their heads in bed sheets and plastic shopping bags, dismembered their bodies, masturbated onto the limbless torsos, then scattered their body parts throughout Dutchess County. Maybe a head in a streambed, an arm in a wooded area south of Catskill, a full torso propped upright (with the feet, hands, and head cut off) against a gravestone in a cemetery called Heavenly Gardens in Cairo. His most famous case involved a six-year-old beauty-pageant winner whom he gagged and bound and tossed into a Dumpster (alive presumably), which he then doused with gas and set on fire. On the macadam underneath the burned-out Dumpster, investigators found three semen-filled rubbers indicating that, for some odd reason, Giles Garvin had felt the need to use a condom while he jerked himself off at the crucial moment when the flames were consuming that poor kid. The fire, incidentally, inside the Dumpster was so intense, that all that was found of the little girl some four hours later (after

Garvin had phoned in the whereabouts of his latest victim) were a couple of fragments of her teeth, which authorities used to make a positive ID. It was some weeks later that forensic scientists were actually able to extract enough DNA from the six-year-old's tooth to match it with skin and blood taken from under Garvin's fingernails. The tiny bit of DNA evidence was all it took to put the mark on Garvin and, in turn, send him away for the rest of his life. The only thing keeping him from lethal injection was the possibility of insanity.

Since Garvin couldn't strangle, burn, masturbate over, or dismember kids anymore, he had become one hell of a good drug salesman, which seemed oddly out of character for him, since drug dealing, at base, was a hustler's business, not a cold-blooded killer's. For his own protection, he spent a lot of time in the cage. New York State wasn't about to make the same mistake the state of Wisconsin had made with Jeffery Dahmer.

On this Tuesday, he slithered out from the dark regions of his cramped cell and pressed his body up against the vertical bars when I was let into the cage by the presiding CO. He gave me a teeth-biting sneer that wasn't much of a welcome wagon as the CO took his time manually releasing the locking device on the cell. He stood there with his short, well-groomed hair and his wiry, vascular, copper-colored body.

I stepped inside.

The CO closed the gate behind me and moved back to his post at the edge of the guard shack where the electronic panels powering the cell doors were located.

For now, I took a seat on Garvin's stainless-steel bunk while he used the rim of the stainless-steel toilet as a chair. He was dressed only in gray inmate pants, his torso exposed. His chest was mapped with scars and pockmarks, trophies earned from attacks by rival gang members. On his left biceps was a tattoo of a rose. A very beautiful tattoo of a red rose. He had a thin, coarse face, like a man who had spent too much time in the sun before coming to the iron house. Tattooed to his cheek, below his left eye, were four tiny blue teardrops. His hair was bleach-blond, neatly cropped, slicked back against his head.

I gave Garvin a Pall Mall, lit it for him. He blew the smoke out slowly through his nostrils. In the meantime, I could hear shouts and jeers coming from the caged animals near Garvin's cell. "I want my fucking lawyer. Rehabilitation, shit. I want my lawyer. . . ." They went on and on, not making sense, but making a plea nonetheless, because that's all they had left to do. But like living beside a railroad track, after a while you just don't hear the trains anymore.

"He had like this scheme going," whispered Garvin a minute or two after I asked him his thoughts on Eduard Vasquez now that he had escaped. "Years ago, Eddy knew he had to buy into the program. It was his way up the chain of command, so to speak. Wasn't long before he was pushing like one thousand, two thousand pounds inside and outside the joint." Garvin looked up at me. His smile was oddly attractive, oddly confident. "Over-the-counter trading he called it," he said, exposing a gold tooth, a shining gem amongst a mouthful of rotting molars, incisors, and cuspids.

"What about the escape?" I said, laying my hands out flat on the cold steel bed.

Garvin faced the sky, blew perfect smoke rings that dissipated against the concrete-paneled ceiling. "Orders would come in from the inmates and visitors. Manhattan street prices prevailed, no more, no less, far as we could tell. Keep market value consistent, that was the motto, like that was the fucking rule. Orders left the prison with the visitors, along with logistical information. . . . You know, like where and when the drop would take place. Same thing would happen if the drop was going to be on the inside. Course, that was much trickier. Shit came in and out with the visitor, hidden inside a deflated balloon stuffed up his ass. Or, more likely, stuff came through in bulk, through the service entrance, with the deliveries and the laundry."

"So tell me something I don't already know, Giles," I said, holding out the pack of cigarettes for him again. "I mean, why does a guy like Vasquez even sell shit when he doesn't have a prayer of seeing the outside?"

Without hesitating he took another cigarette from the pack and lit it off the one just smoked. "Okay," he said, "all right. Like Vasquez was selling so he'd have a nest egg for him and his girlfriend, what's her name?"

"You tell me," I said.

He smiled a mouth full of black-and-brown teeth, the one capped in gold out of place and sparkling in the raw white light that came from the overhead ceiling fixture. "I don't have no fucking names," he said. "But I do know this about Vasquez. He was selling shit so he and his girl could have something to live on down in Mexico when he finally got his chance to split. But like, he couldn't split right away. Like he was waiting for the perfect security personnel, the right guards, you dig it? Eddy, he's a motherfucker for sure, but he's one smart motherfucker. He knew he had only one chance, one shot. He had to get hold of some guards who didn't have no problem taking a bribe."

I put my hand in my pocket and fingered the number-ten-size envelope with Cassandra Wolf's address on it.

"You want to give me the names of the guards who were working with Vasquez?"

"Yeah," he said, leaning back against the concrete wall, laying his tattooed forearm across his lap. "Like I really, really do, Mister Warden sir."

He looked into my eyes with that killer smile. I wondered if it was the same smile he had used when he had lured those kids into his van. I guess this was the part of the one-on-one where I was supposed to feel a slight chill shoot up from the base of my spine. I wasn't sure if my lack of feeling was more an indication of Garvin's lack of effect on me or my own desensitization. On the other hand, there was something very practical and useful going on here and I didn't want to blow it by getting on Garvin's bad side, although I'm not so sure he had a good side at all. Fact is, it wasn't often that an inmate would just open up about a fellow inmate unless some serious shit was going down between them. "So why are you telling me all this, Giles?"

Garvin's already-hard face went noticeably taut. His skin turned fire-engine red. He used his lit cigarette as a pointer when he extended his fist to my face. "Should I say, Mister Warden sir, that Eduard Vasquez, motherfucker that he is, is on my shit list? Should I say that Vasquez, when I get to him, is like one dead motherfucker? Would that be incriminating myself, Mister Warden, sir? Because if it is, like I don't give a motherfuck."

I opened up to the voices of the other caged men. "Hey Warden Marconi, I know you're in there. . . ." I heard the voices until I would not allow myself to listen to them anymore.

In the meantime, Garvin had settled down a little. "But I don't give away information without a price," he said, blowing another stream of smoke into the sweat-soaked air.

"Listen, Giles," I said, wondering just what Vasquez had done to double-cross him, "I can't do a thing about your sentence. Those kids you murdered are too much. But I can make it easier for you in here."

Giles stared at me with translucent blue eyes hidden in chiseled cavities. The four baby-blue teardrops tattooed to his face were bitter reminders of the four children he had murdered and mutilated.

"But first," I said, "give me names."

Garvin looked to one side of his cell and then to the other as if expecting to see something besides concrete and steel and slime. "Okay, Mister Warden, sir," he said, leaning up and resting his elbows on his knees. "But you gotta promise me one thing."

I nodded.

"That when it comes time, you speak up for me."

Garvin had no chance for parole. If the jury hadn't wrestled with the sanity question, they would have sent him straight to death row. I had no idea what Vasquez could have done to betray him.

"No deals," I said. "Any deal gets made, I make it."

Garvin spread his thin legs wide, grabbed his balls. "Blow me," he said.

"You know the score, Garvin," I said. "Word gets out I gave you a deal, my name's shit in the iron house."

Garvin dropped the spent cigarette through his spread legs so that it landed in the toilet. I heard the quick hiss of the doused flame. He leaned back against the concrete wall. When I offered him a third cigarette, he refused, choosing instead to cross his arms against his chest as though in protest.

"Names," I said.

He hesitated for a second or two. "Fuck you," he said. "Like you don't want to help me, then fuck you."

"No deals."

"You just want those names so you can save your ass," Garvin said. "You ain't got no interest in helping me. I read the papers too, Warden. Like, you been slipping since your wife got killed. Like, maybe your mind just ain't on your job no more."

"Yeah," I said, standing up from the stainless-steel bed, nodding for the guard to release the cell door, "I'm a million miles away."

"No deals," Garvin said, "then fuck you."

The cell door opened, electronically this time—an iron cell within an iron cage.

"Go ahead," said Garvin, laughing now, showing me his gold tooth, "waste your time, man. Like 'California Dreamin'.' Just like that stupid-ass song. You be real safe, you be real warm if you was in L.A."

I turned to leave.

"Don't you see, Warden, California was never real. Like California was just a big fuckin' dream. You are the warden, aren't you? Like, you can do anything."

"Yeah," I said. "I'm the big boss, Giles." I didn't have the slightest idea what he was trying to tell me, if he was trying to tell me anything at all. It was rants like this that had spared him from lethal injection when judge and jury handed down their sentence. Nutty rants and raves that made little or no sense.

But then, Garvin had been on the money about one thing.

Since Fran had died, I had been a million miles away. If my mind had been on my job, then maybe—just maybe—I would not have let Vasquez go like that, civil liberties or no civil liberties.

I tossed the pack of cigarettes onto Garvin's bunk and got the hell out.

CHAPTER FIFTEEN

It was quarter past five on a Tuesday afternoon. I took a fresh pack of smokes from the carton stored in the right-hand drawer of my desk. Val Antonelli and Dan Sloat had left for the day, an unavoidable situation that always made me feel a little empty inside. I checked my voice mail. Only one person had left a message. What I mean is, at least six other calls had been placed but the caller or callers had hung up without saying a word about who they were, what they wanted, or why they had to talk to me (but not over the machine).

In the prison business, hang-ups were never a good sign.

Pelton, I thought. Pelton or the press.

Probably both.

I popped a cigarette from the new pack, lit it, and leaned back in my swivel chair. Then I reached over and hit the playback button.

Keeper, Schillinger at Stormville PD letting you know we got dead ends all around. Nothing in Vasquez's cell. Nothing at the road blocks. Noth-

*ing from the California people in Olancha. Just dead ends. We've con-
tacted the FBI, and as I speak, border patrol is doing what they can for us
in case Vasquez is headed south, but who knows. That's it, that's the
score. Just dead ends, you know. Call me back with anything you find
out. Oh yeah, one more thing. I need to tell you that tomorrow we should
sit down and talk about what went wrong on your end.*

Detective Martin Schillinger hung up having delivered his little threat.
Tomorrow he wanted to talk. Over my dead body, I thought. Or maybe
that's what someone had in mind. I found it surprising that he never
once mentioned the photos Dan Sloat and I had handed over to him
inside Vasquez's empty cell. He must have examined them. To me, a
photo of some woman with a heart-shaped tattoo on her neck was a
clue that deserved follow-up. But then, he was the detective and I was
the concerned warden.

I played Schillinger's message back again. When it finished, the
receiver hung up and a dial tone took over. Then nothing. I played the
message back one last time. It didn't change, so I erased it.

I looked at my watch. Five-eighteen on a hot, still afternoon in May.

Happy hour. What was there to feel happy about?

I poured myself a drink anyway, and decided to put a couple down
for all the wrong reasons.

If I called Schillinger I would probably catch him in his office. But
what would I have to tell him about the escape? He'd want the truth
and I had no idea about the truth. I thought about Logan's statement,
about the three armed assailants who had beaten him and Mastriano. I
thought about the little bump above Logan's left eye and then suddenly
I pictured the wide white medical bandage that he had wrapped around
his head, specifically for a television audience. I pictured Mastriano
lying in a hospital bed, his mother sitting by his side, her hands clasped
around his. I pictured Giles Garvin blowing smoke rings up to the
ceiling of his cell.

I took another sip of the whiskey. While the drink was going down
smooth and warm against my pipes, it dawned on me. Giles Garvin.
That stuff he'd been rambling on about, just before I'd left his cell.
California dreamin'. I thought about Schillinger's message, how they

had contacted the people in Olancha, California. I thought about the envelope I found in Vasquez's cell yesterday afternoon. I pulled it out of my pocket and studied it in the white light that came from my desk lamp. There wasn't much to look at, just a typical envelope addressed to Vasquez with a return address from Cassandra Wolf in Olancha. But then I looked at the postmark. The circular mark inlaid over a rectangle was barely legible. But when I put it under the light, I could just about make out the letters. The mark was dated 1 May 1997, but it hadn't come from Olancha, California, at all. The goddamned letter had been postdated at an office in Athens, New York. No wonder Vasquez had eluded the road blocks. No wonder Schillinger and his men had nothing to go on. Vasquez must have somehow made the eighty-mile trek north to meet Cassandra Wolf in Athens.

I sat back in my swivel chair, smoked the cigarette, drank the whiskey.

The importance of what I'd done—withholding police evidence and hampering a state investigation—kicked in, turned my stomach inside out. Maybe Garvin was right. Maybe I was trying to get at the truth just to save my behind for not being more careful when it came to transporting inmates outside the prison. At best, I could just keep avoiding Schillinger the way I'd been avoiding Pelton for the last twenty-four hours. Avoid him and hope he focused his attention on other things, like where to begin looking for Vasquez. But then, I wanted to be the first one to find Vasquez, have him give me the true gen on what was happening to me and to Green Haven.

I poured myself another whiskey. Like bad medicine, I downed it in one swallow. I poured another and drank that down, just as fast. I felt the liquor warm my insides, like an embrace from a beautiful woman, and just as tender. I poured one last shot, took the phone off the hook, closed my eyes, and embraced the woman.

CHAPTER SIXTEEN

I left the office at 6:55 and arrived home fifteen minutes later. I was groggy from the whiskey, but not so dazed that I couldn't catch the rest of the seven o'clock news. Dan Rather spoke from his New York studio to a reporter inside the hospital room of Green Haven CO Bernard Mastriano. Mastriano had attracted national attention. The reporter stood exactly where Chris Collins had stood earlier, at the foot of Mastriano's bed so that you could see him and his mother by his side.

"Has there been any word on the possible location of Eduard Vasquez?" Dan Rather asked the reporter, his face stern and white-looking under that head of hair dyed shoe-polish black.

"No such luck, Dan. All we can tell at this point is that road block and surveillance efforts have proven unsuccessful. In fact, there's speculation that Vasquez may have already escaped the state of New York altogether. Perhaps by now, more than twenty-four hours after the initial breakout, Vasquez has even made it out of the country."

Athens, I thought. He went to Athens, New York, to hook up with his girl.

"Has any reason been given for why such a notorious criminal as Eduard Vasquez would have been allowed to visit a dentist on the outside?"

"Dan, that answer can only come from the warden of Green Haven Prison, Mr. Jack 'Keeper' Marconi, and he's been unavailable for comment thus far."

"Let me get this straight," Dan said, pretending to put his field reporter on the spot. "The warden of Green Haven Maximum Security Prison is not guarding his inmates?"

"That seems to be the case, Dan."

There was a slight pause in the report, as if to allow that little exchange to sink in below the belt of every American tuned in to the broadcast.

"Any word on the present condition of the corrections officer who was struck down?"

"Only that he's unconscious and still in intensive care and will be for some days."

Dan turned in his swivel chair and faced the camera. "William Anderson reporting live from the Newburgh General Hospital room of Corrections Officer Bernard Mastriano, the young man whose life hangs in the balance after suffering a severe beating on Monday afternoon when Eduard Vasquez, a convicted cop-killer, escaped from Green Haven Maximum Security Prison in Stormville, New York."

I got up from the bed and turned off the television. A swift kick in the *cojones* would have been an improvement over the way I felt. I took the envelope out of my pocket and stared at the Athens postmark. I knew I had to go to Athens now. I had no choice. My reputation had just been slandered on national television. Someone was covering up something and gradually making me the scapegoat.

I had to find Vasquez, bring him back.

I took the phone in my bedroom off the hook. Then I went into the living room and spun Bucky Pizzarelli and Zoot Sims again, since it was still on the turntable from the night before. I went back into the bedroom and undressed. I hadn't had any dinner yet. But I poured one final drink. I considered having a few more drinks, maybe even getting drunk. But I couldn't allow that to happen. I couldn't relinquish control when it was still so early in the game. I had to stay cool and sober, because this was no game; it was my life. I put the glass down, turned out the light, slipped into bed, and closed my eyes.

It was only seven-thirty in the evening.

I tried to clear my mind, but it was impossible. In the end I went to sleep to the vision of a heart-shaped tattoo.

CHAPTER SEVENTEEN

I had no way of telling how long I'd been asleep, when the front door opened wide and the living room lights came on. I'd been dreaming of Fran again: feeling her beside me, touching me, her lips pressed against mine, my hands against the small of her back, our naked bodies together in bed. Then the dream shifted suddenly so that Fran and I were prisoners sharing a cell. Logan and Mastriano were breaking in during the middle of the night to shake us down. I could smell the worm smell that comes from the prison galley. I could feel the way the hot summer night made the sweat ooze from my back and from the concrete ceiling overhead. I could see the tight faces of the two guards as they came through the open cell gate, arms outstretched, going for our necks. I could feel Fran in my arms, smell her sweet familiar smell, feel her hair on my lips. Then my eyes focused and I realized I wasn't inside a jail cell at all. Fran was no longer there and I saw the figure of a man standing in my bedroom doorway.

This was no dream.

Zoot Sims and Bucky Pizzarelli had stopped jamming.

My palms and forehead were covered in a layer of sweat.

Too late to reach for the .45 I kept stored under the mattress for just such an emergency. Listen: Even under the circumstances, I made a mental note to store the weapon in a more accessible place. But then it dawned on me: If this man was a burglar, he hadn't been very stealthy about breaking and entering. He wasn't stealing anything.

"Excuse me, sir," the man said. "You up?"

A polite housebreaker.

I propped myself up on one elbow and squinted. Behind the man, I could see two more men. One tall. One short. They were moving around inside the living room of my state-appointed home examining the framed photographs of my wife on the walls and on the tables. They were picking up the picture frames, studying the different portraits, placing them back down again exactly where they had found them.

"Come on in," I said. "Who knocks anymore?"

No smiles came from the big man in the doorway. Not even a crack in his stone face.

"Mr. Marconi?" the man inquired, his low baritone voice now sounding somehow familiar.

I nodded.

"You're wanted in Albany, sir, immediately."

"If not sooner, right?" Definitely a voice I recognized even if I couldn't see the face all that clearly in the darkness of the bedroom. I sat all the way up in bed. "Who wants to see me?" I said. But I already knew the answer to that question. I knew that the men had come in through the front door, without breaking in, simply because they'd had a key. No need to jimmy the lock or break a window or slide down the chimney, for that matter. No need to call the police, because they were the police. They had a key to the place. In fact they probably had keys to all the identical, half a dozen or so, single-story, state-owned homes on this quiet rural road in Stormville.

So that was it, then, that's where I had heard that voice before. The voice of the man standing in my bedroom doorway belonged to a member of Pelton's private staff. If he was the kid I remembered, his name was Tommy Welch. Not a bad kid really. Just a young man robbed from my own staff of COs by Pelton himself when he had come down for one of his surprise inspections a year ago last April. What Tommy lacked in brains he made up for in muscles and loyalty.

"Commissioner Pelton wants to see you now, Mr. Marconi."

I rubbed my eyes. "I'll let you in on a little secret, Tommy," I said. "The state of New York includes a telephone in your boss's budget. Tell him I said to use it."

"He's your boss, too, Mr. Marconi," Tommy tried to remind me. "And my orders are to bring you back with me tonight, so if you don't mind."

I glanced at the digital display clock beside the queen-size bed. Two-thirty in the A.M., Wednesday. Tommy took a couple of steps into the bedroom so that now I could make out more of his clean-shaven face in the light that leaked in from the living room. He wore dark slacks, black turtleneck, black blazer, black mailman shoes. His black hair was crew-cut short and he had sideburns that covered his cheekbones, like Elvis. He was only an inch or two taller than me, but his shoulders were wide enough to fill the doorjamb.

I wiped my hands on my T-shirt. Then I reached over and flicked on the table lamp.

Tommy took a small scrap of paper from his pocket, unfolded it, read it, and put it back. "Mr. Pelton wants to ask you a few questions about the escape of Eduard Vasquez before he faces the news media at a noontime press conference."

"I've got a better idea," I said. "Why don't you and your boys get back in your car and tell Pelton I'll see him first thing in the morning." I turned out the light and slipped back into bed. "And don't forget to hit the light in the living room on the way out." I stretched my legs so that my bare feet slipped out from underneath the covers at the foot of the bed.

First came the footsteps—heavy, power-lifter footsteps. Then the light went back on. Even with my eyes closed, the bright white light burned my eyes through the skin of my eyelids.

"I'm real sorry about this, Mr. Marconi," Tommy said in a deep, whisper voice, "but Mr. Pelton wants to speak with you now. So if you'll get dressed and come with me . . . ."

I leaned up on one elbow, took a good look into the living room. I

could see the two men who had accompanied Tommy Welch. Name-
less men who stood shoulder to shoulder in the hall just outside the
bedroom door. They weren't leaving without me.

I turned over and let out a sigh. "No choice, huh, big fella?"

"No choice, sir."

I slipped out of bed, stood up, felt my lightheadedness give way to
imbalance as I reached out for the end table. "Now I'm going to get
dressed," I said, "if you don't mind."

Tommy glanced at the open window in the wall opposite the open
door. Then he glanced back at me.

"Look-it," I said, just to be more difficult. "Could you please turn
around."

Tommy stood there, his eyes moving from the open window to me
and back to the window again, like I was guilty of something and about
to use the window as a means for a quick getaway. But Tommy was a
good kid really, and he had been a good guard before Pelton had taken
him away from me. He was doing what he did best: following orders.

"Afraid I might run off, Tommy?"

No response other than that stone face staring at me between glances
at the open window.

"Lucky we're just a bunch of dicks here," I said, dropping my draw-
ers, "or I'd really feel stupid."

CHAPTER EIGHTEEN

I sat back in an expensive leather chair, not four feet away from Washington Pelton, commissioner of corrections for the state of New York, and one-time friend to both Mike Norman and myself. It was our first meeting since last Christmas at the governor's wassail party. He hadn't said a word to me since Tommy Welch had escorted me in twenty minutes earlier. Instead, he had buried himself in paperwork that, for some reason, had to be expeditiously processed at four-thirty in the morning. Pelton wore a neatly pressed, black pinstripe suit. A far cry from the stiff, navy-blue uniforms the two of us, along with Mike Norman, had worn when we'd started out at Attica more than twenty-five years ago. The white shirt beneath his suit was finely pressed. Gold cuff links secured the sleeves at the wrists. The tie was silk. Sitting there, I tried to decide if Pelton was dressed for the new day or had never gone to bed the night before.

Regardless of his sleeping habits, I could see through Pelton's act.

He would not look up at me until good and goddamned ready. I could have ranted and raved. I was pissed off enough to grab him by the collar, pin him down on the floor. But then, maybe that's what he wanted. Maybe this was a test to see how far he could push me before I did something stupid like backhand him across the kisser. In the end it would not only have cost me my job and my reputation, it would have put me in jail. I was no longer bargaining from a position of power. Pelton was the commissioner and I answered directly to the commissioner.

For now, I had to be content with looking over his shoulders and studying the many custom-framed photos that decorated the walnut paneling behind his desk. Photos of the commissioner embraced in handshake with New York Governor George Pataki; another of him seated at a round table with Ronald Reagan; another with his arm wrapped around the shoulders of George Bush, broad smiles on their faces. Proud Republicans, the entire bunch.

I sat back and took in the floor-to-ceiling, French-paned windows that overlooked the darkened Albany skyline and the Hudson River in the near distance. Outside I could see the occasional flicker of red neon that came from an electric billboard planted on the flat rooftop of a nearby office building. Pelton's office was dimly lit from the green-shaded banker's lamp positioned in the center of his mahogany desk.

But here's the strange part.

When he finally looked up at me, Pelton's eyes went wide, as though my less than sudden appearance had taken him completely by surprise. He added further to the act by dropping his pen and sitting back in his chair, locking both hands like a headrest behind his gray-haired head. He looked out the window into the early morning darkness.

"Did you get any coffee, Keeper?" His voice was so soft and understated, I barely caught his words. He focused his glance beyond me and directed Tommy Welch to get me that cup of coffee.

"How've you been making out these past few months, Keeper?" he asked. "Since Fran passed away, I mean."

I nodded, as though saying, *Fine, the world is my fucking oyster*. But I didn't like Pelton calling me Keeper any more than I liked entering into any courteous small talk with him, especially about Fran. If it had been twenty years ago, I wouldn't have minded. Twenty years ago, I might have welcomed the small talk. But that was then and since then, we had both changed and gone our separate ways, formed our own alliances and surrendered to our own ambitions. So now I minded.

"They never did find the man who killed her, did they?" Pelton asked.

"You know full well they never found him," I said.

Tommy Welch came back into the room and placed a china saucer and cup on the far end of Pelton's desk. No styrofoam cups in this right-wing office. Before the big man backed off, he placed a finely polished silver spoon on the saucer.

"How's Rhonda?" I said, not able to resist the temptation. "Word's out she's on the wagon."

Pelton pretended to think about it for a second or two. Then he let out a fake laugh. "Keeper," he said, "now you know full well she isn't."

"So you drag me here at four-thirty in the morning to discuss our separate domestic and family affairs."

"No, Keeper," Pelton said, shaking his cranium from shoulder to shoulder. "This has nothing whatsoever to do with your immediate family. This is all about your extended prison family. So perhaps I should get right to the point and dispense with any further niceties."

"Please do," I said. "I'd like to get a shave before work."

Pelton's face went noticeably taut. "Tommy," he said, waving his right arm in the air like a pointer, "send in Mr. Warren, would you, please?"

I heard the door to the office open and then a man walked in and stood between me and Pelton's desk. It was John "Jake" Warren.

"Keeper, Jake," Pelton said, "I'm sure you two know one another."

I didn't get up, nor did I bother with a handshake. Warren had worked for the Commission for almost as long as I had worked for the department. Now he was Pelton's second in command, the man directly responsible for security in and out of state prisons. Ironically he made more money than Pelton, the commissioner's salary not having been raised in more than a decade. But then, Warren didn't need the money, his family owning and operating a good-size machine works in a small Mohawk River town just north of the Albany city limits. Recently Warren had announced his candidacy for state senate on the Republican ticket. An escape, no matter who was responsible, could only hurt his chances for election, since it clearly represented a breakdown in the system that he oversaw. Warren took a seat behind Pelton's desk. Clearly he hadn't been asked to be here in the interest of discussing politics.

"Keeper," Wash Pelton said, "why don't you tell Jake and I just what plans you've established for getting this man Vasquez back."

I took a quick glance around the room, because it suddenly dawned on me that Pelton could be taping this conversation. In that case, I had to answer carefully.

"Taking it by the book," I said. "All the procedural stuff. General lockdown, no authorized field trips of any kind, tightened security, better food."

"But you're not answering my question," Pelton went on. "Haven't you taken any action to get Mr. Vasquez back?"

"I'm not sure I understand?"

"In other words, Keeper," Pelton said, once again looking out his window, "your position in this matter is purely passive."

"What can I possibly do? There's an investigation team on it now. Schillinger from Stormville PD is handling it. FBI's been alerted."

"Yes," Pelton said, "I know."

The room fell quiet for a moment.

And then Pelton said, "Keeper, do you recall Deputy Commissioner Warren having called you about the possibility that Eduard Vasquez might escape?"

"No," I said, my eyes on Warren, getting a good look at his dark blue Brooks Brothers single-breasted suit. "All I've been getting from the Commission are calls for names to scratch from my guard roster."

Warren pushed his horn-rimmed glasses farther up on the crown of his nose. Then he crossed his legs.

"Are you sure?" Pelton asked. I noticed that his voice was getting deeper, more inquisitive, slower than normal—trying his best to convince me of something that hadn't happened at all.

"Yes," I said, sitting up straight in my chair, gripping the armrests with my fists. "No one ever called me about Vasquez. Only about names."

Outside the window, the full moon was plainly visible over the west bank of the Hudson River as it reflected off its surface. In just a little while, it would be the sun's turn to reflect as it rose over the Berkshire Mountains to the east.

"Well," Pelton said, touching his thin lips with the back of his pen, "you'd better get your story straight."

I looked into his eyes. "What do you mean get my story straight?" I said.

"Mr. Warren seems to recall having contacted you."

The light of the full moon cast a pale luminescence over everything in the large room, including Pelton's red face. Somewhere, a church bell sounded, one lonely chime after the other, and stopped after only five chimes.

"No," I said, "I don't recall getting a call from Mr. Warren. I don't think I could forget a thing like that." I tried to make eye contact with Warren. But he sat behind Pelton's chair, legs crossed, eyes gazing down at the floor. Pelton got up and went to the window.

"I know Warren spoke with you," he said.

"Listen, Wash," I said, now feeling the blood boiling inside my head, "I don't care if you are my superior, but I've just been kidnapped from my home."

"No," he said, "not kidnapped."

"Yes, bloody-well kidnapped and brought here to answer questions about an escape I had no way of anticipating. Now you want me to agree to phone calls that never occurred. What the hell's going on?" Now Pelton was looking out the window into the full moon.

"Temper, Keeper," he said. "I thought we were all on the same team here."

"Okay, Wash," I said, my voice lowered a decibel or two, "I'll tell you what. When I get back to work in a little while I can ask Val about any phone calls that might have been placed. She keeps excellent records. She'll know if Warren called."

The room fell quiet for a minute.

And then Wash said, "Keeper, I'm sure by now you have a pretty good idea about what's going on here."

I nodded. "You want me to take the blame for the Vasquez escape."

"I didn't say that exactly."

"You want me to take the blame so that you can save your precious asses . . . so that you can stay up here in this white tower and so Warren here can get his state senate seat. Am I right?"

"I like my job," Pelton said, "if that's what you mean. Jake here, he has his aspirations also."

"This conversation's over," I said, standing up from the chair. "I'm not about to take the blame for anybody else's screwups." I turned to go to the door. But Tommy Welch, loyal as ever, blocked the entire frame.

Pelton shouted: "Superintendent Marconi!"

I turned.

"Sit down," he said. "Please. You don't have to take the blame for this." He took a deep breath.

"Excuse me?" I said.

"All you have to do is admit that Jake called you, warned you, and you simply forgot." The moonlight was disappearing now as the orange haze of morning began to overtake the night. "I'll fix it so that it was all a mistake," he went on. "All you have to do is admit it. And then I'll take care of your little reward." He hesitated a bit between "little" and "reward."

The orange morning light began to sneak its way in through the office windows, drowning everything in its rays, including Pelton's face.

"You're not saying anything, Marconi," Pelton shouted. "This is your fucking life we're talking about here. I'm trying to save it, just like you saved mine at Attica. Don't let pride fuck it up. A lot of money for a lot of people could be at stake."

The morning light became almost too bright to look at.

"Do you know I could have you fired for this escape and brought up on charges for negligence? I mean, for Christ's sake, Keeper, you executed the releases that allowed a convicted cop-killer to just walk outside the gates of Green Haven."

The pressure in my head was suddenly replaced with a sickening, sinking feeling, like my organs were about to slide out from underneath my skin, spill all over the floor.

"Admit it, Keeper, you just haven't been the same since Fran passed on." Pelton was smiling now. "I mean, you haven't really been paying attention, have you?"

I took couple of steps closer to him. "You'll get nothing from me, Wash," I said, "because I didn't do anything wrong."

"You didn't do anything right either," Pelton shouted. He ran his hands through his thinning gray hair, took a deep breath. He looked at me and I glared at him, our eyes locked. His eyes were stone cold and wet. His lips were taut and angry. So this is what it had all come down to, I thought. This is what it was all about. Somebody's dirty money.

"Okay then," he said. "Fuck it." He walked around to the opposite side of his desk, picked up the phone, pounded a button or two on the phone unit. He kept his eyes locked on me the entire time, as though I might just disappear into the woodwork. Warren, on the other hand, stayed seated, staring at the floor. A liar caught perpetrating his own lie in the name of might and right. A true Republican, I thought. A true-to-life right-winger. I heard an electronic buzzing coming from outside the room. When it stopped, Pelton whispered something into the phone. I heard the sound of footsteps on the floor in the hall outside the door. There must have been two or three people, at least, on their way down the corridor toward Pelton's office. Their leather soles slapped against the terrazzo floor of the state building. They were running, not walking. Their quick steps matched the rapid beating of my heart. My stomach collapsed, my chest tightened. I could feel them coming for me as Pelton slammed the phone down. The wood-and-glass door opened and two uniformed police officers came into the room along with Detective Martin Schillinger.

Pelton pointed to me, his arm outstretched across his mahogany desk. Warren leaned over, buried his face in his hands. Behind him was the photograph of Ronald Reagan. Behind him were the photographs of President Bush and Governor Pataki. All those politicians posing for the camera, glowing faces perpetually locked in those twenty-five-cent smiles.

Schillinger looked at me with emotionless eyes and a plump white face. As usual, he was wearing that Burberry trench coat. He said: "Mr. Jack 'Keeper' Marconi, you are under arrest for obstructing justice and tampering with police evidence."

I turned toward Wash Pelton. He lifted a large plastic Baggie from inside his desk. It contained Logan's pistol, the rounds of ammo, and the key to his handcuffs. I knew then that it must have been Mike Norman who'd given the thing away right after I'd left his office. He must have called Wash Pelton, told him that I'd been there, and asked him to process the evidence for prints illegally.

I stared at Schillinger.

He stood there with a shit-eating grin planted on his face. I wasn't about to stand around and allow him to arrest me. I wasn't about to stand around and beg for my freedom either. I did what I should have done the minute I'd been escorted into Pelton's office earlier. I went for the door. But one of the cops grabbed my collar from behind. I swung back with my left elbow and clipped his nose. The nose exploded like a water balloon. He went down. A second man grabbed my arm and pushed me backward. A third man knocked my legs out from under me, at the knees. I hit the floor hard. The cop I'd clipped in the nose grabbed a fistful of hair and pounded my forehead against the terrazzo while the other cops held me down. I met the floor with my face two separate times. Once would have been enough; once would have done the trick. I saw the room go dim and wavy before I felt the pain and tight swelling of the egg-shaped lump that had already begun to form on my forehead.

They picked me up off the floor, one man under each arm.

I surveyed the room, tried to get my bearings. I stared at Pelton, Warren, and Schillinger through a haze of bright stars and wavy light.

"You may read Mr. Marconi his rights, Detective Schillinger," Pelton said. "And don't forget to add resisting arrest."

Schillinger reached inside his trench coat and pulled out a leather wallet. He lifted a small plastic card from the billfold and started reading from it.

"You have the right to remain silent. . . ."

Reading me the Miranda rights just added to the annoyance. What I mean is, I knew them by heart. As another cop drew my arms behind my back and closed the handcuffs so tight around my wrists that I could feel the skin tear, I saw my old buddy Wash standing inside that ray of pale, white sunlight. "I'm sorry, Keeper. Really, I'm sorry. But you leave me with no other choice." He wasn't smiling, but then, he wasn't crying either. Jake Warren remained buried in his hands. Hear no evil, see no evil. He never said one word the entire time. He just took a deep breath, as though relieved, as Schillinger and his men began dragging me out of the room. Like his future would be somehow certain, somehow secure so long as I was out of the picture and behind bars.

BOOK TWO

ALBANY AND STORMVILLE

CHAPTER NINETEEN

Here's how I see it now after twenty-six years: In my mind, the Attica riot was something very much like a short war. During the heat of battle there is no such thing as innocent or guilty, no such thing as right or wrong, no such thing as heaven or hell.

It is all hell.

And when, in the middle of all the madness, the rebel inmates surround the prison chaplain as if they suddenly feel the need to pray, I know for certain that the devil is truly showing his face at Attica State Prison. Instead of reciting "Our Father"'s and "Hail Mary"'s, the rebels order the chaplain to strip down to his Skivvies, socks, and white V-neck T-shirt. They force the meek, round-shouldered Roman Catholic priest onto his knees, hands behind his back. One inmate cuffs his wrists while another inmate bends down and plants a kiss smack-dab on his quivering lips.

The priest has a thin, almost gaunt face. His skin is white, but caked with mud and spit. His lips are blue. Horn-rimmed glasses lie crooked on the crown of his nose, his chin is pressed down against his chest. He is crying, not out of shame, but because a rebel inmate has dressed himself in the priest's habit. The inmate is doing an Indian dance around the half-naked priest, spitting on him, mocking him.

"Though I travel through the valley of death," mumbles the priest between tearful gasps, "I shall fear no evil."

The rebel inmate carries a steel pipe in his hand like a war club. He chants woo-woo-woo and dances that Indian dance all around the crying, praying chaplain. The rest of the inmates break out in laughter. "Fear this," they scream. "Save yourself, Mister Righteous Man," they shout.

The rebel inmate dances and chants. He brings one foot up slowly and lets it down, then brings the opposite foot up and lets it down. His movements are slow, deliberate, and smooth.

He stops dancing suddenly. Just like that.

He coughs up a hawker from deep inside his nasal passages. He rolls the hawker around his mouth for a while until I want to gag on just the thought of it. Then he positions his mouth over the priest's head and lets loose with the wad of yellow-green spit. When the mission is accomplished the inmate stands up straight, takes a step or two back, and brings that metal pipe down hard on the priest's head. It's then that the priest stops crying, stops praying. He makes a wide-eyed look of surprise, as if something inside his body and soul has just snapped. And it has, along with the entire cranium of his skull.

The priest smiles a peaceful smile. He releases a slight breath. A puddle of blood oozes up from the opening in his skull like oil from a well, and for a split second even the rebel inmates are perfectly silent, as though a church service is about to be performed in their honor. A moment or two later, the priest lets loose with a gentle sigh and falls flat on his face.

CHAPTER TWENTY

In the dream Mike Norman sits behind his desk in a darkened office with only a red-and-white neon light flickering outside the venetian blinds. He is pouring brandy into his I LOVE MY JOB! coffee mug. I see the word NOT! on the bottom of the mug when he lifts it high and drinks, allowing the booze to spill over the rim and run down the sides of his narrow face onto his white button-down, soaking it like a layer of sweat.

Laid out on Mike's desk is a Baggie, the word EVIDENCE printed in white letters against a background of baby blue just below the seal. The Baggie is filled with Logan's .38, six loose rounds, and the key to his cuffs. Suddenly Norman has the phone to his ear. His hands tremble. "I've got what you need, Wash," he says. "But it's gonna cost you."

Mike sits back in his chair, reaches down between his legs, grabs a brown paper shopping bag. He puts the bag on his lap. His eyes grow wide and wet. Tears start pouring down his face, off his chin. "I'm sorry, Keeper," he says, reaching into the paper bag with his right hand, pulling out Fran's head.

Now it's me who's crying, only there are no more tears. . . .

The dream shifts to my second-floor office in Green Haven.

Val Antonelli sits in my chair, her stocking feet up on the desk. She smiles, holds her open arms out for me. Then she is gone and now it's Robert Logan who sits behind my desk, laughing. On one side of me stands Marty Schillinger, his big hands planted firmly in the loose pockets of his Burberry trench coat. On the other side stands A. J. Royale, the butcher of Newburgh. He wears a white surgical mask over his mouth. He holds out a fisted hand. The hand is covered with a rubber glove. He opens his fingers slowly to reveal an extracted molar, the long roots stained with blood. . . .

And then they are all gone, just like that.

Now I stand only a few feet away from the banks of a gravel pit. Positioned on the very edge of the pit is a woman I do not recognize. The woman is naked with dark teardrop eyes, shoulder-length hair, and chiseled cheekbones. My insides feel like melting. I want her, bad. I try to reach out for her, but I can't quite touch her. It's then that the gravel pit fills with water. The pit seems to become as wide and as deep as an ocean. The woman looks at me with an expressionless face. She smiles, whispers "Keeper." Using her left hand, she gently brushes back her brown hair to expose a heart-shaped tattoo. She turns and dives into the water, begins swimming away. I jump in after her, but instead of floating, I feel tentacles that rise up from the bottom of the pit, wrap themselves around my legs, and pull me down, deeper and deeper, until the surface is beyond reach and all my air is gone. . . .

The cement-walled holding cell measured twelve feet by ten feet. I'd walked it out at least thirty times since I'd woken up after having been tossed in it early that morning. Side wall to side wall, and back wall to bars. In the center of the battleship-gray concrete floor were two benches positioned side to side, their full length facing the front of the cage. The bench tops were made of heavy oak worn down smooth from age and use. Tubular steel supports served as legs. The steel supports had been bolted into the concrete floor with heavy-duty lugs.

I wasn't alone.

The man in the holding cell was still asleep when the guard slipped me inside and unlocked my cuffs. He was an older man, somewhere between sixty and seventy. He lay on his side on one of the benches, his knees tucked up into his chest. His cupped hands were stuffed into his crotch. He had a wrinkled, chalky-white face and looked like the living dead. He snored, and when he exhaled, his breaths rattled against the concrete walls. Once, he mumbled something I could not understand, and it wasn't until I came close to him that I could smell the whiskey on his breath.

Because of the hour of my arrest, SOP dictated that I'd have to stay in the holding cell until my arraignment, which was scheduled for nine that morning. In the meantime, I sat on the cell floor with my back pressed up against the wall and listened to the echo of the old man's rattling breaths. I waited for my lawyer, Tony Angelino, to show up, along with Val, who would bail me out if the judge demanded it. I lit the first one of the morning and fingered the welt on my forehead and the scratches on my wrists.

Eight o'clock on a Wednesday morning.

I'd been up for nearly six hours, despite the hour nap I'd caught when they first tossed me in here after tagging, printing, and photographing me.

I listened to the workings of the jail as if they were familiar, and they were. The closing and opening of iron gates; the slap of footsteps on the concrete; the sound of muffled, nearly indiscernible voices coming from loudspeakers that echoed in the concrete corridors; the smell of urine and sweat; other invisible prisoners locked in steel cells, shouting to one another, their voices mixing together like blood and poison.

Guard: *You there, stand up against them bars.*

Prisoner: *Go fuck yourself, screw.*

Guard: *I hear you, boy.*

I should have been at home in a prison, with the disgruntled sounds and the greasy, worm smells. Prison was my home away from home. I'd spent more time surrounded by cement, steel, and razor wire than I'd spent with my wife.

Listen: For me, the outside of a prison cell was familiar ground.

Inside was not.

The drunk tossed and turned on the narrow bench. How he managed to make complete turns on a bench that could not have been more than twelve inches wide was a testimony to either his sense of balance or his experience.

When he woke up suddenly, he opened his eyes wide and took a deep breath. He sat up straight, took his hands out of his crotch, brought them up to his face. He rubbed his eyes, ran his hands over his cheeks, and massaged his entire face as if jump-starting the circulation in his congested veins and capillaries. He hacked, coughed up some loose phlegm, and spit it out onto the concrete floor. It was then, just after he spit that wad, that he realized he wasn't alone.

"Who the fuck are you?" he said.

He smiled or maybe it was just a way of positioning his lips. He wore bright blue polyester pants, white socks collapsed at the ankles, and black plastic loafers split at the seam.

I decided to say nothing. On the other hand, I couldn't keep my eyes off the man, as if I no longer had the energy left to ignore him. He stared at me, too, his hands flat on top of the bench, his arms locked straight like pillars, to support a body that might otherwise collapse the second I breathed on him.

"You a pimp?" he said, his voice forced and raw.

I shook my head, laughed.

"Whas so funny?"

"No," I said, looking down at the concrete slab, "not a pimp."

"Dealer?"

"Uh-uh."

"Burglar, hit man? What the fuck are you, then?"

I said, "I'm the warden of Green Haven Maximum Security Prison."

He scrunched his eyebrows. "Man," he said, "you sure look like shit."

I broke out laughing. Nervous exhaustion, I think they call it.

The drunk laughed, too, a high-pitched, squeaky laugh—a laugh I felt in my temples and the backs of my eyes more than heard. A suspicious laugh, as if he were certain the goddamned wool was being pulled over his goddamned bloodshot eyes. He said, "And I'm a fucking senator. Glad to meet you, Warden. I'm fucking Senator Kennedy from fucking Hyannisport." He said Hyannisport like *Hy-anus-port.*

"I don't expect you to believe me," I said, letting out a breath of cigarette smoke.

The drunk lost his smile. He stared out beyond the vertical bars as if there were something to see besides a concrete floor and a cement-panel wall. He turned, looked at me with a perked-up, almost sober face. "Then you must be nuts, I guess," he said. "You must be fucking nuts. Or a pervert. Is that it?"

I answered him by directing my vision to the concrete floor.

"Tell you what, nutcase pervert," he said. "I'm going back to sleep. Wake me when President Clinton comes to bail me out. Or better yet, wake me when Hillary comes." With that he curled up his wilted body and lay back down on the bench. "Fucking warden, my ass," he whispered, pressing his hands together, stuffing them into his crotch.

CHAPTER TWENTY-ONE

At ten minutes after nine in the morning, the judge set my bail at five thousand dollars, much to my lawyer's irritation and mine. "Let's face it, your honor," Tony Angelino had said, smoothing his double-breasted blazer with his big, thick hands, "Mr. Marconi is a respected member of both the New York State Department of Corrections and society at large. I'm quite confident that he is not about to run away from us."

Wash Pelton stood up and directly requested that the district attorney set the bail at twenty-five thousand, minimum. But in the end, because of my reputation as a member of the corrections department, the judge set the bail much lower, despite a two-felony-count accusation plus resisting arrest. (The arresting officer who'd gotten it in the nose with my elbow stood close by with a piece of gauze taped across his swollen face.)

The middle-aged judge, Anthony Sclera—a man I had met on several occasions at the governor's mansion—sat back in his black leather chair, stuck his hands out from under his wrinkled cloak, and crossed them again against his considerable chest. He was heavy-set and out of breath and his white hair stuck up on one side like he'd been dragged out of bed for just this occasion, which may have been the case. He used his index finger to push the round wire-rimmed glasses back onto the summit of his hawk nose while he expressed his deepest regret on the matter of my arrest. He even went so far as to apologize for how and when I'd been taken into custody. It was his solid hope, he said, that the entire affair was nothing more than a mix-up. A simple case of miscommunication. At the conclusion of the morning hearing, the judge leaned up onto his oversized podium, made a frown, and shook his jowls. A court date was set for August ninth, and the gavel came down.

I was escorted out of the courtroom and brought back to the holding cell where I would stay until Val Antonelli arrived to post my five-thousand-dollar bail.

About an hour later, the attending guard came back to my cell. Sure enough, "a good-looking woman named Val" was here to bail me out. I stood up, straightened out my pants, tucked in my shirt. "When can I see her?" I said.

"Soon," the thin black guard said. He waved his hand in the air as if to say, *sit back down, relax, you're not going anywhere for a while.* "She's in the middle of processing all that paperwork. You know, SOP."

I tried to work up a smile.

A frown was easier.

"You could have asked *him* how long the process usually takes," the guard said, referring to my drunken cell-mate lying flat on his back on the wooden bench and snoring. "But then, he's not much of a talker in the morning."

"I bet he talks a blue streak during his first six or seven manhattans," I said. "It's probably the last two dozen that shut him up pretty good."

The guard turned. "I'll be back for you in a few shakes, Warden."

I could just picture the headlines now.

CHAPTER TWENTY-TWO

I should have stayed behind bars just a little longer.

I knew something wasn't right the second Val pulled into the driveway of my Stormville home. Deep gouges had been dug into the lawn. Black tire tracks were burnt into the blacktop. The mailbox had been rear-ended and now leaned out toward the road.

Somebody must have peeled out in a hurry.

Tommy Welch and his men hadn't made that kind of impression on the property when they'd come for me the night before. They were calm, collected, businesslike. Somebody had been at the house between the time of my arrest and the time I'd returned—not the brainiest of deductions, but true just the same.

"Wait here," I said. I opened the door and eased myself out of Val's station wagon.

"I'm coming with you," she said.

I leaned into the open passenger-side window. "Stay here," I said. "Somebody might still be inside."

I knew my .45 was still in the house, under the mattress in the bedroom.

Val cut the engine. She got out of the car. "I'm not staying out here all by myself just because you want to play hero," she said, slamming the car door closed.

Together we stood at the front door. Small aircraft were taking off and landing at the Stormville airfield directly across the street. The day was hot and still and dry. I took the key ring from my pants pocket, found the house key. Val stood close behind. I could hear her long, deep, calming breaths. I went to fit the key into the lock. But the door swung open on its own.

I couldn't understand it.

The wood jamb hadn't been notched out, nor had the metal lock-set been ripped away from the frame with a heavy screwdriver or crowbar. The wooden door had not been kicked in with the heel of somebody's jack boot. Somebody had used a key. Neat and simple. But then they'd left the door open on their way out. They'd torn ruts in the lawn; they'd run into the mailbox.

Sloppy. Or, if not sloppy, then downright intentional.

I pushed open the door. From the foyer I could see that the single-story home had been left in a shambles. The carpeting had been torn up and tossed in a heap into the living room. The coffee table had been turned on its side, the books pulled off the shelves, my entire CD and album collection thrown on the floor. Nat King Cole's "Unforgettable" had been stepped on and crushed, and what really got to me was that when I took a few steps inside, I realized that they'd cut the skins on every one of my goddamned drum heads. No music fan, no matter how sick, would have resorted to that.

There was more.

All the paintings and photographs were either hanging crooked or no longer hanging at all. There was an old photograph of my grandfather and me: Him sitting on the edge of a neatly stacked pile of cordwood just outside the cabin he'd built in the Adirondacks, with me, no more than five years old, sitting on his knee. He was smiling that wry smile of his, his red-and-black mackinaw over his stocky shoulders. The photo had been thrown on the floor, the frame cracked, the glass shattered.

There was the gold-framed mirror Fran's mother had given us as a

wedding gift twenty-five years before. It lay on the floor in pieces. Someone had deliberately crushed it. I stepped on the broken glass, felt it
crunch under my leather soles. Then I felt a hand on my shoulder. I
turned fast, grabbed the hand.

"Jesus," I said, "I could have taken your arm off."

Val took a deep breath. I let go of her. The two of us leaned against
the plaster wall in the foyer.

"My mistake," she said.

"Nobody's here," I said.

She walked into the living room, stepping carefully to avoid the
broken bits of glass. "What the hell happened?"

"Someone left me a message," I said. "And I think I know who."

Val took a few more steps in and scanned the room. "Jesus, Mary,
and Joseph," she said, lifting the remnants of a picture frame off the
floor. Pieces of broken glass fell from the frame and shattered. She held
a portrait of Fran and me in her hands. I recognized it as the one taken
at a studio just after our engagement in 1971. Me with jet-black hair cut
close to the scalp, no mustache, and Fran with long black hair parted
down the center, making her look like an angel. Now there was an X
slashed through her face.

I took the photo out of Val's hands and tossed it into the pile of torn-
up carpeting, books, and albums. "Mother of God," I said, taking a
deep breath.

"I don't want to look anymore," Val said. She went into the kitchen,
started rummaging through the cabinets, through the pots and pans.
When I heard the water running, I knew she was making a pot of
coffee. Leave it to Val, I thought, to bring calm and civility to an
otherwise chaotic and senseless situation.

I went ahead and checked the rest of the bedrooms. Everything
seemed okay. Nothing was missing. Even my briefcase, which contained a copy of Vasquez's file and the number-ten-size envelope I'd
found in his cell, hadn't been disturbed. I returned to the kitchen, took
a beer from the fridge, and brought it out to the porch. Later I would
clean up the mess. As for calling the cops, I knew there wasn't much I
could do but file a report. Besides, I was the one under arrest. And how
did I know it wasn't the cops who had trashed the joint in the first

place? How did I know it wasn't Tommy Welch along with a couple of Wash Pelton's finest?

They'd used a key for Christ's sake.

I lit a cigarette and for the moment just stood there on the porch watching the small planes take off from the airstrip. I looked at the torn-up lawn and the leaning mailbox. I looked at the driveway covered now with streaks of black rubber. I couldn't help but remember the image of my wife being zipped up in a black plastic body bag and stuffed into the back of a Chevy Suburban with black-tinted windows. The bastards who'd X'd her face would pay for that little stunt. Screw with me but don't screw with my wife, dead or alive.

Val joined me on the porch. In her left hand she held an ice pack fashioned from a white-and-blue-checked dish towel filled with ice cubes. In her right, a cup of coffee. She handed me the ice pack. "You want me to help tidy things up for you in there?" Using two hands, she balanced the overfull coffee cup against her lips and took a sip, careful not to burn her mouth.

"I'll manage," I said, holding the ice pack in my hands.

"I'd like to help if I could."

"I know where everything goes," I said, setting the ice pack down on the porch floor next to my chair.

"That's a nasty bump," Val said.

"Too late for ice," I said, taking a hit off the cigarette and following up with a swig of the cold beer. But she was right. I could still feel the tightness of the swelling above my eye. The egg-sized welt throbbed. I suppose it couldn't have been any less conspicuous than a tattoo.

Across the street, a Cessna with white wings and a red-and-white fuselage was coming in for a landing. The small craft descended pain-fully slowly, never straight, always fighting the wild up-and-down currents of air as its black tires came closer and closer to the hot, sunbaked pavement. It landed finally, the wheel that faced me touching the airstrip first, then the weight of the plane coming down hard on the opposite wheel.

"How does a man like you get himself arrested?" Val said.

I drank my beer and smoked my smoke and told her about the gravel pit off Lime Kiln Road, and about the evidence I'd found there. Then I told her about my visit with her old boyfriend Lt. Mike Norman at the Albany Police Department and also about my visit with Pelton, including the illegal part where he'd wanted me to take the blame for Vasquez's escape in exchange for a reward.

"And you think Mike ratted on you?"

"Makes sense," I said.

"You know as well as I," Val said, still holding her coffee cup with two hands, "that Mike Norman is not that kind of man."

I pictured the kind, caring man Val probably wanted to remember from those few months they'd spent together as a couple. On the other hand, I couldn't help but imagine his pale face, his trembling hands, the coffee mug he used for a shot glass. I thought about his ongoing love affair with the brandy bottle and I knew that this was the real reason Val and Mike had never worked out. She could never be content taking second place to a man's drinking problem, and who could blame her. But then I saw Mike Norman picking up his phone once I was out of his office and I saw him dialing Wash Pelton's private line and I heard him saying, "Wash, old buddy, I've got something you might be interested in, but it's gonna cost you, old buddy, it's gonna cost you good."

I might have explained all this to Val, but considering how she'd once felt about Mike, regardless of his drinking, I felt it only right to let it go. Besides, at this point, the only thing I could be certain about was the bump on my forehead.

Val looked out beyond the porch and took a swallow from her coffee cup.

"There's something else I've got to do," I said, careful to drop the subject of Mike Norman.

Val turned back to me.

"I'm going to locate Vasquez, talk to him face-to-face."

"Jesus, Keeper," said Val. "First of all, nobody knows where Vasquez is, and second, even if you could find him, what in the world makes you think he'll talk with you?"

I flicked my spent cigarette butt over the rail of the porch. "We have a common enemy now," I said. "Common legal circumstances, too."

"Except you're white and a respected member of the law enforcement fraternity, and he's Latino and a convicted cop-killer on the loose."

"Correction," I said, "I'm Italian, which makes me no whiter than Vasquez, and what's more, I've just been busted for obstruction of justice and manipulation of evidence. My home's been ransacked by someone who has a key to the front door, and I refused to take a bribe from the commissioner of corrections, who, as we speak, is probably sealing my fate. So, under the circumstances, Val, I don't think I have much choice but to find Vasquez."

"All this still doesn't solve the problem of where to find him."

"I think I know where to start looking," I said. I was thinking of Athens.

Val stepped up to the porch rail and took a deep breath. But then she set her coffee cup down on the rail and, for a time, stayed perfectly still. Some of the coffee spilled when she went down the porch steps. She came back up with the morning paper in her hand and a sour look on her face.

"Read it and weep, boss," Val said.

The headline consisted of only two words, but I had to read it several times before I could absorb it completely. MARCONI BUSTED! Not far under the headline was an old photograph of me, taken at least a decade before for my current ID, from when I had been appointed first lieutenant for Coxsackie Correctional Facility in 1987. The black-and-white photo would have been available in the commissioner's records. In the photo, I'm stone-faced, almost thuggish-looking. The photo looked more like a mug shot than anything else, with my eyes nearly closed and a smile hidden behind a Pancho Villa mustache.

Below the photo was another headline of almost equal proportions. DAY NUMBER THREE FOR MASTRIANO, and it showed a picture of the corrections officer lying in a Newburgh General Hospital bed, his mother by his side, along with Dr. Fleischer, the fierce little man, who was looking directly into the camera. The photo credit belonged to the Associated Press.

"This thing made the morning papers," I said. "Which means Pelton must have leaked the story to the press before he called me into his office."

"They had every intention of arresting you," Val said. "The whole thing was a setup from the start."

"I'm the patsy," I said, feeling very dizzy.

Just then a station wagon pulled up outside the driveway. A white van with a satellite dish on top pulled in behind that. *Channel-13-Newscenter* was printed on the sides of both the car and the van. The two vehicles couldn't have been there more than ten seconds when a Ford Bronco from a different television station arrived from the opposite direction.

I stood up just as the reporters and cameramen began scrambling out of their cars and trucks. "Guess it's about time we made a quick exit," I said.

"Congratulations," Val said, "you're gonna be famous."

"For all the wrong reasons," I said.

We went back into the house.

I locked the dead bolt behind me and turned to Val.

"Listen," I said, "there's no telling where this thing is going and who could be implicated along the way."

Val pressed her lips together. Her eyes were deep and wet. "What are you trying to say, Keeper?"

"What I'm trying to say is, I don't want you to do anything you don't want to do." I put my left hand on her arm and gripped the newspaper with my other.

"You can trust me," she said. "I work for you before I work for anybody else."

I kissed her forehead and pressed her against me. "Thanks," I said.

"As far as I'm concerned, those bastards toss you to the dogs, they toss me to the dogs, too."

Outside the picture window in the living room, I could see a reporter standing on the front lawn, his hand at his forehead like a visor, trying to get a look inside the house.

"They already have, Val," I said. "They already have."

CHAPTER TWENTY-THREE

I suppose people show grief in different ways. I didn't openly weep after Fran died. I didn't cry at her funeral. From a distance, I could see other wives whispering to their husbands, and I knew what they were saying. Shouldn't he be more upset? Shouldn't he be crying?

But Fran's death tore me up all the same.

Repairing those rips and tears over the last twelve months had not been easy. Now, any little thing could set me off, plunge me into the dungeon of despair. A half hour after Val left through a haze of reporters on her way to the office in Green Haven, I went into the living room to pick up the mess. I would have managed it, too, if I hadn't picked up the portrait of Fran and me, the one with the X slashed through her face.

I stared at the photo for a good long while, longer than I should have. Then I gently put it on the fireplace mantel. I went to the bar and poured myself a tall Scotch. It had turned into a Scotch kind of afternoon. I lit a cigarette. My hands shook. Standing there alone in the living room with the reporters walking around aimlessly on my lawn, I knew I should have stashed the photo away, saved it for something. For evidence maybe. But I couldn't help myself.

I took the photo off the mantel and lit the white corner with the Zippo. It caught fire instantly and I tossed it into the open fireplace and sat there smoking while the photograph shrunk and curled up into itself; and I watched my body and the body of my wife disappear in a blaze of orange-and-red-colored flame, and I grieved all over again.

I took a pull on the Scotch and took another look outside the floor-to-ceiling living room windows. People were carrying all kinds of communications equipment, voice recorders, and cameras. They paced the front lawn waiting for something to happen.

I felt like the groundhog.

Maybe if I waited long enough, they would try to burn me out.

In the kitchen, I dialed my office and got Val.

"How you holding up?" she said.

"I feel like O.J.," I said. "Except I didn't do it."

"More like John Gotti," Val said. "Get your ethnicity right. You want to check in with Dan?"

"Why not?"

There was a pause and then the confused noises of the phone being transferred from one person to another.

"What the hell's going on, Keeper?" Dan said. "Pelton called, said by court order you can't step foot inside Green Haven. Said if you did to have you arrested again."

There was that familiar organ-slide feeling in my gut. I made a conscious decision not to explain anything to Dan quite yet. Besides, what could I possibly tell him that he didn't already know?

"Pelton make you acting warden?" I said.

"Just this morning."

"Good," I said, as if that had been the plan all along. "Now I want you to do us all a favor."

"Anything."

"From here on out, you've got to avoid Pelton like the plague."

"Won't be easy, Keeper," Dan said. "I mean, under the circumstances, he wants constant reports. Especially with Vasquez gone and general lockdown still in effect."

"Just ignore his calls as best you can, or if he decides to make a surprise visit, take the back door. Just don't let him get to you."

"Anything else?"

"Sit tight, don't say a word about anything to anybody, especially Pelton and Marty Schillinger. Val will fill you in on everything. In the meantime, I've got a little catch-up ball to play."

After I hung up the phone I went around the entire house and closed all the curtains. The press had gathered enough nerve to move from the lawn to the front porch. They rang the bell a few times, but they knew I wasn't about to open the door. They knew I was still inside the house, but I'd do my best to remain invisible until it came time to get by them.

Now I knew why they called them the press.

I returned to the living room, took hold of the heavy metal poker that leaned against the brick fireplace, and used the blunt end to crush the burned photo of Fran and me into so much soot and ash. It was then I noticed that the photo hadn't burned completely. A semblance of the image remained. I bent down, sifted through the black ash, and picked out the remains.

Fran's face was still there.

I put the cigarette between my lips, reached into my pocket for the Zippo. I started the lighter and brought the flame to the stamp-size portion of intact photograph. Maybe my imagination was taking over but, like the image of her body, the image of Fran's face took some time to disappear. No matter how I put the flame to it. I wasn't the type to heed signs from above, but it seemed like a gesture from divine providence itself.

CHAPTER TWENTY-FOUR

At 12:50 on Wednesday afternoon, I reached under the mattress in the master bedroom of my state-appointed home on the grounds of Green Haven Prison. As luck or providence would have it, the pistol was still there. Even though the mattress had been left askew and the underside searched, it hadn't been searched thoroughly. Maybe Pelton's men assumed no one would hide anything as obvious as a hand cannon under the mattress. On the other hand, maybe they hadn't searched under the mattress at all.

I gripped the .45 and depressed the latch with my thumb so that the magazine slipped out into my left hand. Still fully loaded, I slammed the magazine home and cocked a round into the chamber. Then I gave the pistol a quick polish by using the end of the bed sheet as a buffer. When the gun metal was shiny, I laid the .45 flat on the bed and changed into a pair of jeans and brown cowboy boots. I slipped into a blue-jean work shirt and a charcoal blazer. Checking the safety on the .45 I shoved it, barrel first, inside my belt. Then I turned and looked at myself in the mirror above the dresser. First I looked at myself head on, at the shadowy face, the overgrown mustache, the dark hair now high-lighted with shades of gray at the temples. I turned one way and then the other. With my blazer buttoned, the .45 was well hidden.

At the dresser I opened my briefcase, pulled out the number-ten-size envelope, and stuffed it into the pocket of my jeans. I took my keys off the dresser and held them in my hand while I returned to the living room, pulled the curtain back just a touch, and took a quick look outside the window. I saw Chris Collins waiting for me in the center of my front lawn, her cameraman right beside her, his camera hoisted up on his right shoulder.

By now, three or four other news teams had gathered as well.

Tenacious bunch.

I would have to make a mad dash for the Toyota if I was going to get out unscathed.

I decided to use the sliding door in back, off the kitchen.

I made my way around the back of the house, past the woodpile, then the garage, until I came to the driveway in front. No one had spotted me yet, but I knew the shit would hit the fan once I attempted to unlock the Toyota. I knew I should have invested in one of those electronic locking and unlocking devices long ago.

My head was buzzing. I felt as if the whole world were about to slip out from under my feet. Then I thought, screw it, this is my house, my driveway, my fucking truck. If I want to walk out to my truck, I have the right to do it without being harassed by the press. I took a step out from behind the wall.

"There he is," someone said.

The bunch of them turned and looked at me.

I made a dash for the Toyota.

I didn't have the key in the lock when Chris Collins, along with the other reporters, came running after me. "Mr. Marconi," Collins shouted, attempting to shove a microphone in my face. "What can you tell us about the escape of cop-killer Eduard Vasquez?"

"Not now, Chris," I said, avoiding the microphone and her eyes, attempting to jam the key into the lock.

"Mr. Marconi," another voice screamed, "what about your arrest?"

"Keeper Marconi," came a third voice, "how much money did you get for assisting with Vasquez's escape?"

Oh how quickly they turn on you.

I opened the door and got in. I pressed my foot on the gas and started the son of a bitch. Then I threw it into reverse and resisted the temptation to run as many son-of-a-bitching reporters down as I could.

CHAPTER TWENTY-FIVE

The vigil stretched all the way from Bernard Mastriano's fourth-floor room in Newburgh General, out into the hall, down the full length of the corridor, and into the waiting room where a half-dozen cameramen and photographers from newspapers and television stations were exploiting "Day number three for Bernard Mastriano, the corrections officer from Green Haven Prison mercilessly struck down while in the line of duty."

Somebody had paid somebody an awful lot of money to allow all those media people to be there without reprisals from the hospital staff. The place was so congested that there was barely enough room for the nurses and physicians' assistants to get through with their clipboards and their IV units on wheels.

I pressed myself through the crowd and was nearly knocked over when I read the words, WHO SHALL PROTECT OUR CHILDREN IF WE CANNOT PROTECT OURSELVES? stenciled in black letters on the large cardboard banners. I squeezed past the children carrying smaller banners that read WHO WILL PROTECT ME? in the same lettering. Under the words were drawn perfectly shaped faces with perfectly shaped teardrops coming from perfectly shaped eyes. The entire scene was surrealistic at best, as though some Hollywood director had taken over the hospital and set the scene for a movie shoot.

I squeezed past the reporters and the cameraman getting shots of the children as they stood together, packed into a far corner of the hospital wing, their faces blank, wide-eyed, and confused. I thought, who in their right minds would come up with banners like these? Who the hell would come up with slogans identifying the corrections department as the protector of all civilization? Certainly not the children. Certainly not the average citizen.

No doubt about it, somebody had definitely given somebody one hell of a payday to go to all this trouble.

Moving closer to Mastriano's room I could see the bright portable lamps used by the cameramen. The white lights illuminated Mastriano, made him look like an angel. He was still on his back, but a full bandage had been applied to his head, hiding his black hair completely. An IV was attached to his right arm, just below the elbow. A plastic-and-metal chair had been placed at the head of the bed. I assumed the chair was for his mother. But now it was vacant.

Behind me stood a group of older women, two of whom were dressed in blue habits. All four of them looked at me as soon as I came into the room, but no one seemed to recognize me. They simply went on with their praying—chanting really—rosaries in hand, beads pressed tightly between thumb and forefinger, bodies straight and stiff, faces to the floor—like imitations of the statue of the Blessed Virgin Mary I remembered from Vasquez's cell.

Mastriano lay on the bed facing the white ceiling—eyes closed, thick arms straight and pressed against his sides, shoulders stiff, face cleanly shaven as if his mother had just run a razor over those chubby baby cheeks. And maybe she had. A tightly tucked, baby-blue-colored blanket covered his entire torso.

I sat down in the empty chair, brought my lips to his ear. I wanted to shout out his name. I wanted to see him jump. But I acted calm and cool while the nuns went on praying and the sweat oozed out from the pores in my forehead.

"Mastriano," I whispered. "Can you hear me, Mastriano?"

Hail Mary, full of grace, the Lord is with thee. . . .

"I found your service revolver, Mastriano. Can you hear me, Officer Mastriano?"

I searched for a response, a twitch of a finger, a blinking of an eye, a slight trembling of the bed. I got nothing.

"I would have told you Monday, but things have gotten complicated now. Things have changed now that you've got your friends all around you."

. . . Blessed art thou amongst women. . . .

"I've got the piece, the ammo, and the key to your cuffs."

. . . and blessed is the fruit of thy womb, Jesus. . . .

"I found all that stuff, Mastriano, and when it all comes back from the lab I'm gonna prove the only prints on it are yours and Logan's. Do I make myself clear, Mastriano?"

. . . Holy Mary, Mother of God, pray for us sinners. . . .

"You know what I'm gonna do after that, Officer Mastriano?"

. . . now, and at the hour of our death . . .

"I'm gonna fire your ass. I'm gonna have you brought up on charges for conspiracy in the aiding and abetting of an escaped convict. Are you getting all this, Mastriano? I don't think you're getting all this, Mastriano. You've got to pay attention."

. . . Amen.

Mastriano lay perfectly still. Too still. I mean, he never even flinched. Maybe he was out cold. One thing was for sure, if he'd been awake, he'd have known by now that I'd already been arrested for harboring his pistol and ammo. If he'd been awake, he'd have known I was bluffing.

I had to consider this: Maybe he was injured, after all.

But there was something else to consider: Maybe his unconsciousness was chemically enhanced and not simply faked. What I mean is, if Dr. Fleischer could get away with slapping a bandage on his head, poking an IV into his arm, and allowing all these people and their cameras to invade hospital corridors where the truly sick were trying to get well and the truly terminal were trying to die in peace, then he would have no trouble putting Mastriano to sleep. In the end, it all depended on one thing and one thing only.

Money.

Just how much was Fleischer getting and who the hell was greasing him?

I turned and looked out the open door. A flash went off, stung my eyes, blinded me for split second. A tall man stood behind the photographer. He supported a video camera on his right shoulder. The cameraman must have been filming me the entire time I'd been speaking to Mastriano. The media people weren't leaving anything to chance. And I suppose it was pretty reckless of me to be seen inside Mastriano's room like that, after what had gone down in Albany that very morning.

I sat back, blinked, tried to regain my eyesight.

There was some kind of commotion going on outside in the corridor.

Behind me, the nuns went on praying, unaffected.

Our Father who art in heaven . . .

When I looked up, the false image of a black flashbulb had nearly faded from my line of vision and I was able to make out the face of a plump gray-haired woman dressed in black. Mastriano's mother. On one side of her stood Dr. Arnold Fleischer. On the other stood Chris Collins from Channel 13 news. Collins, in all her tenacity, must have followed me from Stormville, across Route 84, over the Newburgh Beacon Bridge, all the way to Newburgh General. And I hadn't noticed even for a second in my rearview mirror. She looked at me with that chiseled face and those deep black eyes. She wore a blue skirt with a matching blazer and a white oxford shirt buttoned all the way to the top, a silver brooch pinned where the knot of a tie might have been. She held a microphone to Mrs. Mastriano's face—a face that became distorted with rage when she recognized me.

"You," the little woman shouted in a trembling, accented voice. "You . . . you sent my boy out with that criminal, that cop-killer."

She pointed an index finger, thick as a sausage, at my face.

. . . *Thy Kingdom come, thy will be done* . . .

She clenched her hand into a fist and lunged at me. But Chris Collins dropped her mike to the floor and grabbed hold of the woman's right arm while Dr. Fleischer grabbed hold of the other.

"Mr. Marconi," Fleischer said, "I'm going to have to ask you to leave the premises."

Chris Collins wasted no time going to work on me, waving her hand at the cameraman who was still shooting the scene from outside the door, then using the same hand to pull down on her skirt and straighten her hair. The bright white light shined in my eyes again. Collins turned to face the camera. "We have Keeper Marconi, warden of Green Haven Maximum Security Prison in nearby Stormville, with us today. As warden, Mr. Marconi is the man directly responsible for sending Corrections Officer Bernard Mastriano outside the prison walls with Eduard Vasquez, who, until Monday afternoon of this week, had been serving a life sentence for the notorious 1988 slaying of a rookie policeman."

Collins turned to me. At the same time, she pulled Mastriano's mother away from Fleischer and into the picture with me. Behind us, serving as a backdrop, was Mastriano, laid out on the hospital bed. Before I knew what was happening, Collins was subjecting me to the third degree. "Mr. Marconi, can you tell our viewers why you chose Bernard Mastriano for this particular, potentially life-threatening job?"

Mrs. Mastriano broke into tears at the sound of her son's name.

. . . and forgive us our trespasses . . .

Caught off guard, I looked into the camera and said, "That's strictly police business now. I'm here simply to check on the condition of my officer."

"We don't want you here," the old woman screamed. Fleischer took hold of her once more, pulled her out of the way of the camera.

"Can you tell us, Mr. Marconi," Collins went on, "what Mr. Mastriano's injury reveals about the nature of prison policy in general and about the disintegrating nature of the corrections system in this country?"

I looked straight into those black eyes. "Lady," I said, "you have no idea." And then I walked away. But before I left the room, I approached Fleischer, who stood in a far corner between Mrs. Mastriano and the group of four nuns.

I pointed my index finger at his face. "I don't know what you're pulling here," I said, "and I don't know who's paying you off. But in the end I'll have your medical diploma tacked to the wall of a prison cell." Then I made a mistake by poking his chest with my finger, forcing Fleischer to stumble back a little. "I think maybe F- or G-Block for you, pal."

. . . but deliver us from evil . . .

"Listen, buddy," Fleischer screamed, releasing Mrs. Mastriano's forearm. "I'm a Harvard-educated doctor of medicine. You were the one arrested, Mr. Marconi. Not me."

I turned back to him. "Then let's get away from this circus, Harvard boy, and talk about it like real men."

The white camera lights grew even hotter against the back of my neck. You could probably smell the testosterone in the room. For a second or two, I had forgotten about the cameras. Mrs. Mastriano crossed the room, sat down on the chair beside her son. Tears dripped from her chin. Chris Collins stared wide-eyed at the entire scene; her cameraman was almost all the way into the room now, his bulky camera mounted on his right shoulder. I knew that if I stayed any longer, I would do something I'd regret.

"Okay," Fleischer said. "You want to talk, Marconi, let's talk."

He went out the door and disappeared into the crowd.

For thine is the kingdom and the power and the glory, now and forever. . . .

"Amen," I said, glancing back at the two nuns. And then I followed Fleischer out of the room.

CHAPTER TWENTY-SIX

It was as quiet as a morgue inside Dr. Arnold Fleischer's first-floor office in Newburgh General. I stood alone in a square-shaped room decorated the way you might expect from a physician who relied on boasting about his Harvard Medical School education to elevate his character. Numerous diplomas had been tacked to the walls along with more than a dozen citations, plaques, and other advertisements for himself, most of them for delivering papers on the benefits of one medical drug or another, the spelling and pronunciation of which were beyond my energy and will at that point.

I was busy going over how unimpressed I was with Fleischer's credentials when he stormed in like they do on *ER*, slammed the door behind him, and sat down hard behind his desk. He scanned the desktop, opened the drawer, pulled out a pen, and sat back in the swivel chair, clearly relieved that he had something to fiddle with while we had our little discussion. "Okay, Mr. Marconi," he said. "Can I ask what that was all about?"

I shifted my gaze from Fleischer's wall of fame to Fleischer in the flesh. "You tell me," I said. "Monday afternoon, Mastriano was stable. Not a mark on him. Today he's battling for his life."

"I told you we had to perform some tests to determine the extent of his internal injuries."

"I felt his head myself," I said. "There were no lumps the size of a tennis ball or a baseball or a basketball, for that matter. No blood, no nothing. What'd you do, Fleischer, hit him over the head yourself when no one was looking?"

"I'll pretend I didn't hear that," Fleischer said, clicking the push button on his pen and squinting his eyes while he glared out the window overlooking the massive parking lot of Newburgh General.

"What is it then?" I said, pulling a cigarette from my chest pocket and lighting it before Fleischer had a chance to protest. "Mastriano paying you under the table to make his case look worse than it is? Or is someone else your sugar daddy?"

Fleischer turned back to me. "First of all, this is a doctor's office and I would appreciate it if you refrained from smoking."

I blew out a long, exaggerated stream of cigarette smoke. Then I flicked the loose ash onto the carpeting.

"Second of all," he said, "Officer Mastriano *appeared* to be stable Monday afternoon. The injury I referred to yesterday morning on the news, to the back of his skull, was an internal injury we did not pick up until we did the MRI on Monday evening. The bleeding was internal and gradual, not external and out of control."

"Who mentioned yesterday's news?" I said.

Fleischer turned visibly red, like maybe he was giving away too much.

"Listen, Mr. Marconi," he said, "he's leaking CSF. We had to pump him full of steroids to shrink the brain swelling and to stem the flow of blood and fluid. Perhaps I should have clarified that earlier."

I smoked for a second or two. Then I said, "Yeah, perhaps you should have clarified that earlier."

Fleischer clicked his pen a few more times. He sat up straight in his chair, gave me a tight-lipped, wide-eyed look that made him seem a lot older than I'd thought he was only forty-eight hours ago. "I know how upsetting it must be for you to have lost a prisoner—"

"Inmate," I interrupted.

"Excuse me?"

"Inmates haven't been called prisoners since the days of the Sing Sing lock-step," I lied.

But Fleischer bought it anyway. His cheeks were redder than the red seal on his Harvard Medical School diploma. "Okay," he said, "I know how upsetting it must be for you to have lost an *inmate*. Especially a man who shot an officer of the law. I know about fraternity and all that." He waved his right hand over his shoulder, referring to the numerous fraternal and academic institutions on his wall, as if I couldn't see them. "And I also know you must be upset for having to take the blame for the escape. But that comatose man upstairs was hit with something right here and hit with something hard." He made a fist with his free hand and struck the back of his head like he meant it. "He was hit hard, even if I wasn't able to pick up on the actual extent of his injury right away. That's what modern medicine is all about. That's why we developed medical imaging in the first place."

Satisfied with his speech, Fleischer sat back and resumed clicking the back of his pen while gazing out the window.

"Look, Doctor Fleischer," I said in a much calmer tone of voice, "all I'm saying is, as a prison worker, I've seen every kind of head injury there is to see, from stabbings to blows. Every single goddamned one was followed by some kind of bleeding or swelling or both, so don't tell me there might be nothing unusual about Officer Mastriano's condition."

Fleischer actually smiled. "That's exactly what I'm telling you."

"I see," I said. The good doctor had me stumped, or so it appeared. So I decided to make like Barry Sanders and change direction midstride. "What about all those people upstairs? Tell me they're all family."

"Now that the media has latched on to this," he said, his eyes still fixed on the parking lot, "there's little I can do."

Now he was definitely lying, but I wasn't buying it and Fleischer knew it. On the other hand, there was no real point in going toe-to-toe with him anymore. This was his home turf, his ballpark, and I didn't have a warrant and all he had to do was call security and then I ran the risk of another arrest. "Well then," I said, "I apologize if I caused you any inconvenience."

I went for the door.

I heard the sound of Fleischer getting up behind me. "Water under the proverbial bridge," he said, reaching for the door and opening it for me.

Proverbial, I thought. What a smart man.

"You really should consider putting an end to those things," he said, nodding at my lit cigarette, "before they put an end to you."

"Is this Harvard Medical School talking?"

"Just a concerned doctor of medicine," he said. "You must be aware of the risks."

"When you're as desperate as I am to find answers to difficult questions," I said, holding the cigarette up to both our faces, "a few risks here and there are worth it."

"And just what is it you're trying to find out, Mr. Marconi?"

I glanced over Fleischer's shoulder, honed in on the Harvard diploma above his desk. "*Veritas,*" I said, "and a whole lot more."

CHAPTER TWENTY-SEVEN

I did eighty all the way from Newburgh to Albany and made it in just under two hours. I went directly to the Albany Police Department on South Pearl Street where I had no trouble walking into Mike Norman's hole-in-the-wall office.

"What the fuck," I said, instead of hello.

Norman got up from his desk, pulled me into the office, and slammed the door closed. "You shouldn't be here," he said. "You know the trouble you've gotten me into already, Keeper?"

The wall-mounted clock above his desk read 3:35 in the P.M.

"What went wrong, Mike?" I said.

Looking more tired and pallid than usual, he walked back to his desk. His jet-black hair was sticking straight up, like last night had been spent in the office sleeping it off on the couch. And my guess was that it had been. What should have been a finely pressed button-down shirt was wrinkled and stained, and the knot on his brown necktie was pulled down around his chest. Mike ran his hands through his hair as if it made any difference at all and he sat down, hard. Opening a bottom drawer, he pulled out the bottle of ginger brandy, filled his I LOVE MY JOB! mug, laid out a second mug beside that one, and filled it, too.

I drank the brandy in one swallow and slammed the mug back down on the desk.

"Look, Keeper," Norman said. "I don't mean to go ballistic, but if Pelton's busted you, that makes me an accessory. No matter who's in the wrong, that makes me liable for manipulating the evidence, too."

"You knew the risks."

"I never imagined anything like this."

"Pelton's going to pin Vasquez's escape on me," I said. "Why is that?"

Norman poured another shot and drank it down. He squinted his eyes and wiped his mouth with the back of his hand. "You think I ratted," he said, his voice strained and constricted from having swallowed the booze.

I looked him square, in both eyes. "I think you tipped him off," I said. "I mean, for Christ's sakes, the man was holding the bag of evidence in his hands."

"For Christ sakes, Keeper," Norman said, "I had nothing to do with it. You hear me? Nothing."

"I'm supposed to take your word for it?"

"What can I say? You either believe me or you don't or you shoot me in the belly right here or you fucking leave my office."

"Sure," I said.

Norman poured another shot. He took a swallow from the cup, set it down on the desk, not hard. "My hands are tied," he whispered.

"Who set the knots?"

"I'm not exactly at liberty to say." He took another drink.

I reached across his desk, grabbed the brandy bottle, poured myself a second shot. I drank it down, felt the cool heat of the liquid coat the inside of my gut.

"What more can I do for you, Keeper?"

I placed my mug back down on the desk. I wanted nothing more to do with it.

"You can help me get out of this mess and then you can help me bring Pelton down."

Norman took hold of his mug and sat back in his swivel chair so that the light coming from the desk lamp in his otherwise black office made his face glow like a ghost's. At the same time, something inside told me that Norman was truly on his way to becoming a ghost. "Try again, Keeper."

"At least fill me in on what happened yesterday afternoon."

I sat down, crossed my legs, and waited for Norman to talk.

He took a deep breath and looked into his mug. "This plainclothes cop came by only a few hours after you left to go back to Stormville. What the hell was his name?" He opened his desk drawer, scanned the contents, and pulled out a business card. "Schillinger," he said. "Detective Martin Schillinger, Stormville, PD. Big, beefy goofball of a guy in a trench coat; same guy you told me about yesterday."

"My arresting officer," I said.

"Well, he wasn't alone. He had an entourage with him. No one I recognized. He said he had reason to believe I was harboring evidence of some kind that was crucial to the recapture of Eduard Vasquez."

"What'd you tell him?"

"What do you think I told him? I told him I didn't know what he was talking about. That I had only just heard about the Vasquez escape. How could evidence have possibly made it up to my office that fast or at all for that matter? Then he asked me to follow him downstairs to the crime lab." He took another drink, emptying out his mug so that the word NOT! was clearly visible on the bottom.

"You followed."

"You're goddamn right I fuckin' followed. Listen, Keeper, you've been in Corrections most of your life, so I'll spare you the gory details, but are you aware of new SOPs on printing analysis?"

I shook my head no, even though I was somewhat cognizant that fingerprint technicians were becoming real scientists with ultraviolet light-enhancement processing and microscopic imaging. That sort of thing. But as far as any actual procedures went, I didn't know much. It just wasn't part of the warden's job description.

"When the stuff you gave me was sent down to the lab, it would normally have been tagged and bagged and logged in on the computer with both the state and the FBI as admissible evidence. Only this time I worked off the fucking record, so no tagging, no bagging of any kind. Just analysis."

"No registering with the proper authorities," I said. "No way for Stormville PD to know about the stuff unless there was a leak."

"I promised you I'd do this under the fucking table," Norman said, pouring one more drink, "and that's what I set out to do. Now here's the kicker. Somehow this clown . . ."

"Schillinger."

"Somehow Schillinger knew what the fuck to look for and where the fuck to find it in the lab."

"Informant," I said, lighting a cigarette. "Squeaky technician."

"No way," Norman said.

I released a cloud of smoke that boiled in the light from the desk lamp and then disappeared into the darkness. "Could have been any-body in the lab," I said, getting up from the couch. "Let's go pay a visit."

Mike stood up fast. "Keeper," he said, "sit down. You go traipsing through there, you get the whole fucking place in an uproar."

I sat back down. So did Mike. In the end, I suppose he was right. I had to be careful about shooting my mouth off or making any false accusations. Maybe on one hand I had trouble believing he was giving me the truth. On the other hand, I had no real reason not to believe him.

"Those folks downstairs," Mike said, "they're scientists, techies. They got no reason in the world to turn informants. They're like machines, extensions of their scopes and lasers."

"Money," I said. "Money talks."

"What?"

"How much one of those crime techies make a year?"

"Probably thirty. No more than thirty, anyway."

"How can you be sure a lab techie didn't phone a friend of his downstate when you asked him to do the Vasquez stuff off the record?"

"I know these people pretty well, Keeper. They're on the up-and-up."

"And we're not?" I said.

"You're not," Mike said.

An uncomfortable silence followed that I nearly filled by calling my old buddy Lieutenant Mike Norman a son of a bitch.

"What about you," I said. "How deep you in now?"

"Keeper," he said, holding his mug with two hands, "I'm playing dumb the whole way. Don't ask me how that stuff got in the lab. It could've happened a hundred different ways. For all I know, the stuff spontaneously fucking appeared out of the blue. Maybe aliens dropped it."

"Aliens," I said, stamping my cigarette out in the metal ashtray next to the base of the desk lamp. "Sure."

Norman got up, which told me there wasn't anything left to talk about.

A thin waft of smoke rose up from the ashtray, clouded his sunken face.

"Now get out of here and don't come back for three years, Keeper. I'm sorry, man, but a pension's a pension, and you're a hot ticket these days."

I stood up and took a look at the calendar tacked to the wall behind him. The entire first week of May was close to being x-ed out. Soon he'd be working on the second week.

I went for the door.

"Keeper, wait," Mike said.

I turned.

"Sorry it went bad."

"Lots of people sorry these days, Mike. Me included."

He put his hands on his hips. His .9 millimeter Glock was stuffed up under his left armpit. His armpits were soaked with sweat and his white shirt stuck to the sides of his ribs.

"Maybe I should have gone right to the Stormville cops," I said, "instead of taking matters into my own hands. It's just that I knew Robert Logan's statement was a phony."

"Tell you what, Keeper," Mike said, going for the door. "When this thing blows over, we'll go to lunch. We'll do something better than Jack's, something a little more personal. We'll do Italian in your honor. How about Citones on Quail Street?"

"William Kennedy's hangout," I said. "Pulitzer Prize–winning pasta."

"I'll be counting the days," Mike said, "until this thing is finished and you're off the hook."

"Hey," I said, taking one last glance at the x-ed-off calendar behind his desk, "I like my job, too." I forced a smile, but I wouldn't call it a happy smile. Because I knew then, for certain, that my old Attica buddy Mike Norman was a liar.

CHAPTER TWENTY-EIGHT

But then, Mike Norman hadn't always been a liar. Once upon a time, Mike Norman was a happy-go-lucky young kid trying to make a name for himself in the Department of Corrections. We all were like that—Mike Norman, Wash Pelton, and me. Cocky, young, crazy. Lucky, for Christ's sakes. And get this: We'd set out to make a difference in the lives of those prisoners. Until September of 1971, that is, when the prisoners made all the difference in our lives.

And there's no denying that Mike was affected the most.

Even now I can see him lying on his side, knees tucked into his chest, arms wrapped tight around his shins, fingers locked in place at the knuckles. I can see his black hair sticking up straight on the left side of his head. His face is thin and filthy with saliva and dirt. A patch of dry blood stains the small space between his upper lip and nostrils. Eyes wide, he gazes straight ahead into an imaginary distance. He doesn't seem to see the iridescent glow of the tower beacons or the small gathering of inmates who are shooting up with drugs lifted from the psycho ward. He doesn't seem to see the rebel inmates granting interviews to special reporters allowed inside the yard, any more than he sees the famous William Kunstler, long-haired lawyer for the people, seated at a long folding table conducting negotiations with the Panther leaders. He doesn't see the sharpshooters poised on the stone wall or the helicopters making their perpetual flybys. He doesn't feel the power of the propeller-driven wind when they buzz the yard. He doesn't see the puddles of blood or my bare feet. Mike sees only what he sees. And I cannot imagine what that is. And I'm not sure I want to know.

CHAPTER TWENTY-NINE

I met my lawyer, Tony Angelino, at the Miss Albany Diner on Broadway beside the old RCA building, the six-story, concrete monstrosity that was topped off with a fifty-foot-high, plaster-of-paris Nipper the dog. Nipper sat doggy style on the flat roof, his tail end pointing to the banks of the Hudson River like an insult. Nipper was a magnificent leftover from the old days when the RCA company had run and operated the building—back when Albany had been a budding metropolis for gangsters like Legs Diamond and political gods like Erastus Corning before the city had paved over the trolley tracks and integrated the districts that had originally been divided between the Irish and the Italians and the Polish and the Canadian French, and you knew where you stood just by sniffing the particular aroma of whatever dishes were being cooked for the evening meal.

My own grandparents had come from the Ancona region of Italy directly to Albany after a brief stay on Ellis Island where my two-year-old father was nearly shipped home, having contracted a severe case of influenza during the long journey. In Albany my grandfather went to work for a local grocer, then for an automotive parts distributor; then he began a construction company, and, yes, his father's brother was responsible for having invented a wireless communications system that the world would one day embrace as radio, although this afforded no special privileges to my father and his family once they arrived in the States. During the Depression, he also moonlighted for some of the more ambitious and money-hungry local politicians, driving trucks full of "near-beer" from Albany to Hartford and back again in the middle of the night under blackout conditions. In those days, there was a lot of money to be made working for the local politicians.

Sometimes it was the only money.

Years later, the corruption in Albany had supposedly been squelched by honest taxpayer coalitions. On the other hand, what had once seemed like a budding metropolis now seemed devoid of life itself—a small city filled to the brim with state workers making lower-than-middle-class wages, perpetually trapped in an overcast atmosphere best described as prison-gray.

On the other hand, if you wanted to find it, you didn't have to look too hard around Albany to uncover corruption both on the street and on the political level. Just last year the city treasurer, Ernest McDaniels, had been busted for taking a kickback from a contractor who wanted the contract for the new train station that would occupy four square blocks of razed downtown property. Now both men were doing time at Auburn. In the end, I suppose, the difference between the politicians of the past and those of the present is that now you can't flaunt the fact that you're on the take.

Tony Angelino was a staff lawyer for Council 84 on Colvin Avenue in the west end of the city. Council 84 was the New York union that represented law enforcement officials throughout New York State, including New York City. He had already started on a plate of eggs over easy and buttered toast when I came through the narrow door of the old Miss Albany Diner.

"Breakfast at four-thirty?" I asked, taking a seat on the empty stool directly beside the short, square-shouldered lawyer.

"If you remember correctly, paisan," Tony said with a deep, careful voice, "my breakfast was interrupted this morning by a plea for help from a certain guinea warden I know." He wiped the edges of his

mouth with his napkin and took a quick glance at the lap of his pin-
striped suit to make sure he hadn't spilled any egg yolk during the
exchange of conversation. "Hey, Cliff," he said across the counter to a
short, balding man with a white apron wrapped around his thick torso,
"coffee for my paisan."

I watched Cliff retrieve a white ceramic mug from the stainless-steel
shelf above the grill.

"How you holding up?" Angelino said, placing a good-sized portion
of egg onto a triangular piece of toast and then stuffing it into his
mouth.

"Not bad for a guy who's been kidnapped from his own bed, held at
gunpoint by the police, busted across the forehead, accused of harboring evidence and obstructing justice," I said. "Not bad when you consider I've been tossed into jail, printed, photographed, and booked. Not
at all bad now that my reputation has been slandered in the newspapers
and on national television. Not bad when you consider my house has
been ransacked and the assholes who did it have a fetish for slicing
giant X's through photographs of my dead wife."

I let out a breath.

"Glad I asked," Tony said.

I took a sip of the coffee and looked around the old diner that had
been here since my father was a kid growing up less than a mile from
here on Colonie Street, smack between the redbrick rectory of Sacred
Heart Church and the western bank of the Hudson River. The counter
was made of light oak that had been covered some years back with a
white laminate top. The walls were covered with a stainless-steel paneling that hadn't quite managed to live up to the title of stainless, display-
ing as it did the brown-green marks of spattered grease. The big, boxy
gas-fired grill took up most of the wall space directly across from Tony,
and the floor was covered with white-and-black asbestos tiles. The Miss
Albany was an old diner that looked like it might have been a trailer at
one time. But now the place was an Albany landmark, a steadfast survivor amongst the abandoned lumber yards and steel mills that, once
upon a time, made Broadway and the banks of the Hudson River seem
like a hopping, if not a somewhat seedy, destination.

Frank Sinatra crooned over the loudspeakers while I sipped my
coffee.

"So you've decided to take my case," I said.

Tony puckered his lips and blew on the surface of his coffee. "It'll probably cost me my job," he said. "A union lawyer representing an indicted lawman would be a definite problem."

"Don't do anything you'll regret," I said.

"I wouldn't get up in the morning if I didn't plan on doing anything I would regret later on."

"We can sit here and philosophize all day, Tony. But you got to think about number one, no matter what. So I'll understand if you want to say no."

"Listen, Keeper, I've been thinking about going out on my own for a long time now."

"I thought you liked the Council."

"It's not that," he said. "I'm forty-two. Maybe it's that midlife thing and maybe it's not. But I feel like I got to make a move. This might be as good a time as any."

"Glad to be of assistance," I said.

"And besides," Tony said, "I think Pelton is crooked and I think I might get as much enjoyment out of seeing him come down as you will."

We said nothing for a second or two while Cliff cleaned the grill by scraping away at it with an inverted spatula.

"We used to be friends, you know, Pelton and me," I said.

"So were Martin and Lewis."

"And Lennon and McCartney."

"And Marcia Clark and Chris Darden."

"More than just friends or law partners."

"She enjoyed that extra long, good thing, paisan."

"We're a team then?"

"Yeah we're a team," he said, biting into another triangle of toast. "Paisans, like O.J. and Johnnie Cochran. Only don't get in the habit of calling me at four in the morning to bail you out."

I had another sip of coffee and took in the soothing voice of Old Blue Eyes. I didn't know what it was about Sinatra that made me want to light up a cigarette and pour myself a tall whiskey.

Night and day, day and night . . . you are the one. . . .

I tapped out the swing beat on the counter with a butter knife.

"Always the skins, man," Tony said.

"They call me the keeper," I said.

The afternoon sunlight poured in through the wide diner windows behind me, and I could feel the radiant heat on my back. Outside the diner, the Broadway of the 1990s was now empty. But I tried to imagine a long time ago when it must have been filled with cars and trucks and women (when they still painted their faces, instead of piercing their noses) and men (when they still wore fedoras and oversized overcoats with shoulder pads, and smoked filterless Camels as they walked the sidewalks).

Angelino wiped up the egg yolk on his plate with the last of his toast. "Let's move to a booth," he said, lifting his stocky body up from the stool, "get down to business, Keeper."

We set our coffees back down and took seats across from each other in the empty booth behind us. Before anything else was said, Tony took out a small tape recorder not much larger than his palm. He pressed the PLAY and RECORD buttons on the little machine simultaneously.

"I'm gonna ask you a couple of basic questions," he said, "just to get the blood moving, get a feel for what could be going on."

I nodded. From here on in, Tony was running the show.

"Have there been any wrongdoings at Green Haven that you've been privy to in the three years since you were appointed warden?"

The question was more like an understatement. Angelino knew the answer almost as well as I did. My war against corruption on the inside had made headlines for more than two years. Up until the time Fran had died, that is. After Fran lost her life, I seemed to lose my enthusiasm for fighting what was a losing battle anyway. Who was I to be fighting the drugs, booze, gambling, sex, the gifts for guards, the favors, and extortion? Or to be more accurate, who was I to be fighting it all alone?

Tony's point, I knew, was this: Did I make any enemies while acting as warden? The answer? Of course. Just ask Eduard Vasquez or Giles Garvin or any number of mob connections I had put a lid on—the likes of Edward Farrelli, Franky Evangelista, and Joseph "The Thumb" Ricardo.

"The problem," I said, "is this: Along the way I set up a couple of guards with wiretaps."

"Illegal move, number one," Tony said, making a mark in a small, flip-top notebook he pulled out of his shirt pocket.

"It was the only way to snag guards and convicts who were working together to bring in contraband. I knew Vasquez had been running the show. He and, to an extent, Giles Garvin. And they knew that I knew. It's just that I could never catch them in the act. Even with the taps."

"They were probably on to the taps."

"It wasn't until yesterday when I talked with Garvin that I realized how much stuff was being passed through," I said.

"Garvin opened up to you?"

"Guess he figured it was safe now that Vasquez was out," I said. "But I think there's more to it than that."

"How?"

"Garvin said something about Vasquez being on his shit list."

Tony nodded, wrote something down in the notebook. "What would you say if I said I thought Pelton could be taking off the top?"

"Possible," I said. "Could explain why he kept me purposely understaffed. Could explain why none of the dope pushers were ever indicted."

"Could explain a lot of things," Tony said.

"It's a long shot," I said. "I mean, come on, the guy's the commissioner for Christ's sakes."

"Sure, it's gonna be tough to prove," Tony said. "But not impossible."

I took a breath, tightened my lips. "Could be just the thing to save my ass."

"Any of those *tapped* men come forward, Keeper, you're done. Prisoner or no prisoner. Proof of Pelton's involvement or no proof. You obstructed justice, even before you were *busted* for obstructing justice. What you got now looks bad, but what you'll have if those *stupidos* come forward is a six-figure fine and five years' lockup minimum. Can you imagine what they'd do to a former warden inside an iron house?"

I was silent for a minute while the tape recorder continued running and Tony sipped his coffee.

"Listen, Tony," I said. "What if somehow I get to Vasquez, get him to admit he escaped, that Logan and Mastriano helped him, and that I had nothing to do with it?"

"Now, paisan, you're defying all logic."

"Just consider it," I said. "You know, for shits and giggles."

Tony sat back in the booth, both hands still wrapped around the coffee mug. "Well, seeing we're only talking shits and giggles, I'd say you could prove you weren't implicated. At the very least, you'd sway a jury that way."

"Christ, Tony," I said, "I'd blow the whole thing out of the water."

"At the same time, paisan, you'd open up a whole new can of worms."

"But it would make Pelton awfully nervous, that is, if he really did have any part in the drug trade."

"And just how do you plan on getting an escaped convict to come forward?"

"Hey, if Vasquez won't come to me . . ."

Tony sat up straight. "You're not thinking of doing something really stupid?" he said. "As your counsel, I should remind you, you leave Stormville, you jeopardize the terms of your bail. Listen, paisan, you're under what amounts to house arrest. You're taking a chance just by being here."

I took a sip of my coffee. "Vasquez's girlfriend lives in a town in southern California called Olancha, right?" I reached into my pocket and pulled out the crumpled number-ten-size envelope, pointing to the postmark with my index finger. "Well," I said, "what do you make of this, Tony?"

Tony picked up the envelope and held it out before him at arm's length. He squinted and adjusted his arm like a telescope, until he could read the postmark. "Athens," he said, hitting the STOP button on the tape machine and now holding the envelope only inches away from his face. "No wonder the FBI turned up nothing."

"Exactly," I said. "Vasquez could be right under our noses and no one knows about it except you and me."

"Okay, say he *is* in Athens? Just what do you think you're gonna get from Vasquez if you can find him? Just what do you think he's gonna say? *Take me, I'm yours?*"

"It's the only chance I've got, Tony," I said. "My only shot at re-demption. Maybe I can convince him that Pelton is more of an enemy than I am."

Tony leaned into the table. "He sees you," he said, "he's gonna kill you, Keeper. Take it from me. You go down to Athens, you're a dead man. Vasquez won't consider you a friend, believe me."

Cliff came over and topped off our coffees. Out of the corner of his mouth, he asked me if I wanted something to eat. I told him I didn't. It didn't seem to make a difference to him either way. He went back behind the counter to take care of a customer who had just walked in. The customer, who wore a long wool overcoat in the middle of a hot spring day, took a stool at the counter. A long wool overcoat and it must have been eighty-five degrees outside, and sunny.

"There's something else I should tell you," Tony said.

"What now?"

"Just this morning, Pelton nominated Mastriano and Logan for a citation and a promotion."

I felt the blood fill my face.

"At the same time," Tony went on, "Pelton wants to compensate them for their physical and emotional troubles. A bonus, if you will."

"Well I'll be goddamned," I said.

Tony got up from the counter, shaved some bills off the thick stack he kept in the pocket of his pants.

"Give it to me straight, Tony," I said. "Just what the hell do you think is going on?"

Tony took a deep breath, adjusted the two buttons on his double-breasted blazer. He looked directly at me. "In my opinion, paisan, Wash Pelton's gonna try and bring you down."

"I'm aware of that already."

"Yeah, but he's gonna stop at nothing. He's not interested in convincing the public that you let Vasquez go free out of simple negligence. He wants to convince Johnny Q. Public that you were paid to let him go. In other words, he'll try to make it look like you were part of a much larger crime syndicate. Pelton could actually be putting you in his own shoes, making you take the rap for something gone way out of control for him. This could either be the fruition of a long-range plan or something he's doing as a last-ditch effort. Who knows?"

"You mean to tell me I might have been stepping on Pelton's toes the past three years and not even realized it?"

"If he's involved in what I think he's involved in, the last thing he needed was an overzealous warden stemming the flow of drugs and contraband into Green Haven."

I made a fist, brought it down hard on the tabletop. "Bastard's turning the tables on me," I said. Coffee spilled over the rim and made a puddle on top of the Formica. Cliff made an about-face at his grill. So did the man seated at the counter. He was still wrapped in his overcoat, like it was cold and snowing outside instead of hot and sunny.

"It's okay, Cliff," Tony said. "My paisan's a little upset."

Cliff looked at me for a second or two with eyes that seemed more searing than his grill. His round face, on the other hand, was as cold and white as old bacon grease. He had faded tattoos on both forearms — Navy tattoos — one an insignia, the other a hula-hula dancer with a grass skirt. He held a stainless-steel spatula in his right hand. After a second or two, he let out a short breath. Then he turned and flipped a couple of eggs, over easy.

"Listen," Tony said. "That business this morning at your house? The ransacking? In my opinion, just a scare tactic. Probably from Pelton, to make you know he can get at you whenever he wants. He knows you can't get away with accusing him of doing such a thing because, after all, he is the commissioner. An accusation would be ludicrous, especially after your arrest." Tony got up and took his brown Mike Hammer fedora off a hat rack that was attached to the booth back. He placed the hat on his head carefully, so that it didn't muss up even a single strand of his black hair. Then he pulled down the brim, shading his eyes. He took a toothpick out of the shot glass atop a small table by the door and placed a hand on the door knob. All I could see from where I sat were his head and shoulders on the other side of the booth back.

"Still not going to be easy to sleep knowing they're out there," I said, resting my hand on the .45 stuffed inside my belt, hidden by my blazer and the tabletop.

Tony took his hand off the doorknob and laid his heavy arms on top of the booth back. He set his chin on the backs of his hands and, at the same time, glanced over at the grill to see if Cliff was watching. When he saw that Cliff was distracted, he brought his right hand up and made a trigger-pulling motion with two fingers. "Listen up," he said. "I got a little story for you that might put you at ease."

"A story," I said, "now?"

"Just relax and listen," he said. "Once upon a time there were three little pigs who left their mama to go out into the world and build homes of their own. Now, the first little pig built a house of straw. One day the big bad wolf came by and blew it down. The pig ran like a bat out of hell across town to his brother's house, which by the way, was made of wood. But the big bad wolf had been tailing his ass and when he caught up with the two pigs, he blew in that house also. The two pigs screamed 'Mamma mia' and managed to escape to their oldest brother's place—a house built the right way, you know, the Italian way with bricks and mortar."

"I've heard this one before, Tony."

"Let me finish, paisan," Tony said. "Now, the two younger pigs were in a panic, screaming that the big bad wolf was after them and that he would be there any second to destroy the brick house and make roast pork with rosemary out of them. But the oldest pig was calm and cool. He told his bothers to settle down, relax. Even if it didn't seem like it at the time, he had everything under control. Just to prove it, he picked up the phone, dialed a number, spoke with someone for a few seconds, and then hung up. A few minutes later, sure enough, the old wolf was at the front door shouting off like a drunk son of a bitch about huffing and puffing and caving in the entire joint. While the two younger pigs huddled in a corner trembling in fear, the oldest pig sat back and relaxed. But just then, there was the sound of a car racing up the road. The car skidded to a stop right outside the door. A bunch of rounds were fired—shotguns, grease guns, Uzis, you name it. Then the car sped away. 'What the hell was that?' the youngest pig asked the oldest pig. 'That, my little brother,' he said, 'was the Guinea Pigs.' "

Angelino laughed and pushed back his fedora just slightly, enough to expose some of his forehead.

I sat back. "I'm not sure I get it," I said.

"What I'm trying to tell you, paisan, is not to panic. I'm prepared to help you fight this son of a bitch Pelton no matter what it takes. Even if I have to call in a few of my underworld pals to lean on the big bad wolf a little. If you know what I mean."

"Guinea Pigs," I said. "Friends of yours."

"I prefer to call them business associates," he said. "And they're available whenever or wherever I want them. Capice?"

"Capice," I said.

Angelino laughed unlike any lawyer I had ever known. It was a tongue-in-cheek laugh that said, fuck the law, what's right is right. It felt good to know he was on my side, working for me. He gave me a wink and a smile, and pulled the brown fedora back down over his forehead. He twisted that toothpick around inside his mouth. But before he left, he took a good look at the guy in the wool overcoat who had both hands wrapped around the coffee cup like it was snowing outside. Tony turned back to me, made like a pistol with his forefinger and thumb, pointed it at his temple, and twirled it around a few times. Then he exited the Miss Albany Diner the only way possible: by way of the front door.

CHAPTER THIRTY

Inside the Toyota, before turning over the ignition, I took one final look at the color-Xeroxed file Val had lifted from the microfilm in the prison archives. Rap sheets, medical histories, two photos of Vasquez—one a snapshot of him seated in a cheap aluminum lawn chair, a shotgun laid out flat across his lap, another a blow-up from mug shots taken during his 1988 arrest in New York for shooting that rookie cop at point-blank range. There was a third photo, too, but not of Vasquez. A blurry, color shot of a woman who had to be his girlfriend, Cassandra Wolf. Her hair was brown and her face white, her eyes black and heavy. The color Xerox was a little distorted. But even with the distortion, I could make out a small red mark on her neck, down near her shoulder. Just a small mark, about the size of a thumb print. Maybe a birthmark, maybe a tattoo. It was hard to tell because the mark was cut off by the edge of the photo. But then it came to me. I thought about the heart-shaped tattoo from the photos now in Schillinger's possession. Could Cassandra Wolf be the mystery girl in the orgy shots? Whatever the case, it wouldn't take an Einstein to figure out that, wherever I found Eduard Vasquez, I'd find Cassandra Wolf.

The thing to do, I thought, as I noticed the tall man in the long wool overcoat exiting the Miss Albany Diner, was to go to Athens, no matter what my lawyer advised, and find out for myself.

BOOK THREE

ATHENS

CHAPTER THIRTY-ONE

Thursday, midday, I opted for the scenic route north from Stormville and followed the Hudson River for seventy stop-and-go miles. I made it to Athens about an hour and a half later. Athens, with its run-down wood-framed buildings and sleepy sidewalks, was the sort of small town Fran might have described, once upon a time, as quaint. I, on the other hand, might have called it a dump.

One main artery ran through the center of the downtown—a road that paralleled the Hudson River, which ran wide and dark under the gray cloud cover. Judging by the proximity of the river, I guessed that Athens had been built inside the flood plain, which may have made it a constant source of anxiety for some of its residents, especially when you considered how many American towns had been wiped out by floods during the past few warm, wet winters. Whatever the case, the town was made up of dozens of two- and three-story asphalt-clad houses and buildings that occupied both sides of Main Street. An occasional coffee shop or hardware store was interspersed amongst the residences. Cars and pickup trucks parked on the diagonal against the curb, the hoods and bumpers pressed up against parking meters with red flags clearly flying, as if the police had simply given up collecting revenues from parking violations.

I took it slowly, driving through the town at ten to fifteen miles per hour, and kept a watchful eye out for Vasquez on the off chance that he might be reckless enough to be walking the streets, maybe taking in a little sight-seeing, despite the fact that there were no sights to be seen. I knew that finding Vasquez on the street like a common citizen would have been next to impossible. But then, I had no other plan in mind but to cruise the streets and find what I could find until something turned up.

I took three separate trips up and down the main drag, doing my best to get a good look through the wide, square-shaped picture windows of the eating establishments. I gazed at the faces of the passersby. Sad-looking people in blue jeans and T-shirts, mostly, who returned my stares with squinty-eyed suspicion.

After a while, I decided to turn off onto another side street that ran parallel to the Hudson River. But the effort was futile. That was when I decided to pull into the Sunoco station at the northern edge of town. When all else fails, my father used to say, stop at a gas station, ask for directions.

This wasn't the new-style gas station with islands of computerized, self-service pumps, shiny aluminum paneling, and colorful neon. This was an old station, the kind I remembered as a kid, with revolving black-and-white numerical displays on the pump faces as opposed to computerized readouts with accompanying robotic voices that say thank you when you've finished feeding them your plastic money.

The station itself was something my father and grandfather might have built decades ago. Squat and square-shaped, the flat-roofed building had been constructed from cinder blocks covered with a coating of yellow plaster that, over the years, had faded to off-white from too many summer suns. Outside the picture window was an oversized tin placard shaped like a Coke bottle. The long thermometer embedded in the center of the bottle read eighty-seven degrees—a record, I guessed, for this early in May, although I could have been wrong.

The decor on the inside of the station was hardly an improvement. Fran would have called it a charming time capsule—a relic from an era gone by. I would have called it a dive and Fran would have said that I had little appreciation for what could easily pass as art deco. One thing was certain: the place smelled like gasoline and motor oil—not a bad smell really. But then, it wasn't a good smell either. Just a heavy industrial odor that tickled my sinuses.

A calendar was tacked to the wood paneling behind a metal desk and it featured a full-color photo of a bleach blonde in a red string bikini and high heels. In her right hand she held a torque wrench, in her left a long rubber hose, while a banner draped like a bandolier around her waist and shoulder read Snap-On-Tools.

On the desk sat a black rotary-style phone next to an adding machine and a mound of little yellow credit slips. A radio on a metal shelf gave the play-by-play of a noontime Yankees game.

Big Daddy, hero of the '96 World Series, was at bat.

The guy seated behind the metal desk was asleep, with his feet up on top of the credit slips. He wore a button-down shirt with a football-shaped emblem glued to the left chest pocket, the name Henry sewn into it in red curlicue letters against a white background. Henry had thick black hair that looked like it had been soaked in a grease pit.

I slammed the door closed.

It took little less than a split second for Henry to sit up straight, feet back on the floor. He began counting receipts, but then he got ahold of himself and raised his head to take a good, slow look at me. Once it registered that I wasn't the big boss, he took a breath, tossed the yellow receipts back onto the counter, and sat far back in the swivel chair, looking more relieved than exhausted.

I gave him my best stranded-stranger smile.

But Henry's expression never wavered. "What?" he said.

Big Daddy took a swing and missed. Strike one. A hum from the crowd at Yankee Stadium.

"Hi there," I said, raising my voice a full octave. "Jeez, I'm passing through on my way to Montreal and, jeez, I was wondering if you might recommend a hotel where a tired guy could spend the night." I stretched my arms, let go with a fake yawn.

Henry squinted, sat up straight, and leaned up against his desk. "Haven't I seen you before?"

I imagined Big Daddy knocking the dirt out of his cleats with the heavy, wide bottom of his Louisville Slugger.

I brought my right hand to my face, rubbed the stubble of my day-old beard. "I can't see how," I said. But then I glanced over Hank's shoulder into a corner of the room that contained a newspaper vending machine nestled between a glass-topped peanut dispenser on one side and candy dispenser on the other. Like everything else in the gas station, the dispensers were relics. You had to slip a quarter into the slot and turn the silver-plated knob 360 degrees to release a handful of junk that had probably been stored for more than a decade in the clear glass containers. As for the newspaper vending machine it housed the *Poughkeepsie Standard.*

"Warden Indicted" read the headline, and just a for a split second I felt like I was reading about a total stranger. But the headline was accompanied by a photograph taken a decade ago. I had lost some hair since then. So recognition for Henry may not have been that instantaneous. But just to be safe, I looked to the floor and turned the collar up on my charcoal-colored blazer.

Big Daddy swung and missed. Two down.

"Yeah," Henry said, bringing his right hand up and rubbing his chin so that a few of the yellow credit receipts floated down to the floor. "You look real familiar to me."

Big Daddy set up one last time to the commotion in the stadium.

I took a quick glance through an open interior door that led into the garage. The far wall inside the garage was covered with dozens of mufflers that hung from an overhead ceiling-mounted rack. I turned back to the attendant. "You ever hear of Midas Muffler, Henry?"

When he nodded, a thick strand of greasy hair fell down onto his forehead.

"The commercial where the customer looks into the camera like this." I made a stern, tight face. "And then he says, 'I'm not going to pay a lot for this muffler!' "

Henry beamed with an ear-to-ear grin. "Yeah, yeah," he said, "I know it."

"That's me," I said.

Henry took his hands away from his face, set them in his lap. "I'll be damned," he said. "Never seen a film star up close before."

"Now," I said, "how about that hotel?"

"The only place around is the Stevens House Bed-and-Breakfast over on the corner of Livingstone and North Water Streets."

"Expensive?" I said, making that same tight, stern face. "I don't want to pay a lot for that hotel." Maybe I was pushing it too far.

"Cheap," Henry said, "for a man of your means." He sat back once more in that swivel chair, ignorant of the credit slips that continued to float down to the grease-and-gasoline-smeared floor. "Jack Nicholson and Meryl Streep filmed some of *Ironweed* over there on the second floor."

"Jeez," I said. "Jack and Meryl."

"You know them?"

I crossed the finger on my right hand. "Jack and me are like this," I said.

"No shit," Hank said.

"Who should I see at the Stevens House?"

"Just tell them Henry Snow sent you."

I glanced at my picture and my headline.

"What did you say your name was?" said Henry, his eyes squinty and curious.

I hesitated for a second or two—maybe longer than I should have.

Big Daddy swung and missed again. Three strikes and a loud buzz of disappointment from the New York fans. I remembered seeing Mickey Mantle make a rare strikeout when I was a boy, having made it to the ball game with my father on the bus trip the Italian American Benevolence Society of Albany sponsored once a year.

I took a quick look at the bowling trophies and plaques displayed on the same shelf as the radio broadcasting the game. Some of the plaques had been service awards issued by the Sun Oil Company. The most recent award had the year 1972 embossed in fake silver plate attached to a fake marble base.

Nineteen seventy-two, the year Wash Pelton, Mike Norman, and I might never have seen had we not survived Attica.

"Sonny Rivers," I said. "My stage name."

"Can't say I know the name," Henry Snow said. "But it sounds like it could be famous."

I put my hand on the door, took one last look at the newspaper headline and photo. But then Henry turned and looked at the headline, too.

Time for Sonny Rivers to make his exit, stage right. "Hey thanks," I said, turning the knob on the old glass-and-wood door.

"Don't mention it, Sonny," Henry said.

And then I left.

But as I climbed back into the 4-Runner, I could see that my newest buddy, Henry Snow, had already picked up the phone. I turned over the four-by-four and glared at him through the plate-glass window that took up a whole quarter of the station's facade. For a second or two, our eyes locked. But Henry kept right on talking into the receiver as if convinced that he could see me, but that I had no way of seeing him. Glass tends to fool some people that way, as if transparency works only one way. Maybe it was just a hunch, or maybe just a bad feeling. Maybe my nerves were getting the best of me. But as I turned out onto Main Street, I felt certain that Henry Snow was calling the cops.

CHAPTER THIRTY-TWO

The Stevens House was an old townhouse that took up an entire street corner. It had a high Victorian-style roof with gables atop all four corners. The gables were visible from where I parked the Toyota on the opposite side of North Water Street. With its tall shutters and dark, heavy oak doors, the place looked more like a haunted house than a bed-and-breakfast.

The west bank of the Hudson River cut across the flat landscape directly to my right. A jetty made up of black boulders reached out to the center of the river. At the farthest point of the jetty was a lighthouse, the base and tower of which had also been constructed of heavy stone blocks. The lighthouse beacon cast a bright yellow light against the cloud cover.

I turned back to the Stevens House and decided to wait and watch out for a dark, wiry-looking man who fit Eduard Vasquez's description—a man with his ID number tattooed to his knuckles and a mouth with a hole in it where a molar had been extracted. I waited for a woman with brown hair and a small, heart-shaped tattoo on her neck. I would have waited and watched until dark, had I not heard the unmistakable wail of police sirens.

CHAPTER THIRTY-THREE

Not everything about the Attica riot was fear and loathing and silent desperation. There were moments of real heroics. I don't mean Arnold Schwarzenegger–style Hollywood heroics where I suddenly, single-handedly, take out each and every one of the rebel inmates with my bare feet and knuckles. What I'm trying to get across is this: Just staying alive constituted honest-to-God heroics.

For example, I still see myself dragging Mike Norman by his feet back to the wall of D-Block, keeping him between me and the stone foundation. Wash Pelton follows, sets himself right beside me. Two rebel inmates—one black, one white—watch over us. Other inmates stare at us, the guards who have become the prisoners. From here I can see the sudden reflection of the sun in the scopes of the sharpshooters during the occasional breaks in the clouds.

The rebel inmates lift their shivs and spears and assume a sort of attack formation. When they begin to close in, I can see the whites of their eyes. I can see their jagged, broken blood vessels. I can almost smell their sour breath. It's then that something strange happens to me. All fear leaves my body. It just seems to drain out through my bare feet like water from a sieve. It's as if, along with the realization that I'm a short-timer, a great burden has been lifted from my shoulders.

CHAPTER THIRTY-FOUR

I kept the Toyota at an even thirty-five per until safely outside of town. Then I shot up Route 9 to Highway 87, fast lane. When I came to the first available rest stop about fifteen minutes later, I pulled around back of the wood-and-stone building and parked between two green Dumpsters.

The rest stop resembled a ski lodge more than a tourist trap for wayward and exhausted motorists. Bolted to the exposed fieldstone interior, a colorful neon sign advertised a Burger King and a Santo Pizza Parlor. Another smaller, much less conspicuous neon sign advertised an ATM like an afterthought.

Since I hadn't eaten all day, I chose the lesser of the two evils and ordered two giant slices with sausage from the Santo pizza joint. I covered the slices with Parmesan and ate them while standing at a green Formica counter that wrapped around a seating area with identical pea-green tables and chairs. The tables were filled to capacity with families mostly—eating now, tasting later. Middle-class travelers, I imagined, en route to early vacations upstate at a time of year when the cost of lodging was still cheap. And there were others. Men and women eating alone. One slice of pizza cost four dollars, which meant I'd blown a ten-spot on two lukewarm slices of sausage-covered. My mother would have called the cardboard-thin pizza a disgrace. But then, when it came to my mother, any pizza other than her own was less than edible.

I glanced at a family of four seated in the far corner. Mother and father in their mid-to-late thirties with two young children—a boy and a girl. The cherubic faces of the children barely cleared the table as their little hands awkwardly maneuvered the oversized slices of pizza to their undersized mouths. Throughout the meal, the mother and father never once looked at each other, never once spoke a single word. It made me sad to look at them. I also knew that if I thought about it hard and long enough, I would begin to feel a certain desperation for them.

But then, I knew I had to clear my head, stay focused.

I finished the pizza and wondered about the California return address handwritten on the envelope. Had Athens been a deception or merely a temporary stop—an out-of-the-way place for Vasquez and Wolf to regroup before making their escape to California? Connections and possibilities, possibilities and connections. Maybe Vasquez had simply planted the envelope. Like everything else I'd found along the way (the orgy stills, the .38, the key to Logan's cuffs, etcetera, etcetera), maybe all of it had been a plant from the start, designed to manipulate me and the cops. Maybe Cassandra Wolf and Eduard Vasquez were hiding out in Athens for a few days—until things had died down, the road blocks were taken up, the fugitives given up as missing. Or maybe, as a last possibility, they had attempted to deceive everyone, to make us believe that they were headed back out to California when in fact they had no other plan but to hole up in a small town located not far from Green Haven Prison.

As the young mother tried to maintain her composure while placing a stack of napkins on the orange soda her little daughter had spilled, I recalled the first rule about going after the location of an escaped convict. Check on his significant other, first thing. Nine out of ten times, an escaped convict could be found in bed with his girlfriend or wife or lover, making up for whatever time together they had lost. It would amaze some people to know just how many escaped convicts could foul up a foolproof escape plan for a romp in the hay. It happened more than John Q. Public knew. It just wasn't publicized.

As the young family got up and left their table, I wiped the last of the overpriced pizza from my mouth, pulled the envelope from my jeans pocket, took one more look at the California address and the Athens postmark. Just a red-lettered, mechanized postmark barely visible even in the light from the overhead fixture. Vasquez wasn't your basic, run-of-the-mill prisoner. If I had to make a choice, I'd say he had set up a deception that hadn't been entirely carried out yet.

But it was then, as I stacked the now-empty tray in its designated place on top of the Formica-covered garbage receptacle, that I noticed him again. The guy in the long wool overcoat who had been drinking coffee in the Miss Albany Diner. He was standing at the ATM machine, making a cash withdrawal. At first I thought I might have been imagining things. But after a few quick looks, I knew for certain it was him. I also knew for certain that I was being tailed, and not just by the cops. I knew I'd have no choice but to let him follow me until I was presented with the perfect opportunity to ditch him. But then, there was another option. I could always flank him, come up on him from behind, stick the .45 in his face, demand information on who had sent him.

But from the looks of things, he had other priorities. Because as soon as the cash dropped from the machine, he stuffed it into his overcoat and made for the exit.

By this time, it was already one-thirty on a Thursday afternoon. I didn't want to chance going back home to Stormville. The place would be surrounded by cops and reporters. Some of the cops would know me as a friend. Some of the reporters would know me, too, but not as a friend. I had no choice but to go back to Athens. I also had to dump the Toyota. The fire engine–red 4-Runner was more like a red herring in Athens and everywhere else in New York State, for that matter. The second the police found out I was nosing around Athens, an APB would go out with the red Toyota established as the vehicle to ID. Judging by the police sirens I'd heard in Athens, I had to assume that the bulletin had already gone out. And on top of it all, there was the matter of the overcoat man.

There was an information booth located between the ATM and a small souvenir shop. The woman behind the booth was reading from an oversized fashion magazine, W, with a very attractive black-and-white photograph of Cindy Crawford on the cover.

Older, slightly overweight with silver-gray hair puffed up like a bee-hive, the woman behind the booth was no Cindy Crawford. I must have looked at her for a full minute before she finally caught on that I was standing there. When she did look up, it was all very theatrical, with a long breath and the bifocals removed from the crown of the nose very carefully, very pompously. The temples of the diamond-studded half-glasses were attached to a hair-thin silver chain, and she allowed them to dangle against her chest.

"Yes," she said, eyes wide but not interested.

Yes must have meant, can I help you.

"Where can I rent a car?"

Old Beehive let out another breath and held her place in the magazine using her forefinger and thumb like a clothespin. She nodded over her left shoulder, drawing attention to the pamphlet shelves built into the same wall as her information booth. Dozens of pamphlets and colorful brochures had been neatly stacked and alphabetically organized, all of them promoting one rent-a-car agency after another. The usual—Hertz, Budget, Rent-a-Wreck, and about a dozen independents. I picked up a Hertz brochure and checked out the address stamped on the back.

Seven fifty-five Pelham Way, Catskill.

I stepped back to the information booth, "This close by?" I asked, holding the address out for Beehive to see. She licked her index finger and flipped a couple of pages of the magazine. She had those little half-glasses on again. The little fake diamond studs embedded in the cat's-eye frames seemed to enhance her silver beehive, make it so luminescent that I almost had to stand back and take a breath.

"Next exit," she said, "northbound. Go left off the exit." She forced a fake smile. "Will there be anything else?"

Not to be outdone by Old Beehive, I forced a fake smile of my own. "You've been very helpful and courteous," I said.

"Tell me another one," she said, licking her index finger and flipping another page.

"Nice hair," I said, but I don't think that's what she had in mind.

CHAPTER THIRTY-FIVE

Southbound on Route 87.

This time in a rented Chevrolet Impala with a white hood, off-white side panels, dark-green trim, and a license plate enclosed in a yellow plastic frame with the Hertz logo on top.

I'd felt less conspicuous in the Toyota.

I switched on the radio, hit scan, and surfed for a local news station. Station 540 appeared on the digital display in light-up yellow numbers.

"Day number four for a corrections officer struck down in the line of duty," the anchorman announced, "and a warden indicted for corruption and manipulation of evidence. Those stories and more top our news."

Then, without warning, I felt all the air leave my body. I tried to breathe but I couldn't, and it was as if my lungs had spontaneously collapsed. I felt cold, and the open highway in front of me turned to a wavy blur, and my mind spun, and I swore an entire squadron of cops was tailing me. But I must have slowed down without knowing it because the man behind me in a pickup truck laid on his horn. I gripped the steering wheel so tightly that I could feel the tension in my wrists, and I had no choice but to pull off onto the shoulder of the road. I got out of the car and ran down into the ditch and back up the embankment, all the time trying to get a breath but getting only enough air to stay conscious.

Standing there, on the edge of the tree line, with the rented Impala parked where any cop who happened to be passing would notice, I wanted to die.

In my imagination I saw myself in shackles and cuffs.

I'm being led down a concrete corridor with a low concrete ceiling and a yellow stripe along the floor. I'm brought into F- and G-Blocks, the ghetto blocks, and all the inmates come to the front of their cells to greet me, their former warden, the man who came down hard, the man who tried to empty their cells of the drugs and the booze. Big men, small men, black men, brown men, white men, all with their bodies pressed up against those bars—hollering and jeering and whistling and shouting and screaming for my ass. And me, with my head between my legs, knowing full well that I'm a dead man. No former warden in any prison has got a fucking chance, if he wants to stay alive.

I tried to take three distinct breaths and I tried not to think about any kind of future whatsoever. Christ, there *was* no future. I tried to recall just what the hell had gone wrong along the way. How could I not have seen this whole thing coming? How could I not have suspected Pelton as he arrogantly robbed me of my corrections officers when I was already so poorly understaffed? How could I have been so naive as to think I could have single-handedly removed every drug, every still, every needle and flashpan in Green Haven? How could I not have known that important people were making money off the drug and contraband trade? I had always been aware that some of the COs were on the take. But I never had imagined Wash Pelton on the take. And here I was, standing at the tree line trying to get a breath, blaming myself for something that was beyond my control. I had only tried to do my job. If I had to guess just where I had made the mistake, I would have to have said that I hadn't made a mistake at all. I would have to say that Pelton had made the mistake when he'd appointed me warden of Green Haven Maximum Security Penitentiary.

But now I *was* making a mistake by not getting back into the rented

Impala and doing what I'd intended to do in the first place. The sooner I could locate Vasquez, the sooner I could get to the bottom of what had happened out there on Lime Kiln Road, and the sooner I could catch Logan and Mastriano in their lies, the sooner I'd be out of this mess. Of course, it all depended on finding Vasquez, and then it all depended on him talking without killing me first.

By now I was breathing more comfortably so I walked back to the car and got in. The second I pulled out, I noticed a blue sedan pull up behind me, not exactly on my tail, but about three car lengths behind. The sedan was obviously the kind of unmarked car an undercover cop would drive, but there was no way to be sure. I tried to get a good look inside, but the glare from the windshield made it impossible to see anything but shadows and darkness. I tried instead to get a look at the plates but even from that distance, I could see that there was nothing official about them, nothing indicating local or state police. But then, that didn't mean anything either. The driver could still be an officer of the law and if I had spent any more time on that embankment, he would have pulled me over. For now, I had to maintain those steady breaths and the speed limit and not give this cop (if he was a cop) any reason to believe that I was anyone other than some jerk who had happened to stop by the side of the road to relieve himself.

Whoever and whatever he was, persistence was one of his finer qualities. After a few miles, he decreased the distance between us and practically pulled up onto my fender.

I adjusted the rearview to get a better look at him. Now I could see that it wasn't a cop driving the sedan at all, at least not a uniformed cop. The man in the car was the overcoat man. How he had managed to follow me all the way out to the Hertz office and back without my noticing was anybody's guess. I knew then that he had to be a professional, and I knew there would be no getting around the son of a bitch. Especially if he worked for the law. I also knew I couldn't pull a gun on him any more than I could blow him away.

Jesus Christ, I thought, as I punched the gas pedal of the Impala, just who the fuck can I trust?

No one, a little voice inside my head told me.

CHAPTER THIRTY-SIX

The overcoat man tailed me all the way to the Athens exit. But after I pulled off and paid my toll, he was suddenly nowhere to be found. Ten minutes later, I reached the outer limits of town. Things had changed in the time I'd spent away. Now Athens was lit up with dozens of red, white, and blue flashers from the cop cruisers and ambulances that blocked off the roads. All along Main Street I could see the reflections of the flashing lights in the picture windows and storefronts of the two- and three-story crackerboxes that lined the main drag.

Yellow barricades had been set up around the perimeter of the downtown. I could only drive in so far before I had to turn the Impala around and cut across one of the narrow side streets that would lead me to North Water Street and the Stevens House. But North Water Street was just as congested as Main Street with cops, fire trucks, onlookers, and on-the-spot satellite crews.

I parked the rented Impala in the middle of the road because I couldn't go any farther without running someone or something over. I took a quick look at the river. The Hudson flowed thick and gray-black on an overcast afternoon. A barge floated in a southerly direction toward Manhattan, pushed along by a red-and-black tug.

I got out of the Impala and walked along the sidewalk toward the corner of North Water Street. I moved on past the old buildings, some of them covered in wood-slat siding, others covered in rust-colored asphalt shingles made more for roofs than facades. Along the river, the tug pushed the barge past the glowing yellow light from the lighthouse.

I pushed and shoved my way in toward the front door of the Stevens House. I saw her then, in the very second that I broke through the crowd—Chris Collins reporting live via satellite for Newscenter 13. The same cameraman I'd seen inside Bernie Mastriano's room at New-burgh General now supported a shoulder-mounted video camera and aimed it in the direction of Collins's face. The camera was the only reason she did not get a look at me right off. She stood only a few feet away from me, with her back to the Stevens House entrance. The glow from the camera-mounted spotlight made Collins's wide black eyes light up like big black marbles. Her hair was parted just to the left of center and hung down stylishly, curling below the ears, barely touching her narrow shoulders. She wore a bright red suit with matching blazer and miniskirt. Intent eyes stared into the camera, away from me, di-rectly at her viewers.

Collins held the aluminum-tipped microphone to her mouth. The black head touched her red lips. I stepped back into the crowd before she had a chance to spot me. At the same time, the cameraman lifted his right hand, palm up. Like opening a switchblade, he snapped his index finger into position. He brought his arm down fast, pointed di-rectly at Collins. Her legs went rigid, high heels pressed together, left leg bobbing just a little at the knee. Then everything about her went absolutely tight, absolutely rigid.

On the air.

"A significant portion of the mystery is solved this Thursday after-noon," she said, a slight smile growing on her strong, confident face. "Eduard Vasquez, convicted cop-killer and recent Green Haven es-capee, has finally been found, but not alive. The slain body of Vasquez was discovered only moments ago by a group of law-enforcement offi-cials who'd received a tip from an anonymous caller who, it is alleged, recognized a suspicious, as of yet, unidentified man driving the streets of Athens in a red Toyota 4-Runner."

A team of paramedics hauled a stretcher out the front door of the Stevens House. One man at the feet, another at the head, two on each side. Vasquez's body was on the stretcher, a dark red blood stain on the white sheet where it covered the face. You could see the imprint of his nose, lips, and sunken eyes. Cops in uniform followed the stretcher out the door.

"Vasquez appears to have taken a bullet at close range," Collins went on, "with a heavy caliber firearm, sources told me just moments ago. But for now, that's all the vital information police officials will offer. However, when asked to confirm rumors about whether or not Jack 'Keeper' Marconi met the description of the 'suspicious man driving the streets of Athens,' Martin Schillinger—the detective in charge of the Vasquez apprehension operation—refused to comment. What he was able to tell us is that Marconi does indeed own a red Toyota 4-Runner that fits the anonymous man's description."

I pictured Marty Schillinger's chubby white face. Then I saw the real thing following the uniformed state troopers out of the Stevens House. I took another step back, pressing against the wood-slat exterior wall of the bed-and-breakfast so that I was no longer in Schillinger's line of sight.

"There is also speculation that Keeper Marconi was spotted by more than one witness walking side by side with Cassandra Wolf, Eduard Vasquez's long-time girlfriend. Although nothing is official, such allegations make Marconi and Wolf prime suspects in the shooting death of the deceased cop-killer. The thirty-two-year-old Wolf, who had been sharing a room with Vasquez here in the Stevens House bed-and-breakfast under the assumed name of Hewlet, also fled the scene at approximately the same time that Marconi was purportedly seen."

I looked away from Collins, beyond the crowd, out toward the tugboat and the barge it pushed. In my mind I sprinted through the crowd, dove head first into the river water, swam to the barge, stowed away to New York, and made my way south from there to Mexico. I'd change my name, grow a beard, grow my hair, blend in, drop out.

I felt sick to my stomach and deprived of oxygen.

"This is Chris Collins reporting live from Athens."

She relaxed her arm, let the mike drop against her thigh, and took a deep breath. The cameraman had already moved away from her and shifted his focus to the EMTs who had loaded Vasquez's body into the back of a black Chevrolet Suburban with tinted windows. The same kind of truck that took Fran away one year ago. The crowd grew so quiet that you could hear the small waves breaking on the western shore of the Hudson, the tugboat and barge having cut a heavy wake when they pushed through.

The townspeople of Athens fixed their eyes on the final scene—with the red, white, and blue lights from the cop cruisers flashing off the rear windows of the Chevy Suburban after the heavy double doors had been closed and secured. Call it shock, call it another panic attack, I must have fallen into a semiconscious state. Because when Henry Snow, the gas station attendant, stepped out of the crowd in his light blue uniform, raised his oil-slicked right hand, and shouted out my name, it didn't quite register, didn't quite sink in. Until I heard the distinct sound of shoe leather slapping against concrete.

It happened fast.

I heard the order shouted by Marty Schillinger to apprehend the man in the dark blazer. But just before that, I made an all-out dash for the Impala, gaining maybe ten or twelve steps on the cops.

With cowboy boots slapping hard on the pavement and air shooting out of my chest and mouth, it was like the Impala was in one of those dreams where you reach out for something that isn't there. The closer I came to the car, the farther away it appeared. Cops shouted, threatened to shoot. A distinct, all-at-once high-pitch cry from the crowd told me that weapons had been drawn.

At the Impala, I searched through the pockets of my blazer for the small key ring with the yellow plastic attachment shaped like a little number *1* and word *Hertz* printed on it in bold black letters.

The cops worked their way closer, service revolvers drawn.

My brothers, my fraternal order.

I looked over my shoulder, once. The crowd was on the ground, men and women on their stomachs, some of them lying on top of their children.

I could see them all now—Chris Collins alongside Schillinger, microphone in hand, cameraman behind her, filming the scene for history, posterity. "Warden Gunned Down after Jumping Bail." What a story it would make. Uniformed cops on their knees behind their black-and-whites, using the cars to shield their bodies. Shield them from what? All sidearms drawn, aimed at me.

The sharp crack of the revolver echoed off the walls of the buildings along North Water Street. So did the shots that followed.

Who had given the order to shoot?

Someone had to have given the order.

Maybe someone thought I'd gone for my gun. But I hadn't gone for my gun. I was going for the keys to the rented Impala. I searched until I found them, finally, in the right-hand pocket of my blue jeans. But not before a slug blew a hole in the windshield.

"Shoot the tires," one cop screamed. "Go for the fucking tires."

He was right. That's what I would have done. Shot out the rear tires. But no one shot out the tires. No one shot at me as I managed to get back into the car. I turned over the engine, threw it in reverse, fishtailed and hit a Volkswagen Beetle on its driver's-side panel, then sideswiped the tail end of a red pickup on the right. The rear windshield exploded the second I threw the floor-mounted automatic transmission into drive.

Don't look back, Keeper. Never look back.

Bastards had no idea what they were doing.

My fraternal order. Just what the hell did they know about the truth?

I could have gone for my gun, returned their fire, called it self-defense. But what good would it have done? In the end, going for my gun would have been the foolish thing to do. Not a smart move at all, not with my right foot putting the pedal to the metal, not with the rented Impala veering dangerously to the right side of the road, not with the unmistakable feel of a cold pistol barrel pressed up against the back of my head.

CHAPTER THIRTY-SEVEN

Planted on her neck, a heart-shaped tattoo.

A small red heart about the size of a man's thumb print, plainly visible just above her left shoulder when she turned to see if the cops were still on our tail. The associations came to me, fast. Vasquez's cell in G-Block . . . the manila envelope underneath his mattress containing the pornographic stills . . . an unidentified woman with a heart-shaped tattoo on her neck . . . an unidentified man with a scar under his chin . . .

Associations.

Connections.

"Did you kill him?" My right foot pressed down on the gas, I was trying to prevent the Impala from veering off onto the soft shoulder.

"If you only knew," said the young woman, with the piece pressed to the back of my head.

"But did you kill him?" I had to hold the wheel tight to keep it from going ditch-bound.

"If only you really knew me," the woman said in a flat, expressionless voice. The barrel was pressed hard against the back of my skull. Maybe .32 caliber. Maybe smaller. What difference did caliber make at point-blank range?

"Somebody had to kill him," I said, gazing into the rearview mirror at the heart-shaped tattoo on her neck where her long hair fell to her shoulders. Definitely the woman from the porn stills. Definitely Cassandra Wolf, Vasquez's girlfriend. "If it wasn't you, sister, then who was it?"

I felt her warm breath on the back of my neck.

"If you only knew what I was like," she said, "you wouldn't even ask the question."

I took that as a definite denial.

In my estimation, I had about a mile-and-a-half jump on the cops. By the time I turned off Route 9 for the less-traveled Route 27, I'd increased the distance to maybe two or three miles. Still, it was only an estimate. But it could also have been wishful thinking. I knew that no matter how many miles I put between me and the cops, there would be another pack waiting ahead. The trick would be to get as far away from the area as fast as the rented Impala could take me, before the road blocks went up. Meanwhile I had to deal with a woman who had what I guessed to be a Saturday Night Special pressed up against my head.

I took another good look at Cassandra in the rearview.

"How'd you find me?" I said.

"That's funny," she said, jamming the barrel of that pistol against skin and bone, "I was about to ask you the same thing."

"I mean it," I said, taking a deep breath, trying to shrug away the pistol but only making it hurt that much more. "Tell me how you found me?"

"When the police raided the Stevens House," she said in an unaffected, nearly monotone voice barely audible above the racing engine, "Eddy threw me into the bathroom."

"They had reasonable suspicion?" I said, knowing full well that the possibility of my presence in town, thanks to Henry Snow, the gas station attendant, must have tipped Schillinger off as to the whereabouts of Vasquez and Cassandra Wolf.

"Eddy tried to stop the police at the door," Cassandra said.

"Let me guess," I said, speaking to her through the rearview, "they kicked the door in."

"I climbed out the window, onto the fire escape, made a run for the river."

"Jesus," I said, "they didn't think of blocking the fire escape."

"We're not talking brain surgeons here," she said. "I hid in the public ladies' room near the lighthouse."

"You must have seen me when I got out of the car."

"I saw everything from the ladies' room," she said, voice cracking now, showing the first signs of stress and pressure. "When you got out of the car, I went to get in, but—"

"But what?"

"I couldn't at first."

"What do you mean you couldn't?"

"I mean I couldn't get into the car."

"I don't get it," I said. "It's not like I locked it."

"The minute you took off, some guy in a black overcoat started poking his nose around inside the car."

I pictured the man from the Miss Albany. I hadn't lost him after all. "Just what the fuck was he looking for?" I said.

"How the hell should I know?" she said.

I slowed around a curve in the road, making a right turn, heading for Route 87 north toward Hudson. Nobody ahead of me, nobody in back. Still lucky, but not for long.

"You going to keep that thing pressed up against the back of my head forever?" I eased up on the gas just a little more. "We're on the same team here, sister."

"I'm not your sister," Cassandra said. "So don't speak to me like I'm a second-class citizen. Got it, brother?"

"Maybe I'm a little cranky," I said. "But then, they think we both killed your boyfriend, and you've got a gun to my head, and some freak in a wool overcoat has been tailing me all fucking day."

"Just drive," she said, "and watch your fucking language. There's a lady present."

I could feel the jab of the barrel against the sensitive, bony portion of my head, just to the left of the right ear lobe.

Enough was enough.

I sped up, gradually this time, the engine of the Impala revving and the warm air pouring in through the hole in the windshield. The double-and single-story homes on both sides of the road whizzed by. At just the right time, I gave the wheel a slight turn to the left. I braced myself, hit the brake, leaned into the turn, spun the wheel sharp, counterclockwise, resisted the G-force by leaning into the door. The Impala fishtailed 360 degrees. Cassandra Wolf flew back hard against the right side of the car, and the pistol was knocked out of her hand. I was sure because I heard the thud of the pistol against the carpeted floor.

It was the sound I was listening for.

I threw the transmission into park and lunged like a diver over the opening between the two front bucket seats. The pistol was on the floor by her feet. I grabbed it before she could and I aimed it at her face, point-blank.

"Now we do things my way," I said.

"Go ahead," Cassandra said, laughing hysterically, barely able to get the words out between laughs. "Shoot."

Sweat ran down my forehead, stinging my eyes.

"You're crazy," I said, running the back of my free hand across my brow.

I turned and saw a car coming. It was still a ways back, but coming up fast. My eyes stung badly from the sweat pouring into them, and I couldn't make out the type or style of the car. I didn't know who the hell was driving it. Maybe a cop, maybe the overcoat man. I didn't know shit about anything. All I knew was this: We didn't haul ass right then, we'd both have something to cry about.

I took the aim away from Cassandra's face and planted a bead on the oncoming car.

"The pistol," she said, "it's not loaded."

I turned to her, quick. "What do you mean it's not loaded?"

"The cops were breaking down the door," she said, pressing both hands down flat against the floor of the car. "I didn't have time to escape *and* load the gun."

I cracked the cylinder on the black-plated .32. No bluff. All six chambers were empty.

The car was clearly visible now. A white car, whiter than the Impala. Maybe an unmarked cop car. Maybe not. I had no plans to hang around long enough to find out.

I tossed the empty .32 in Cassandra's lap and swung around into the driver's seat.

"See," she said, "I told you it wasn't loaded."

I pulled the Colt .45 out of my belt, held it up for Cassandra to see. "This one is," I said.

I pulled the car ahead, just a little.

Just then, as the white sedan passed, I ducked down, then sat up again in time to see it turn into a church parking lot just ahead on the left.

Not a cop after all.

Definitely not the overcoat man either.

I got only a quick glance, but the guy driving the car had a head of gray hair, and he was wearing something that looked like a black T-shirt. A priest maybe. Who would have guessed?

But I had learned a valuable lesson.

I knew that I had to ditch the Impala and go after my third car in a single afternoon. I had to find a safe house and make a plan. Now that Eduard Vasquez was dead, Cassandra had to be a part of that plan. Cassandra Wolf had to take the cop-killer's place.

CHAPTER THIRTY-EIGHT

It was a small, white, old New England–style church with colorful stained glass, clapboard siding, and a steeple shaped like an inverted icicle mounted on an A-frame roof. Directly across the street was a funeral parlor that, in my mind, seemed oddly convenient. Attached to the rear of the church was a good-size, two-story Cape Cod–style house with dormer windows and a small front porch. I pulled into the lot and drove slowly past a wooden placard with Church of the Nazarene engraved on it in black letters against a white background. A daily mass schedule was printed below that.

I drove all the way around the church to the back of the house. In the meantime, Cassandra got up off the floor of the car and balanced herself on the edge of the backseat. Shards of broken glass covered the vinyl seat cushion. Through the rearview I saw her face, her dark teardrop eyes, her high cheekbones, her full red lips, her equally red, heart-shaped tattoo.

I pulled up to the two-door Pontiac Grand Prix—the same car that had passed me a few minutes before. "I've got an idea," I said. Then I killed the engine on the rented Impala and stuffed the keys into the pocket of my blazer. "But tell me something first," I said, turning to Cassandra, "how are your acting skills?"

The plan went something like this: Cassandra would ring the rectory doorbell, plead her case to the pastor, explain to him that her car had broken down and was now stranded alongside the road a ways back. The breakdown occurred while coming back from her sister's house near Catskill. Now she had to get back to Albany to pick up her daughter from Public School 21 on Clinton Avenue, and if the priest knew anything at all about Albany, he'd know what a dangerous neighborhood Public School 21 was located in. It was very late in the afternoon. She was an hour late. There was nobody in Albany for her to call. She and her daughter, they were all alone in the world now that her boyfriend had split. . . .

The pastor would ask her to at least phone the school. But Cassandra would insist she didn't have time for that. She'd be unreasonable, she wouldn't be thinking straight. Please! she'd scream. In the name of God you have to drive me to Albany!

She'd be one hell of an actress, appear panic-stricken, desperate.

The pastor, being a man of God, would have no choice but to act the role of the good Samaritan.

I had a clear view of Cassandra from the driver's seat of the Impala as she walked to the screen door of the rectory and rang the doorbell. If all went as planned, we'd be on our way out of town in five minutes or less.

But for now, I had to wait and hope that her acting abilities were as good as her talents for evading the police. Of course, she couldn't deny her film experience, but that kind of film didn't take a whole lot of talent.

She was better than I could have hoped.

It took only about ninety seconds and Cassandra had the pastor by her side, the two of them making a beeline for his Pontiac Grand Prix.

From what I could see, the pastor was older than me by four or five years, with very thin arms and legs. His belly, on the other hand, was enormous and hung over his black polyester pants. A black collarless shirt was unbuttoned at the stomach, exposing a white T-shirt underneath. He held a key ring in the fingers of his right hand. Nearsighted, he held it up to his red face while peeling back key after key until he came to the one for the Grand Prix.

Cassandra wiped both eyes with the backs of her hands. She was good. She was very good. Not only had she fooled the pastor into believing her story about a stranded daughter, but she had forced tears. But then, her boyfriend had just been shot and killed, so the tears may have been real, not an act at all.

The pastor unlocked the passenger-side door for Cassandra. He went around to the driver's side and got in.

That was my cue.

I got out of the Impala, gripped the .45 in my right hand, barrel pointed down at the macadam. I moved fast and silent, careful not to alert the pastor, who, with shaking hands and trembling fingers, was inserting the key into the steering column. The driver's-side window was rolled down so it must have been a complete surprise to him when I raised the .45 and stuffed the barrel into his ear.

"Don't move, Father," I said.

The pastor stiffened, gripped the black steering wheel, white-knuckled. "In the name of sweet Jesus," he said, "don't kill me."

All life seemed to drain from his face. He breathed heavily, sucking air in and blowing it out fast. I hoped his heart was still good. If his gut was any indication, a massive coronary was imminent. But it was a chance I had to take.

"Shut the car off, Father," I said. "Backseat."

I unlatched the door, held it open for him. He started sliding out as ordered. But when he was all the way out and standing in the lot, he began to breathe faster than his lungs could soak up the oxygen.

"Nice going," Cassandra said. "Now the fucking priest is having a fucking heart attack."

I grabbed the pastor's shoulders, put my face in his red face. "Breathe, Father," I said. "Take your time and breathe."

"Can't . . . get . . . air," he said, in a voice so forced I could actually feel the pain and struggle in my own lungs.

"I'm not going to hurt you," I shouted, my heart pounding against my rib cage. "I just need you to get into the back of the car."

"Right . . . pants . . . pocket," he said. "Breathilator . . . right . . . pocket."

"Get his fucking breathi-whatever," Cassandra shouted.

"I fucking heard him," I said, feeling around in the right-hand pocket of the pastor's black pants. When I found the breathilator I pulled off the cap and stuffed the round inhaling end into his open mouth. The pastor took a breath while I squeezed down on the device at the same time. What a team we made. By the time I took the breathilator away, he was already beginning to breathe normally.

"The good Lord," he said, between breaths, "has blessed me with many things. Good lungs is not one of them."

"You okay now?" I said, taking a look around the parking lot to make sure we hadn't been spotted.

"Yes," he said. "Better."

"Good," I said. "Now get back into the car."

The pastor stuffed himself into the back. No arguments, no struggles, no heart attacks. I took another quick look around. Nothing but a slightly overcast afternoon and the wavy, miragelike heat rising off the blacktop.

I got in and started the car. "Take the pastor's belt off and tie his hands at the wrists."

Cassandra's eyes were wet and heavy looking, and she faced the floor of the car.

"There's no need for that, my son," the pastor said in an even, steady voice, a fabricated voice he might have used during his Sunday sermon. "I'll give you no trouble."

"Do it," I said, pulling out of the lot and turning left northbound.

Cassandra turned, extended her slim body into the back, reached for the pastor's belt, and unbuckled it. I watched in the rearview as she slid the belt out from between the loops and told the pastor to hold his wrists out. Then she wrapped the belt around them until the slack was gone and the belt was buckled tight.

There was a pause for a second or two while I drove past the open fields browning in the unusual summerlike heat and past the scattered wood-framed cottages and bungalows.

"You're that warden, aren't you? And you're that young woman. You murdered that escaped criminal, that man who killed the policeman with the pregnant wife. Not that he deserved to live, but who are you to judge?"

I kept the speed at an even forty-five. Not too fast, not too slow.

"Would it help, Father," I said, "if I told you that both of us are innocent?"

"Your guilt," the pastor said, "is entirely your affair, as is your inevitable council with the Almighty Himself. What does not have to be inevitable is your lack of repentance. What you need to ask yourself, my son, is this. Just what do I profit through my corruption that I should gain the world but lose my soul? Why must I lie, cheat, kill? Son, you can still be saved so long as you admit to your crimes, turn yourself in, turn your soul back over to Jesus Christ, your Lord and Savior—"

"Cassandra," I said, "gag the pastor."

I reached into my pants pocket, pulled out a hankie.

"I won't be able to breathe," he said.

"Make sure his nostrils are clear," I said.

"See," he said, "this is exactly what I'm talking about, case and point."

"Sorry it has to be this way, Father," I said, as Cassandra turned and stuffed the hankie into the pastor's mouth. "But I believe your opinion about the state of my salvation is not relevant."

Of course, the pastor had no way of responding. But he was not to be silenced either. He mumbled something nearly indiscernible through the gag. Something that sounded like, "May God have mercy on your souls."

CHAPTER THIRTY-NINE

I had left my cellular phone inside the Toyota, leaving me with no choice but to call Val Antonelli from a wall-mounted pay phone outside a twenty-four-hour supermarket located just a couple of miles south of the Albany city limits. But before that—before I got out of the Pontiac—I made the pastor lie down on the backseat, out of sight. In the meantime, Cassandra, through the opening between the bucket seats, kept the barrel of the .45 pointed in the direction of the pastor's head. What the Father did not know was that I had discharged the clip and slipped it into my pocket before handing the piece over to Cassandra. It was one thing trusting her with the .45. It was quite another trusting her with a loaded .45.

"Superintendent's office," Val said.

"You alone?" I said.

"Where are you, Keeper?" Her voice suddenly muffled, but urgent all the same.

"Pay phone."

"Vasquez is dead."

"I know," I said.

"I saw the special report on television. You were running away."

I let out a breath. "I didn't do it," I said.

"Of course," Val said. Voice funny, distant.

"Listen carefully," I said. "I'm running out of change and time. You have to call me back."

I read off the number displayed behind the clear plastic tab embedded in the chrome panel of the phone box.

Val hung up without saying good-bye.

I wasn't entirely convinced she'd call me back, but it was a chance I had to take.

I took a quick look at the Pontiac while I waited (and prayed) for the pay phone to ring. Of all times to lose the cellphone. Cassandra sat in the passenger seat, gripping the two-and-a-half pound, unloaded .45 in her right hand, holding it steady on the pastor. She made a fist with her free hand and rested it in her lap. Her face lacked even a semblance of expression—mouth closed, teardrop eyes staring through the windshield, heart-shaped tattoo looking out of place but somehow natural on the smooth skin of her neck.

The phone rang.

I felt a wave of relief when I pulled the receiver and put it to my ear. "Tell me what you know?" I said.

"FBI came snooping around this morning," Val said. "There was a bag of something. Dope, heroin, something; I don't know what. A bag of cash, too, inside your desk drawer under lock and key."

I felt like my legs had been chopped out from under me.

"They found two bags, Keeper. How am I supposed to feel about that?"

"Plants," I said, taking a deep breath, trying like hell to regain my equilibrium. "Don't you see, Val? Setup."

"Of course," Val said, in that strange, unfeeling, monotone voice.

"Jesus, Val," I said. "You have to believe me."

The silence that followed verged on unbearable. I gazed into the Pontiac at the ever-still pastor and the ever-still Cassandra Wolf with .45 in hand.

"I told you before, Keeper," Val said finally, in a whisper voice. "I work for you first."

There, I thought. She'd said it, said exactly what I'd wanted her to say. But it was the way she'd said it. A funny, unsure, trembling voice.

"You have to do me a favor," I said. "I'm heading north to my cabin in the Adirondacks. I want you to meet me at Exit 28 of the Northway tomorrow morning at nine. Pull off the exit and wait. You won't see me, but I'll see you."

"You have a cabin in the Adirondacks?"

"My grandfather's before he died," I said. "Then my father's until he died. He left the place to me. I haven't been there since I was a kid, but I don't know where else to go."

"Sure," Val said, as if she didn't quite believe my cabin story either.

"Now," I said, "you're going to need a pencil and some paper."

I waited until Val was ready.

"Go," she said.

"I want you to bring me a first-aid kit and some food. Enough stuff to last two people a couple of days. Also, two shotguns."

"Jesus Christ, Keeper. Where am I supposed to find—"

"Just call Tony Angelino at Council 84. He'll help you."

Val wrote down the instructions.

"Two twelve-gauge shotguns," I said. "Remington 1187s if he can get them. Four boxes of shells, plus a box of .45 caliber rounds. I need a pair of black jeans, black combat boots, black turtleneck, black watch cap. You know the sizes."

"Guns," Val whispered. "Guns and combat boots."

"Here's where I really need your expertise," I said. "I need an identical set of clothing for a woman."

"Cassandra Wolf sort of woman?" Val said.

"Yeah," I said. "That sort of woman."

"What's her size?"

I took another quick look inside the Pontiac. "She's a little taller than you I guess, maybe a hundred seven, a hundred ten pounds, average hips, better than average chest, I suppose."

"Sounds like an eight," Val said. "Lucky you."

"Also," I said, "I need some cash."

"Anything else, Keeper?"

"Anything you can think of that I might have missed."

"Who's gonna pay for all this?"

"Just tell Tony Angelino to put it on my tab."

"He's gonna love that, Keeper," she said. "A union lawyer financing a fugitive."

I could feel the uneasy silence oozing through the line.

"You have to be guilty to be a fugitive, Val."

"I'm sorry," she said. "It's just that I saw you running away on TV. Away from the police, I mean. And there was the stuff in your drawer."

"I didn't do it, Val. Neither did Cassandra Wolf."

"It's just the way it looked."

"Remember," I said, "you don't have to do anything you don't want to do."

I pictured Val's soft face, her brown eyes, and well-sculpted black eyebrows. I pictured the way she reached for the ceiling when she stood up from the swivel chair inside my office at Green Haven. Scared and anxious, that's all she was. So was I.

"Keeper," she said, releasing a quick breath. "I'm with you all the way."

"You do this for me," I said, "you become an accessory after the fact."

"Listen, Keeper," Val said, "I'm thirty-six years old. My husband took off on me six years ago. Other than Mike Norman, I haven't had a steady relationship in almost as many years. I have to do something for me. Take a stand. Maybe this is my stand."

"I won't let you down, Val. I swear it."

I gazed once more inside the Pontiac. Neither the white-faced pastor nor Cassandra stirred. Just a blank look on her face, and a .45 in her hand.

"Remember, Val," I said. "Exit 28 of the Northway. Nine o'clock sharp."

"I'm already on it."

"You're my angel, Val Antonelli."

"You bet your sweet ass I am," she said.

BOOK FOUR

IRONVILLE

CHAPTER FORTY

Nineteen seventy-one is the year Attica State Prison goes insane.

Here's how:

I sit cross-legged and barefoot in a mud puddle in D-Yard. Mike Norman sits directly across from me mumbling something that makes no sense. His eyes are dark and glassy, his face sunken and pale. His yellow jumpsuit is soaked through to the bone. He is covered in mud. So is Wash Pelton. He sits beside me, so close I can feel his trembling shoulder rubbing up against my own. His knees are tucked up into his chest, arms wrapped around his shins. He is crying again. I feel my own eyes welling up. Everything around me—the stone wall, the soupy earth, the overcast sky—is gray-brown. A high-pitched whistle goes off inside my head. When I hear the screams of the CO who is being castrated with a double-edge razor, I have to hold back the tears and the shakes. My body goes numb as the officer is pushed to his knees. His pants are pushed down and his skinny legs are exposed, the white skin streaked with veins of mud. I see the patch of black hair that surrounds his cock. Two rebel inmates hold him by the arms and by the hair on

his head. They press his knees into the mud. He screams in agony as
the razor cuts through the pale flesh and opens up the purple artery, the
blood spurting five feet into a rainy sky. The scream is the kind of
primal scream you feel more than hear. It is a scream that goes beyond
anything human. I try to turn my mind off to the blood, rain, mud, and
death. I try to turn my mind off completely. But I know this corrections
officer and because I·know him I feel he is a part of me. He is forty-
seven years old and the grandfather of a new baby boy.

John Pendergast has been emasculated with a razor blade.

He lies bleeding to death in the middle of D-Yard.

I am eighteen years old. My name means nothing to the rebel inmates. My death would mean everything.

"Our Father," we begin to pray together on the muddy floor, "who
art in heaven, hallowed be thy name. . . ."

CHAPTER FORTY-ONE

At five o'clock I got back into the white Pontiac and drove out of the Supermarket parking lot. I knew I had to do something about the pastor. If I were a real killer, this would have been the part of the mystery where I'd have to bump him off, execution style. Just one shot from the .45 to the back of the head would do the trick. Then I'd lose his body in a patch of heavy woods somewhere off the highway, well above the Albany city limits. North, above Lake George.

The pastor knew too much. He could finger Cassandra and me in a lineup. At the very least, I'd have to take him with me, lock him up in the potato cellar underneath my grandfather's cabin. He knows too much, I'd keep telling myself. It's either him or me.

But I wasn't a killer and it made me sick to my stomach to be thinking like one. Maybe I was beginning to unravel from the inside out. Maybe I was beginning to disintegrate. Maybe, with my back up against the wall, I was becoming one of them.

•   •   •

There was an orange-red sky on the horizon, and a steady north wind bucked against the Pontiac, making it veer to the right. I pulled off the highway onto the ramp for Pottersville, not far from the Pottersville Inn—a century-old, three-story, wood-framed building that took up one full square block in the small upstate town.

As I came to the end of the exit and made a left turn onto the road to the inn, I was suddenly stricken with vivid memories of my grandfather. It was thirty-five years ago and we were on our way from Albany to his cabin. But first he turned off the highway for a "cold one" and led me into the inn. Driving now through Pottersville I could still see the long mahogany bar and the wide, gilt-framed mirrors behind the shelves of bottled liquor; I could see the giant moose head mounted above the ladies' room and the fire going in the woodstove; I could smell the burning hardwood and stale beer and the distinct, steamy fish smell from my grandfather's oversized mackinaw as the snow melted off it. Then I remembered my grandfather's callused hand wrapped around my smaller hand, and I smelled the sweet smell of Scotch-sour on his breath, and I recalled the weird feeling in my stomach when I realized, even at eight or nine years old, that this short man, with black-and-gray stubble on his face and a halo of light brown hair around his head, was my father's father and how different the two men looked and how differently they acted—one slow and methodical and tender, and the other (my father) fast and direct and always occupied.

I pulled the Grand Prix over to the soft shoulder.

Cassandra turned to me. "Why are we stopping?" she said.

"This is where the pastor gets out," I said.

She opened her eyes, wide. Her first real emotional response since we'd borrowed the pastor's car. "But he can recognize us now," she said. "We can't just let him go."

"I'm not a kidnapper."

"Short-term memory can be a real bitch," she said. "Trust me. I used to study stuff about the brain, how it works."

"What college?" I said.

She rolled her eyes. "The University of Bad Breaks," she said.

"I see," I said.

"I used to take correspondence courses, before Eddy hired me on."

"So you think we ought to keep the pastor with us."

"All I'm saying is he can spot us now."

"We're innocent, remember?"

"Innocence never kept anyone from jail. You of all people should know that."

"That's a chance we'll have to take."

Cassandra retreated back into herself again, as if I had scolded her. But then, she didn't seem quite like the kind of person who could be easily scolded by anyone, least of all me. She gazed down at the rubber foot mats of the Grand Prix and tried to tune me out, just like that.

"Listen," I said. "By the time he finds his way back to Albany, we'll be long gone."

But she said nothing, as if I couldn't possibly convince her that letting the pastor go was the right thing to do. I reached around the bucket seat anyway and pulled the gag out of his mouth. I undid the belt tied around his wrists, tossed it onto his lap. "End of the road, Father," I said. "You're free to go."

He wiped away the white patches of dried saliva that had collected on his lips, and he coughed. "You mean you're not going to kill me?" he said in a strained voice.

Cassandra laughed suddenly and glanced over her left shoulder. "Would you like us to kill you, Father?"

"You two are wanted murderers."

"I think the padre here wants to be a martyr," Cassandra said.

"That's enough," I said.

But Cassandra turned away and shook her head and laughed a little bit more. When she moved her head quickly, her shoulder-length hair bobbed, exposing the red, heart-shaped tattoo on her neck.

"Despite public opinion, Father," I said, "the lady and I are not Bonnie and Clyde."

I got out of the car and pushed the driver's seat in toward the steering column so that he would have an easier time getting out. At the same time a car passed and then another. As far as I could see, neither driver seemed to suspect that anything was wrong.

"You have any money, Father?"

The red-faced, gray-haired pastor gave me a look like the skin was melting off my face. He padded his pants pocket with open hands. "I wasn't planning on needing any," he said, clearly fearing a mugging.

I pulled the roll of bills out of my pocket, peeled off two tens. "Here," I said. "Now I'm going to ask you, as a Christian and a man of God, not to call the police for at least one hour. That's all I'm asking. And I'm asking you in the name of the Father."

The pastor stood there, mouth open, little tufts of gray hair blowing in the wind that trailed each passing car and truck. He said, "One hour." His stringy hair stuck up on one side and the bald spot in the middle of his round head made him look like a friar more than the pastor for the Church of the Nazarene. His collarless shirt now hung out of his pants. He had two tens folded up in his fisted hand. "You did not harm me," he said, looking down at his hand. "You are letting me go free. You've given me money. Maybe you are innocent, maybe you are not. But I will give you the hour you ask for." He took a deep breath and raised his face to mine. "Then I'm going to call the proper authorities and tell them what I know."

"I'm sorry, Father," I said.

He started to walk away. But before he got far, he stopped and turned back to me. "What about the car?" he said. "The car belongs to the parish."

"I'll take good care of it," I said, trying to work up a semblance of a smile. "I'll return it when I no longer need it."

The pastor looked down at the ground, most likely convinced he would never see the car again. And he was certainly justified in thinking that way. But then, for a second or two, both of us were drawn to Cassandra. She sat motionless in the Grand Prix, her eyes peeled on the Pottersville Inn just ahead. She seemed transfixed by the old building. But then, I had the feeling that she saw something completely different.

"She going to be okay?" the pastor said.

"Her boyfriend was just blown away by the very same people that want to see me go down," I said.

"I'll say a prayer for both of you," he said.

"Do it now," I said, getting back inside the car. "Do it often."

CHAPTER FORTY-TWO

We got to the cabin at a little past seven-thirty.

The five-room cabin had been built by my grandfather in 1947, just a couple of years after he'd come back from the war in Europe, where, during the Battle of the Bulge, he'd taken rounds in the leg and the shoulder from a Tiger tank-mounted machine gun. He'd set the cabin into the base of what some locals referred to as a very small mountain called Old Iron Top because of the way the metal aggregates in the bald, granite hilltop glistened in the sun when it shined down directly at noontime.

The cabin had been constructed of timbers felled from the forest that surrounded it. The roof was framed in the shape of an A and shingled with wood shakes that had been replaced only twice that I knew of since the old man had died from stomach cancer back in '81. The cabin had been set so far into the base of Old Iron Top that you could access the roof from the back without using a step ladder. Coming up the paved drive I was besieged with childhood memories of warm summer nights, and of sneaking out the bedroom window and shimmying up onto the roof, and of how in the morning my grandfather would swear he'd heard animals running around overhead during the night.

When I tried to wake Cassandra, she wouldn't budge. Maybe it had been days since she'd slept so soundly. Or maybe Vasquez's death had had some kind of tranquilizing effect on her. Some sort of shock to the system. Whatever the case, she slept like the dead, and I was thankful for it.

Like we had done to the pastor only a short while before, I took off my belt, wrapped it carefully around the wrist of her right arm, and at the same time slipped it through an opening in the passenger-side door handle. I secured the belt as best I could without jarring her and started my walk up the drive with the silence of the black forest all around me and my .45 in hand—a round chambered, safety off. I made it to the stack of piled firewood stored under a carport connected to the west side of the cabin, and moved on slowly until I reached the side door. In the light from the headlights, I could make out the little black mailbox bolted to the wall beside the door frame. The golden eagle that had once been attached to the black box was gone now, leaving only an outline.

I stepped up onto the first of the three wooden risers and slipped my hand into the small space between the mailbox and the exterior cabin wall. The key was there hanging by a small nail, just like I hoped it would be. It had been my grandfather's idea to hide the key in that space. Now it was left there by the caretakers so renters could access the place in the summer and early fall months.

I slipped the key into the lock, twisted it, felt the deadbolt give way cleanly and smoothly. I opened the door and stepped inside and smelled the familiar mud-and-wood smell. It was a very personal smell that had not changed in all the years since I had last stepped foot inside the place. Feeling my feet on the rough plank floor, I walked blindly but confidently—the .45 leading the charge—knowing my way across the sitting room and into the kitchen where I knew a wrought-iron lamp would be bolted into the log wall above the kitchen table.

I felt for the lamp.

It was still there. I reached inside the lampshade, felt for the switch, and then there was light.

In the kitchen, cast-iron pots and pans hung from metal hooks above the black gas stove, and white plates were stacked on the exposed pine shelving beside the cabinets. There was the same black rotary phone I remembered as a kid, sitting on a small table in the far corner of the room, below the window and behind the kitchen table. I picked up the handset, brought it to my ear. The phone worked.

I returned to the great room and took a good look at the fireplace my grandfather had constructed with Adirondack fieldstone cut out of Old Iron Top. The fireplace rose up through the ceiling. A railroad tie had been mounted above the box to serve as a mantel. I gazed at the cross-beams that supported the roof—exposed beams that, once upon a time seemed so massive to me and so high off the floor. Now I could reach the beams by raising my hands above my head.

I took a quick second or two to listen for anything out of the ordinary. When I heard nothing, I went back to the kitchen and pulled down the shade on the window. Another house or cabin could not be found for five miles in any direction, but I knew it was not unusual for the occasional car to pass by along the hard-packed east-west road. Why draw unwanted attention in a place where even a sudden shift in the weather was cause for an Ironville town meeting?

After all, if the cabin was going to be my safe house, it had to be safe.

I slipped across the kitchen into the short hall that accessed the bathroom and two back bedrooms, aiming the .45 into each room as I passed. Nothing but empty walls and empty beds. Back out in the great room, I eased the hammer back on the .45, clicked on the safety, and slipped the piece into my belt.

The light shining into the cabin from the headlights on the Pontiac reminded me of the white spotlight that lit up my office at Green Haven on those occasions when I worked well into the night, which was more often than not now with Fran gone. It also reminded me that I had to get Cassandra inside before she woke up. I had no idea who she really was or what she was capable of. She had gone along with me so far, but then her ass was on the line as much as mine was. I knew she could easily undo that belt and run off, and I wasn't about to allow that to happen.

When I checked on her and found that she was still asleep, I carried in some of the wood from the stack under the carport. Maybe it was warmer than normal down in Albany, but up here it was colder than a witch's tit. I cut up some kindling using a small hatchet that hung by a strip of leather from a rusty sixpenny nail pounded into the log wall. Using some newspapers left behind in an old wooden vegetable crate and my lighter, it didn't take a lot of effort to get a good fire going.

When I was certain the fire could sustain itself, I went out and drove the car up under the carport to keep it hidden. Then I unraveled the belt from Cassandra's wrists and slipped it around my waist. I cradled her in my arms, carried her into the cabin, and laid her down on the mattress in one of the bedrooms. In the kitchen, I searched under the sink for anything resembling a rope. But I found nothing. So I took a towel from the bathroom, tore it into two long strips, and used them to secure one of her wrists and one of her ankles to opposing posts of the single bed. I covered her with a black-and-white-checkered blanket left behind by a summer vacationer. Then I returned to the kitchen of our new safe house and began my search for food and, God willing, booze.

CHAPTER FORTY-THREE

As luck or God would have it, I found two cans of beef stew, a large can of baby peas, and an entire case of Beaujolais still packed away neatly inside its cardboard case. I set the .45 within arm's reach on the counter while Cassandra continued sleeping in the back bedroom. Then I mixed the stew and peas together in the same pan.

I reached under the sink to open the gas valve. The gas hissed as it passed through the line and fed the stove. I lit the front burner with my lighter and stood at the stove to watch the stew heat and to think about my next move. But very soon the thick gravy began to bubble and it was suddenly impossible to think logically what with the aroma of beef stew filling the cabin.

I guess it was impossible to sleep, too. Because that was when Cassandra started screaming.

Perfect timing.

I grabbed the .45, rushed into the bedroom. She was struggling to free her limbs from the bedposts. She popped her head up from the pillow. With the pale moonlight shining in through the window against her face, her expression reminded me of the *Exorcist*.

"Just what the fuck do you think you're doing?" she said.

"Protecting my assets," I said, knowing I shouldn't have.

"Fuck you," she said.

I was waiting for her head to spin completely around.

"Listen," I said, "I can't take a chance on you running off."

"Just where the hell would I go?" she said. A good point, considering that we were miles away from any kind of civilization and light-years away from New York City, her home turf.

I began undoing the knot in the cloth strip wrapped around her ankle. "At this point," I said, "I can't take any chances. It's only a matter of time until someone knows we're here, and then the cops will find out, and then it's all over."

"So," Cassandra said, shaking out her now-free ankle.

"So," I said, starting on her wrist, "I have to know I can trust you."

"What was all that shit with the priest? A nice little act? I mean, I could've bolted right there and then. But I didn't. Because I know you're in trouble, and you know I'm in trouble, and maybe we can help each other out, right?"

When the last strip of cloth was undone and Cassandra could sit up, she slapped me.

"Jesus," I said, bringing my hand to my stinging cheek.

"That was for not trusting me," she said.

I might have slapped her back if she hadn't started crying.

She looked weary now, not in the moonlight, but in the dim light that leaked in from both the kitchen lamp and the fire. She ran her hands through her thick hair, got up off the bed, and marched into the kitchen. I followed her out and noticed how she paused just long enough to get a quick look at the beef stew cooking on the stove. Then she went into the great room and sat down in front of the fire.

I followed her in.

She brought her knees to her chin, wrapped her arms tightly around them, stared into the flames. "First comes the denial," she said, wiping her eyes. "Then comes the grief. Just wait till I get to the angry part."

The case of Beaujolais was under the kitchen table. I took out a bottle and opened it with a corkscrew I'd found inside the junk drawer next to the sink. I ladled some of the beef stew into a couple of bowls and poured some red wine into two coffee mugs. Mugs in one hand and plates in the other, I managed to carry everything into the living area of the cabin and set it down by the fire without spilling even a single drop of wine or gravy.

Cassandra took one look at her plate and turned back to the fire.

I sat down, picked up my plate, and set it carefully in my lap. "I think it's time we had a little talk," I said in my best diplomatic, let's-make-peace tone of voice.

Cassandra dipped the tip of her index finger into the thick stew, brought it to her lips and tongue. Her teardrop eyes glistened from the fire and her crying.

I took a bite of the stew. It was hot and tangy on my tongue—canned, but tasty all the same.

"I'm ready to listen if you're ready to talk," I said. But I could see that it would be no use pressing her. Cassandra was in too much pain to talk. I suppose I couldn't blame her. Her boyfriend had just taken a round in the back of the head, point-blank. I knew what it was to lose someone you loved.

"Would it help," I said, "if I told you it can only get better?"

She looked at me with a blank stare and said, "Look who's predicting the future."

I finished off my beef stew and wine in silence. I finished it all, right there on the rough wooden floor of my grandfather's cabin, in the exact spot where he used to sit after an afternoon fly-fishing Putt's Creek, the narrow stream that ran parallel to the east-west road.

I took the empty bowl into the kitchen and put it in the sink. I filled my mug with more wine. I knew the time was ripe for me to get some answers. I also knew the longer I waited, the longer it would take for me to figure out just who was responsible for this mess. I stood there in the kitchen with the wine in my hand and it was all I could do not to grab hold of Cassandra and make her spill the truth right there and then. But all she could manage right now was tears. And I couldn't blame her.

It was getting close to eleven o'clock. I hadn't slept in what seemed like days. Maybe this was as good a time as any to get a little rest. There was no telling when I'd get the chance to sleep again. So that's what I decided to do. Get some rest. While I had the time and the opportunity.

Maybe I was taking a bigger chance than I realized. But Cassandra was still sitting by the fire, on her own, when I took the bottle with me into the bedroom so that she could be left alone with her thoughts about a past and a future I knew she wanted nothing to do with.

CHAPTER FORTY-FOUR

But then I knew all about the power of the past, about the power of sleep. I knew that sleep could make my past come alive again in dreams, so that one second I am staring at the cabin ceiling and the next it is morning inside Attica State Prison on the fourth and final day of an insurrection that has already claimed a dozen lives and will claim dozens more before it is finished. I am walking the catwalk—the narrow concrete platform that spans the perimeter of D-Yard's interior—thirty feet above the naked ground. The walk is protected on both sides by connected lengths of pipe railing. My right hip rubs against the railing as I walk toward the place where the catwalks from this and the other three yards merge in the center of the Attica State Prison complex to form a cross. The area in the center, where the catwalks intersect, is called Times Square by inmates and COs alike.

A rebel inmate presses a shiv up against the back of my neck where the spine meets the brain and pushes me along by the collar of my yellow prison jumpsuit. He presses the razor up against the tight flesh surrounding the spine, until I feel the eye-watering sting of a blade on the verge of popping through the skin.

Up ahead, another inmate holds a black-plated service revolver against Wash Pelton's skull. Like me, Wash is dressed in a yellow inmate jumpsuit. Unlike me, he is lucky enough to have a pair of work boots to protect his feet. He struggles with the pistol-bearing inmate, trying to break free from the arm the man has wrapped around his neck. He pushes and pulls until the rebel inmate clips him on the back of the skull with the service revolver. Wash goes down on his knees, onto the concrete.

I try to keep up with the pace of the inmate who pushes me along. I haven't eaten in three days, haven't slept in four. I can't maintain my balance.

It seems like hours pass before we finally make it to Times Square. It's there that Wash Pelton is pulled back up to his feet by the rebel inmate after having been literally dragged. Then the inmate forces the barrel of the revolver into Pelton's mouth. That's when Wash begins to cry. Tears and saliva drip down the barrel of the revolver. The hum from the crowd of inmates that fills D-Yard dies down. All eyes are on Wash and myself and a third hostage who takes his position by my side. Norman is unconscious or catatonic, I don't know which. He shows no sign of waking. Two rebel inmates hold him up, one on each arm. The inmate on his right points the skinny barrel of a prison-issue M-16 at his head. But the M-16 has no effect on Mike Norman.

There are puddles of muddy water. There are piles of clothes and garbage. In a far corner of the yard a fire is blazing. It had rained hard all night. And the corrections officers had been left out in the rain. No one except Mike Norman slept. From over the prison PA system comes the tinny voice of the commissioner of corrections for New York. "Give up your hostages or you will be met with force." No one pays even the slightest attention to the voice. Not the hostages or the inmates. The commissioner, after all, addresses us from outside these stone walls.

Above us a black-and-white state police chopper makes a flyby. The rebel inmates aim their weapons at the helicopter. From Times Square I can make out the squad of state troopers poised along the west wall. Sharpshooters with scopes and rifles (.270 caliber sniper jobs, I assume) aimed in my direction. The rebel inmates are dressed in corrections officer uniforms. The hostages are dressed in yellow inmate jump-suits—suits designed specifically for transporting prisoners outside the prison walls. I wonder if the state troopers can tell the difference be-tween a hostage and a rebel inmate from that distance. I wonder if it will really matter to them once the shooting starts.

Behind the row of sharpshooters the live television crews are water-ing at the mouth, hoping for one or more of our heads to be blown away. What a scoop it would make. What a report. What had become a gentle hum among the rebel inmates in D-Yard has once again become screaming. "Kill the motherfuckers. Blow their fucking brains out."

The two inmates who support Mike Norman lay him down into a shallow pool of water that has collected inside a depression on the concrete catwalk. The white inmate who has forced the blunt barrel of the black-plated service revolver into Wash Pelton's mouth pulls back the hammer, closes his eyes, faces away. . . .

CHAPTER FORTY-FIVE

I woke up to the sound of footsteps on the roof. I didn't know quite where I was until I focused my eyes on the half-light that leaked in from the fire in the great room. I wasn't sure if I had truly heard footsteps on the roof or if it had been my imagination, the result of a dream, the recollection of which had disappeared as fast as it had come.

I felt for my gun.

Then I looked at my watch and realized I had only been out for an hour. But it felt like ten hours of drugged sleep. Taking a deep breath, I got out of bed and made it to the bathroom with eyelids at half-mast. You might say I was operating on instinct, on a physical knowledge of the cabin interior that had not left my body in more than three decades.

At the sink, I threw cold water on my face and took a good look in the mirror. I gazed at the heavy brown eyes, at the three-day-old growth, at the unkempt Pancho Villa mustache, and at the thick black hair cut close to the scalp. I felt more than tired, more than exhausted, as if my body had waited until this very moment to feel everything it was supposed to feel since the trouble had begun on Monday afternoon when Vasquez bolted from the iron house.

Despite the persistent chill in the cabin (even this late in May), I took off my shirt and gazed at the washboard ripple of my stomach muscles and the way my chest heaved, defined and elastic, when I took deep breaths. Maybe all the running and body building had kept me in some kind of shape, but I also knew that the cigarettes were getting to me, making my lungs ache, killing me. Although the real pain would take its own sweet time.

But something else was also taking its own sweet time.

Since Fran had died, I hadn't slept well, or eaten well, or been without a bottle of Scotch or Jamesons close by. Since Fran had died, grief alone had made me drop eighteen pounds in twelve months. At that rate I'd be down to eighty pounds in five years. A frightening prospect. Standing at the sink, with the hot and cold water running down against the white porcelain bowl, and staring at my white face in the mirror, I knew it was time to begin living again. The trick was learning to live without the grief and without the guilt. The trick was to create a life worth living, a life no longer conscious of death.

I made a cup with my hands, filled it with cold water, splashed it over my face and chest. I felt unbearably cold until I dried my face with the towel and hung it back on the rack behind the door. It was only after I looked up again that I saw his face in the mirror. With the water running, I hadn't heard him slip out from behind the plastic shower curtain. He was dressed in a full-length wool overcoat and he held a bowie knife the size of my leg up against my Adam's apple.

"Don't make a fucking sound," the overcoat man said, covering my mouth with his free hand.

How could I make a sound?

His hand smelled like sweat. I felt dizzy, weak. His were the footsteps I'd heard on the roof. I hadn't dreamt them after all. The footsteps were as real as it gets.

The water was still going steady, from both spigots, swirling down the drain of the sink.

He took his hand away from my mouth slowly. At the same time, he pressed the blade tighter against my throat so that it was an effort just attempting a swallow.

"Now," he said, voice smooth and evenly toned, like a professional. "We're going to take a walk."

"Who sent you?" I said.

He rapped me on the side of the head with the blade. The rap stung, but I knew the damage was nil.

"No talking," he said.

I raised my hands in surrender.

"Turn off the water," he said. "Use your right hand, nice and easy."

I lowered my hand and brought it to the cold-water faucet. I twisted, clockwise, all the time wracking my brain for a way out of this, searching the immediate area for a knife, a comb, a razor blade, anything that would give me a fucking semblance of a chance.

"Come on," he whispered. "The next one."

I put my hand on the hot water faucet and hesitated.

"Now," he said. "Do it."

The hot water steamed up onto my bare chest and face. I could feel the sting of it as it splattered into the white porcelain sink. I began to turn the knob. But instead of turning it counterclockwise, I slowly turned it clockwise, opening up the valve, the hot water pouring out faster and heavier and hotter.

"No," he said, still using that evenly toned whisper, but somehow more urgent now. "The other fucking way."

And that was when he fell for it. He reached out to the faucet with his free hand. But I grabbed his wrist and held his hand down under the scalding water and went for the knife. The overcoat man screamed and yanked back hard. He stumbled backward a few steps and I brought my fingers to my throat to see if he'd cut me. When he raised the knife to drive it into my chest, I looked closely at the blade to see if it was streaked with red. But before I had a chance to see, his body crumpled and collapsed.

Without thinking, I went down for the knife.

Standing over me was Cassandra.

She had buried the kindling-wood hatchet smack into the back of his head. He never knew what hit him.

I dropped the knife to the floor and got back up on my feet. For a second or two, Cassandra and I stood there stunned, looking at one another with blank faces, breathing hard but steady.

Then I went down on my knees again. "Grab a towel," I said.

She did.

I held the towel in one hand and jerked the hatchet out of the skull with the other. Blood came rushing out along with the blade. I pressed the towel up against the wound and got a good look at his face. His eyelids were blinking and his mouth was opening and closing, but no sound was coming out and I was fairly certain that his life had left his body before his nervous system had had a chance to register it.

I laid him down on the floor, the weight of his head pressed against the now blood-soaked towel.

"Oh Christ," Cassandra said, bringing her hands to her face, turning her head. "Oh my Jesus fucking Christ."

I had no way of telling if her reaction was the result of what she had done or of recognizing whom she had done it to, or both.

I felt the jugular for a pulse.

Nothing.

I brought my ear to his mouth, listened for breathing.

Nothing.

I shook the bastard. "Who the fuck sent you?" I said. But it was all useless.

All I could get out of him was a death rattle and even that stopped after a few seconds. He was gone and I knew it.

I pressed his head back down onto the towel and looked up at Cassandra.

"You recognize this son of a bitch?" I said.

She had her back to me.

"I'm talking to you," I snapped.

"No," she said.

"You're lying," I said, bounding up.

She said nothing. I grabbed her shoulders, turned her around. She was crying.

"Who the hell was he?" I said. "You saw his face and you recognized him. Who the fuck was he?"

"I don't know," she screamed. "I'm telling the God's honest truth. For Christ's sake, please. . . ." Her voice just trailed off.

I let go of her, took a deep breath, and glanced back down at the dead man. The bath towel was saturated now and there was a small puddle of blood on the floor behind his head.

"How the hell do I know if you're telling the truth?"

Cassandra gritted her teeth and looked at me wide-eyed. "Because I just saved your ass," she said, with a voice that made the hairs on the back of my neck stand up stiffer than the overcoat man's dead body.

"Oh Christ," she said, tearing the plastic shower curtain right off the metal rings and draping it over the body.

"There," she said, walking out. "I did my part. Now you clean up the rest."

I took a deep breath and proceeded to do exactly that.

CHAPTER FORTY-SIX

It didn't surprise me one bit that I found nothing on the man after going through his pockets. No wallet, no ID, no photos, no badge (thank Christ), not even a goddamned stick of gum. He was a thorough professional, probably a freelancer. And I was quite sure he had been sent either by Pelton or Schillinger or both. It only made sense for them to place a tail on me seeing that I posed such a threat. What did surprise me was how the hell he located us all the way up here. He must have tailed us the whole goddamn way.

Under the cover of night, I dragged his body out to the woods behind the cabin and buried him in a shallow grave marked with a stone cairn and piles of oak leaves and pine needles for camouflage. It wasn't much but at least his body would be hidden until I devised some kind of plan for disposing of it before the stink of decomposition took over. I'm not sure exactly why I did it, but before I covered him in dirt I put the knife back in his hand.

It took about an hour to clean up the mess in the bathroom and to

burn the blood-soaked towels in the fire. By the time I got settled, it was
going on two o'clock in the morning.

Cassandra was a tough one.

She never lifted a finger to help with the mess. She sat by the fire
taking deep, calming breaths, her shoulders shaking, trying to bring
herself to grips with the fact that she had just buried a hatchet in
somebody's skull. Like Eddy Vasquez's sudden death, this was something she had to swallow. But in another sense, it was something I had
to swallow too. Cassandra had saved my life and I knew I should be
grateful. And I was. Not for my life necessarily, but for providing me
with at least one very good reason to place my trust in her.

I sat down beside her. She seemed somewhat calm now, although I
had no way of knowing for certain just how she really felt.

"Thanks," I said, staring not at her, but into the fire.

"For what?" she said.

"For preventing that asshole from planting that knife in my solar
plexus."

"Oh," she said. "That."

"Yeah," I said. "That."

I looked at her, saw her make a slight, corner-of-the-mouth smile,
then break down in tears once more.

"You did what you had to do," I said.

"No," she said in a soft, whisper voice. "That's not it at all."

"What then?" I said, trying my best to stay calm and patient, despite
the fact that I needed answers and needed them quickly.

"I'm not sure that I loved Eddy at all after he shot that cop," she said.
"It's just that I felt this need to be there for him once he'd been put in
prison. Like my being there somehow gave him a good side or somehow destroyed the bad. And now that he's dead, I can't help but feel
like I somehow let him down."

She hesitated for a few seconds.

Her entire body was trembling, and for good reason.

"But there's something else, too," she said. "I can't help but feel
relieved."

I felt the heat from the fire on my face, but in my brain I pictured
the overcoat man coming up on me from behind, knife in hand. "How
can I help?" I said. But what I really wanted to say was this: Just what

the hell do you know and how do I know you're going to tell me the whole truth and nothing but the whole truth, regardless of the way you just saved my ass? . . .

Of course, I'd have to be gentler than that, cut down substantially on my cursing, at the very least.

"You don't know what I'm going through," she said, louder this time, more forceful.

I looked at her eyes, wide and brown, filled with fire both real and reflected.

"I almost feel good, like this weight has been lifted from my shoulders because I know I won't have to be there for him anymore, won't have to play his or anyone else's games. Like I can live a life of my own now that Eddy has lost his."

I put my hand on her knee. She made no attempt to move it. "Don't confuse relief with guilt," I said. "From the moment he killed that cop, his going down was only a matter of time." I wasn't sure if I should have said it like that, but I said it anyway, because it was the truth and I wanted to get beyond this whole thing as soon as possible. But the facts were plain enough: Eduard Vasquez shot a cop, point-blank. A cop with a pregnant wife. He had to pay, one way or the other.

Cassandra put her head down again, chin against chest. She wiped the tears from her eyes with the backs of her hands. But then, suddenly, she snapped her head up so that her heavy eyes and long black eyelashes once again reflected the radiance of the fire. "That's it," she said. "I'm not going to mourn for a man I did not love."

"Good," I said, lifting my hand from her knee to her shoulder. "Then let's get to work."

I checked the time.

Two-fifteen in the A.M.

Before I knew it, daylight would be breaking over the valley and Val Antonelli would be waiting for me at our rendezvous off Exit 28 of the Northway. That is, if the bastards didn't get to us first. What I mean is, if the overcoat man had been sent by Pelton or Schillinger and he didn't return or contact them at some designated hour, somebody was going to become a little suspicious.

I got up, tossed two more chunks of wood into the fire. Sparks shot up and a couple of air pockets burst like intermittent blasts from a light-caliber revolver. It was hard to believe in a way. A fire during the month of May, during an unusually warm spring. But that was the difference between the north country and the suburbs that surrounded Albany only a hundred fifty miles or so to the south. As I sat back down again, I knew that even during the summer months it was not unusual to get a frost up here.

"Now look, Cassandra," I said, in as steady a voice as I could summon given the circumstances. "I want to ask you some questions and I want you to tell me the truth." I tried looking her in the eye, but she looked away as if the effort were just too painful. "We have to be honest with each other, help one another out as much as possible, hold nothing back. Or else we both risk going away for a very long time. Do you understand what I'm saying?"

She stared at the fire like it was her lifeline, like we had all the time in the world. I took her by the shoulders, shook them just enough to get her full and undivided attention. "Do we understand one another?" I said.

She said nothing. Instead she nodded her head yes.

"Good," I said, standing and pulling the .45 out from under my belt, checking the safety and the round I had chambered earlier. "First question. How'd you get mixed up with a crook like Vasquez?"

"So you want to know about Cassandra's fucked-up past, is that it?"

"It might help if we start from the beginning," I said, pacing now from one end of the great room to the other. "It'll definitely be a start if I get to know you a little better."

Cassandra laughed, but I wasn't sure why.

As for me, I pulled back the shade on the picture window just enough to get a look outside, slightly anxious that the overcoat man might not have been alone when he tailed us here.

Cassandra cleared her throat as if about to make a speech. Then she breathed and started in. "In '87," she said, "I was working as a waitress in one of those cheap Mexican buffet joints down by NYU. I was barely getting by, so I decided to answer a classified to become an exotic dancer. You know, a stripper. No prior experience required, the ad said. You provide the gash, we provide the cash."

"The ad said that?"

"At the same time," Cassandra said, "I was taking some home-study courses from the Sally Struthers television correspondence school where, I'm proud to say, you never have to set foot inside a classroom."

"In what?" I said, peeking out the window once more, but seeing only the flat, black darkness.

"I already told you in the car," she said.

"The brain."

"Psychology, to be exact," she said.

"So you were an intellectually motivated student, slash, exotic dancer, is that it?"

"A very broke dancer, slash, correspondence student," Cassandra said. "I had bills to pay, and dancing more than paid for them. I even had my own apartment on the West Side. Try supporting that on waitressing money."

"Dancing was cost-effective," I said.

"I guess that was the sensible side of it all," she said. "But then there was the other side."

"What do you mean?"

"I used what I was doing at work to come up with a topic for a term paper. "Striptease," I called it, "For Fun or Money?' "

"What'd you get?" I said, now leaning against the windowsill.

"For what?"

"For a grade?"

"For a grade?" she said. "They didn't even bother to grade it. The teacher wrote a little note saying that my topic had little to do with the intention of his course and that it might help if I turned myself in to the pornographic hot line or the rape crisis center or the dysfunctional family Web page or some shit like that."

I wasn't sure why, but part of me wanted to laugh.

"I guess they weren't used to term papers written by strippers," Cassandra admitted.

"Which was it for you, then?" I said.

"Which was what?"

"Dancing," I said, picking up a scrap of kindling from the floor and tossing it into the red-yellow flames. "Fun or money?"

"I'm not sure," she said. "Like I told you, it was a way to make the green. But it wasn't like I hated it either, you know."

I sat down next to her again, sat the .45 in my lap, barrel pointed to the fireplace, and gently brushed away the hair on her shoulder exposing the heart-shaped tattoo. "What about Vasquez?" I said. "What about this tattoo?"

"He saw me dancing one night and offered me a job in Tribeca that paid almost twice the cash, and suddenly I've got this career."

"But what about the tattoo?"

"All his dancers had their mark," she said. "Their brand you might say."

"Yours came in the shape of a heart," I said.

"You catch on quick, Mr. Marconi," Cassandra said. "Do I call you Mr. Marconi or is it Warden Marconi or General Marconi?"

"Keeper," I said, in the interest of killing off any formality. Besides, she knew by now what people called me. "What I don't understand, though, is how a smart kid like you could be coaxed into being branded by Vasquez?"

"Lots of recreational drugs went with the job," she said, "which, by the way, kind of added to my term paper."

"Research is research," I said.

"I ended up doing a couple of films for him. Nothing heavy. Strictly cheesecake. But by then the drugs were becoming an everyday event and I was snorting a lot of shit and making more money in a single week than my father made in three months when I was growing up. All of this went into the paper."

"I'm beginning to understand your teacher's concern," I said, getting up from the floor once more, replacing the pistol in my belt, and going for another bottle of wine. "Suddenly the researcher becomes the subject."

"I was making the green," she said, "and getting off on the excitement. My father struggled for years selling wholesale toilet paper from the dining room table of our flat in Queens and then died a lonely, broke old man. I wasn't going to let something like that happen to me."

"What about your mother?"

"My mother?" she said, grabbing the fresh bottle of wine from my hand. "My mother died not long after my tenth birthday. And as for my father? Holy Christ, they should have buried him alongside her."

"After a while," Cassandra went on, "I had no idea what I felt or what I was doing. It was like suddenly the mythical Cassandra—the babe who's supposed to be able to tell the future—can't make any sense out of her past or present. It wasn't like I was worried about having a future. It was like I didn't want a future at all."

"Drugs, pornography, correspondence school," I said. "It all adds up."

"I fell into this trance," she said, taking another sip of wine from the bottle and passing it back to me. "Did you know there's been studies done as to why women turn to hooking or stripping or both?"

"Women who normally wouldn't turn to that sort of thing," I said.

"Yeah," she said. "Some shrinks think that these women work from some kind of . . . how do they put it . . . some kind of pathological base, but not identical pathological bases, if you get my drift."

"Pathological, as in crazy?"

"Do I look crazy to you?"

"I hardly even know you," I said. "But here I am, needing you." The memory of her burying that hatchet flashed through my mind.

"Believe me," she said, "the word pathological can even mean that some women are born into this kind of thing. Doesn't matter if they're rich or dirt-fucking poor like I was, they're attracted to the allure of it all, attracted to the trance. They don't give a rat's ass about doing anything else."

"In other words," I said, "it's not just a way of making a quick buck, after all."

"You're not going to believe this," Cassandra said, "but some prostitutes don't need the money at all."

"So much for mythology," I said. "But what about you? What snapped you out of the trance?"

She took a breath and another swallow of wine. "One night in 1988," she said, "as Eddy and I were coming back from the club in his Mercedes, he ran a stop light. A cop tailed us and made us pull over, close to the sidewalk. When the cop came up to the car, Eddy opened the door and slammed it into him. It caught the cop by surprise and he fell back hard. I screamed at Eddy to stop it, but he just backhanded me, told me to shut the fuck up.

"I couldn't believe it. I'd seen him mad before, but not like this. He just went berserk, like the cop triggered something off inside his brain. He shot out of the car and kicked the cop in the head and dragged him into an alley on the opposite end of the sidewalk. It was late night and dark, and you know how it is in the city when it's hot and people just hang out at all hours of the night. Some people had gathered, a few black kids and a black woman I remembered whose eyes were as big as pools, even through the tinted windows of Eddy's Mercedes. It took only a second or two, but then I saw the flash and heard the pistol go off.

"I got out of the car and screamed, 'What the hell are you doing?' But Eduard never answered. He just pulled the trigger again."

Cassandra fixed her eyes on the fire now. Finally, she was opening up to me. At the same time, I knew she was trying to come to grips with a past gone horribly wrong.

"I started to run," she said. "I ran as far as I could for as long as I could. And then I ran some more. The next morning I found myself outside the doors of Penn Station. I wanted to go straight to the police but I was afraid of what they'd do to me. So I went into Penn, went downstairs and called 911 from a pay phone, told them I knew who killed the police officer. I gave them Eddy's address and by the time I got up the nerve to go back there, Eddy was under arrest. That black woman with the big eyes, she had given the police a description of Eddy, too. A description that must have matched mine.

"But here's the strange thing. During the time Eddy was being questioned, he never let on that I was with him. Even though witnesses were sure there was a girl with him at the time. But then, he's always held that over my head, along with the fact that I called the police. I mean, it's one thing that I told him I turned him in. It's another he didn't kill me right away. It's why I stayed with him, even after he went to jail. It's why I did everything."

"Because if you left him," I said, "he'd have had you killed."

"I was a part of his brood, his property."

"Branded property," I said.

Cassandra took a deep hit off the bottle. "But with Eddy Vasquez," she said, now looking into my eyes, "you always knew where you stood. You were either his friend or his enemy; you were either alive or dead."

Three o'clock was approaching, fast.

If time is relative, then the speed of time had doubled since Cassandra and I had made it to the cabin just a few hours before. But for now there was little to do but look at the fire and drink the wine left behind by the summer people and hope that Eddy Vasquez's girlfriend could feed me all the information I needed to know. I also had to be sure I could trust her and that she wouldn't go running off on me somehow. On the other hand, it would not be a bright idea to tie her up again if I was to consider her my ally. These were the things that were going through my head that night.

But in my thoughts I pictured that rookie cop on his knees on the hot, piss-covered concrete of a New York back alley. I imagined the feel of the barrel pressed up against his head and I wondered if he'd known for certain that his time was up. I wondered if he'd known what had hit him when the first shot exploded. I wondered if he'd heard the sound of the exploding round before the bullet had penetrated his skull.

I knew that only a cold-blooded killer was capable of that kind of execution. An animal who flew off the handle when provoked. As the keeper of the iron house, cold-blooded killers were my business, my trade.

Cassandra put her hand on my leg and leaned in close. "I heard about your wife," she said. "You must think about her a lot."

She kept her hand on my leg.

"I'm having a little trouble shaking her," I said.

"Oh," she said. "I see."

"What do you see?"

She tried to work up a smile. "Looks like you haven't gotten far beyond the guilt and remorse stage," she said.

"Hark," I said, "the Sally Struthers student, slash, exotic dancer speaks."

There was a thick silence that seemed to cover everything in the room like glue.

"Listen," she said, removing her hand from my leg, her voice trembling, "I speak from my own goddamn experience."

When she started to cry again, I felt the sudden urge to hold her tightly against my chest. I wanted her to hold me, too. But I didn't know her and she certainly didn't know me. Not that knowing one another was a prerequisite for commiserating together, each of us over our separate losses. But then, I also knew that getting so close to her at a time when she was so vulnerable would be a grave mistake. For me and for her.

She wiped her eyes and forced a smile. "I'm not just sad," she said, "and I'm not just wiped out with a token dose of the guilts."

"What is it then?"

"I'm happy, too," she said, letting go with a strange-sounding laugh drowned in tears and sniffles.

"I'm not sure I understand," I said.

"I'm all mixed up," she said. "Right now, I'm sad and I'm guilty and I'm scared and most of all I'm happy because that son of bitch is dead, and I feel like I don't deserve a second chance at living my life without Eddy over my head."

Then Cassandra did something extraordinary. She took off her boots and socks and sat up straight and took another long drink of wine. She stood up and began doing a dance, moving her narrow hips from side to side, gyrating with her stomach and midsection. She closed her eyes and let her hair fall to one shoulder so that I could see the heart-shaped tattoo pulsing with the muscles in her neck. She held her arms out away from her breasts and twisted her hands and fingers in and out and all around, her every limb and digit separated from her body but somehow in sync and all the time whispering a song I'd never heard before but beautiful and attractive; with the firelight surrounding her, she was like an angel or an apparition.

For a moment she seemed suspended, her bare feet hardly touching the plank floor. But then she was suddenly in my arms, her face only inches from mine, and I could feel her heart beating, and I could smell her sweet breath, and I was taken in by her teardrop eyes, and I wanted to touch her. Time had just stopped and all that she'd confessed about living with a cold-blooded cop-killer had never happened and I badly wanted to kiss her and feel her mouth with my mouth, but I knew it was not me who wanted to kiss her, but someone inside of me whom I could not trust to take control.

I pushed her away. "No," I said.

"No," she said, "as in no you can't or no you won't?"

"Both," I said.

"For Christ's sakes, your wife is dead and gone."

I stood and pulled Cassandra up by her arms. I put my face in hers and shook her, hard. "Now look," I said, "since your boyfriend took off from my prison my life has gone to shit and it's taken a Herculean performance to keep some semblance of it together."

Cassandra was wide-eyed now and silent, regardless of the tears that streaked down her face.

"So you listen to me, sister. What I don't need now is some half-baked psychoanalysis or exotic dances or temptations of any kind. Do you hear me? What I need is answers, you got that."

I let her go.

"I'm sorry," I said, brushing back my hair with both hands in an attempt to regain control. "Maybe I don't know what I need."

Cassandra stepped back, wiped her eyes.

"What you need," she said, now picking up her socks and boots from the floor, "is a really long steel shank."

"What for?" I said.

"To kill the bug that is lodged inside your ass."

What was supposed to be a safe house suddenly didn't seem so safe anymore. I had to get the hell out, even for a few minutes. I went outside and lit up a cigarette. As I smoked I looked up at the stars and breathed in the cool mountain air and tried my best to regain some semblance of my ever-diminishing composure. The stars were so bright up north, unencumbered by the lights of the city. Layers and layers of them. I thought about Fran and I thought about the rookie cop lying dead in a back alley and I thought about the overcoat man rotting in the woods and I thought about going to prison and I thought about Attica and I thought about the way Cassandra had just danced for me and I thought about so many things I didn't know what the hell to think next.

None of this shit matched the warden's job description.

Then she came out, took the cigarette out of my hand, and took a deep drag. She raised her head just a little when she exhaled, allowing her hair to fall back against her shoulders. In the light of the moon, she was truly beautiful. There was no other way to put it. But I couldn't allow myself to be taken in by the beauty. I had to concentrate on the problem at hand. Hell, the *problems*.

"Hey," Cassandra said, her arms crossed at her chest for warmth, "I've got an idea."

"I'm all ears," I said, as antisocial as possible.

"Let's start over," she said, handing back the cigarette. "Like we never even met until this very moment."

The two of us had our eyes locked on the moon and stars. But then we both turned to each other at the same time.

"What the hell," I said, cigarette tucked in the corner of my mouth, right hand extended for her to shake. "Keeper Marconi, Green Haven Prison."

"Cassandra Wolf," she said, taking my hand, curtsying slightly. "Eddy's Blue Bayou."

"Pleased to meet you, Cassandra," I said.

"Same here, Keeper," she said.

I stamped out the butt with the sole of my boot, blew out the last breath of smoke. "So Cassandra Wolf of Eddy's Blue Bayou, what would you like to talk about?"

"What if I were to tell you I was in possession of information that could change your life?"

"What'll it cost me?"

"How's about a drink?" she said, a smile now planted on her face.

"You read my mind," I said. "How's a Beaujolais circa 1995 sound to you?"

"A very happy year as I recall," she said, turning for the cabin door.

"Funny you should say that," I said. "That was the last year I remember being happy."

CHAPTER FORTY-SEVEN

"It was supposed to be a simple operation," Cassandra said, as we stared into the dying firelight, an empty bottle of Beaujolais on the wood-plank floor between us beside the full bottle I had just uncorked. "Eddy would handle the trade and the customers, while Wash Pelton handled the up-front money and the security. To make the whole thing work, Eddy had to latch onto some guards he could trust. Guards who had no problem taking a bribe."

It was going on three-thirty in the A.M. Neither of us had slept, except sporadically. And although Cassandra had finally started on the information I needed to know, I got the sense that she was choosing her words carefully, stopping midsentence to take little breaths or to release a sigh that I assumed contained as much guilt as it did sadness.

"Let me think," I said, as sarcastically as possible, "guards from Green Haven Prison who have no moral quandaries about taking a bribe. Must have taken Vasquez forever to find two men to fit those qualifications."

"Of course, he immediately found two men willing to sell out," Cassandra said, taking a swallow of wine.

"Money talks in the iron house," I said.

"Loud and clear," she said. "They came up with a system of outside visits, all of them under the pretense of visiting a dentist. Pelton had to get them on the outside, free, at least for a while. You see, Mister Marconi—"

"Keeper, please."

"Okay then, Keeper," Cassandra said, catching her breath. "When it comes to making some serious cash, those iron bars and concrete walls can be a real problem."

I nodded.

"There's this dentist," she said. "A. J. Royale."

"We've met," I said.

"A real ladylike kind of guy. He agreed to work with Eduard and Pelton for a price. He got paid a flat fee per visit and in turn did some kind of dentistry work on Eddy's teeth, just to make the whole thing look good. Afterward, he'd co-sign the release form in exchange for a pile of cash, I don't know how much. Since Eddy had to be on the outside at least six or seven times in order to make the plan effective, A. J. Royale agreed to do a root canal on a perfectly good tooth. A molar that eventually had to be pulled because the tooth went bad. For six months Eddy saw the dentist once every three weeks. You should know about that, Keeper. You signed the releases for his outside visits."

"I recall them," I said. "All six or seven."

"Don't you see?" Cassandra said. "You were the main man, Keeper. The whole operation would have been dead in the water without you."

"Glad to be of service," I said under my breath, but the humor was nowhere to be found.

"Pelton and Eddy figured that in three months they could clear six hundred grand, cash. They would split four hundred, fifty-fifty. The remainder would be divvied up between whoever helped out indirectly."

"Even a serial killer like Giles Garvin?"

"That's right," she said. "And it worked out all right, for a while anyway. Until Eddy and those guards, Logan and Mastriano, started taking stupid-ass chances."

"How stupid?" I said, pouring some of the wine into my coffee mug, taking a drink.

"After visiting the dentist, they'd change into civilian clothes right there inside the prison station wagon and they'd find a nice cozy bar and they'd set up shop for a while. Eddy would meet me in some hotel room we'd prearrange and we'd have sex for an hour. Or at least, he'd try, but it was all pretty useless. I just didn't want him anymore, not like that."

"You don't have to explain."

"Afterward, Logan and Mastriano would rendezvous at the hotel room and they'd change back into their corrections officer grays, Eddy into his yellow jumpsuit. They'd head back to the prison but not before I produced a list of buyers and the up-front money that came from Pelton."

"You did his dirty work."

"Pelton wouldn't meet with Eddy directly," she said. "Claimed it was too risky."

"Then who would supply you?"

"The lists came directly from Pelton's second-in-command, Jake Warren. He'd meet us at the prearranged spot, which was usually the hotel. He'd toss us the list and we'd toss him Pelton's cut of the money. Then, on their way back to Green Haven, Logan and Mastriano would pull into the Stormville airstrip where Marty Schillinger would be waiting for them. He'd oversee the retrieval of the drop and the payoff for the dealer. After that they'd bring the stuff in through the service entrance around back and begin dispersing the rest of the payoffs and the buys."

Jesus, I thought. The operation had been going on at the airstrip directly across the street from my house in Stormville, and I'd never known the difference. I thought about all the nights I'd sat outside slow-drinking whiskey and smoking cigarettes while the planes came in and took off again.

"Tell me more about Garvin," I said. "He seemed pretty agitated when I tried getting some information off of him on Tuesday."

Cassandra ran her hands through her soft brown hair and touched her heart-shaped tattoo with two fingers. "Giles Garvin," she said, "that horrible son of a bitch." She hesitated for a minute, as though choking on her own words. "I'm sorry," she said, "but it's hard for me to believe I was involved with a creep like that."

I drank some more wine while I waited for her to compose herself.

"Giles Garvin, Martin Schillinger, Tommy Welch," she said along with a deep breath, "all of them assisted Eddy in handling the inside trades to prisoners and guards. But mostly, his customers were visitors coming into the prison to see their quote, loved ones, end quote." Cassandra made quotation symbols with her fingers. Then she said, "Schillinger and Welch would get their payoffs directly from Pelton, but Garvin was supposed to get his payoff from Eddy since they were both on the inside. You have to understand, I never once met Garvin, but I knew who he was and what he had done to those poor kids."

"So why's he so bent out of shape?" I said.

Cassandra's face lit up. "Jeez, don't you get it, Keeper?"

"No," I said. "I don't."

"Listen, when Eddy took off on Monday, he left with Garvin's share for three months' work. Ninety thousand dollars. Cash Eddy had already shipped to Olancha, California, where I keep a trailer just outside Death Valley. He stuffed the cash into three plastic baby-dolls and packaged them inside a cardboard box. I shipped them out by way of the Athens post office."

I pictured the envelope I'd found in Vasquez's cell with the Olancha address and the Athens postmark. Then I pictured Marty Schillinger traipsing around Vasquez's cell in his Burberry trench coat like he had no idea in the world who the cop-killer was or how he could have escaped from Green Haven. I pictured Tommy Welch standing in the door frame of my Stormville home and I knew he would have been capable of tearing me in two if Pelton gave the order because sometimes loyalty and devotion to duty have nothing to do with right and wrong.

"I was all set for leaving the country once Eddy managed the escape. If he *could* manage the escape, which turned out to be a piece of cake."

"Let me guess," I said. "There never were any masked bandits to steal Vasquez away from Bob Logan or Bernie Mastriano."

"On Tuesday Eddy and I heard Logan's story on television. He was nearly in tears he laughed so hard. Especially the part about those two taking a terrible beating. Don't you see, Keeper? Once Bob Logan and

Bernie Mastriano discovered Eddy and me missing from the hotel rendezvous in Newburgh, they must have panicked and beat each other up just to make it look like they were attacked by a bunch of 'shotgun-carrying assailants.' "

"Okay," I said, tossing another log onto the fire. "So you were free. What next?"

"We had our cut of the money to live on, plus Garvin's. More than enough to start over in Mexico or South America. But then Eddy got greedy. Once he was out, he turned the tables on Pelton. Told him that if he didn't get more money, he'd expose the entire operation. He threatened to send an anonymous letter to *The New York Times*. He would accuse the entire department, including Pelton's main man, senatorial hopeful John 'Jake' Warren. The accusation itself, Eddy figured, would be enough to make Pelton jumpy. So instead of heading directly to the California desert, which had been the original plan, we holed up in Athens.

"But it all went bad because something happened that none of them had counted on. Pelton retaliated. He made you take the fall for Eddy's escape. He set you up, Keeper, as a scapegoat for the entire deal. He made you take the fall not only for Eddy's escape but for Logan and Mastriano's misfortune in the field. He managed to get to you just as Eddy was getting to him. And, after all, you'd signed those releases. It was something no one had counted on and it made Eddy's plan completely worthless so long as the cops bought into it. You'd been a tough man to get around during the first couple of years of your appointment, Keeper. You were shaking down cells, drug-testing inmates and guards. Eddy was even aware of the wiretaps you'd planted on a few of the guard and inmate informers. But then something happened to you, some kind of shock. Your wife died and you backed off. You kind of retreated into yourself. Maybe you didn't realize it at the time, but you must have been clinically depressed. One thing was for sure, things got easier for Eddy then. That's when he said yes to Pelton's plan—only a few weeks or so after your wife was killed."

Cassandra said nothing for some time. As for me, I thought about melting into the woodwork. Since that was impossible, I went to the window, pulled back the shade, and looked out onto the blackness of the early morning. I took a breath and glanced at my watch, again. Four in the morning. In just two hours' time, it would be daylight. "I found photographs of you and another man inside Vasquez's cell," I said, finally.

Cassandra swallowed a breath and chased it with some wine, as if the breath were that bitter. "Pelton began to demand a different kind of payoff," she said. "That is, once Eddy was safely behind bars after each of his field trips outside the prison gates. At first I kept the news from Eddy. But then I told him because I didn't know what to do anymore. I didn't know how to make Pelton stop. But do you know what Eddy told me? He told me he expected me to do exactly what Pelton wanted. When it came to Wash Pelton, he said, neither of us was bargaining from a position of power."

She took another deep swallow of the wine, and then she refilled my mug.

"But there was a way to get back at Pelton without him knowing," she said. "Eddy came up with the idea of making the still photos, since I couldn't exactly send a video to him inside the prison."

"VCRs are hard to come by inside the iron house," I said.

"Exactly," Cassandra said. "We could somehow use the stills against him. That is, if we could get them into the right hands, at the right time. In order to make it work, I had to steal a video while I was with Pelton. Then I'd have the stills made and I would ship them to Green Haven. Eddy would take care of things from there."

"Tell me," I said, feeling sudden warmth from the thousand-watt bulb that ignited inside my brain, "is Marty Schillinger on the video, too?"

Cassandra looked at the floor surrounded by the half-light from the dying fire. "Yes," she said, "that creep, Schillinger, too."

Why couldn't I have seen through the forest earlier? I pictured the three stills I'd found in Vasquez's cell. The unidentified man with the scar on his neck just above the breastbone. It was Pelton all along. The scar left over from the blade the rebel inmate had pressed up against his throat during the Attica riot. I thought I'd found the photos by accident. Now I knew they had been planted by Vasquez for some-one to find, for someone to use against Pelton. That someone had had to be me all along. He must have known I'd shake down his cell once he escaped. And then I went and handed them over to Marty Schillinger, who couldn't grab them out of my hands fast enough.

"You could have done better with the stills," I said, stepping away from the window, back toward the fireplace. "You can hardly make out Pelton. And you didn't get Schillinger at all."

"The video is that bad," she said. "It was the best I could do. I mean, it's not easy trying to convince a video mechanic that the skin flick you'd like to have transferred to stills is purely for your own enjoyment. And think of it this way. Pelton's been in the news a lot lately. Can you imagine the attention I would have gotten if I'd left it up to a total stranger to develop a clear photograph of Wash Pelton in bed with two other people—one of them another man, the other the girlfriend of a convicted cop-killer? Jesus, Keeper, I had to be a little smarter than that. I had to take another route."

I knelt down next to Cassandra.

"So now what?" she said.

"We're going to get that video back," I said. "And the money."

"It's in Olancha, like I told you. It's all inside the same big box."

"I have friends who can take care of getting it back," I said. "In the meantime, you have to stick with me. You and that video are my way out of this mess. I'll see to it that you get some sort of immunity by testifying against Pelton and the rest of them, even if they do try and charge you as an accessory in Eddy's escape once we're cleared of his murder. I'll see to it that you get the money you need and a one-way ticket to Mexico."

"No way in hell," Cassandra said, slapping the wine bottle down on the plank floor and knocking over one of the empties. "I'm not about to testify for anybody or anything." She started to lift herself up from the floor, but I reached out, grabbed hold of her arm, and pulled her back down.

"Christ," she said, "you're hurting me." She gripped her forearm where I had taken hold of it.

"You are going to testify because I'm going to make it all right for you," I said. "Don't you understand? We prove you were a victim of circumstances, the courts go easy on you."

Cassandra relaxed her grip and looked down at her lap. "I've done questionable things," she said, under her breath.

"You've also done nothing they can keep you in jail for," I said, "so long as you agree to cooperate."

She raised her head. "Well then, what if I don't want to go to Mexico, after all?"

"Even if you're off the hook, you'll always be looking over your shoulder. Pelton's a powerful man. Who knows what kind of connections he's got. That dead man outside in the overcoat is proof. The way I see it, you've got no choice. But before we do anything, I've got to get Mike Norman, Wash Pelton, and Marty Schillinger in one place at one time."

"When do you plan on pulling this off?"

"I'll start on it tomorrow morning after I meet up with a friend. With a little luck we could be out of this in a couple of days."

"And what happens to me if your plan doesn't work?"

"We could always stay here," I said.

"For how long?"

"Until the wine and the Dinty Moore run out."

As the night wore on I could not keep myself from remembering.

On a Monday morning a year before Fran was killed, I sat at the kitchen table of the Albany home I saw only on weekends. The sun poured in through the wide kitchen window beside the table, and gazing outside I could see the green grass and newly budding trees at the perimeter of the yard and a black-and-white cat I had never seen before walking aimlessly across the lawn. My morning newspaper was laid out flat beside my coffee cup. The headline read, "Warden Tightens Belt on Prison Security!" There was a photo of me sitting at my desk on the phone inside my office on the second floor of Green Haven Prison.

On this Monday morning, Fran sat across from me nibbling on a piece of toast coated with a thin layer of strawberry jam. "You're still making friends, I see." She wore only a terrycloth robe because she wasn't expected at school for another hour and a half.

"Don't kid yourself, Fran," I said, folding the paper in half and placing it back down on the table next to my third cup of coffee since five that morning. "The inmates would rather have it that way, believe it or not."

Fran had her long hair pulled back in a ponytail. When she smiled, small dimples formed in the lower corners of her prominent cheeks. She placed a small piece of toast in her mouth and squinted her eyes as if to say, How.

I leaned back in my chair and, looking outside, watched the black-and-white cat move stealthily over the lawn, nose to the grass, sniffing out the grubs. "It's all very simple when you think about," I said. "If I'm not in charge of the prison, then the gorillas are in charge."

"And what are the gorillas like, Keeper?"

"Nice fellas," I said, as the cat jerked a grub out of the lawn with its claws, "who like to rape and kill for fun."

Cassandra got up from the floor and went into the bedroom. She returned carrying two woolen blankets and a pillow. She spread out the first blanket on the floor in front of the fire and placed the pillow on the far end. Then she lay down on the makeshift bed and covered herself with the other blanket. She reached out for my hand. "I know it's corny," she said. "But will you stay here with me, at least until I fall asleep?"

I nodded and smiled. Rather, I attempted a smile.

But as Cassandra slowly drifted off to sleep, I felt myself sinking into a gorge of self-pity. I had been duped by the men I had worked with and trusted. By Wash Pelton and Marty Schillinger and Mike Norman, even though a part of me could not help but believe that Mike did what he did, not out of spite, but out of pure desperation.

When I was a boy, my father once told me that there are three points of realization that occur in a young man's life. The first is the knowledge that his parents will die one day. The second is that he, too, will die. The third—and this is the most important—is the knowledge that he must create a life worth living.

But I think there is a fourth point of realization that my father left out. What he didn't tell me is that a man is on his own in this life. No matter whom he trusts or whom he loves or whom he calls his friend and confidant, he is on his own. And the sooner he realizes it, the better.

I tuned my thoughts to the events of the past five days.

First, there was the bogus story of Logan and Mastriano's escape. Truth is they must have panicked when Vasquez took off while they waited for him at some bar in Newburgh. The entire story about three shotgun-packing assailants in a black van was nothing more than a fabrication—a fiction designed to fool me and, at the same time, arouse public sentiment. If what Cassandra told me was true (and as a warden who has spent his career trying to sift through inmates' lies in order to get at the truth, deep down inside I felt she was on the level), then I had no further reason to believe that the statement Robert Logan had issued in my office on Monday afternoon contained even a semblance of truth. If I had to come up with a motive for Logan's lie, it would have been this: Logan and Mastriano must have put the pressure on Wash Pelton because they weren't about to take the blame for Vasquez's sudden escape. They had been involved in the drug racket from the beginning. They knew too much. On the other hand, they were the most obvious patsies available to Pelton. Pelton, sensing the two guards meant business, must have paid off Dr. Fleischer to fabricate the serious blow to Mastriano's head. Now I was certain that Mastriano's coma had been faked and that Fleischer was pumping him daily with something to keep him out of it. In fact, I had the distinct feeling that Pelton was going around paying off everybody and his brother in order to keep his scam under wraps.

Then there were Cassandra's porn stills that were now in Schillinger's possession. Would he have used the illicit photographs against Pelton? First he would have had to get the original film and destroy it, along with any copies that might have been made. If Lt. Martin Schillinger was really on the video, like Cassandra said, then she and Vasquez had made a mistake by not making stills of him—no matter the quality of the film, no matter who might have found out about it later. It was a missed opportunity no matter how you looked at it. There was, however, one proverbial ace-in-the-hole. And it was this: If Schillinger and Pelton cared even the least little bit about their reputations, their careers, and their lives, they would want that video back—stills or no stills.

All I had to do was to get ahold of that film. The film would allow me at least a little power to bargain with. But before anything else, I had to trust in Cassandra, believe that she was telling me the truth. But then, how does a man go about trusting a woman who had been an integral part of a convicted cop-killer's pornography ring? How do you learn to trust a woman who saves your ass by axing a man in the head when all she had to do was knock him cold? How did I know I wasn't being duped all over again?

I had to go with instinct.

And now, watching her sleep on the floor of the cabin my grandfather'd built with his own two hands, bathed in the golden firelight that came from the fieldstone fireplace, I wanted to believe that she was telling the truth.

Now I pictured Mike Norman. I saw his thin red face in the flames of the fire. He must have known about Pelton's drug operation even if his knowledge was based on rumor, because he had used the evidence I'd picked up at the Lime Kiln gravel pit directly against me. My guess was that he'd seen an opportunity to make a quick buck and had taken it to Pelton without thinking about what could happen to me, not to mention himself. Pelton would pay Norman anything he asked if he believed it would present the perfect opportunity for me to be convicted in his place. Was it true that innocent men went to prison and stayed there for the rest of their lives? It was true, absolutely true. And I had never considered the reality of it as much as I did right then. Because an innocent man going to prison is what really was at stake. This wasn't about corruption and conspiracy in the prison system or about exposing the people who perpetrated it. What was at stake was my life. Of all people, a warden—indicted for crimes he did not commit. A warden sentenced to life would be sentenced to death. Once incarcerated in an iron house, I was a dead man; no two or three ways about it. That's what this was about. These were the stakes. Because in prison there was no such thing as a guardian angel.

I sat on the floor of the fifty-year-old cabin, but for some reason, I did not feel the floor beneath me. Beside me, Cassandra slept soundly. The tattoo on her neck rose and fell with the rhythm of her silent breathing. I had to trust her, whether I liked it or not. At least, I had to believe I could trust her. Together we were on the run. Like me, she had been accused of the murder of Eduard Vasquez. I had to believe she was innocent, because what would she have gained by killing him?

To be honest, she had a lot to gain.

She had three hundred thousand dollars cash to gain and a videotape she could use to blackmail Pelton for even more money. Still, I had to go with instinct, and my instinct told me she was innocent. After all, if she had killed Vasquez and managed to elude the police, why would she have come this far with me?

I believed this: that Cassandra Wolf had not shot Vasquez. The trigger man had to have been Wash Pelton or Marty Schillinger, or both. Or more likely, it had been Tommy Welch acting on Pelton's orders, or maybe even the overcoat man.

Cassandra slept soundly, breathing steadily, like a baby. She was no baby, though. She was a grown woman on the run. And I needed her more than anything else in the world. I would guard her with my life. Maybe protection was her reason for staying with me. But then, maybe protection had nothing to do with it at all.

CHAPTER FORTY-EIGHT

The next morning I parked the Pontiac in an observation area overlooking the Champlain valley to the south. Getting out of the car, I cut through the second-growth woods at a jog, keeping the road in view to my right until I sighted the glass-and-metal-paneled exit booth at the edge of Exit 28. From within a small patch of pines and birch trees located beside a garage used to house snowplows and dump trucks for the Champlain Valley Department of Transportation, I waited for Val's Town & Country station wagon to pull up.

At exactly one minute before nine A.M., the car rolled into the exit. I watched Val pay the toll, then drive slowly out onto the Champlain valley road. The closer she came the easier it was to see her lovely sandy-brown hair and her deep, almond-shaped eyes and the more I felt my lungs deflate, my heart swell. She drove slowly, twisting and turning her head, surveying the open road, until she finally decided to pull the wagon over to the shoulder, not ten feet away from the asphalt drive that led up to the metal doors of the DOT garage.

I walked out of the woods and made my way downhill to the car.

Other than the one uniformed man in the two-bay toll booth, I was certain no one had seen me. I opened the passenger-side door of the wagon, slipped inside, and smelled the good, sweet smell of Val. I wanted to take her in my arms and kiss her and hold her, swallow her. But I knew there was no time for that.

"Drive," was all I said.

I told Val to make a right-hand turn into the observation area.

"I have everything," she said.

"I knew you would," I said.

The observation area had been built along a natural clearing in the mountainside. The clearing looked out onto a view of the southern portion of the Champlain valley, where it abutted the northern portion of Lake George. The observation area itself was nothing more than a concrete sidewalk and a short, knee-high wall made from fieldstones topped with polished slate.

I got out of the car and unlocked the trunk to the Pontiac.

Val opened the hatch of the wagon.

Without a word, we made the exchange of clothes, food, and weapons. Val tried not to show that she was nervous. She kept a straight, tight face the whole time, never once smiling or, for that matter, submitting to a frown. Her face was flat and expressionless, her motions direct and to the point. When the exchange was over, the two of us got into the car.

She wore dark slacks, a white, button-down shirt, and a blazer. Her shirt was unbuttoned at the collar and a gold crucifix hung from a gold chain against the smooth bronze-colored skin of her chest. But now I could tell by the sudden downtrodden expression on her face that something wasn't right. Something besides the obvious. She wouldn't look at me directly. When I tried to catch her glance, she looked away and pinched the underside of her chin like she somehow forgot it was attached to her face.

"Val," I said, grabbing her elbow. "What's wrong?"

Looking down at the floor of the station wagon she started to cry. She reached behind the seat and picked up a copy of the morning's *Times Union.* She laid the newspaper in my lap, headline staring at me.

"APD Officer Found Hanged!"

I folded the newspaper in half and slammed it against the dash of the wagon. The impact was like a blast from a .45 and just as shocking. Val jumped and emptied her lungs of oxygen. I let the paper fall to the floor, sat back in the seat, and drew a deep a breath.

"I'm sorry," I said.

"I know," she said. "So am I."

I took her in my arms and held her, and she held me.

"Do you really believe Mike could have killed himself, Keeper?"

"What I think is that Pelton could have made it look like a suicide."

Now that we had calmed down, I was holding Val's hand and giving her the play-by-play behind the Vasquez-Pelton drug operation. I relayed exactly what Cassandra had told me just hours before, without altering a single detail of her story.

"It's true," I said. "Mike turned the evidence I found at the gravel pit over to Pelton. But he must have done it out of desperation, for the promise of money."

"In turn," Val said, "Pelton may have considered him a security risk. I mean, the last thing Pelton needed was for Mike to get drunk and shoot his mouth off."

"Wouldn't take much to make Mike look suicidal," I said. "I know how you felt about him, Val, but we both know he was a hopeless boozer, and we both know that the department had continually passed him by, right? Attica was a long time ago but the scars stay with you forever and there's no way in hell they were about to let him forget about his breakdown."

"But my God, Keeper," Val said, squeezing my hand hard, "that was so long ago."

"So long ago but not long enough. When you saw what we saw during those four days, twenty-five years may as well be twenty-five seconds." I stopped there, but I wanted to go on. I wanted to tell Val that you never forgot the smell of the dirt or the look of the rain when it fell in sheets into puddles filled with the blood from a man who's been castrated, or a man who's had his skull pounded in with an iron bar. It never leaves you, I wanted to tell her. There wasn't a single day at Green Haven that I didn't think about it. I never pretended for even a second that Attica couldn't happen again, because it would. And when it did, it was going to be worse, and more officers and inmates and civilians were going to die, but they wouldn't die easily. I wanted to tell her all this. But I let it go.

Val pulled her hand away and used the other to rub the feeling back into it. "I'm sorry," she said.

I took a deep breath. "I'm the one who's sorry," I said. "It's just that those feelings are so ingrained and I never talk to people about Attica, except to myself."

For a minute or two we said nothing. Then I said, "I just can't help but think that Pelton had Mike killed."

"To Wash Pelton," Val said, "Mike's failings must have seemed like an opportunity."

Below the article about Mike's suicide was a smaller headline.

"Warden and Cop-Killer's Girlfriend, Fugitives!"

Planted below the headline was the face of the pastor whose car I'd stolen. A small caption beneath it read, "I asked them to place their trust and forgiveness in the Lord." Below that, another headline advertised, "Day Number Five for Corrections Officer Mastriano!"

I folded the paper in half once more and this time slid it into the space between the arm rest and the bucket seat. "The three stills I found in Vasquez's cell on Monday afternoon," I said, "were lifted off a home video Pelton took of him and Cassandra having sex. She claims that Marty Schillinger, of all people, is in the same video."

"Let me get this straight, boss," Val said, her eyes nearly popping out of her skull. "Not only has Pelton been running a major drug ring inside our own prison, but he and Martin Schillinger have been making pornographic films with Vasquez's girlfriend?"

"By the looks of things, Vasquez and Pelton forced her into it. Vasquez didn't like it, but claimed he wasn't bargaining with Pelton from a position of power, which was probably an accurate assessment."

"Tell me something, Keeper," Val said. "Why should a man like Vasquez make such a difference in Cassandra Wolf's life? I mean, how did he hold so much power over her?"

"She was there the night that rookie cop took two slugs to the back of the head," I said. "She ran from the scene and called the cops. She turned her own boyfriend in, and for all these years he's held it over her head, made her feel like an accomplice and a traitor."

"And you believe her?" Val said. "You think a little guilt trip is enough to make a girl stay with a man who kills and runs drugs, even when he's in prison?"

I thought about Cassandra lying on the floor of my grandfather's cabin, her chest rising and sinking with steady, even breaths, and I pictured her eyes and the tattoo on her neck that appeared to pulse when she swallowed. It was true, I had no idea who she really was, what she had done, or what she was capable of doing. I could have told Val about the overcoat man and about what Cassandra did to him for me, for my life. But then I thought better of it. Knowing I was that vulnerable would not sit well with Val. It would only make her more concerned, more nervous. On the other hand, maybe Val's concern was something I just wanted to believe in.

"Listen," I said in as soft a voice as I could summon. "I believe Cassandra is telling the truth."

"But don't you think you're forgetting one thing, Keeper?" Val said, taking my hand once more. "Maybe it's not your heart that's speaking to you at all," she said. "Maybe it's your conscience. Maybe you feel you have no choice but to believe that Cassandra is telling the truth."

From the front seat of Val's station wagon we could see the mountains and the lush green valley to our right and the empty Champlain road to our left.

"Let me get this straight, Keeper," Val said. "Pelton was having sex with Vasquez's girlfriend and getting it all on tape."

"Like I already told you, Pelton was the sugar daddy for the drug operation, and now everyone is trying to blackmail him for more money, or so it appears."

"So then Pelton's been trying to pin this thing on you from the start, to try and save himself when news of the operation goes public."

"I'm going to beat Pelton out of the gate," I said. "But first you have to do me another favor." I lit a cigarette and blew the initial hit of smoke out the open window.

Val nodded.

"I want you to call Tony Angelino for me. Tell him I want to hire his Guinea Pigs."

"His what?"

"I'll explain another time," I said, taking another hit on the cigarette. "I want them to retrieve the videotape of Pelton and Cassandra, and the three hundred grand."

Val smiled. "Location," she said, pulling out a pen and a cocktail napkin that said *T.G.I. Friday's* on it out of her blazer pocket. She triggered the ballpoint and, at the same time, spread the cocktail napkin on her thigh for something to write on.

"It's at a post office in Olancha, California. It's a big cardboard box, like the kind televisions come in, and it's addressed to Cassandra. Inside the box are three baby dolls. You know, oversized plastic dolls for little girls who like to play mommy."

"I remember, boss," Val said.

"Inside one of those dolls is a videocassette. Inside all three dolls is the three hundred grand. All in big, unmarked bills. Tell him there's a hundred grand in it for him and his Guinea Pigs. All he has to do is get to it."

"Maybe Tony's got an L.A. contingent who can have it in hand by tonight," Val said.

"If I know Tony," I said, "that's the case exactly. Just have him send the entire package overnight express to me at the Ironville post office."

"What name do they use?"

"Use my grandfather's name," I said.

Val wrote fast. "Go ahead," she said.

"My grandfather's name was Pasquale," I said, taking a quick drag on my cigarette. "Pasquale Marconi."

"There's just one thing that bothers me," Val said.

"What is it?"

"Can you trust Tony?"

"As much as I can trust you," I said.

Val smiled. "What next?" she said.

"Then I want you and Tony to arrange a meeting."

"With?"

"Schillinger and Pelton," I said. "I want them both at the cabin tomorrow night at nine o'clock sharp. Tell them I'm aware of the truth now—the drug deal, the blackmails. Tell them I want to work it all out, that I know I made a mistake by running. Make it sound like they set me up real good and now I realize there's no getting out of it without doing things their way. Ask them for their complete assurance, complete protection, and secrecy. No cops. Make sure you tell Pelton that all I want is my job back and that I know I made a mistake not working with him in the first place. Tell him I looked tired, haggard, scared, defeated. Really pour it on."

Val looked out the window for a second or two. Then she looked at me and said, "What's Pelton got to gain by coming all the way up here, Keeper? You're already taking the rap. I mean, Pelton and Schillinger, they're on easy street."

"I'll have the magic videotape by then," I said. "They refuse to come up here, I'm going to deliver it directly to Chris Collins at Channel 13 news."

"What if they still don't go for it?" Val said. "Couldn't they just claim the film was made for private viewing?"

"Then I'll have no choice but to bring Cassandra in on my own terms, throw us both on the mercy of the court, if there ever was such a thing. That way, she'll have her chance to testify not only about what she witnessed inside the hotel room in Athens yesterday afternoon, but about the entire drug operation. A jury will either believe her or they won't. But one thing is for sure, a trial will make a big stink for everyone involved with Pelton, including Schillinger and Jake Warren, our illustrious senatorial hopeful."

"So a little road trip may be worth it to them," Val said.

"It's important that I meet them on my own terms, on my own playing field."

"I get it," Val said. "Your turn to join the blackmail squad."

"Time to clear my name of this thing, once and for all."

Val smiled for the first time since she'd arrived. It was a sly, corner-of-the-mouth kind of smile that made me want to melt into the bucket seat. "I'll need detailed directions to the cabin," she said.

"Tell Tony Angelino to be in his office tomorrow evening at five o'clock," I said. "That's when I'll call him with the directions. In turn, he can relay them to Pelton and Schillinger."

"You could just cut to the chase, give me the information right now." She balanced the ballpoint pen above the *T.G.I. Friday's* napkin as if to exaggerate her point.

"The less you know the better," I said. "A lot can happen between now and tomorrow night."

As if on cue, Val and I glanced at the headline reporting Mike Norman's apparent suicide.

"If they can get to Mike Norman," I said, "they can get to you and Tony. So take care of yourself. I need you." I flicked the spent cigarette out onto the parking lot. Sparks flew up when the butt hit the pavement.

Val returned the pen and paper to her pocket, took my hand and squeezed it. She moved in closer and I breathed in her sweet smell and looked into her eyes.

"You'll be happy I wanted it this way," I said.

"Especially if they torture me, boss," Val said, coming even closer, but not yet touching.

"You are one pleasant administrative assistant," I said, my lips only inches from hers, nearly touching, but somehow better than touching.

"Pleasant," she said, "is my middle name." And then I laid one on her.

CHAPTER FORTY-NINE

I got out of the car, closed the door behind me, and leaned inside the open window.

"You sure you're going to be okay?" Val asked. How she was able to maintain a happy face was a testament not only to her strength, but to her blind faith in me.

"I am now," I said. "But you and Tony's Guinea Pigs have to come through for me. Otherwise this thing is shot to hell, and I go straight to jail, do not pass go, do not clear my name, do not save my reputation or my life."

Val pressed her lips together. "I'll make the necessary arrangements right now," she said. "But I have to know you're going to be all right." She went to turn over the ignition, but I reached inside the car and took her arm.

"Val," I said, "do you know what they'd do to a former warden inside an iron house?"

She nodded and placed her hand on my hand.

"Don't worry about a thing, boss man," she said. "Not about me or Tony or those Guinea Pigs."

I squeezed Val's forearm arm gently. When I let go, she turned over the ignition and smiled again. But I knew the smile was forced. The big eight-cylinder on the Town & Country revved for a few quick seconds, then settled down to a gentle purr. Val put her hands on the steering wheel. She looked small sitting behind the big black wheel, almost fragile. But deep down, I knew she wasn't anything like that.

"One hundred thousand bucks," she said. "Sounds very reasonable."

"Tony has to come through," I said, leaning away from the window. "Tomorrow morning. Ironville post office. Attention Pasquale Marconi." I thought about Cassandra's testimony. I had to believe she'd told me the truth. I had to believe in the power of instinct.

"It'll be there," Val said, switching the automatic transmission into reverse.

I stood away from the car so she could back out. Then she pulled out onto the Champlain road and left me in the observation area, more alone than I'd ever felt in my life.

It was all I could do to wait until Val's car was out of sight before I doubled over, went down on my knees, and heaved. The acid from the bile in my stomach burned the insides of my chest, my throat. The bile soured my mouth, made tears run down my face. That was my excuse for the tears, anyway. The salty tears ran between my lips and combined with the sour taste in my mouth.

I left a clear brown puddle on the black lot.

My body felt like it had been ripped inside out.

I closed my eyes, winced from the burning pain. I saw Mike Norman's face. Tommy Welch sat in Mike's dark office in Albany. I saw Mike downing shot after shot of ginger brandy out of his I LOVE MY JOB! mug. Tommy Welch was holding a .9 mm. porcelain Glock to Mike's head, ordering him to drink up.

Then, when the time was right, Tommy would unbuckle Mike's belt, slide it out from under the loops, wrap it around Mike's neck and run it back through the buckle. He would strap the belt to one of the overhead steam pipes that rose up the wall and ran across the ceiling.

Tommy would lift Mike up with an arm and a shoulder. Mike's emaciated body would be like lifting a baby for a muscle-man like Tommy. He would stand Mike up on the chair and just walk away.

Out of desperation, Mike would manage to balance himself for a second or two on the swivel chair. He would be sober suddenly, and he would try to shout, but no words would come. He would try to go for the .9 mm. usually kept in his leather shoulder holster. But in his position, a move like that would mean certain death. And besides, his piece would have been long gone. With his fingers he would try to make a space between the belt and the flesh of his neck, but the belt would be too tight and he'd be too drunk, though somehow sober at the same time. He'd leave claw marks where the belt was. And as the windpipe in his throat closed up, he would reach out for Tommy as if his killer could also be his savior. But Tommy would already be gone, out into the night, and Mike would realize that he was already as good as dead and that the life he had left was merely a formality. That's when Mike would lose his balance on the swivel chair. That's when he'd fall away, and there'd be no one in the office to hear the distinct, sharp crack of his neck.

Listen: Mike's death may have been suicide.

It may also have been murder.

To me, it didn't matter what anyone called it. It was murder no matter how you looked at it.

CHAPTER FIFTY

In a state of mild shock, I drove back to the cabin. I'm not sure where my feelings had gone, but one thing was certain: I wasn't feeling much of anything anymore. Suddenly, after having collapsed in the observation parking lot, it seemed like someone had peeled off my skin and scraped away the nerve endings. At the same time, I had to believe that I was over the hump and that Val, Tony Angelino, and Cassandra were working with me now as one big happy family. Even the Guinea Pigs were on my side. In any event, I had to stay in control, clear my head, stay positive.

I got back to the cabin at around ten o'clock that Friday morning, just four days after Vasquez had escaped from Green Haven Prison, just one day after his murder. I turned the car around in the drive and backed it into the carport, beside the woodpile. I got out and opened the trunk. Then I took the cabin key out from behind the old black mailbox and unlocked the side door. But when I went inside to find Cassandra, she wasn't there.

I looked in the kitchen, the two bedrooms, and the closet-size bathroom. I pulled back the shower curtain, looked inside the empty shower. I looked behind all the doors, inside the closets, under the bed.

No sign of her anywhere.

The sensation of being trapped somewhere between feeling and not feeling suddenly disappeared as fast as it had hit me. Now I couldn't help but give in to the wave of dread that swept through my veins like a three-stage lethal injection.

Here's how lethal injection worked:

First, you were strapped down on a black gurney, arms extended like in a crucifixion. Then an execution technician (who cannot be a doctor or a registered nurse because their code of ethics forbids it) swabbed your forearm with alcohol to prevent infection, of all things, then probed your arm for a vein. When the vein was found he inserted a needle into it. The needle was connected to an intravenous line that channeled sodium Pentothal into your veins to knock you out. After that, panchromium bromide and potassium chloride were introduced. The first paralyzed your diaphragm, collapsed your lungs, and made it impossible to take a breath. The second stopped your heart from pumping. How long your brain continued to receive and transmit messages and brain waves was undetermined.

During the first death by lethal injection that I witnessed, it took nearly a half hour to kill the man. The tube that had been attached to his arm broke away. The witnesses were sprayed with the deadly chemicals and the condemned inmate began to convulse and foam at the mouth and nostrils. His eyes were wide open the entire time.

During "my" second death by lethal injection, the execution technician gave the inmate too weak a dose of the chemicals, causing him to choke and heave blood for nearly fifteen minutes before he died with a blue face.

The third and last time I witnessed an execution, the conditions were considered perfect all around though the "patient" heaved and spit and choked and even broke a rib from the strain.

I'd witnessed three lethal injections during my time in the department, all of them in states where execution was still legal. If I ever found the man who'd killed Fran, I'd see a fourth. That is, if I ever got myself out of this mess. But first I had to find Cassandra. Without her and her testimony, I faced jail. What I faced in jail was more horrible and just as deadly as lethal injection.

I took a deep breath and lit a cigarette. I sucked in the smoke and felt the rush of nicotine and the slight rise in blood pressure that always accompanied it. I knew I had no choice but to try and relax, to try and think logically. It was a beautiful spring day with unusually warm temperatures. Maybe Cassandra had spring fever, literally. Maybe fourteen hours spent in a five-room cabin had become too confining for her.

I had to do something to prevent myself from thinking, because I didn't want to suffer the anxiety that went with thinking. So I busied myself with transporting the supplies from the trunk of the Pontiac to the cabin. I made every attempt to be as organized as possible, making slow deliberate movements under the assumption that this would make the time pass faster. Maybe, I thought, she would come back while I was working.

I placed the extra clothing on the bed in the back bedroom and stacked the few canned goods on the exposed shelves in the kitchen. I put the milk and the beer in the refrigerator, and the three loaves of white bread on the table my grandfather had built into the kitchen wall. I checked the chambers and the chokes on the two Remington 1187 twelve-gauges to make certain they weren't loaded, and then I leaned them against the waist-high bookshelves beside the fireplace.

When there was nothing left to do, I started thinking again, and this gave new life to the old anxieties.

In the seventeen or so minutes it had taken to transfer the supplies from the car to the cabin and to arrange it systematically, Cassandra had not come back. I knew then, as I slammed the trunk of the Pontiac closed, that if she was not coming back to me, I'd have to go looking for her.

And that's exactly what I set my mind to doing.

CHAPTER FIFTY-ONE

I searched the perimeter of the cabin looking for footprints. But the earth around the cabin, although muddy in spots, was fairly dry from the strange bout of spring heat that had affected the entire northeast, even as far up as the Adirondack mountains (although the nights were still cool, if not downright cold).

I swatted a black fly from the sweat-covered skin on the back of my neck and I walked the length of the driveway, downhill, until I came to the hard-packed east-west road. I looked across the road and across the trout stream, and I surveyed the empty field beyond it.

Again, not a thing.

I turned west and then faced east.

Nothing but open road and the constant hum of black flies.

Suddenly, I felt like the lost one.

Standing there in the middle of the open road, I turned and faced my grandfather's cabin. Directly behind it, I could see Old Iron Top, its bald, granite summit sparkling in the late-morning sunshine.

And then it hit me. That's where I would find her.

•   •   •

I walked back up the drive and went to the edge of the second-growth forest surrounding the base of Old Iron Top. The trail my grandfather had cut decades ago was still accessible about thirty yards southwest of the cabin. The summer renters must have used the trail often because the narrow footpath was still freshly cut. Footprints were plainly visible in the mud. Cassandra wore cowboy boots similar to my own. But the heels on her boots were shorter and flatter. The prints at the beginning of the trail could not have been made more than an hour earlier. I could even see how the groundwater that had been squeezed away from the dirt had puddled in the heel area of the print.

Here's what I did before I entered the woods:

I pulled out the .45, pointed the barrel up toward the tops of the trees, and chambered a round, safety on. I slipped the piece back through my belt, this time against my backbone, and walked into the woods.

Maybe the forest had lived without me for more than three decades, but there was something about it—about the birch trees and the scattered sections of pine and the grouse that nearly made my heart stop when it drummed and took off from the soft, pine-needled floor—that made it seem like time had stood still. But the forest was not the same, and I knew it had changed as I had changed. But then there was the rich smell of vegetation, there was the way the sunlight broke through the leaves and branches of the trees, and the way the mosquitoes buzzed around my face that made it all seem the same. These were sights and sounds and feelings you just did not get inside a maximum security prison. A few feet in, I felt the tingle of a spider web that broke off against my face when I unknowingly walked through it. My blue-jean work shirt turned damp at the arms from the dew that clung to the vegetation even at midmorning on this hot spring day, and the world seemed suddenly foreign to me. Foreign but the same.

The dimensions of the trail were as I remembered them, too.

The trail dipped at first, descending for about twenty-five yards until it reached the base of the hill where the trail went severely vertical again. I wasted no time starting the climb, wishing, after five or six raised steps, that I was wearing hiking boots instead of cowboy boots. In a word, these boots weren't made for hiking. But then, what choice did

I have? I moved uphill, the branches scratching and snapping at my face, stinging the sensitive facial skin beneath the three-day beard growth. A small twig poked me in the eye, filled me with enough pain to draw a tear.

But I didn't stop for anything, not even to take the breath that I desperately needed.

One thing was certain: I was drowning in my own inhalations. Too many cigarettes for too many years. As the arteries pressing against my temples began to pound with blood, I promised myself that if I got out of this mess, I would quit smoking for good. I would get my life back together, start living the good life again—like a man who cares about the life he's got left.

But in the woods, I began to drown in something else, too. I couldn't shake the image of Cassandra being left for dead on the summit of Old Iron Top. This time it I was seeing the future, and the future in my mind was crazy, morbid even. What if Pelton's men had followed us out to the cabin, gotten to Cassandra this morning when I was with Val? What if Pelton's men had dragged her into the woods and shot her or sliced her neck with a straight razor? In my mind, I pictured a razor moving across the smooth bronze flesh of Cassandra's neck the same way I had witnessed a CO die at Attica. As I forced myself up the hillside, I knew that with Cassandra dead I was as good as finished— porn film or no porn film to use against Pelton. I needed Cassandra alive to testify on behalf of what she'd witnessed, not only during the last five days, but during all the years of her relationship with Vasquez.

Maybe it was the lung-scraping breaths or the way the blood pulsed and boiled inside my skull, but I couldn't prevent an image of Cassandra's head cut completely away from her body, just the way Fran's had been when the black, four-door Buick sedan ignored the do-not-enter and slammed into the side of the car at sixty-five-per in a thirty-mile-per-hour zone. It had taken only a split second for Fran to be thrust forward, her head and shoulders through the windshield, the jagged edge of which, like a razor, took her head clean off at the base of the neck, her body slumping back into the passenger seat like nothing had ever happened. Like our lives had not been changed by the split second of time it took for a windshield to shatter. And then nothing but the sight and sound of the battered Buick tearing away from the scene of the accident, only the back of a man's shaved head visible . . .

How do I describe the shock, the timelessness of the moment, the rapid beating of my heart, the buzz in my brain that sucked the air out of my lungs, filled them with the poison of instant grief? The sickness rose up from my stomach and spread through my body and my veins, like rigor mortis.

All I could do was close my eyes, try to convince myself that the accident had been a figment of my imagination, like a nightmare. But they had revived me in the hospital bed I'd been strapped to some thirty-six hours before, and they had made a point of telling me the entire story of the accident, detail for detail, as if I had not been a part of it or the cause of it, or as if I had not been stained with my wife's blood or as if I had not been there to smell the smoke or feel the fire. As if I had not seen the flashing red-and-white lights of the cop cruisers and useless ambulances. As if I had not seen the tears shed, not for Fran, but for me. And when I asked them why they had to tell me all this so soon and in such detail, they said, "So you'll believe it."

They called themselves doctors, priests, and friends, and they surrounded my bed and told me the story of my wife's death as if the reality of it was good for me. You must tackle the grief head-on, they'd said. The Lord dishes out only what you can handle, they'd said. The death of my wife was like a commendation from the Lord because He knew I could take it. Your wife, they said, she's an angel now.

Go fuck yourself, I said.

I felt the anger boil inside my gut, and I would have killed them all if I'd had the chance. I would have ripped their heads off. But all I could do was lie in the hospital bed and feel my face distort and my muscles wrench because they had me strapped to that mattress and they had the God-fucking awful nerve to tell me the truth about my dead, decapitated wife and the bald-headed man who'd gotten away with it.

And somehow, one year later, I was climbing a hill I had not climbed in thirty-five years. And as my lungs began to collapse from the strain, it did not seem possible that it had taken only thirty minutes to make the entire climb, because it seemed to have taken much longer when I was a kid. And when I reached the peak of Old Iron Top, I could plainly see Cassandra through openings in the heavy vegetation surrounding the rocky clearing. She stood on the rock face, dressed in blue jeans and a white button-down shirt that was now unbuttoned. Under the shirt was an elastic band, like an Ace bandage, only wider. The flesh-colored elastic was wrapped flat around her entire stomach as if to hold it in, like a makeshift girdle. And as she began to button her shirt up over it, I could only assume that Cassandra was pregnant and didn't want anyone to know about it, least of all me.

I quickly moved to the left of the trail and ducked down in the tall grass while Cassandra buttoned her shirt. She ran both hands through her long brown hair so that I could see the tattoo on her neck, and then, from where I crouched in the tall grass, I saw her pull that .32 caliber pistol out of the pocket of her jeans. I saw her walk to the opposite side of the clearing and toss the pistol into a patch of thick briars. She made a quick check of the surrounding area and only when she was certain no one had seen her did she begin to make her way back across the rocky summit toward the trail. I was forced to lie down flat in the grass and remain as still and quiet as humanly possible. More than humanly possible. Because, after all, she was about to pass right by me, and I did not want her to know that I had seen everything and that I now knew for certain that she was not the woman I had thought she was.

CHAPTER FIFTY-TWO

I waited there in the tall grass for more than three minutes after she'd passed. During that time I held my breath and listened to the steady, rapid pulse pounding against my temples. I could only hope that she would not make out my tracks in the soft earth. I hoped her concern about getting rid of that .32 and concealing her pregnancy was so great that she wouldn't worry about footprints.

When all was clear, I moved out of the grass and sprinted across the granite clearing. Stepping down into the thick vegetation, I fought my way through the briars and pine scrubs. I squatted and felt with my hand around the area where I thought the pistol might lie. It took about five minutes of tearing and scraping the skin on my left forearm, but eventually I found the piece resting on a nest of thick tree roots.

I stood up and began picking the briars away from my shirt and pants. Maybe it was the cold, almost slimy feel of the tree roots, but for some reason I began to picture a nest of snakes and I moved back onto the clearing as quickly as I could. I cracked the cylinder of the snub-nosed revolver and brought the six-round chamber up close to my face.

I smelled each chamber separately. The pistol had been fired in the past three days. I was certain of it. The smell of the exploded gun powder was that fresh, that pungent. The question was this: Had Cassandra fired the pistol? If not, then why would she go to all the trouble of hiding the piece on Old Iron Top?

Standing on the open rock face, I knew that the answer most likely lay in the events that had gone down in Athens the day before. Maybe the answer lay with Vasquez. But then, Vasquez wasn't about to talk.

CHAPTER FIFTY-THREE

On the concrete floor of the Times Square catwalk, three buck steers pin Wash Pelton down on all fours. They pull his pants down and stick it to him from behind. They make no attempt to squelch his screams because the louder he screams the more they like it, the more it turns them on.

Oh God, I say, as his screams burn a hole through my skull. Get me out of here.

To my left, the blunt barrel of a black-plated .38 service revolver is stuffed inside Wash Pelton's mouth, while a shiv made from a razor blade planted inside a plastic toothbrush handle is pressed up against his throat. The rebel inmate holds Pelton's head back, mouth open. He manages this by grabbing onto a fistful of hair, pulling the hair back like the reins on a horse. Wash Pelton gags on the pistol barrel. I see his eyes rolling in their sockets while the rebels take turns on him. His Adam's apple does a bobbing dance. Blood runs from the gash in his neck. Sweat oozes through the pores of his forehead, runs down his face, off his nose, mixes with the blood on his neck.

I try and turn away, but the inmate who has hold of me won't allow it.

Pressed against the back of my head is a spoon that's been lifted from the mess hall. The spoon has been scraped along the concrete floor of a prison cell until razor-sharp. Directly to my right, the barrel of a police-issue M-16 is aimed, point-blank, at Mike Norman's head. But Norman can't stand up. Norman lies on his stomach on the wet concrete floor of Times Square. A black-and-white helicopter hovers overhead. Below, a crowd of twelve hundred inmates faces us, the hostages on parade. They wave their fists in the air, not in solidarity, but in defiance, a show of force. Why give a sign of peace when you can wave a fist?

I lower my head, stare at my bare feet flat against the gray concrete. I feel the edge of that sharpened spoon suddenly pressed harder against the back of my head, ready to spear the skin and bone.

"On three," the inmate behind me says. "We execute on three."

CHAPTER FIFTY-FOUR

I managed to make the hike down from Old Iron Top without falling, despite the smooth-soled cowboy boots. I jogged the entire way, feeling the muscles in the backs of my legs tense up as I grabbed onto the thick branches and tree trunks lining the narrow footpath. The day was growing noticeably hotter, even in the shaded woods, and by the time I reached the bottom, I was drenched in sweat and out of breath.

When I came to the edge of the woods, just a dozen or so yards from the cabin, I waited until I was certain that Cassandra was inside and had no plans for coming back out. I crouched and moved quickly to the Pontiac. I found the car keys in my pocket, opened the trunk, and peeled back a portion of the black carpeting. I slipped the .32 out of my pants and put it in the trunk, then I pressed the carpeting back in place and closed the trunk as quietly as I could. I turned, took a breath, and walked into the cabin like nothing had happened at all on the summit of Old Iron Top.

• • •

Cassandra was already asleep on the floor in front of the fireplace, on the same wool blanket she had slept on the night before. I knelt down, shook her shoulder. She stirred and looked up at me with glazed eyes. She gave me a dreamy smile, and for just a quick second, I had the distinct sensation that she was going to kiss me on the mouth.

"What took you so long?" she said, yawning and curling back into the blanket, hands pressed together as though praying, only using them for a pillow under her head.

I sat down on the floor and did my best to suppress the urgency building up inside my sternum. It was a sensation that screamed, *Tell me everything you know; hold nothing back!* But I knew I had to take it slowly, carefully, not give Cassandra any reason to back away.

I felt the gentle heat from a fire now reduced to glowing embers. "You never told me," I said, "who pulled the trigger on Vasquez."

She leaned up on her right elbow, tilted her head slightly so that it nearly rested on her shoulder. Her smooth, long hair gravitated toward the floor. Other than her breathing and the steady hiss of the fading embers, there were no other sounds inside the cabin.

"Who pulled the trigger, Cassandra?" I pictured the black-plated .32 she'd tossed into the briars and pine scrubs. I could smell the freshly fired gunpowder. I pictured the way she'd wrapped the Ace bandage around her waist so as to conceal what was growing inside her.

She sat up straight but stared at the floor. Until I grabbed her shoulders. "I want to know," I said in a forced whisper. "No matter how much it hurts." I was so close to telling her what I'd seen only minutes ago on the granite clearing of Old Iron Top that I could almost taste it. But that would have been the wrong thing to do. That would have put her on the defensive and that's not what I wanted at all. I wasn't after the truth about who'd pulled the trigger on Vasquez, so much as I was after the truth about Cassandra. I had to be sure I could trust her. Because if she could lie about the murder and if she could conceal her pregnancy, then she could easily lie about the victim-of-circumstances role she'd played in Pelton's drug operation.

"Keeper," she said, "stop it."

I let go of her shoulders. She took a deep breath and then another. "Like I told you," she said, in a long, drawn-out voice. "Yesterday afternoon, Martin Schillinger and Pelton came to see us in our room at the Stevens House."

"Pelton and Schillinger together," I said. "You're sure about that?"

"I worked with them for a long time," she said. "I made that God-awful movie with them. I know what they look and sound like."

I nodded.

"They pounded their fists against the door, threatened to knock it in if we didn't open it right away. Eddy took the .32 from the desk drawer and stuffed it in my hand, he pushed me into the bathroom and locked the door behind me. And all the time I'm hearing the sound of fists and feet kicking down the door. And just like that, they were in."

"You couldn't see them," I said. "But you could hear them."

"I heard them fighting, struggling. Then I heard the shots."

"How many shots,?"

"Two," she said, with a shaky voice that verged on tears.

I stood up and, using the pointy tip of my cowboy boot, stamped out a lit ember that had popped out of the open fireplace.

"Two shots," Cassandra repeated. "Back-to-back."

I wondered how many chambers had been fired from the .32. Two, maybe three. I couldn't be sure. There was no sure way to tell.

"Did you hear what Pelton and Schillinger said before they shot Vasquez?"

"Pelton called Eddy a 'back-stabbing bastard.' He called him some other things, too, but that's what I remember most. They fought and some glass broke and then they must have had Eddy down on his stomach because Pelton said, 'Let me see the son of bitch's face.' And the room went silent for a minute and I wanted to unlock the door and run out of the bathroom and blow them all to hell."

"But the .32 had no bullets."

"I didn't know that then," she said. "I thought I'd lose it right there. Christ, I was afraid. You know, *fear*—a normal reaction to danger."

"I know what it is," I said.

"I called out for Eddy, but he wouldn't answer. Then came the first shot and I thought I would fall dead on the floor like the bullet had hit me. I heard Schillinger. He said, 'Shoot the motherfucker again and then shoot the bitch in the closet.' And then they shot Eddy a second time. But before they started after me I was already out the window, down the fire escape, and making a run for the river."

"So Pelton was the trigger man?"

"I don't know," she said. "I couldn't see, remember?"

"But whoever did it, used two caps," I said. "You're sure about that."

This time, Cassandra wouldn't answer. My questioning was getting to her. I could see it in the wear and tear on her face. Maybe she was telling the truth, maybe she wasn't. There was no way to be certain one way or the other. All I knew was that I had seen her, up-close-and-personal, tossing that .32 into a patch of heavy vegetation on Old Iron Top where no one would ever find it. But then, maybe she had other reasons for tossing it away and maybe those reasons had nothing to do with the shooting death of Vasquez. In the end, what it came down to was whether or not I could trust Cassandra. I had been racking my brain over it for almost twenty-four hours. I had to choose, one way or the other. If I chose not to trust her then I had to make her a prisoner, lock her up in one of the rooms and tie her to the bed until I was ready to haul her in to the authorities on my own terms. On the other hand, if I chose to trust her, I had to make her an asset, an ally to the cause, which was nothing other than getting out of this mess as fast and as cleanly as possible. I had to choose; there were no two ways about it. The sooner I made the decision and the commitment, the better off I'd be. What little time I had—before the police or Pelton's goons, or both, had me trapped—was precious.

Choose, Keeper, whispered the voice inside my head. Choose now.

I looked at Cassandra on the floor, her head hung in sadness.

I chose to trust her.

With that clearly in mind, I decided to pursue another avenue. Instead of focusing on the killer, I decided to focus on the weapon. "Cassandra," I said, "were you able to see the pistol they used?"

She was crying now. Long, drawn-out tears. "I told you before," she said. "The bathroom door was closed."

That's when it hit me.

I pulled out the .45 and discharged the clip. I began to empty the rounds, one by one, into the palm of my hand. There should have been eight rounds in the magazine. But only six were ejected from the clip.

It hit me a second time.

When Pelton's men raided and ransacked my Stormville home on Wednesday, as I was detained in the Albany County lockup, they must have found the .45 under the mattress and taken the two shells they would eventually need to kill Vasquez and pin the whole thing on me. Of course, I couldn't be sure. But the alternative was to believe that Cassandra had killed Vasquez and was now lying about it along with everything else. But I had no way of knowing just what caliber round Vasquez had been shot with, and it was possible that my .45 had only had six rounds in the clip to begin with. So in the end, I had no real way of discerning the truth.

Using my thumb, I pressed the shells back into the clip. Cassandra wiped the tears from her face and took some deep breaths, composure regained. I couldn't get the image of that Ace bandage wrapped around her torso out of my mind. I wondered how many weeks or months along she was. She couldn't have been that far into the pregnancy, because she was only just showing.

"What do you plan on doing now, Keeper?" she said. "We can't stay up here forever and I can't take any more of your goddamned third degree. I saved your life, for Christ's sakes. Remember that."

With the .45 in hand, I stood by the heavy wooden door that led to the carport, beside the corner where my grandfather stored his fly rods. I turned and looked at Cassandra. "What do you mean?"

"What I mean is, after all that, you're not thinking of leaving me, are you, Keeper?"

I slammed the clip back into the .45 and returned the weapon to my belt. "I need you," I said. "And I think you need me. But there's something we have to do first, and like I told you before, it involves getting Wash Pelton and Marty Schillinger in one place at one time. And that place has got to be here, in this cabin, because this is my turf and this is where I'll have the most control."

I went into the kitchen and took a beer out of the refrigerator. I cracked the tab with my thumb and took a deep drink. Cassandra followed me. She suddenly seemed far from tears, curiosity and concern having replaced fear and loathing.

"What about all the others?" she said. "What about the guy who turned you in? What about Mike Norman?"

I drank the rest of the beer in one long swallow and fired up a cigarette. "Norman's dead," I said. "They found him late last night, hanging from a steam pipe in his office in Albany."

Cassandra went pale. She reached out to the kitchen table for balance.

"It could have been suicide," I said. "Or it could have been murder. But the result was the same." I took another beer from the fridge and opened it. As opposed to the last one, this beer would get sipped.

"They got to him, didn't they?" Cassandra said. "The bastards got to him, too, just like they got to Eddy and almost got to us." She stood up straight and breathed and took the beer out of my hand and drank deeply. "How can I help you?" she said, handing the beer back to me. "Just tell me what to do and I'll do it. Please, just tell me."

My father used to tell me that when things got bad, all you had to do was sit down, regroup, think things out, and make a plan. Just the act of making the plan, he said, seemed to make you feel better, like you were in control again. And that's what I was about to do. And I think the strategy was about to pay off because Cassandra seemed to perk up just a little bit.

"Cassandra," I said, "how good are you at working a video camera?"

CHAPTER FIFTY-FIVE

There was a removable panel in the wood floor of the great room between the fireplace and the door. While most of the cabin had been built on a concrete slab, my grandfather had dug out a small cellar to use as storage for onions and potatoes. Occasionally he used it for smoking trout or perch or venison strips. Just a room in the ground, maybe six feet deep by eight feet wide, accessible only by a removable panel and a stepladder. A great hiding spot for me when I was a kid.

I turned on all the lamps in the great room, and I got on my knees and began feeling around for the edges of the removable panel. The edges had been smoothed out in the many years since the cellar had been used and had I not known it was there, I would never have known the difference. Dirt had filled the tiny groove between the square panel and the planks that surrounded it so that the surface of the cabin floor appeared perfectly homogeneous. But once I began my search, I found the edges right away.

I went into the kitchen and took two steak knives out of the drawer. I got back on my knees and stuck each blade into opposite ends of the panel while Cassandra stood over me. I braced myself and lifted the panel off the floor.

As I'd expected, the hole was dark, and a cool, moist air rose from it. I asked Cassandra to look under the sink for a flashlight. She found one and brought it to me. I hit the switch and shined the bright light into the hole. The place was covered with spider webs and, aside from the insects, seemed absolutely dead. Until I heard the distinct sound of something scurrying back and forth on the dry plank floor at the bottom of the hole. I must have disturbed some animal. From where I lay on the floor, I could see the shriveled remnants of petrified potatoes and onions left behind by my grandfather on the wooden shelves lining the walls of the cellar. Still, I wasn't able to make out the far side of the crawl space—the portion covered by the cabin floor.

"I'm going in," I said.

"Better you than me," Cassandra said.

With flashlight in hand, I eased myself down onto the stepladder, pressing my weight onto the top rung to make sure it was sturdy enough to support me. Shining the flashlight on the floor, I stepped into the hole. The change in air temperature was immediate. The hole was warm but clammy, and the air smelled like worms. I swiped away at the spider webs and ducked under the floor structure and it was then that I discovered the source of the animal sounds. In the far corner of the otherwise empty space, a family of snakes had taken up residence. Garden snakes, the biggest I'd ever seen. The snakes were piled up into one corner like a stack of black-and-yellow garden hoses. Maybe four of them. I wasn't the type to be spooked by the occasional spider or rat or multilegged insect. But snakes were a different story. Just the sight of a snake, even on television, had a way of making me catatonic if only for a few seconds until I was able to pull myself together. So here's what I did: I pulled out the .45, emptied the entire six rounds into the bastards, watched their black-and-yellow flesh bounce and tremble from the blasts.

The entire cellar lit up like the Fourth of July.

"Jesus, Keeper," Cassandra screamed. "What the hell's happening?"

I climbed up the ladder, the three dead snakes in hand.

"Oh my God," Cassandra said, backing away fast. "Oh dear sweet Jesus."

"Don't worry," I said. "They're dead and the hole is now clean."

"So why should I be worried?" she said, as I went for the door of the cabin, opening it and tossing the dead snakes out beyond the woodpile. "What's that hole got to do with me?"

"That cellar," I said, closing the door behind me, "is going to be your post tomorrow night during the party."

"Party," she said. "What party?"

"The TV party we're going to have with Wash Pelton and Marty Schillinger."

CHAPTER FIFTY-SIX

It took some doing to convince Cassandra that the cellar would be clean and that no snakes could possibly get into it again. And she agreed that snake phobias—like all phobias—made little sense, considering that garden snakes, at least, were harmless. I told her that for a student of the prestigious Sally Struthers school of correspondence, she had certainly covered a lot of territory. Knowing the truth about fear, she said, didn't make it any easier for her. "Me neither," I said, although my sympathy did little to calm her nerves.

We took the car into town and rented a VCR. Then we drove thirty miles to the closest Radio Shack in the little ski town of North Creek. As luck or providence would have it, I was able to charge a video camera along with a thin, flexible scope that could take pictures from any place and any position at any time of day. The snakelike lens cost about ten times what the camera cost, but would be worth its weight in diamonds if my plan succeeded.

By the time we got back to the cabin it was late afternoon. I set the camera up on its tripod in the potato cellar and I attached the video probe. It took a bit more convincing, but eventually Cassandra climbed down with me.

"All we have to do," I said, forcing the black, superthin camera lens through a knothole in the floorboard beside the access panel, "is snake this baby through here."

"Bad choice of words," Cassandra said, examining the controls on the video camera.

In the meantime, I climbed out of the cellar and stood near the door to the cabin. "Can you see me?"

"Right on," Cassandra said. "You look about three feet taller and twenty pounds lighter." I suggested that the vision must be a real improvement. Cassandra laughed and disagreed saying she preferred solid, muscular men to skinny wimps.

Next I repositioned the TV so that the screen faced the cellar and the camera lens. "How about the TV screen?" I said.

"I'm getting the whole thing," Cassandra said. "You and the TV." She came back out of the cellar, brushed away some of the dust and dirt from her pants. "There's just one thing that's got me perplexed," she said.

"What is it?" I said, moving away from the door and pulling back the shade on the picture window, making my usual check outside.

"Why don't you just make a copy of the video once you get ahold of it, and send it off to the governor or some bureaucrat like that. I mean, why go to all this trouble?"

"We don't have time for all that," I said, letting the shade fall back. "Besides, it's not the film I'm so concerned with, it's Pelton's and Schillinger's reactions to the film that I'm more interested in."

She nodded.

"I want to see their faces when I get them to admit that they pulled the trigger on Vasquez, and I want them to see my face when they admit that they set me up to take the fall, and I want to record the event on tape—not just for the governor, but for all the world to see."

Cassandra turned away and stood in front of the picture window that looked out onto the east-west road and the trout stream alongside it. "You may have a tough time getting them to do that," she said.

"Who knows," I said, "I've been known to get lucky from time to time."

"Not lately."

CHAPTER FIFTY-SEVEN

The next morning, I drove to the Ironville post office to retrieve the box that Tony Angelino's Guinea Pigs had (God willing) found and overnighted from Olancha. The post office was a small brick building with a slate roof and old, single-paned windows. The Formica counter held a cash register as well as a weight scale for packages. On both sides of the counter were walls of post office boxes. The boxes were the same old, wrought-iron-style compartments I recalled from my youth when I'd ridden shotgun beside my grandfather going to pick up his mail on Saturday mornings. On display in a glass booth below the counter were the featured stamps of the month, which, it turns out, were the faces of jazz legends the likes of Duke Ellington, Mel Torme, and even the chairman of the board himself, Sinatra. Maybe one day there'd be a stamp of the keeper and his famous drums.

On the drive from the cabin to the post office I'd wondered how good an idea it had been to use my grandfather's name on the package. Considering that things never changed this far north, there was the distinct possibility that the man or woman working behind the counter would have known my grandfather. Luckily, the kid behind the counter could not have been more than eighteen years old. He had long hair parted in the middle. The hair had been died yellow as opposed to natural blond. It probably hadn't been washed in two, maybe three weeks, and it hung down in clumps, like starchy spaghetti. He wore a T-shirt, on the front of which was the visage of Kurt Cobain, the self-assassinated rock star who seemed to be the model for the kid's obsession with the same straggly yellow hair, the same it-sucks-to-be-alive expression, and the same three-day-old growth. Below Kurt's picture were the dates 1967–1994. It bothered me to know someone could be so young, so rich, and so resentful of the world. Maybe old Kurt's death was really murder, a cover-up for something else? Maybe someone should have interrogated his wife?

I stepped up to the counter. "Package for Marconi," I said.

"First name," the kid said.

"Pasquale," I said.

"What?" the kid asked, eyebrows upturned.

"Pasquale," I repeated. "It's Italian for Patrick."

"Hang on," the kid said. He turned and went through the swinging, restaurant-style door that led to the distribution area in back. It seemed like the entire operation would be a piece of cake. But then I spotted a stack of the FBI's most wanted posters tacked to the bulletin board on the plaster-coated wall beside me. I imagined my face there for all of Ironville to see as they retrieved their junk mail. All twelve hundred people. The five-by-seven, black-and-white poster would show my face, head-on, and a left-side profile. In the photo, I would be frowning, my mustache covering my upper lip, my eyes dark. My face would not have been shaved in many days and the salt-and-pepper stubble would match the slicked-back salt-and-pepper hair on my head. My thick, muscular neck would meet my overdeveloped trapezius muscles at the bottom of the photograph. My neck would support a thin chain supporting a placard with a seven-digit ID number, and to the innocent bystander, I would appear more like a hitman than a lawman.

Kurt Cobain returned with a box cradled in his skinny arms. "This just came in, overnighted from California."

I signed for the box and took it in my arms. Then I did something very strange. What I mean is, I should have sprinted for the door, jumped into the Pontiac, raced back to the cabin. Instead I found myself hesitating for a second or two. "It's a shame," I said, nodding toward the Kurt Cobain T-shirt. "I understand he was a father."

"Yeah," the kid said, "so what?"

"Maybe," I said, "old Kurt never thought life was worth living."

"You sound like my father," the kid said, now leaning against the counter. "He likes to sit inside the trailer, watch satellite TV, drink beer, and talk about the good life. Whatever that is."

"It's life any way you look at it," I said. "And it's the only one you got."

The kid frowned.

I left.

CHAPTER FIFTY-EIGHT

Back at the cabin, I opened the package with a steak knife, slicing through the layers of duct tape and cardboard, careful not to destroy any of the contents in the process. When I peeled back the folds, I found three plastic baby dolls inside, just as Cassandra had said I would. The baby dolls were protected with piles of crumpled-up newspaper. I pulled out the paper and tossed it into the fireplace where it quickly caught fire.

Beneath the newspaper, I found the money, neatly stacked.

There had to be hundreds of hundred dollar bills. Thousands actually.

"You took a real chance shipping cash this way," I said.

"What choice did I have," Cassandra said, "UPS?"

For a moment or two, I just looked at her. Then I said, "Yeah, UPS would have been good."

I picked up the first doll, placed it against my right ear, shook it, discovered a slight rattling.

Cassandra held her hands out to me, took the doll into her arms, and cradled it, as if the doll were a real baby. She turned it over and pulled up the white taffeta gown the toy-maker had dressed it in. The back of the doll had been cut up along the spine and then sewn back together with fishing line. Not a very neat job, but it seemed to have done the trick. Cassandra put the doll down on the table.

"Cut along there," she said, pointing to the suture in the doll's back.

I opened the baby doll's back with the steak knife and uncovered more money and one compact videocassette. The cassette was a lot smaller than the VHS-style cassette I was used to—more compact, more modern, I supposed. The cassette contained no stick-on label, no identification of any kind.

I cut through the backs of the other two dolls and found three hundred thousand dollars, of which I would owe Tony Angelino one hundred thousand. The remainder would go to Cassandra Wolf. For Mexico and a new life, for her and her baby.

I held the videocassette in my right hand, held it up to Cassandra's face. "How do you know for certain that this is the one?"

With her right hand she pointed to the TV and the attached VCR and said, "I put the package together myself, but if you have to be sure. . . ."

"Not a bad idea," I said. "That is, if you don't mind me looking at the film."

Cassandra looked at me with sad eyes and a slight smile. "If it's for our freedom," she said, "then I suppose it's for a good cause."

I smiled and for a second or two we said nothing.

I reached out for her arm. "You going to be okay?" I said, slipping the cassette out of the transparent plastic protector.

She crossed her arms tight, as though embracing herself. "Maybe we should pop some popcorn," she said, "really make a show of it."

"Hey," I said, "a flick isn't a flick without the popcorn."

But it wasn't the least bit funny.

The picture on the video was blurry, with only a bed and a bare wall for background.

"Where did Pelton film this?" I said.

Cassandra sat behind me on the wood-plank floor in what had become a near permanent perch beside the fire. She had both arms crossed and locked tightly at the chest, a wool blanket wrapped around her torso. She was rocking back and forth, as though freezing. "At the Coco's Motor Inn," she said, "near the Albany airport."

"Hotel-no-tell," I said.

In person, a very tragic-looking Cassandra stared into the newly stoked fire—a fire on what had become a very warm afternoon. But then, I think the fire was necessary. I think the fire helped Cassandra cauterize her memory of Wash Pelton. In the video she wore black stockings and a black garter belt, no panties. Despite the way the film moved in and out of focus, I could plainly see the heart-shaped tattoo on the left side of her neck. I knew the film was nothing more than a porn film, whether it was meant for Pelton's private viewing or not. Still, I couldn't help noticing how beautiful Cassandra looked with bare breasts and flat stomach, and there was the way she moved in the bed, smoothly, not the least bit abrupt, her eyes closed the entire time.

Wash Pelton, on the other hand, looked terrible. He had undergone a drastic change in the years since we had been corrections officers together. His gut had become large and fleshy, his arms lanky, if not atrophied. The same went for his legs. His appendage was long, veiny, and purple. The little bit of hair he had on his head was snow-white. In a word, he had gone soft. Irreparably soft.

I knew I could have watched the film from start to finish without Cassandra interfering. She knew the stakes as well as I did. But once I saw the jagged scar on Wash's neck, I knew without a doubt that I could make a positive ID in a court of law. And a positive ID is exactly what I needed to turn the tables on Pelton.

But then another man appeared in the viewfinder. A tall, portly man. Schillinger, of course. He stood in front of Cassandra, took hold of her hair, pulled her up onto the bed.

I turned and looked at the real-life Cassandra sitting on the floor staring into the fire, that wool blanket wrapped around her on a hot spring day in May.

Enough was enough, I thought.

I got up, hit the eject button on the machine, pulled the cassette tape out, and slipped it back into the plastic case. I took a pot out of the kitchen and placed the video inside it, along with some of the cash. I filled two more pots with the rest of the cash. Then I took up the square panel from the floor and stored the pots in the far corner of the cellar, in the exact place where I had shot the snakes. When I was finished, I climbed back up the ladder, secured the cellar, and got two beers out from the fridge. One for me and one for Cassandra, courtesy of my love, Val Antonelli, and my lawyer, Tony Angelino.

By that time, it was going on four o'clock. I needed to call Tony with directions to the cabin so that he could feed them to Schillinger and Pelton. But what if they decided to blow the whole thing off? What if they decided to take a chance on me exposing the video to the entire world? What if they figured I was already screwed or way beyond screwed, video or no video? What if they knew for certain I was going down, not only for the aiding and abetting of Eduard Vasquez's escape, but also for his murder?

If it all happened that way, then prison was inevitable.

The corrections officers would not bother protecting one of their own. In the maximum security prisons of the 1990s, the gorillas were in charge, not the hacks or the screws. Certainly not "the man." The COs would stand off to the side while the inmates held me down flat on the concrete floor and cut away my flesh piece by piece with a shiv made from a disposable, prison-issue razor. The inmates would hold me down by the arms and legs and cut along the back, making shallow slices, then deeper slices. They would peel the skin, roll it back, expose the fleshy-white underlayer until no skin was left on my back. Then they would string me up by the neck, maybe slice my gut so that my intestines would spill out onto the cold concrete.

Anything I imagined could come true, and worse.

Schillinger and Pelton had to take the bait.

I felt a hand against my shoulder. I turned fast, grabbed it.

"Jesus," Cassandra said.

I dropped an open beer to the floor and pressed her up against the wall of the kitchen. "Don't ever do that again," I said. I released my hold on her. "I'm sorry," I said. I pulled out a cigarette and lit it.

Cassandra wiped her eyes, combed her brown hair with open fingers.

"You need help," she said. "Maybe if you had found a way to resolve your wife's—"

"Don't," I said, pointing the lit cigarette at her in place of my index finger. "You have no idea."

The white foam spread out in all directions on the floor.

She took a step toward me. "Don't talk to me about being alone. You're not the only one who's alone. You've got no right to think you're the only one who is alone."

I pictured her image on the video and I pictured what she was doing to Wash Pelton in that white room. I pictured what she did with Marty Schillinger. Then I saw her tossing that black-plated .32 off the side of the granite clearing and into the heavy growth on top of Old Iron Top.

Maybe she was right.

More accurately: I had no right to feel like the only one who had suffered.

I bent over, picked up the now empty beer can, and placed it on the kitchen table. Then I put my hands on Cassandra's shoulders, pulled her toward me, into me. "I'm sorry," I whispered.

"Maybe you're just scared," she said. "But then who the hell isn't?"

CHAPTER FIFTY-NINE

At four o'clock, Cassandra and I changed into black jeans, black turtle-necks, and black lace-up combat boots. I pulled a black watch cap over my head. We painted one another's faces with black face paint to make the get-up complete. I slipped on a pair of black leather gloves that fit so tightly that they might have passed as a second skin, and I spent the next half hour squeezing my hands in and out of fist position so as to loosen up the gloves and make sure my trigger finger was free.

I laid out the Remington 1187s on the kitchen table and loaded the weapons with five two-and-three-quarter eight-shot all-purpose magnum loads. I handed one of the shotguns, barrel up, to Cassandra. "You know how to use this thing?"

She pulled back the chamber device on the semiautomatic and popped the release. The cabin was filled with the sharp, solid, metallic sound of a round being chambered. "Eddy Vasquez was my lover," she said, depressing the safety latch on the trigger as if that was answer enough. Then she went into the great room and pulled up the floor-board panel. She climbed down and leaned the shotgun against the wall beside the ladder. When she climbed back out of the hole, she said, "Maybe you'd better make that call now."

"It's the only thing left to do," I said.

Using the old rotary phone in the kitchen, I dialed the number for Tony Angelino's private line at his office inside Albany's Council 84. The time was four-fifteen.

He answered after the first ring, not bothering with a formal hello. "Go," is all he said in his raspy baritone.

It took me a little less than fifteen seconds to give him precise directions from Albany to Ironville and the cabin.

"Sounds like my L.A. Guinea Pig contingent came through," Tony said.

"Pelton and Schillinger are definitely coming?" I said.

"Pelton was happy you came to your senses. Said he'll figure out a way to back you up, if you'll only give him back that video."

"They ask about copies?" I said. "What if they think we made copies?"

"I told them it was a chance they'd have to take, paisan. I told them all you wanted was your name back, and your job, and that it would not be in your best interest to further piss them off. That you wanted to work with them now, not work against them. Capice?"

"And Cassandra?"

"Told them you sent her on her way. That she's probably in Mexico by now."

"No cops," I said.

"No cops," Tony said.

"And you're sure they bought it?"

"Sure," he said.

"I'll be in touch," I said.

I drank five more beers in the next two hours. I could have drunk more. The adrenaline or the fear or both seemed to burn the alcohol away as fast as I put it in. Cassandra drank nothing. She made no comments about my drinking. She seemed calm, casually sitting on the floor in front of the fireplace in her black jeans and turtleneck, the fire having been allowed to die completely for the first time since we'd arrived. For now, the cabin interior was lit with the dim light that came from the brass table lamp on top of the three-tiered bookshelf abutting the stone fireplace.

We said very little. Not even small talk. I paced the cabin floor and drank beer and said nothing.

Nothing seemed like the easier alternative.

CHAPTER SIXTY

Blood runs from the base of Wash Pelton's neck, down the front of his yellow inmate jumper. It hits me then: Why bother holding a shiv to a man's neck if you already have the barrel of a .38 service revolver pressed up against his head?

In the four days since the rebel inmates took control of D-Block and D-Yard, they have not fired a single round. The murdered COs were cut open with shivs, not blown away by bullets.

Beatings and shivvings, but not bullets.

The situation is simple, but deadly.

The rebel inmates have firearms, but they don't have bullets.

As the afternoon of the fourth day wears on, the rebel inmates make their demands once more. Demands for food, money, medical supplies, helicopters, weapons, freedom, and, of course, bullets. Lots of bullets. With fists raised high and bandannas wrapped around their heads and sunglasses covering their bloodshot eyes, they scream insane orders over government-issue bullhorns from the center of Times Square to the state troopers who line the west wall, sighting us in with their .270

caliber standard-issue sniping rifles. Their firearms are loaded and locked.

No question about that.

The question, on the other hand, is this: Do the troopers have orders to take out three corrections officers in the interest of saving the lives of two dozen others?

CHAPTER SIXTY-ONE

At exactly one minute past eight o'clock on a warm Saturday night in May, just five days after convicted cop-killer Eduard Vasquez escaped from Green Haven Maximum Security Prison—and just two days after his assassination—two egg-shaped headlights broke through the darkness of the north country. What I guessed was a state-owned, four-door Ford Taurus rolled slowly along the east-west Ironville road until the driver turned off and pulled into the driveway that led to the cabin.

I moved away from the picture window and turned toward Cassandra. "You know what to do," I said, keeping my eyes planted on the headlights, remembering her pregnant condition.

"Yes," said a voice in the darkness, "I know what to do."

The white light from Cassandra's four-battery flashlight sliced through the thick darkness like a laser beam. From where I stood, I heard her lifting the wood panel off the floor. I heard her steps when she climbed down the ladder. I heard her replace the panel.

What happened next was up to me.

And luck.

•   •   •

I pulled the .45 out from behind my back, pulled back the slide and felt the good solid feel of racking a live round. Using my thumb, I clicked on the safety and stuffed the piece, barrel first, behind my belt buckle. I jogged into the back bedroom and picked up the twelve-gauge Remington with the flashlight I had duct-taped to the barrel. I opened the bedroom window and climbed out hind end first, so that I was sitting on the windowsill with my legs still in the room. Then I stood on the sill and heaved myself up onto the roof.

I shimmied up onto the wood shakes, crawled on my chest and stomach, propelled myself with my legs, arms, and hands, feeling the brittle wood shakes crack underneath my weight. I slid up to the apex of the A-frame and looked down on the driveway. From this position, I watched the headlights cut through the blackness of the early evening. The car moved slowly up the hard-packed dirt road, sweeping up pebbles and stones against the underside of the carriage until the driver turned into the driveway and stopped.

The headlights from the car shined on the front of the cabin but not in my eyes. From my position on the roof I was able to see Tommy Welch squeeze his massive body out from behind the steering column. And I was able to see Wash Pelton get out of the passenger side. And I saw Marty Schillinger crawl out of the backseat.

"What in God's name is going on here?" Pelton said. "Keeper Marconi, you here?" His strained voice echoed against Old Iron Top and then drifted out over the grassy fields opposite the Ironville road. When Pelton took three or four steps forward I was able to see that he wore a black business suit tailored to fit his soft, middle-aged body. He wore a bright red tie that showed well in the light that came from the headlamps on the Taurus. He looked out of place in the middle of the Adirondack forest. Unfortunately for him, the tie would make a good target if I needed one.

Tommy Welch pulled out his service pistol and assumed a sharpshooter's stance—legs spread, feet flat, knees cocked, arms out straight, two hands supporting the grip of the .9 millimeter Glock. Like the turret on a tank, he shifted his aim from left to right to left again. He seemed more suited to the occasion, with his work boots and jeans and jean jacket with the sleeves cut off.

"Keeper Marconi," Pelton shouted again, this time with his hands cupped up around his mouth like a megaphone.

I felt the wood shakes snapping and breaking underneath me.

Tommy Welch pivoted, waving the Glock in the direction of the east-west road, as if suspecting an ambush.

"Put that thing away, Tommy," Schillinger said, "before you get lucky and shoot yourself." Schillinger looked like a pulp-fiction detective with his shin-length Burberry trench coat.

"This your idea of a joke, Marty?" Pelton said, now looking at his partner.

I held my breath and considered Pelton's and Schillinger's attitude toward each other a good sign. No conveyance of even the most minimal courtesies between them. Antagonistic allies at best.

"I don't fucking joke," Schillinger said. "You should know that by now."

"Let's just get back in the car and go," Pelton said, now stepping toward the Taurus.

It was then that I shined the barrel-mounted flashlight on the three men.

Schillinger and Pelton brought their hands up to their foreheads in a mock salute to shield their eyes. Tommy Welch pivoted on the balls of his feet, aiming the barrel of his .9 millimeter at the source of the light.

"Lose the piece, Tommy," I said.

All three looked up at me, squinting their eyes as if straining to see me.

"Lose it now."

But Tommy Welch wouldn't listen. He just planted a solid bead on me with his weapon as I spread my legs and anchored my weight against the roof. I pulled open the chamber on the Remington 1187 and, purely for effect, released it again. No other sound in the world carries more weight than the sound of a twelve-gauge semiautomatic when it's locked and loaded. The metal against metal sound echoed and bounced off the south face of Old Iron Top, as if, somehow, the old hilltop were alive and well and on my side.

"Do it, Tommy," Wash Pelton said with an even, businesslike voice.

"Yeah, dummy," Schillinger said, "lose the fucking piece."

Tommy turned and gave Pelton and Schillinger a disgusted, sour look. He tossed the piece a few feet away, onto the lawn. "I told you he was gonna try and shoot us," he said. "Just like he blew that drug addict Moscowitz away."

"We don't know that for sure," Pelton said.

"Moscowitz wear a wool overcoat?" I said.

"Yeah," Schillinger broke in. "The drug addict did wear a wool overcoat. Cold, all the time, the freak."

"Old Tommy here is not so dumb after all," I said.

Tommy let out a laugh. "Told you, douche bag."

Schillinger bobbed his head. "Keep laughing, fat ass," he said. "Pretty soon you're gonna be roadkill, too."

"Both of you, stop it," Pelton shouted while remaining perfectly still, hands up. "Let's hear what he's got to say."

"Move closer to the cabin," I said, feeling the sharp sting of the splintered wood shakes piercing my black jeans, needling the skin on my stomach, chest, and thighs.

No one moved.

"Closer to the cabin," I said again. "Move away from the car."

"This wasn't part of the deal," Pelton said.

"Tony told us no cops, no guns," Schillinger said.

I braced myself and let off a round that shattered the windshield on Pelton's Ford Taurus. "Move," I said.

The explosion bounced off the south wall of Old Iron Top and echoed into the empty valley across from the east-west road.

"Move!"

Now, the three men walked toward the woodpile under the carport, in the direction of the door. It was all I wanted.

"Open the side door and walk inside," I yelled, shifting my weight back down off the roof, maneuvering my legs onto the sill of the open bedroom window. "And lock it behind you."

"You're digging yourself into one hell of a giant chasm, Keeper," came the sound of Pelton's voice. "In my estimation, you're about to put the proverbial screws to yourself."

I slid back into the bedroom and ran toward the front of the cabin, shotgun barrel poised ahead of me. "Stand right where you are, gentlemen," I said, loud enough for Cassandra to hear me through the floor-boards. The three men stood only a foot or two in front of the closed door, within perfect range of the video probe. "Now," I said with a smiling face, "I hope you guys are movie fans."

CHAPTER SIXTY-TWO

Dry-mouthed, hands wrapped tightly around the smooth wood stock of the Remington 1187, I aimed the barrel at the chests of men I had once considered fraternal brothers. I shined the barrel-mounted flashlight in their eyes, kept them in constant view, especially Tommy Welch. No telling his capabilities in the name of loyalty, allegiance to duty, and good old-fashioned recklessness.

I sidestepped to the bookshelf, keeping the shotgun steady, and reaching under the lampshade, I hit the switch.

"You're a wanted fugitive," Schillinger said, his long arms dangling against his loose-fitting Burberry trench coat. "I should warn you, in case you're planning something stupid."

"Something more stupid than this?" Pelton said. "I thought we had a nice peaceful exchange set up?"

I could only hope that Cassandra was getting all this on tape under the floorboards of the cabin.

"Look, Marty," I said, feeling the weight of the shotgun on my left arm, feeling the tightness of the leather glove on the trigger finger of my right hand, "I'm entirely aware of your partnership with Pelton. So stop the good-cop–bad-cop routine before my finger gets itchy."

"You're in a position," Schillinger said.

"I don't want to hurt your feelings," I said, "but you know how it is when you don't have control of your own future."

"I do now," Schillinger said.

"We kept our part of the bargain, Keeper," Wash Pelton said, arms out stiff by his side, fingers moving in and out of fist position. "Now give us the film and I'll see about getting you cleared of this thing."

If I squeezed the trigger of the twelve-gauge just a fraction of an inch, one round alone of the eight-shot magnum loads would have been enough to take off all three faces. Someone might live through the experience, but what would have been the point of carrying on without a face?

I picked up the remote control for the television and VCR with my left hand, all the time holding the shotgun in my right. I turned on the machines and began to roll the porn flick.

"Now, gentlemen," I said, "watch carefully. What you see may change my life for the better."

There were a few seconds of static on the screen. But through the blur, I could make out Wash's face and the scar on his neck as he sat on the edge of a bed inside a room at the Coco's Motor Inn. Cassandra was down on her knees. All I could make out of her was her naked back, the garter belt wrapped tightly around her waist. But when she leaned into Wash — between his legs — you could clearly make out the heart-shaped tattoo on her neck, just above her left shoulder.

From where I stood by the bookcase, I could see the sweat break out on Pelton's forehead. I could almost hear the anger flush into Schillinger's face. As for the ever-silent Tommy Welch, I could see his eyes moving from the screen to me, then back to the screen.

I knew this: He was looking for the perfect opportunity to jump me.

But I also knew this: I had to keep all three in one spot long enough for Cassandra to get a shot of them, long enough for them to admit to setting me up.

•   •   •

On the screen, Pelton scrunched the muscles of his red face. He was close to something, I could tell. I recalled the feeling. You could see his lips move but you couldn't hear what he was saying. Cassandra moved her face out of the way when he finally did come to it. She turned to the camera, opened her eyes wide, disgusted and terrified. When Pelton was through, she held her face down. In a word, she looked defeated.

Then Schillinger came into the picture.

At first all I could make out of him were his skinny legs. But then I could see all of him when he bent over, grabbed Cassandra by the hair, and pulled her onto the bed. I couldn't hear the words he said, but I could plainly hear Cassandra crying out in pain when Schillinger yanked hard on her thick brown hair.

Now that Schillinger had clearly made his presence known inside the cabin *and* on the video, it was time for me to lose my weapon. To add emphasis (and drama), I slid back the chamber of the Remington 1187 four distinct times, forcing out four unspent shells. It was an important move losing that shotgun. But it was definitely not in my best interest to continue being the aggressor. It was important for them to think I was the victim.

The heavy shells made a thumping sound on the floor. I handed the shotgun over, stock first, to a shocked Tommy Welch. He looked at me like my brain had suddenly oozed out of my face through my nostrils. I bent over, picked up each shell, one by one, and put them in the pocket of my black jeans.

"Sorry about the greeting, boys," I said. "But I had to make sure it was safe."

Wash appeared to be tongue-tied.

Schillinger appeared to have gone mute.

But then Tommy let the surrendered shotgun fall to the floor. He grabbed me, turned me around, threw me face first against the bookshelf, knocking the brass lamp over. A half-dozen or so books cascaded to the floor.

He held on to me, his thick forearm around my neck.

"Wait," Pelton said. "Let's hear what he's got to say."

I felt the pain shoot up my back and down my neck between the shoulder blades. Tommy had twisted my arms behind my back. He pressed them up, palms out. I took as deep a breath as I could with my constricted diaphragm, tried to stem the pain, tried to stay calm, clear-headed. It was my one and only shot.

"I say we off the motherfucker now," Tommy said. "I say we kill him, take the video and our chances."

"We need him alive," Wash said.

Schillinger took a few steps forward. "You mean you're nothing without your fall guy," he said. Exactly what I wanted him to say. Precisely. That was the good-luck part of the proceedings. But there was the bad-luck part, too: Schillinger reached into his trench coat, came out with his own .9 millimeter Glock. "I agree with Tommy," Schillinger said. "I say we kill the son of a bitch while we still have the chance. That's the only reason I agreed to come up here in the first place. To see that this fuck-face bites the big one."

Schillinger handed the pistol over to Tommy, who then jammed the weapon against my temple. I heard the distinct sound of the hammer being thumbed back. My eyes watered, my heart skipped a beat and verged on stopping altogether.

But then Pelton screamed. "I said no!" There was an explosion, and I felt my body freeze, and Tommy Welch broke his grip on me and dropped down flat and lifeless to the cabin floor.

I turned fast and saw Pelton with a pistol in his hand, and I saw right away that it was a fancy chrome-plated .38 with an eight-inch barrel and a walnut grip, and there was a thin trace of smoke rising up from the barrel.

Pelton raised the weapon, aimed it at the back of Schillinger's head. He cocked the hammer a second time, and Schillinger dropped the Glock. When I kicked the Glock away toward the other end of the room, it smeared the puddle of dark red blood that gushed out of the exit wound in Tommy Welch's head.

"Now," Pelton screamed. "We listen to what he's got to say. Got it? Then we decide what to do with him."

Schillinger slowly backed away. It was hard to make out his face in the dim light. On the television, Cassandra was on her knees, straddling Wash like a horse while he lay on his back and pulled her long hair back like a rein. Her mouth opened painfully wide, and I could clearly see the pain and strain on her face. But then I could see something else on the film too. Something I never would have guessed. Schillinger stood on the edge of the bed, very near the prone Wash. At first, what I saw didn't register. At first, I couldn't believe what I was seeing. But then I knew I couldn't deny it. There was no denying it whatsoever. In the video, Wash let go of Cassandra and flipped over on the bed onto all fours. Marty Schillinger was on him from behind doing something I had seen happen to him once before at Attica; only this time, he wasn't screaming or trying to get away.

In all the craziness, both Schillinger and Pelton must have forgotten about the video, because together they turned and looked at the screen. "Jesus H. Christ," said Schillinger.

"What difference does it make what he knows?" Pelton said. "All you want is your name back. Am I right, Keeper? You just want out of this mess."

"Something like that," I said. "But first, I want to settle the score."

CHAPTER SIXTY-THREE

"I gave you a chance to get out of this with a slap on the wrist," Wash said, standing near the cabin door, the chrome-plated .38 in hand, eyes on both me and Schillinger. "And I would have compensated you nicely for your troubles."

I gazed at the screen. Schillinger's head was hanging back in ecstasy while he worked on Pelton, faster now, the flesh on his white ass cheeks trembling as Cassandra sat back on the bed and stared at the floor.

"Maybe all of this could have been avoided," I said. The hole in Tommy Welch's head was still gushing dark red blood.

"Sure," Pelton said.

"Pelton would have killed you anyway," Schillinger said.

"You shut up," Pelton said, waving the gun at his head. "I never wanted anybody killed nor have I killed anyone . . . of importance, that is."

"You're forgetting about Vasquez."

"Not my doing, Detective Schillinger."

"Let me guess," I said, shifting my eyes from the naked bodies on the television screen to the fully clothed bodies in the dimly lit cabin. "I'm sure it never once dawned on you, Wash, that if I took the blame for the escape, I would also be accused of running the drug racket that was about to hit the press once your partners managed to pull off their separate backstabbings."

"It wasn't supposed to work that way, Keeper," Wash said. "I never counted on Mike Norman and," nodding at Schillinger, "my good friend Marty here betraying me."

"I just want what I have coming," Schillinger said, looking directly at Wash and the barrel of that .38.

"So what happened, Wash?" I said. "Let's see. I'll bet as soon as I left Mike's office on Tuesday he got this bright idea and gave you a call and offered you a sale you couldn't refuse? A few thousand dollars in exchange for evidence that could put Keeper Marconi away and make it look like he'd been perpetrating the drug racket inside Green Haven, maybe even make it look like I was the one who helped Vasquez escape. After all, I signed the orders allowing him outside the prison grounds, and no matter what, I was the one who approached Mike with illegally obtained evidence."

"In essence," Wash said, "that's what happened."

"I guess it's true," I said, "that I initiated the whole thing through Mike — created a window of opportunity for you. You might even say I could be hating Mike right now, cursing his soul. But, you know what, I'm convinced the poor pathetic bastard must have called you out of desperation, to make a quick buck. In my heart I can't believe that he would have done anything to hurt me. Not really. And you might have given him a few bucks and his bad conscience might have been a lot easier to handle with a wallet of cash pressed against his backside. But maybe, just maybe, you'd had enough of paying people off."

"After a while," Wash said, the .38 still steady in his hand, "people thought of me as Fleet Bank."

"You'd already paid Logan and Mastriano to keep their mouths shut," I said, catching the rapid, wet finish of Schillinger's act with Pelton on the screen. "And this is after you paid off A. J. Royale for performing an unnecessary root canal on Vasquez. And you had to pay off Doctor Fleischer for putting Mastriano into a fake coma to gain public sentiment and, at the same time, make me look like the bad guy, the insensitive warden. Because all wardens are insensitive tyrants, am I right? You must have figured that you could either take care of Norman with a payoff or have him killed."

"I had no intentions of going into the hit-man business," Wash said, shifting his grip on the heavy pistol.

"Choosing the less violent alternative, you gave Schillinger one last payoff to be distributed to Mike Norman in exchange for the bag of evidence. On Tuesday afternoon Marty returned with the evidence you would use against me on Wednesday morning, but what you didn't know at the time was that he'd kept the payoff for himself, probably telling Norman that it would be delivered within a couple of days. But when Thursday came around, all Lieutenant Mike Norman got was a visit from Marty Schillinger and Tommy Welch."

Pelton was staring at Schillinger now. Schillinger was looking at Tommy Welch on the floor. As for the video, it was finished and all you could see on the screen was snow.

"How is it you're privy to all this information, anyway?" Wash said. "I mean, you're no detective, Keeper. You're a goddamned warden."

"I paid a second visit to Mike only a few hours after my arrest on Wednesday. He told me flat out that Marty had come in and taken the evidence away from him, no explanations, no nothing. And I believed him."

Pelton moved closer to Schillinger, put the barrel of the chrome-plated .38 up against his temple.

"So how'd you and Tommy Welch do it, Marty?" I said. "Get Mike good and stinking drunk behind closed doors? Then string him up with his own belt once he passed out, make it look like the suicide he was sure to pull off ever since his nervous breakdown at Attica? With him dead, there was no chance for him to open his mouth about what was going down in the New York State Department of Corrections. Because Mike had been doing little jobs for you guys through the years, hadn't he? But he could only be trusted just so far, because he was a drunk and he wasn't renowned for being too stable. In fact, Mike might have been gone from the department a long time ago had he not been considered a tragic hero—a survivor of those four bloody days in September 1971. You remember those four days, don't you, Wash?"

I might have looked into Wash's eyes, but instead I got a good look at

Schillinger. The sweat poured off his brow, into his eyes, down his puffy red cheeks, and onto his Burberry trench coat. I could tell that he wanted nothing more but to wrap his hands around my throat and squeeze till Kingdom Come. But he could do nothing about it. There was nowhere to run and hide. He just had to stand there and take it. That was his only option.

"And you were next on Schillinger's and Tommy Welch's list, Commissioner Pelton," I said. "But Marty here didn't want to do it so soon after he'd pumped Vasquez."

"You're full of shit, Keeper," Schillinger mumbled.

"You were going to wait until the cops picked up me and Cassandra and slapped us with first-degree murder. And you knew I'd go to Athens, Marty, because you'd planted that envelope on the floor of Vasquez's cell on Monday afternoon. You knew I'd find it and if I didn't find it, you would have picked it up yourself and pointed it out to me. You knew I'd be curious enough to go to Athens. You'd shoot Vasquez, and when witnesses would testify to seeing my 4-Runner there, I'd naturally take the blame. But somebody had beaten you to the punch. When you went to kill Vasquez, he was already dead. Still, no matter who killed Vasquez, the result was the same. The case against me and Cassandra would be open and closed. All that would be left would be to make sure Pelton had an accident. But you had time for that."

There was a thick silence for a slow second or two, with only a clear blue screen on the television and a high-pitched whistling that indicated the porn video was about to run out of tape, and I found myself praying to Christ that the camera was still rolling under the floorboards and that Cassandra was all right. But just then, as I pictured the blood from Tommy Welch's head dripping through the cracks in the wood panel into the potato cellar, Schillinger suddenly looked at me and screamed, "Bull-fucking-shit." And just like that he took hold of Pelton's revolver. "It's him," Schillinger shouted while he and Pelton struggled for control of the pistol. "It fucking had to be him. We left the fucking room together. Wash must have gone back to Vasquez's room, shot the fucker dead."

Schillinger screamed and clawed at the pistol but Wash had the advantage with his chubby index finger already wrapped around the hair trigger; it went off and Marty dropped like a stone. He went down right beside the body of Tommy Welch, his blood and his soul draining out of his face like water from a faucet.

For a second or two, Wash and I just stared down at the two dead bodies. Then Pelton raised his head to me. "I didn't kill anybody," he said in a strained, out-of-breath voice. "I didn't kill Vasquez. Christ, I needed him alive because I wanted my fucking money back. This son of a bitch must have killed him, no matter what he said, he had to have done it. Or you, Keeper, but somehow I don't think you're capable. No, Schillinger must have killed Vasquez. Just like he killed Mike and would have killed me. The son of a bitch." He extended his right arm, held out the pistol, and emptied another round into Schillinger's body at the exact moment that he said, "bitch."

Schillinger's dead body jumped when the bullet hit it.

I stood there watching the bleeding body as if I wasn't in the room at all, like my body was still there but I was somewhere far away, like in a dream. I knew that it didn't make even an ounce of difference who'd drawn whom into the smuggling and murder business, or who'd abused whose power or who'd double-crossed the other or if I had created an accurate scenario of what went down during the last five days or not. In the end what difference did any of my assumptions make? This wasn't a case of whodunit. It was a case of don't-blame-me. What I mean is, it didn't really matter who took the blame for killing Vasquez, as long as it wasn't Cassandra and as long as it wasn't me.

CHAPTER SIXTY-FOUR

"Seems to me we've been here before, Wash," I said, taking a step forward, closer to where he stood. At the same time, I recalled that September afternoon when the rebel inmate had held the barrel of the black-plated .38 service revolver inside Wash's mouth and pressed a shiv against his neck, making the jagged scar that still existed today.

"You turned out to be some kind of hero," Wash said. "This time I have the power to save your life or take it away."

"What made you do it, Wash?" I said, now standing as still and as nonthreatening as possible. "Why go to all the trouble of arranging a drug deal that was destined to fail? After all we believed in?"

"What we believed in once upon a time, my friend," he said, "is pure fantasy now. What we believed in was destroyed when Attica went down. They took away our power, handed it over on a platter laced with gold to the inmates. It was either us or the gorillas. Or there was a third option."

"We could just join the gorillas," I said.

"Precisely," Wash said.

"What do you know about us or them?" I said. "How much time have you spent inside a prison lately, other than to make a surprise inspection and take away my officers?"

"I was there, Keeper," Wash said, shaking the barrel of the chrome-plated .38 in my face. "I was there a long time before I entered the political arena. I felt the pressure, maybe more than most, because of what happened to me at Attica."

I knew what Wash was referring to and I knew it involved the four men who'd held him down on the concrete floor of Times Square.

"I felt the pressure too, Wash," I said, "and I never gave in to the gorillas. Not once."

"Yes, you fucking well did," Pelton screamed. "You signed the releases for Vasquez a half a dozen different times. You knew he'd killed that rookie cop. You knew he was high risk and that you could have vetoed the releases. But you signed them anyway."

He was right.

"Come on, Keeper," he went on, "after Fran died, nothing was important to you anymore. So you let the gorillas take over in force."

"My wife had nothing to do with this," I lied.

"You went soft."

For a moment, I zeroed in on the chrome barrel. If he'd let loose with a round right then, I would never have known the difference. It would have been lights out, no pain, with the hope that I reached heaven an hour before the devil knew my soul was up for grabs. Right then, standing on the blood-soaked floor of my grandfather's cabin, death seemed very near, and it was doing a job on me.

"Listen, Keeper," Wash said, softer this time, "when we started out in this system, there were thirteen thousand inmates for twelve maximum security prisons in New York. Now there's twice as many inmates living under the same twelve concrete roofs. And do you know what the governor expects of me? My assignment is to cut more officers, cut more programs. Now you tell me, Keeper Marconi, just what does the governor know about prison?"

He kept the barrel of that weapon pointed at my face like it would somehow help him drive his point across. A point that was absolutely valid, but had little to do with saving my life. I was defenseless and Wash knew it.

"Maybe you had no choice but to go soft, Keeper. We all go soft at some point when the fight becomes pointless. Fran's death was just the catalyst for your experience. If it hadn't been her, it would have been something else. And as for Mike Norman? He'd barely gotten out of the starting gate before he crumpled under." He started bobbing the weapon as though about to collapse under its weight. His finger was pressed against the trigger. I knew he might shoot me and not even intend it. "There is nothing more we can do for inmates. There is no such thing as rehabilitation, certainly. Never was. Nowadays, you either give up, or you give in. You gave up is all. I gave in."

The Remington 1187 was on the floor, not far from my feet. But it wasn't loaded. I had dechambered the four unspent rounds myself. My only chance was to jump Pelton or call for Cassandra. But counter-attacking Pelton would have blown my entire plan out of the water. I had no choice but to remain the victim for as long as possible.

But then something happened. Something I never would have expected given the dead men on the cabin floor. Pelton took a deep breath, lowered the pistol, eased back the hammer, and simply pocketed the weapon. He spent a second or two rubbing the feeling back into his shooting hand, and then he bent over and pressed the manual eject switch on the rented VCR. When the video was ejected, he popped it out of its VCR adapter and slipped it into his jacket pocket. He straightened up and looked me in the eyes. "You're certain no further copies of this exist?"

"No copies," I said, standing cautiously still despite the disappearance of his weapon. "I can't be sure no one else made any. But Cassandra assured me, before she left."

Pelton nodded. "Well then, we had a shaky start, but I think I've seen enough to know you mean business."

"Okay," I said, not quite grasping his reference to two dead men as a shaky start.

"I'll make sure you're cleared of this mess," he said. "As soon as I get back, I'll make the necessary calls."

I nodded.

"Then I'll send someone up here to take care of the bodies."

"The overcoat man . . . what's his name?"

"Moscowitz."

"He's buried out back, underneath a pile of dirt and stones."

"I see."

"Key'll be in the mailbox," I said.

"Sorry all this had to happen," Pelton said, running his hand through his gray hair as he turned for the door. "But people change. Things change. You saved my life once. I can't take that away from you. No matter what, you saved my life. I owe you that. Consider this the fulfillment of a twenty-six-year debt of gratitude."

I stood still as a statue while the pools of blood grew larger and combined. And just like that, Washington Pelton left through the side door, alone. But as sincere as he may have sounded, I knew he was lying about clearing my name. It was a gift I had, an ability to spot a liar at twenty paces, and it may have been the only thing I'd gotten out of working inside a prison for all these years. I knew that Wash Pelton had no alternative but to make me go down for the entire ball of wax. And frankly, I was a little insulted that he assumed I'd bought into his empty promise of vindication.

But there were more immediate problems at hand.

As soon as I heard the Taurus make the turn out of the driveway onto the gravel east-west road, I stepped over the puddles of blood and removed the panel to the potato cellar. Cassandra looked up at me.

"You get it?" I asked.

"You want to see it now," she said with a killer smile. "Or do you want to see it later?"

"Grab the money," I said. "We're taking a little trip."

"Where to?" Cassandra said, handing up one of the pots filled with cash.

"See an old friend of mine who works in television."

"No business like show business," she said.

I felt the weight of the three hundred thousand dollars in my hands, and I laughed.

CHAPTER SIXTY-FIVE

I see the quick muzzle flash from the west wall a split second before I hear the sharp crack of the warning shot. When the round explodes against the concrete floor, it sends stony shrapnel into my face, stinging my chin and lower lip. I feel the edge of the shiv pressed up hard against my throat. But not hard enough to break the skin. I hear the breathing of the rebel inmate who holds me tight, forearm wrapped around my neck. I feel his body pressed against mine, his heart beating through my body. To my right, Mike Norman lies on his chest, facedown on the concrete walkway. He is motionless, has been for more than a day. For all I know he is already dead and there's not a goddamned thing I can do about it. The M-16 is still aimed at his head.

An M-16 without rounds.

On my left is Washington Pelton. Blood flows steadily and thickly down the front of his yellow inmate jumper. His Adam's apple bobs up and down. His face has the chalky-white color of death. My face must appear just as lifeless. He is my mirror image. The troopers aim, their sniper rifles steady, just waiting for the word, not even the whole word, just the first sound of the word.

Fire!

If I don't do something now, I am going to die, one way or the other.

We're all going to die—in the name of terror or in the name of the law.

Campfires spit red-and-yellow flame and black smoke. Steel tables are on their sides, facing the wall like a barricade. The tables have been wrapped with razor wire. As the canisters of tear gas come hurling into the muddy yard and as the poison clouds rise from them like a gentle mist, I know that all negotiations have failed and that the only reason for keeping the corrections officers alive is suddenly lost to the wind like the pungent gas that begins to sting our faces, burn our eyeballs.

When the troopers storm the west wall, I take a deep breath and elbow the rebel inmate behind me in the ribs. I grab his wrist, jam my fingernails into it, feel the nails dig in. He drops the shiv and together we go down for it onto the concrete catwalk. But I'm quicker than he is, more desperate. I grab the shiv, swipe it across his neck. The flesh of his thick, hamlike neck opens up red and white. Blood spurts out, stains my face. He is dead before he hits the ground.

Rifle shots ring out in succession.

I am curiously aware of everything around me, as if four days without food has somehow, suddenly, enhanced my senses.

I see the rebel inmates take hits, one after the other. I see them drop dead in the yard.

I hear the cries of the wounded, the screams of the gut-shot. I am up and running for the inmate with the shiv pressed against Pelton's throat. I catch the inmate from behind, run the blade across the back of his neck while he stares distracted and shocked at the hordes of troopers pouring over the walls.

I have just enough time to run the blade through the thick skin, digging deep until I feel the edge of the blade skip across his spine, finally piercing his spine, severing the nerve bundle. His reaction to the blade buried in his neck is more immediate than it was for the appearance of the troopers. He throws his head back, drops the shiv and the empty .38 onto the concrete catwalk. He falls back, looks up at me with wide-open eyes. He moves his mouth, but he cannot talk. Pelton falls beside him, takes hold of my leg. He is panting, bleeding, crying.

At least he is alive.

And as for Norman? He lies on his face, oblivious or dead. I don't know which. The rebel inmate standing over him presses the trigger of the M-16 again and again, only no rounds burst from the barrel. The rebel inmate flips the M-16 over, butt first. He lifts the weapon by the barrel with two hands, swings it back like a war club.

I have to stop him.

I can make it if I lunge after him.

But I can't move.

Wash Pelton has me by the leg. He won't let go of my fucking leg. The rebel inmate takes a deep breath, tightens his stance. The butt of the rifle is up. I reach out for Mike, but I can't reach out far enough or fast enough. Then it happens. Two separate shots from a sniper's rifle nail the rebel inmate square in the chest. The sound of the bullets entering his barrel chest are like a baseball bat swung fast and hard against a feather pillow. The inmate's eyes go wide. His body is not thrust against the stone wall of D-Block like in the movies. He just goes wide-eyed, lets out a breath, and drops down onto Mike Norman.

It's then that Pelton stands, takes hold of my hand with his, holds them up to surrender to the uniformed men come to save our lives.

BOOK FIVE

HOME

CHAPTER SIXTY-SIX

It was my turn to cook. At least that's what I told Val when she arrived at my home in Stormville on a Sunday night nearly three weeks after the escape.

"Shouldn't I be cooking for you, boss?" she said, spooning out the strips of stir-fried boneless chicken and fresh vegetables drowned in a marinara sauce and pouring it over a bed of hot pasta. "I mean, as a celebration of your recent exoneration." She wore a cashmere V-neck sweater and a tan skirt, white pantyhose, and little brown shoes with buckles.

"*Salud*," I said, lifting my glass of Chianti. "Keeper Marconi is not going to jail after all. In the words of the grand jury, hastily assembled on my account I might add, 'No Bill of Particulars is to be filed against Mister Marconi.' "

"I especially enjoyed the part where the judge apologized to you for the hell you were put through," Val said.

"I felt I deserved every word," I said.

We clicked glasses and listened to Zoot Sims skillfully hit highs and lows on his soprano sax. From the dining room, I could see the television in the living room. I had the picture on with the sound down because Val and I were both waiting for the Channel 13 news to begin at six. When it did, I got up from the table, turned down the volume on the stereo and, using the remote, turned the sound up on the television so we could hear, loud and clear, Chris Collins's report from the Albany County Courthouse.

"Today Commissioner for the Department of Corrections, Washington Irving Pelton, was arraigned on numerous charges, including drug trafficking and conspiracy, as well as the murders of former Green Haven Corrections Officer Thomas D. Welch and Stormville Police Department Detective Martin Schillinger," said Collins, from where she stood on top of the marble steps of the county courthouse. She wore the red minidress with matching blazer that I liked so much. Her hair seductively framed her face, making her black eyes seem even wider than they really were. Behind her a group of reporters rushed Wash Pelton as he was escorted out of the courthouse by an army of navy-blue uniforms. Pelton kept his head down and used the wide collar of his raincoat to block his face. His wrists were locked in cuffs. "Pelton was arrested late last week at his home in Albany after a hidden video camera captured not only his confession that he was the ring leader of a massive drug operation inside and outside of Green Haven Prison, but also his confession that he'd shot — point-blank — both Welch and Schillinger. The videotape is said to have come directly from Green Haven Warden Jack 'Keeper' Marconi, although sources have not yet made a positive ID regarding who made the tape available to Newscenter 13. What we do know is that Judge Sclera, overseer of the grand jury, acquitted Keeper Marconi just this morning of all charges stemming from the escape of cop-killer Eduard Vasquez from Green Haven. And in light of recent events, charges against Marconi and Vasquez's long-time girlfriend, Cassandra Wolf, for the murder of Vasquez will be dropped.

"In other developments, Cassandra Wolf agreed to give full testimony concerning her knowledge of the major drug-running scheme that had plagued Green Haven for the last twenty-four to thirty-six months. In return, Wolf should receive total immunity. For now, she has been released on her own recognizance. According to inside sources, Wolf is willing to implicate all parties involved, living and dead. Reports also indicate that Corrections Officers Logan and Mastriano are among those Wolf has set her sights on exposing.

"And in further developments," Collins went on, "Doctor Arnold Fleischer was arrested last evening at Newburgh General for his role in artificially manufacturing Mastriano's coma, which had attracted the attention of the entire nation. Also arrested was A. J. Royale, the dentist from Newburgh, who, it is said, performed unnecessary dental procedures on Eduard Vasquez in order to justify the many field trips outside of Green Haven. And Republican senatorial hopeful John 'Jake' Warren was found attempting to board a plane bound for Switzerland only four hours after being released from custody this afternoon. As of now, pending arraignment for his role in the Green Haven conspiracy, he awaits trial without bail inside the same holding cell at the Albany County Jail in which Keeper Marconi was detained a few weeks ago."

I pointed the remote at the television and cut the power. "Looks like Chris Collins has her Emmy award–winning story," I said, sitting back down at the table.

"Don't you want to see the rest of the report?" Val said.

I took a mouthful of the hot chicken and pasta, tasted the rich marinara sauce. I washed it down with a swallow of wine. At the same time, I shook my head. "She's just going to tell us that Wash Pelton is also the number-one suspect in the killing of Eduard Vasquez, and she might speculate on whether or not Pelton will get life or lethal injection if convicted of all three murders." I took another bite of food.

Val took a small sip of the wine and sat back. "He's white, boss," she said. "He's rich. He's a politician. People in high places owe him money and favors."

"Ten years," I said. "Tops, after the reduction of charges, of course."

"With parole," Val said, picking at the food on her plate, "he'll be out in seven."

Bucky Pizzarelli filled the silence for a time, until the music was drowned out by the Cessnas taking off from the Stormville airstrip. It felt good to be eating a meal in my own home and sitting at my kitchen table with Val.

Christ, it just felt good to be free and clear.

"What about you, Keeper?" Val said. "What are you going to do now that things are going back to normal?"

"Things will never be normal."

"You know what I mean, boss."

"I'm not going back to the iron house," I said. "You can count on that."

"What will you do?" Val said, setting her fork down. "You're a prison man. You can't just start a new career at your—"

I reached across the table and pressed my hand against her mouth. "Don't say it," I said. "Don't say the A word."

She smiled and it felt good looking at her tan, chiseled face and her brown hair and the way it hung down on the smooth skin of her exposed neck. "Don't worry," I said, "I'm not about to leave town or anything crazy like that."

Using her thumb and index finger, Val twisted her wineglass by its stem. "Of course, that's none of my business," she said.

"Look, Val," I said, "I'm toying with the idea of going out on my own. You know, like a private investigator. Only a guy who specializes in prison-related crime. Drug trafficking, money laundering, murder, breakouts. The whole ball of beeswax."

Val took a breath as if relieved. She nodded her head with approval. "Only makes sense," she said. "The prison is a society unto its own. Its own rules and laws. Its own government and social order. No one knows it better than you, boss. Except maybe the COs and inmates themselves. Certainly not the governor, certainly not the politicians. Makes sense you taking it on privately. You know the system like the back of your hand."

I reached across the table, took Val's hand in mine. "Just like I want to get to know the back of yours," I said. I felt that good feeling in my stomach. The feeling that comes when things between a man and a woman are new and wonderful.

Val smiled like an angel and she squeezed my hand then gently pulled away.

"We'll work on that a little, too," she said.

CHAPTER SIXTY-SEVEN

In the darkness of the early morning, Tony Angelino's black fedora made him look more like a shadow than a man. Sometimes I wondered if he really *was* more shadow than man. We stood outside the Miss Albany Diner on Broadway on the first cool morning since spring had begun that year. Through the window of the diner, you could see a single exposed lightbulb burning brightly over the counter. I couldn't see him from where I stood, but I knew Cliff was inside prepping the grill. It was four-thirty on a Monday morning. For obvious reasons, Broadway was even emptier than usual.

"Sorry to get you out of bed again," I said to Tony, handing him a manila envelope. "This should make it worth the trip."

In the darkness it was hard to make out Tony's face. But I could feel his smile and I could see his breath as it vaporized in the cool morning air.

"And this is for you," he said in a low whisper voice. He handed me a brown paper bag that contained an undersized videotape, along with a

few things I had asked him and his Guinea Pigs to get for me at the last
minute.

"Think they'll start a full-scale investigation into the missing porn
video?"

"They might, paisan," Tony said, shrugging his shoulders. "And on
the other hand, they might not bother. That porn video is the least of
Pelton's problems now."

"The second video, the one Cassandra and I made at the cabin, is
the important one," I said. "That should be enough to make a convic-
tion stick."

"Cassandra wants to see the porn film destroyed, huh?" Tony said.

"Can you blame her?" I said, gripping the video tightly with my right
hand.

Tony nodded empathetically.

"So," I said, "what do you think the DA's gonna say when he finds
out that the commissioner of corrections' favorite home movie is
gone?"

"He'll say something smart, like 'What do you mean my fucking
porn flick is missing?' "

Tony and I shook hands like paisans. Behind him I saw Cliff through
the picture window. He was moving in and out of the light, setting
up the booths with ketchup bottles, knives, and forks. By now I could
smell the good smell of peppers and onions and home-fried potatoes
sizzling on the grill. Tony released my hand. I tucked the package into
my leather jacket, zipped it up.

"You're not going back, are you?" Tony said, obviously referring to
Green Haven.

"I don't see the use in it," I said.

"I heard you handed it all to Dan Sloat?"

"Dan'll make an excellent warden," I said.

"What are you gonna do, paisan?"

"Keep busy," I said. "I've got Val and her kid. I've got my drums."

"What are you gonna do for money, I mean?"

"Work for myself," I said. "Private investigations. Specialize in
prison-related crime. Cutting-edge stuff. Wave of the future. You know.
That and quit smoking . . . maybe."

"Word's out the attorney general's office is looking for an unbiased

special investigator with prior prison experience, in light of recent trage-
dies, that is."

"I'm their man," I said.

"Call me if you need a lawyer or the Guinea Pigs, Mister Visionary.
Call me for lunch or call me for dinner. But, Keeper, don't call me
before breakfast."

"Sure," I said.

Tony tugged on the brim of his fedora. He turned and jogged up the
three steps to the door of the diner. In the bit of light that leaked out
through the diner window, I could finally make out his face when he
turned to me one last time and winked. He opened the glass-and-wood
door and went in. "The usual, Clifford," he said, his deep voice coming
over loud and clear through the plate glass. "Sunny-side up with coffee.
And hey, paisan, let's have a smile."

CHAPTER SIXTY-EIGHT

I was driving the Toyota as the sun came up over the mountains beyond the Hudson River directly to the east. My cup of coffee sat in the holder on the dash; I held a cigarette in my left hand. I blew a stream of white smoke out the window, turned onto Marian Avenue, and found the house that now belonged to the widow of the cop slain by Eduard Vasquez in 1988. She had moved back to Albany with her young son to live with her mother, who, the record showed, was also a widow.

I rang the doorbell to a yellow, single-story, clapboard house that needed a paint job in the worst way. A young woman, dressed in a frayed pink robe, came to the door. Poking his head out from behind his mother's robe was a little boy of about eight or nine. The young woman with cropped black hair and brown eyes did not recognize me. Not at first anyway. "Can I help you with something?" she said, making a conscious effort to keep the boy behind her where he was protected.

"I have a package for you, ma'am," I said. "May I?" I opened the screen door and handed her a manila folder, exactly like the one I had handed Tony Angelino earlier. This package also contained a hundred thousand dollars. Money that Cassandra insisted belonged to this woman and her son. "A hundred grand won't bring back her husband or that kid's father," Cassandra had told me during the drive from Ironville to Albany, "but it will give her back some of her life."

I agreed.

The woman took the package from my hand, opened it. "I don't understand," she said.

"Money from an overlooked policemen's fund," I said. "But there's one catch."

Now the woman pressed her son into her leg with one hand, gripped the manila envelope with the other.

"Don't tell anyone where it came from."

I winked at the little boy. His fine, sandy-brown hair was buzz-cut short. When he gave me a smile, I could see that one of his top teeth was missing.

"Have a nice day," I said, and then I turned and walked across the overgrown lawn toward my Toyota. But before I got in, the woman called out to me from her front door.

"Keeper," she said. "You're Keeper Marconi."

I turned.

"I never believed you killed that prisoner," she said. "Not for a second."

I smiled at her and her son. Then I turned and walked away, without saying another word. The hero that I was.

CHAPTER SIXTY-NINE

Cassandra stood on a pier made of heavy timbers covered with two or three coatings of asphalt. She wore a Levi's jacket on this cool morning and the same pair of black jeans she'd worn at the cabin in Ironville. I approached her from behind. She turned quickly and smiled.

"You're late," she said. The wind off the river blew the hair away from her face so that the heart-shaped tattoo was exposed in the early morning sunlight.

"I had things to take care of first," I said. In the distance, an oil tanker moved upriver slowly, almost motionlessly, heading for the petroleum processing plant that took up a good-sized chunk of riverfront property immediately south of the port.

I reached into the right-hand pocket of my leather bomber jacket and pulled out the small videocassette. "You do the honors," I said.

"No, you do it," Cassandra said, her hands in the pockets of her jeans. I felt inside the cassette and pulled out the black videotape. I pulled until most of the celluloid littered the pier. Then I kicked the whole thing into the river. Together, Cassandra and I watched the tape slap against the surface of the river and float away toward oblivion while the gray-and-black tanker inched silently forward.

Now it was time for something else.

I reached into my jacket and pulled out the .32 Cassandra had used to kill Vasquez.

Her face turned noticeably pale as I held out the piece.

"You must have seen me," she said. "You must have seen me climb the hill behind the cabin. You saw me and you said nothing."

"What I didn't see or hear was you firing the two rounds on my .45 when I went to sleep that night at the cabin. My guess is that you went outside and far enough down the road so that the explosions wouldn't wake me. You leaving the cabin like that gave the overcoat man the chance to sneak in and hide himself in the bathroom. When you were finished, you snuck back into the bedroom and returned the weapon to the table next to the bed, where I was still out cold."

"I'm not a killer," Cassandra said. "Pelton and Schillinger and Eddy were killers. I knew all about them breaking into your home. Look, I panicked. Blowing off the two rounds seemed like the thing to do at the time, the thing that would save my life if we got arrested. I thought if they implicated you, they'd let me go."

"It never dawned on you that if Vasquez was shot with a .32, it wouldn't matter how many .45 slugs were missing from my gun." I looked down at the tanker-made waves that crashed against the cement pier. "None of it matters now," I said, taking her hand and giving her the pistol. "I understand why you did it. When I saw that film of you with Pelton and Schillinger, I knew how difficult it must have been for you to be involved with Vasquez for so long."

Her hand trembled as she tried to grip the .32. I felt the warm sun on my face and the cool breeze that tempered the warmth. The tanker was enormous and very close now.

"What do you want me to do?" she said.

"It depends on what you want to do," I said.

We stood there not saying anything for a time that seemed forever. When Cassandra turned and tossed the pistol into the river, I felt like I had been swimming underwater for far too long and had only made it to the surface in the nick of time.

"I have something else for you," I said. I handed her the other items Tony Angelino had given me.

"What's all this?" she said.

"Passport," I said, "credit cards, driver's license. A few other assorted necessities for starting over. You already have enough cash."

"I don't get it," she said. "What's going on?"

"You'll find out," I said, "as soon as you make it over to where that tanker is about to dock. There's a man there that you have to see. His name is Captain Ralph and he's sailing this afternoon for Brazil. You're going to be on that ship."

"But what about my testimony?" she said. "I'm supposed—"

"Don't worry about that," I said. "You get involved in a court of law, somehow they're going to find out who shot Vasquez, and that'll be the end of you."

Cassandra looked down at the passport, opened it, and read the name stenciled under the photo.

"Martha Stewart," she said like a question. "Do I look like a Martha Stewart to you?"

"That's Tony's Guinea Pigs for you," I said, noticing the tears forming in Cassandra's eyes.

She took a deep breath and smiled. "I never could have imagined things turning out like this."

"For both of you," I said, placing my open hand gently on her belly.

She looked up fast. "You know about my angel, too?"

"I hope it's a girl," I said, "and I hope she's as beautiful as you."

Cassandra laughed, but at the same time, a tear ran down her cheek, and it kept going until it reached her heart-shaped tattoo. "I guess it would be wrong for me not to thank you," she said.

"Just promise me you'll be on that boat," I said. "That'll be thanks enough."

She wiped her eyes with the backs of her hands. "I guess I have no other choice," she said. And then she kissed me gently and started walking toward the dock. She was on her way to Brazil.

A few minutes later I was still standing at the empty pier, with the river water moving flat and slow and the wind cool and picking up as the bright morning wore on. I knew I could have asked Cassandra whose baby she carried. Deep down, maybe it was a bit corny of me, but I knew I could have asked her and that she would have told me if the father was Vasquez or Pelton or Schillinger or the overcoat man, for that matter. But then, knowing for sure that it was one of these men would not have been a good thing. And besides, letting it go presented a second possibility. Just suppose the baby's father was not one of the above? Just suppose the baby's father was a nice, hard-working young man whom Cassandra had not mentioned in the interest of protecting his identity? It wasn't likely, but just the same it was the scenario I preferred to believe.

CHAPTER SEVENTY

Mike Norman's body was finally taken out of cold storage and buried at the Albany Rural Cemetery around noon on a warm bright day in early June. He received full pomp-and-circumstance, including three dress-uniformed cops who fired twenty-one rounds into the sky from black, police-issue M-16s.

I stood away from the fanfare, far away from the crowd that had gathered by his grave, even farther from the podium where Mayor McMan delivered a eulogy that included a plea for reform in the corrections department in light of recent calamities. He called for more prisons, more officers, more programs for violent offenders, better medical conditions, fewer field trips. Because, after all, Attica survivor Mike Norman would have wanted it that way.

While the mayor spoke, I crossed the flat green landscape until I found a rectangular plot that, at five feet by ten feet, measured little less than a prison cell. It was a grave I did not visit often, but I knew it as a silent peaceful place, especially at midday with the sun yellow and red over the hills to the east. The cemetery had been laid out on a hillside a

century and a half ago and on a clear day you could see through the tall
maples and oaks to the Hudson River below; you could see the morning
sun reflected off its glassy surface. Overhead, tall pine trees shaded the
plots. When their pine needles shed, even the footsteps of the visitors
were muffled, so that the place reverberated in silence.

In the Albany Rural Cemetery, you always felt like you were being
watched, even when you were certain you were alone. Sometimes you
were sure that you could hear the voices of the souls speaking to you,
but then you would realize that it was the sound of your own heart
beating, your own voice inside your head.

Silence was the reason Fran had chosen this place not two months
before she'd died. One Sunday morning over coffee she'd said that if
she went before me, she would like to be buried here, under the shady
silence of the trees, with the river in the distance.

I remember looking at Fran with a worried smile. I'd told her she
was crazy, that she shouldn't say such things, that such things could
become self-fulfilling prophecies. That she was way too young. That she
had a whole lot of life to live yet.

"But I think you knew something I didn't, Fran," I said now, "even if
you weren't entirely conscious of it."

Fran's headstone was hewn from the whitest marble I could find.
Small and smooth, it was buried flat in the earth, not like the usual
arched headstone that began to lean with time until it fell to the
ground, more dead-looking than the person it was meant to honor.

I wanted Fran's marker to be perfect forever.

The engraving below the etching of an angel read

FRANCIS GORDINI MARCONI
B. SEPTEMBER 14, 1952–D. MAY 13, 1996

It said nothing else, her epitaph too personal for the world to know.

I turned toward the entrance to the cemetery. I could see a woman
coming toward me, walking slowly along the dirt path. With the sun
behind her, surrounding her like an aura, it was impossible to see her
face. But for a second I felt my heart fall away from my chest and the air
leave my lungs. I stood up straight and waited for her, and when sud-

denly I saw her face and knew for certain that it could never again be
Fran, I felt foolish and sad.

But I wasn't sad for long because the woman was Val, and she looked
at me and smiled, her face lit up by the orange, cathedral-like sunlight
shining in through the trees. I looked into her eyes, and I saw that she'd
been crying. She carried a single red rose, and she knelt down, and laid
the rose on Fran's grave. Bowing her head, she made the sign of the
cross, brought her hands together, and closed her eyes. After a minute
passed, she made the sign of the cross once more and then reached out
with her right hand to touch Fran's headstone. She stood up, took my
hand, and held it tightly.

"You okay?" I said.

"I was going to ask you the same thing," she said. We understood
one another and moved on back toward Mike's service. I stopped before
I got too close. From that distance I could see that the mayor had
stopped talking and that a priest was sprinkling holy water on the mahogany coffin. He chanted some prayers I recognized, but I had forgotten most of the words. An Act of Contrition, a Hail Mary, and an Our
Father. And then he sprinkled the coffin with more holy water.

Val's hand in mine, I turned and looked into her eyes, and I knew
that a new life was about to begin, for her and me.

"I want to leave now," she whispered.

"I'm ready," I said.

Val squeezed my hand as we headed for the cemetery gates.